P

Kill

"*Kill Your Friends* is the most exc   /."
                                        ...zine

"Brilliant. It made me ill with laughter. The filthiest, blackest, most shocking, most hilarious debut novel I've ever read." —India Knight

"The antihero of John Niven's *Kill Your Friends* is magnificently eloquent in an utterly sewer-minded way. . . . A vicious, black-hearted howl of a book. . . . A realistic portrait of the music industry, doing for it what *The Player* did for Hollywood. Having spent ten years in the business, [Niven's] insider knowledge, coupled with the kind of headlong, febrile prose that would have Hunter S. Thompson happily emptying both barrels into the sky, results in a novel that is cripplingly funny in the way that only the very darkest comedy can be."
                        —Chris Power, *The Times* (London)

"To call John Niven's *Kill Your Friends* a satire of the music industry is a wicked understatement. It is an all-out assault, a withering, scabrous, and often repulsive attack on every part of the filthy machine. . . . Stelfox is a creation of unparalleled awfulness—chronically sexist, racist, and everything else-ist. He is funny, too. . . . You laugh though you know you shouldn't. . . . As an eye-watering self-evisceration on the part of the Man, this takes some beating."
                        —*The Independent* (London)

"[A] dazzling comic novel. . . . This book is fantastically funny. The humor isn't so much dark as dismally black. No one is to be trusted; no one is to be liked. And yet, have violent sex with prostitutes, excessive use of drugs, and attempted murder ever been this entertaining? . . . Buy this book and give it to your friends. Five stars."
                        —*Time Out* (London)

"The Scot's debut is a dark, gruesome, and frequently hysterical satire of this period, told from the perspective of desperate A&R man Steven Stelfox. It's *American Psycho* meets *The Player*, as witnessed by a writer with Hunter S. Thompson's eye for the grotesque."

—Ted Kessler, *Q* magazine

"Steven Stelfox, the antihero of Niven's debut novel, is an A&R psycho. . . . [He] shares key traits with Bret Easton Ellis's Patrick Bateman: a large disposable income, extreme shallowness, a soul as moribund as a licked-clean coke wrap, and a somewhat casual attitude to the well-being of his fellow humans. But where Bateman is as cold and sharp as a sushi knife, Stelfox is viscerally livid, spewing bile over all he sees as he shags, snorts, and slaughters his way through 1997. The delight is Stelfox's irredeemably poisonous, often hilarious, and utterly filthy inner voice."

—Lottie Moggach, *London Paper*

"[A] brilliant satire on the Britpop generation. Increasingly desperate A&R man Steven Stelfox resorts to murder to shore up his failing career and keep his nose powdered. It hits all the right notes."

—Henry Sutton, *Mirror*

"Like the product of an unholy union between Bret Easton Ellis and Martin Amis, John Niven has delivered a gleefully amoral morality tale, set in the manically unprincipled world of the music business at the height of Britpop. . . . Through a whirl of drugs, violence, and unashamed sexual deviance, the reader is alternately shocked and left crying with laughter."

—*Bookseller* (London)

"*Kill Your Friends* gladly hammers the final and needed nail into the coffin of self-serving and undignified spin that was 'Cool Britannia.' It exposes a world that seethes alongside us and in which we all collude but whose nasty little machinery is rarely glimpsed. The novel is furiously, filthily funny, and, I imagine, tragically true."

—Niall Griffiths

"Brilliant. . . . Hilariously scabrous. . . . Niven's mix of truth and fiction means *Kill Your Friends* might just be the best book ever written about the music industry. I say 'might' because I've not read them all, but I've read an awful lot and his is the most savage, the most unforgiving, the funniest, and the cruelest."   —Rob Fitzpatrick, *Word* magazine

"Like *American Psycho* meets *Spinal Tap* . . . except it's more evil, more shocking, and much, much funnier than that."
                                                    —Doug Johnstone, *Scotsman*

"Anyone working in or trying to get into the music industry should read this book. Niven grotesquely portrays the short-term disposability of this world with a great eye for detail and a stockpile of hilarious insults. Throw in some murder and major brand obsession and you have an indie *American Psycho*."   —James Brown

"A very funny, morbid, and sensationalist read, and a total page-turner."
                                                    —Tim Newbound, *Rock Sound*

"This razor-sharp account of the last heyday for the British music industry—Britpop's zenith in 1997—follows cocaine-fueled A&R man Steven Stelfox as he jaunts around the world trying to sign the next big band. Stelfox is a despicable, truly hateful character, but author John Niven (himself a music industry veteran) has written him with such skill, inside knowledge, and savage humor that you can't put the book down. . . . A truly hilarious read. . . . Highly recommended."
                                                    —*City AM*

"One of the most evil, vicious, despicable characters ever. I couldn't put it down."   —James Dean Bradfield, the Manic Street Preachers

KILL YOUR

FRIENDS

ALSO BY JOHN NIVEN

Music from Big Pink

KILL YOUR FRIENDS

A Novel

John Niven

HARPER PERENNIAL

NEW YORK • LONDON • TORONTO • SYDNEY • NEW DELHI • AUCKLAND

HARPER ● PERENNIAL

Originally published in Great Britain in 2008 by William Heinemann.

This novel is a work of fiction. Any references to real people, events, establishments, or-
ganizations, or locales are intended only to give the fiction a sense of reality and authen-
ticity, and are used fictitiously. All other names, characters, and places, and all dialogue
and incidents portrayed in this book, are the product of the author's imagination.

P.S.™ is a trademark of HarperCollins Publishers.

KILL YOUR FRIENDS. Copyright © 2009 by John Niven. All rights reserved. Printed in
the United States of America. No part of this book may be used or reproduced in any
manner whatsoever without written permission except in the case of brief quotations
embodied in critical articles and reviews. For information address HarperCollins Publishers, 10 East 53rd Street, New York, NY 10022.

HarperCollins books may be purchased for educational, business, or sales promotional
use. For information please write: Special Markets Department, HarperCollins Publishers, 10 East 53rd Street, New York, NY 10022.

FIRST U.S. EDITION

Library of Congress Cataloging-in-Publication Data is available upon request.

ISBN 978-0-06-169061-7

09 10 11 12 13 RRD 10 9 8 7 6 5 4 3 2 1

To Helen

The music business is a cruel and shallow money trench, a long plastic hallway where thieves and pimps run free and good men die like dogs. There is also a negative side.

—Hunter S. Thompson

January

The Kula Shaker and Jamiroquai albums both go double platinum. Warner Brothers have an 18.4% share of the albums market. 'Say What You Want' by Texas is the biggest airplay record in the country. The Pecadilloes and Embrace are hot new bands. Last year the British music industry generated over a billion pounds in revenue for the first time ever. The new Gene album is called Drawn to the Deep End. *Polydor A&R Director Paul Adam says, 'I have big aspirations that this is their crossover record.'*

'A&R (artist and repertoire): *The branch of the music industry concerned with finding and nurturing new talent.*'

I'm smoking and looking out of my office window while I listen to some guy, some manager, crapping away on the speakerphone. Five floors below me a group of black guys – probably some band – are lounging in the car park. The glass is bronzed, honey-coloured, and they can't see me. It's icy winter out there and their breath rises with the smoke from the spliff they're passing around, shrouding them in a pewter cloud. Beyond them, along the Thames at Hammersmith Bridge, is a gigantic poster of the Labour guy, Tony Blair. A slash has been ripped across his face where his eyes should have been and a pair of red eyes – hellish, demonic eyes – burn out instead.

Back down in the car park and one of the kids is actually leaning against my car now, his hands in his pockets and his back arched against the silver Saab as though it were the counter of his local KFC. I keep an eye on him as my mind wanders back to the voice coming out of the speakerphone. It's saying stuff like this:

'And EMI, Virgin and Chrysalis. Warner Chappell are doing the publishing and they've, well, I shouldn't be saying this yet, but . . .'

Don't tell me, they've got a major TV advert confirmed?

'They've got a major TV advert as good as confirmed.'

'Wow,' I say, sounding like nothing.

'But you know we like you,' the cretin says.

'Yeah, great, send it over.'

'It's a rough mix. Your ears only?'

'Sure.'

'Great. Bye, Steven.'

'Bye,' I think for a second. 'Mate.'

I hang up as Rebecca comes in. It's almost eleven, the crack of dawn around here. 'Good morning,' she says, placing a stack of mail on the coffee table, next to a pile of demo tapes of new bands – Cuff, Fling, Santa Cruz, Magic Drive, Montrose Avenue – which Darren, one of the scouts, has left for me to go through.

'Rebecca,' I say, not turning from the window.

'Mmmm?'

'Could you please interrupt whatever you're doing, run downstairs and tell security to get that fucking great *darkie* off of my car?'

She shrieks, pretending to be horrified, and joins me at the window.

'God, who on earth are that lot?' she says, chewing on a strand of her fine, long blonde hair.

'Fuck knows. Probably some imminent signing of Schneider's. The Jew is using the black man as muscle. Against us.'

'You're *terrible*!' She gives me a little elbow as she heads

4

for the door, pleased because I'm in a good mood. 'There's your post. Don't forget, you've got the business affairs meeting at twelve.' Rebecca is tall with full gobbler's lips. Great legs. Decent rack. But the face is beginning to go – little crow's feet creep around the eyes, grooves deepening at the corners of the mouth. She is a couple of years older than me – dangerously close to thirty – and terrifyingly single. She needs to be sorting this out and she knows it. Today she's wearing a tartan miniskirt a foot wide, trainers and a tight black T-shirt that has the word 'WHORE' picked out in little diamond studs. Like all the girls who work here – apart from Nicky, our Head of International, who is so ugly it actually makes me angry to have to be in the same room as her – Rebecca dresses just the right side of prostitution.

'Rebecca,' I say as she reaches for the door handle.

'Mmmm?' she says, turning round.

'The hotel?' I am off to Cannes next week for MIDEM and so far, depending on whom I choose to believe, either Rebecca or our worthless travel agents have failed to get me into a suitable hotel.

'I'm on it, Steven. Relax.' She turns to leave.

I believe her because Rebecca, like most girls, loves to organise things for you. She's never happier than when she's got the travel agent on one line, BA on another and copies of *The World's Great Hotels* and the Zagat and Harden's guides flattened out on the desk in front of her. It strikes me as very odd that she enjoys planning these trips for me even though she will take no part in them, will in no way benefit from them. I cannot comprehend planning something from which I will not gain anything. Something about the girl mind, I suppose – taking pleasure from knowing that the flight will arrive in time to make the restaurant reservation, that the hotel will be lavish and unexpected.

'And, Rebecca?' She turns back again, trying not to sigh. 'You look nice today.' (Carrot and stick.)

'Thank you,' she replies, smiling coyly. Well, as coyly as a girl who probably sucked a minimum of thirty cocks last year is capable of smiling. 'So do you.'

She's not wrong. I've just spent a month on holiday – Thailand–Vietnam–Australia – and I'm tanned to the fucking eyeballs. I'm wearing a black cashmere V-neck sweater, black jeans and black suede loafers, all of which are box-fresh.

She leaves and I flip through my post, mostly waxy Jiffy bags containing demo tapes, feeling the usual reflexive anger at the attempts at spelling my name – there's 'Stalefox', 'Stellfax' and one mongoloid has even gone for 'Stellarfix'. It's Stelfox. Steven Stelfox – before settling down with the new issue of *Music Week*. Some guy who works there has died. Heart attack at thirty-two. Nasty. Very fucking nasty.

As I turn the pages I feel the floor shake, concentric rings ripple in the black coffee, and I look up in time to see Waters come lumbering past the glass wall that separates my office from the rest of the floor. He's really something, Waters. Six two, six three, about eighteen stone. He's clutching a piece of paper and trying to look purposeful in a ludicrous attempt to mask a mammoth hangover. He's red-faced and pouch-eyed, with blips of sweat dotting his forehead. (Doing anything, lifting a cassette, dialling a telephone number, causes Waters to break into a filthy rapist-sweat.) He wearily flashes me a devil sign, extending the pinkie and forefinger of his giant left paw. He is trailing his rat-dog, a little Jack Russell, behind him. He thinks bringing the fucking thing into the office makes him eccentric and interesting. It makes him look like a cunt. Like the brontosaurus, his colossal frame is powered by a brain the size of a grape, and this grape-brain itself, none too dynamic to begin with, has been further buffoonerised by years of chronic chang abuse. I nod a needlessly business-like hello, just to rub his lateness in, and pick up the TV remote.

I watch VH1 for a bit – Blur, Radiohead, Oasis and the Brand New Heavies – and am about to turn it off when there's a little preview of the upcoming Brit Awards. We get Dodgy, the Chemical Brothers, the Prodigy, Longpigs, Mansun. I light another cigarette and watch as Ellie Crush is interviewed. 'Yeah,' she says, 'I know there's people out there that fink a woman can't do all the stuff I'm doing. That she's a puppet? Yeah? But, y'know, I'm here, writing the lyrics and checking on the arrangements and doing all of that stuff. Yeah? My songs come from in *here*.' She flattens a hand sincerely across her heart.

Crush, nominated for Best Newcomer, is a twenty-one-year-old east Londoner who was signed by Parker-Hall over at EMI. Her critically lauded debut LP was released last spring and charted at no. 63. And, mercifully, it looked like that was that. Game Over. See you later, Sooty. Then, gradually, horribly, it started to sell. Word of mouth. Suddenly they got a single playlisted at Radio 1 and the album went gold. I do not want to contemplate what might happen to the fucking thing, what might happen to Parker-

Hall, if Crush wins Best Newcomer. I make a note on my 'to do' list to put a matey call in to the fucker.

'Cause that's what it's all about,' Crush says to the interviewer, *'integritty.* Yeah?' I turn the sound down as she goes on to discuss gun control or something.

It's interesting, I remember being at her signing party a year ago when someone used the phrase 'artistic integrity' in her presence. Her brow knotted and she asked her manager – not rhetorically – 'Wot's "integritty"?' I mean, here is a girl who can barely read. A girl who, just twelve scant months ago, would have sucked the curdled sweat from a tramp's dimpled nutbag to obtain a record deal, and yet here she is talking about 'integrity' and Christ knows what other nonsense. When they sell no records, it's a nightmare. When they sell lots of records – it's a whole other nightmare. Because then these fools, these one-GCSE merchants, these casualties with half a fucking thought to rub together, they suddenly think that the fact that a few hundred thousand of the Great British Public (yeah, those *animals*) enjoy their ditties and respond on some primitive level to their doggerel, means that they have something of value to say about anything from the FTSE to the Middle East peace process. So, the next time you see some Mercury Music Prize/Brit Award/Grammy-nominated diva up there giving it the whole 'I am a strong independent woman with interesting ideas' bit, remember this – it is only because of the tiniest quirk of fate, a deranged quiver of serendipity, the most unlikely of miracles, that her big speeches are not climaxing with the words: 'I'm sorry, sir, this checkout is closing,' or 'Anal is an extra twenty quid, mate.'

There is talk of the Ellie Crush record starting to take off in America. Were this to happen it is conceivable it could sell millions of copies rather than the few hundred thousand it takes to constitute a reasonably big record over here. I know Parker-Hall has two points on the record because I got his lawyer drunk at a Christmas party. If the record properly took off in America Parker-Hall might well become a millionaire. He's twenty-five. Two years younger than me. Admitting the possibility of his success into my head makes me reel back. I feel faint. Sick. I take my mind off the subject by smoking another cigarette and doing some expenses, noticing with some surprise that I managed to spend nearly two thousand pounds on 'entertainment' last December.

Actually, it's not strictly true that my mind is *on* the subject, or any subject, for very long. Here's the deal with the inside of my head: picture a giant bank of screens, dozens of them, reaching high into the air, like you see at NASA, at Mission Control. At any given time many of them are simply showing hardcore pornography: banks and banks of close-ups – some so close they are pixellated to the point of image-degradation – showing troublingly large cocks punching in and out of cunts, lurid dildos violating angry rectums, cocks gliding stiff and imperious between lubed breasts. Other screens show financial stuff: graphs of London house prices, City traders screaming in their striped blazers, pie charts of record-industry market shares, bricks of cash being stacked up, balance sheets, red figures, black figures, recouped acts, unrecouped acts. A few screens show bands and singers: acts I've signed in the past, new acts we're thinking about signing, successful acts I wanted to sign and didn't (the most haunting images). A small row of distant monitors, tucked away high up in a dusty corner, randomly shows footage of colleagues and rivals being baroquely tortured.

There are guys in my head too. The technicians in their short-sleeved shirts, with the pens in the breast pocket and the little headsets on and their styrofoam cups of coffee. They sit slack-jawed in front of the monitors. They aren't happy about any of this. They know it's not good. But they can't seem to do anything about it. They run around and shout at each other. They gather anxiously around blinking computers. They shake their heads over crazily spooling printouts and mutter, 'This can't be right, goddammit,' but the monitors just go on showing what they show.

That's what it feels like in there – like there's a Mission going on, but there's no Control.

Before I go down for the meeting I pick up my paperback copy of *Unleash Your Monster*, by the American self-help guru Dr David S. Hauptman, and open it at random: '*In every age men are born who, in their hearts, in the black of their blood, are warriors. But, for most of us, there are no longer wars to fight. What must they do, these men?*'

As I leave my office I can hear the sound of celebration – laughter and corks – coming down the hallway from the accounts department. 'What are those clowns so fucking happy about?' I ask Rebecca.

'Oh, Rick's just found out he's going to be a dad,' she says cheerfully, and I realise that she's genuinely happy on his behalf.

This astonishes me on two counts: 1) actual happiness at someone else's good fortune in which you have no personal stake, and 2) why is this guy celebrating the fact that he has terminated his life? You might as well run out of the doctor's surgery screeching with joy as you wave your positive cancer test around. The notion of children makes me ill. The thought of having one . . . when you see those guys in the supermarket, wheeling the trolley around while their brats whine and wheedle and some blundering sow questions every little thing they take off the shelves. I mean, just the fucking idea of it, the very word: *family*. Whenever I see it, on travel brochures, on house schedules (*family holiday, family room*), I feel sick.

Also I'm thinking, Rick? Who the fuck is Rick from accounts?

So here's what I do. I listen to music – singers, bands, songwriters – and decide which ones stand a good chance of commercial success. I then arrange for them to be recorded in a sympathetic manner and we, the record company, sell them to you, the general public. Sound easy? Get fucked – you wouldn't last ten minutes.

Now, I don't have a perfect track record. No one does. But I'm pretty fucking good. On average I only get it wrong maybe eight or nine times out of ten. That is to say, if you played me ten pieces of unsigned music I might instantly dismiss three or four acts that might go on to enjoy enormous success. I have thrown the demo tapes of bands that are now megastars, bands whose records you own, across the room with tears of laughter running down my face. I have berated and insulted subordinates for having the temerity to play me tracks that have subsequently sold in their millions.

It's very likely that I'll applaud three or four tracks that will turn out to be absolute, grade-A, Bernard Matthews turkeys. We, my label, have spent millions, literally millions, of pounds signing and developing music that, as it turned out, no sane person wanted to hear.

Which perhaps begs the question, what kind of music do I like? Incredibly, you really do get asked this from time to time. Usually by some new kid, some earnest junior product manager who has tagged along to lunch or by a member of some band you're trying to sign. The new kid will be quickly dismissed with a curt 'fuck off' and the guy from the band you're trying to sign will get a sincerely delivered litany of seminal bands and songwriters; 'Yeah,' you intone sombrely, 'Dylan, Joni Mitchell, the Clash, Husker Du, the Band, Lennon.' (Delete as applicable to the musical tastes of the retard you're talking to.) What kind of music do I like? Asking a major label A&R manager this question is like asking an arbitrageur what kind of commodities he likes. Or saying to an investment banker, 'Hey, what's your favourite currency?' I have very wide musical tastes. 'Eclectic', as spastic musicians say when they're trying to sound clever in interviews. I don't care which genre something comes from – rock, trance, hip hop, Bulgarian fucking heavy metal – *as long as it's profitable.*

Finally, though, out of those ten tracks, I'd probably get at least one right. As long as I manage to do that every couple of years, then I'm doing incredibly well. I'm ahead of the curve. I mean, there are guys who *never* get it right.

Here's the important thing to say about meetings – nothing important ever got decided in a meeting. The place to get your own way is over lunch, in someone's office, in the corridor, over drinks, dinner, *anywhere* but in a fucking meeting. What meetings are very good for, however, is stitching people up – undermining, belittling and humiliating them.

This is particularly the case in gatherings where there are representatives present from several different departments. In the Business Affairs meeting I am now tooling into there are people from Legal (Trellick), Accounting (Leader-kramer), A&R (myself, Hastings and Waters, who are my colleagues, my fellow A&R managers, and Schneider, Head of A&R and our immediate boss) and International (Nicky). At the head of the curving glass-topped table sits Derek Sommers, the Managing Director. At forty-five Derek is, by some distance, the oldest person in the room. Katy, Trellick's PA, takes the minutes.

A useful trick in meetings like this is to try and have a little nugget or two about everyone else's business filed away. Something that they should have known, or that they haven't done that they said they'd do. You then slip your carefully sharpened nugget in at the correct moment – usually in the form of an innocent question or observation – and retire to a safe distance. Business Affairs is an especially good forum for this kind of backstabbing because the stakes are high. Every A&R man has his roster graphically analysed; how much you've spent on this act, how many records they've sold, what's still to be spent, how much more can we sell. There's nowhere to hide because it's like looking at a bank statement; there's credit or debit. And, believe me, we don't spend too long talking about the credits.

'Paul, the Rage LP?' Trellick says, turning to Schneider and sweeping a raft of thick blond hair back off his forehead. James Trellick is a generic toff, the end product of a lineage of fine dining and arse-fucking the poor that stretches back to the Domesday Book. He's tall and pointlessly handsome with the questing, jutting cleft chin that seems to be standard issue to his class. But it's the voice that really does it; an oak-and-gilt Etonian baritone, the sound of someone brought up to run the empire.

'Nearly done,' Schneider says, leaning back, eating a green apple. 'He wants to have a playback for everyone in a couple of weeks.' Schneider is like a weedier, discount, Jewish version of Trellick; similar clothes not filled out so well, a more minor public school, his voice a thinner, reedier take on Trellick's fruity rumble. Today his dark hair is slicked back and he has recently taken to wearing glasses, black-framed designer jobs the clown undoubtedly thinks make him look more intelligent. He will take them off and chew thoughtfully on them during meetings. Rodent-like, Schneider has a victim's face. The happenstances of time and geography surrounding his birth have provided him with opportunity, but there's no getting around it – if Schneider had been born a few decades earlier and a few hundred miles east of here, he'd have toppled off the train, blinking into the sun at Birkenau or Belsen, to find the guards falling over each other to get stuck into him. He nibbles on his apple and talks on, about release dates and lead times. He appears relaxed. He's not.

Truth be told, Schneider has signed one too many turkeys on the bounce and his position as Head of A&R is increasingly shaky. He signed 'drum'n'bass superstar' Rage two years ago and the debut album *Phosphor-essence* (fuck me) was the dance and style press sensation of last year, going gold and picking up a Mercury nomination along the way. However, a gold record means fuck all when you follow it up by dropping two million quid on signing four absolute donkeys in a row. You need platinum sales to insulate yourself from that kind of failure. Rage's new record is, Schneider hopes, his big Get Out of Jail Free card. Ominously, though, Rage has been working on the record in total isolation in a residential studio for the last four months and we haven't heard a note yet. Rumour has it (and rumour is always right, however briefly) that he is *battering* the chang. Grams and grams every day. As I brought the Rage deal in when I was a scout I'm still involved in the project. But at a safe enough distance, because Rage, I suspect, is a one-trick pony. A talent vacuum. He's also the nastiest piece of work you could imagine.

'And do we have a final tour support budget yet?' Derek asks.

'Just about,' Schneider says, tossing his apple core into the bin, 'Steven and I are having lunch with him and Fisher next week, over at MIDEM, to finalise everything.' (Schneider, in his turn, is trying to keep me close to the project, just in case the whole thing goes properly tits up and he suddenly needs an Oswald.)

'Good, good, make sure and cc me on the budget as soon as you have it please,' says Trellick, as he turns to face Rob Hastings now.

Hastings is thin as a guitar string and as nervy as a freshly released paedophile. His rabbit eyes are already shooting around the room – trying to work out where the next attack might be coming from – while his bucky little rabbit teeth wrap themselves around one of the filthy roll-ups he always seems to be smoking. He does not dress like the rest of us either; no black cashmere V-necks, no chisel-toed Prada or Kurt Geiger for Hastings. He wears untucked flannel shirts with shredded elbows, decrepit jeans and Dr Martens. I admit it, the guy is something of a puzzle to me. Someone told me that Rob told them he can comfortably live on a hundred quid a week. All he does is the odd pint, a curry here and there and the occasional lump of hash. He drives a VW. *He rolls his own cigarettes.* (Why isn't the dribbling megamongol spending his entire salary – and more – every single weekend? Why isn't he doing mountains of bugle and whores? Where are the five-star holidays and the Montecristos? Why isn't he dropping stacks of dough in Paul Smith and Armani? He earns enough. I mean, what the fuck is going on here?) He's a genuinely nice guy who has good taste in music and treats people with dignity and respect and the closest he ever comes to a hit record is when he has a wander round HMV on a Saturday. That's right, he's a fucking loser and how he ever got into A&R is completely beyond me. On one level I simply do not care if Rob lives or dies, but, on another, there have been times when I've been very glad he's here because he's made me look good. I could comfortably be lobotomised and still do my job better than Rob Hastings. All Trellick and Derek see, however, is the charcoal strip of the bottom line, which directly affects their bonuses, and consequently either of them would gladly have Rob fired. Fired? They'd have him fucking killed if they could. 'Raawb,' Trellick drawls, 'can you give us an update on the Sound Collective, please?'

There's lip-biting as Rob hauls himself upright in his chair for his weekly beating on this subject.

The Sound Collective – a loose affiliation of DJs, rappers, producers and MCs from Southend – were signed by Rob about eighteen months ago on the back of a couple of gushing articles in the dance and style press and a few late-night Radio 1 plays. Rob has been 'developing' them since then and we are no closer to releasing a record now than we were when we signed them. In fact, my mother is probably closer to releasing her debut album than the Sound Collective, who believe that our role is to shovel mountains of cash into their account and keep our fucking white mouths shut. We have now spent about four hundred grand and haven't heard a bar of music.

Rob rolls a cigarette between his fingers and goes for nonchalance, 'Update? Yeah, sure. Uh, I went down there last week. It's, ah, it's really coming together.'

Trellick: 'Aha. Good. Could you be little more specific?'

'Man, you wouldn't believe how the studio's coming together. They've painted the live room a sort of sky blue.' People look at him. I wonder if he's stoned.

'Good. Good,' says Trellick, losing patience. 'Do we have any music yet?'

'Not yet, no. The thing is MaxMan, their rapper, he had to go back to Trinidad to . . .' He blathers on about what these shiftless spear-chuckers have been up to with our money. Some people frequently dig their own graves in these meetings. Rob is building himself a fucking mauso-leum. Derek is colouring, turning from mauve to vermilion to fluorescent, the colour of his shirt.

Derek, in his turn, dresses like what he is: a wealthy, psychotic, tasteless, middle-aged queer. Grotesquely over-weight, he favours billowing shirts by Versace and Ralph Lauren – in fuchsia pink, emerald green, canary yellow and candy-striped combinations of all three – which are worn in a doomed attempt to disguise his enormous girth. His black hair and little beard are flecked with silver, the hair thinning on top now while remaining in a luxuriant thatch around the sides. His normal facial expression, the one he uses when he's 'off', when he isn't trying to present a certain persona, is really something: the hooded eyes rotate slowly, scanning, evaluating. The faintest flicker of a smile, or a sneer, trembles like an electrical current across his thin top lip while, above it, the crimson nostrils – the colour a painful reminder of the hellish quantities of cocaine and poppers he undoubtedly forced up there the night before – rhythmically flare gently or rapidly, according to his mood. I mean, he looks like fucking Caligula or something, mad and ravaged, cold and violent.

Rob is still going. 'And Massive Attack, Goldie and James Lavelle are all keen too. But the outboard equipment wasn't really up to scratch so we to had to replace most of it and –'

'Yes, Rob, I understand.' Trellick raises a hand to silence him. 'However, we're now,' he consults his notes, 'four hundred and seventy-eight thousand pounds in the hole on this act and we're no closer to having –'

'Look, James man, I know the situation is, y'know, frus-trating,' says Rob, trying to be assertive, 'but the, the creative process, man. Sometimes you can't, y'know, rush it.'

There's collective astonishment at this nonsense. I inter-rupt, directing my comments at Trellick.

'Yeah, James, hang on, it's not like nothing's happening. There's definitely a vibe for the band out there –' I manage to keep a straight face. Rob, the total cuntfuck, is nodding away, thinking I've come to his defence – 'and Rob's doing some good stuff to support it. I mean, those T-shirts look fantastic.'

Derek's head snaps up – a starving attack dog shown sirloin – 'T-shirts? What fucking T-shirts?'

Jackpot. In a misguided fit of craziness (and, I suspect, under extreme pressure from our coloured friends down in Southend) Rob had got a few Sound Collective T-shirts made up. Just a few, but spending company money on having T-shirts made for a band who are half a million quid unrecouped and who have yet to release a record is a bit like taking a full-page ad out in the *Sun* to announce yourself as winner of the lottery before you've even bought the ticket. Rob had quietly and proudly shown me one of the shirts a few days ago and I was pretty sure Derek had no idea.

Rob swallows. 'Yeah. I had a couple of T-shirts m—'

'YOU'RE MAKING FUCKING T-SHIRTS FOR A FUCKING ACT THAT DON'T EVEN HAVE A FUCKING RECORD OUT AND ARE HALF A MILLION FUCKING POUNDS IN DEBT TO US! *ARE YOU OUT OF YOUR FUCKING MIND?*' Derek's fury is so total and instant that, for a second, I think little Katy is going to burst into tears.

'But Derek, I thought if –'

'I DON'T GIVE A FUCK WHAT YOU THOUGHT! IF WE DON'T HAVE A FUCKING SINGLE FROM THIS BAND BY THE END OF THE MONTH WE'RE PULLING THE FUCKING PLUG! DO YOU UNDERSTAND?'

'But —' Rob is going down, drowning.

'DO YOU FUCKING UN-DER-STAND?' Derek pounds his fist on the table six times, with 'understand' getting three of them. Total silence. People admire the oatmeal carpet. Draw on their notes.

Derek is generally in a pretty bad mood. I don't know, maybe the experience of spending his entire adult life having men spray their burning jism over his face and back, of hearing them growl as they pump another radioactive load deep into his mouth or rectum, has soured him on life. I mean, it'd definitely fuck me off, being used as a human toilet for a quarter of a century.

In fact, this whole business of pumping and groaning and roaring and whatnot is really old news for hardcore queens like Derek. For ultra dark-side faggots in the nineties the idea of having some moustachioed arse-demon clad head to cock in studs and leather pummel away at you until your Gary looks like something out of a medical textbook has become a bit quaint. A Norman Rockwell painting. The bender equivalent of a married couple's Friday night, lights out, sheets over you, missionary position fumble. A few months back one of the kids from the marketing depart-ment had been up all night clubbing and found himself drinking in some hardcore after-hours place in the East End, one of those real HIV dens where the proper, certifiable queers round off their evenings. He wandered through a salty fug of amyl nitrate and GHB into a dimly lit back room where he bumped into Derek – chained to a wall, half naked and bleeding, with a couple of muscular Bethnal Green irons giving him a good beating.

Now, they say that an organisation's value systems, its

core beliefs, are shaped from the top down. Given that its Managing Director's idea of a reasonable evening's entertainment involves paying a couple of rent boys to kick the living shit out of him, it seems logical enough that greed, viciousness, duplicity, exploitation, hedonism and aggression feature prominently among the values our company encourages and rewards.

'Yes,' Rob finally whispers.

I mouth 'sorry' at him. He nods as if to say 'not your fault' and goes back to staring at the table, tears in his eyes. I nearly wet myself. Nicky shoots me a look. She is much smarter than Rob and may well have understood where my 'help' was coming from. I return her glare pleasantly, looking at her properly for the first time and noticing that today, as part of an ongoing and doomed attempt to disguise her unimaginable bulk – which the A&R department sweepstake variously puts at between sixteen and twenty stone – she is wearing some sort of muumuu, or sack, or kaftan. On some days she sports the sort of Lycra leggings you only ever see incredibly fat boilers wearing, the kind which make their thighs look like two immense black puddings. Her mouth is just a tiny little hole – a Polo mint lost in the enormous fleshy pudding of her face. The face itself is framed by lank greasy black hair and seared by angry clusters of spots, by deep ravines of acne. Most beasts of Nicky's stripe get thrown the odd break – the big tits, say, or the good complexion, or nice hair or something. Nicky got fucked out of the lot. Sometimes, when she's talking, I'll steal a glance at Trellick or Schneider as they listen to her, their expressions saying the same thing: how the fuck do you have the nerve to leave the house and show your face among decent society? Obviously Nicky was hired directly by Derek. As she has tits and a cunt she is completely invisible to the demented homo. Nicky is un-doable. You could not do her. She could not be done. If, by some chemical derangement, some alchemy of ketamine and smack, you woke up in bed to find Nicky next to you, you'd have two options: emigration or suicide. A plane ticket or an exhaust pipe.

'OK, boys and girls, moving on then,' Trellick announces, rapping his notes on the table, 'unsigned bands.' Waters starts yabbering on about some indie groups he's been to see; Ultrasound, Tampasm, Grouch, Angelica, Disco Pistol.

Later, as we leave the meeting and file down the corridor, Trellick sidles up to me and whispers, 'What is the meaning of life?' 'To drive your enemies before you and hear the lamentations of their women,' I reply automatically as, ahead of us, Hastings scuttles down the stairs.

'The object is to find a winner. The process makes you mean because you get frustrated.'

Simon Cowell

A couple of words for all you hopefuls out there in unsigned bands: Fuck. Off. Seriously, your parents are right. You may as well spend your guitar-string money on lottery tickets – your chances will be much the same. We receive upwards of three hundred unsolicited demo tapes every week. There are five other labels within our corporate group, all receiving about the same volume. That's fifteen hundred demos a week. There are six other corporate groups, EMI, Universal, Warner Bros, Polygram, BMG and Sony, most with several labels within them, all receiving at least the same amount as us, and probably a little more. That's over ten thousand little packages of hopes and dreams arriving every week. (And arrive is often all they do – the vast majority of these packages are never opened. They just lie in boxes and sacks around the A&R floor, where they seem to breed and multiply, spilling over the carpets and taking up sofa space until Tom, our work experience, has to lug sacks of them down to the incinerator where your hopes and dreams are – rightly – burned in the fires of hell.)

Occasionally, if it's a rainy afternoon and we're really bored and want something to do, a few of the A&R staff will gather in someone's office, roll ourselves a couple of thick spliffs, uncork a bottle of red, and go through one of the sacks marked 'UNSOLICITED DEMOS'. These sessions usually end with two or three of us on our hands and knees on the floor howling, gasping for breath, ribs and facial muscles aching.

To this ten thousand we should add (conservatively) another couple of thousand to cover the demos received by all the independent labels. That makes roughly twelve thousand demos a week received by the whole industry – well over half a million a year. In any given year my company will maybe sign something like ten to fifteen acts. The whole UK industry probably signs – at most – a couple of hundred artists every year. Out of these two hundred, in a very good year, you might have twenty or so who break through to some degree, who get their records on the radio, their pictures in the music press, and who fill decent-sized venues. Out of this twenty maybe half will eventually recoup the money invested in them. That's right – ten acts out of over half a million hopefuls will make themselves some real money. And yet a lot of aspiring musicians really believe that getting signed means they've made it, that the physical act of signing a recording contract means they're on the way to fame, riches and drinking Bono's Cristal at the Grammys.

Here's what's more likely to happen: on the back of a spurious 'buzz' from the music press, a few packed gigs in tiny clubs and a couple of late-night radio plays, some idiot like Rob Hastings offers you a record deal for, ooh, let's say, a hundred grand. Great! (You now owe us 100K.) You pack your job in *Quadrophenia*-style and take your parents out to the local Chinese for a slap-up feed where you tell them you'll 'never work again'. You leave Bolton (or wherever) and get off the train at Euston thinking to yourself, 'I am the fucking king.'

You're keen to get cracking on that debut album. However, the odds are that it will take Rob – or some cretin like him – months to make up his mind about a producer. He will then, inevitably, choose the wrong one. This guy will spend two or three months destroying what little talent you had to begin with and you're back to square one. Not content with getting the wrong producer the first time, Rob will pick the wrong guy a couple more times. By the time you've gone through this process three times it's a year down the line, the record still isn't finished, and your initial recording budget has tripled to about three hundred grand. (You now owe us 400K.)

By the time we finally get a single released your great mates over at press and radio could no longer give a good drop of spunk if you're dead or alive. They liked you a year ago. They've got new bands to play with now. In fact, I'll go you one further – the music press *hates* you now. You've gone from being the next Sex Pistols to the last Black Lace in twelve short months. So you get zero airplay and just a tiny smattering of reviews in the likes of the *Aberdeenshire Gazette* and the *North Wales Chronicle* (both of whom love the record; unfortunately no one who reads these papers is under sixty-five or lives within a hundred miles of a chart return shop).

In an attempt to rebuild your profile we send you out

on the road. But you've got a record company behind you now. Why would you travel in a Transit van like in the old days? So you get a fucking great tour bus the size of an aircraft carrier, six totally superfluous roadies, an outlandish catering company run by a pair of titless Notting Hill dykes and a light show with the equivalent power of the sun. Of course, you're still selling zero records and playing tiny venues so you're only getting paid about five hundred quid per show. However, the roadies/aircraft carrier/titless dyke/sun combo is costing something like five grand *a fucking day*. But – hey – we still believe in the band, man, so we underwrite the shortfall. You play twenty dates losing thousands every night, bringing your debt to us up to something like half a million quid. Oh, and by the way, your hundred-grand advance is now long gone. Where did it go? Well, let's see: tax, 20 per cent to your manager, and huge legal fees (your lawyer – some utter lowlife like Trellick – spent a lot of time arguing about pointless clauses in order to line his own pockets) leaves maybe twenty grand. You pay yourselves the princely salary of two hundred quid a week each. Alas, thanks to hanging out with animals like me and Waters, you all now have chronic chang habits, so this doesn't go far. Assuming there are four of you in the band, this means a monthly wage bill of about three grand. You're broke in a year. So we start advancing you extra money to cover the wages. A few months of this and you soon rack up another twenty Gs.

Finally we release your debut album. The *NME* expends a hundred words – and no photo – to call it 'undiluted piss'. We optimistically press five thousand copies. We sell seven hundred in the first week and two hundred in the second. Then, well, that's it. No more. Not another copy troubles a chart return machine anywhere in the world. Ever. Thanks to a combination of your mediocrity and our gross incompetence your debut LP – the crystallisation of all the energy, insight and ambition of your young life – has sold nine hundred copies. With retail discounts you have generated maybe four thousand pounds' worth of income. You are finished. Game fucking over. You are twenty-two years old and six hundred thousand pounds in debt to us – a bunch of subhuman demons who were your best friends a year ago but who would now gladly slit your throat and dance in your blood if we thought it would help us claw back a penny of your debt.

But sadly that's not an option. We take the loss on the chin, chalk it down as a write-off, and you get the coach back up to Bolton where you lie around your parents' house drinking lager and crying for a few weeks until you go crawling back to your old job painting houses, stacking shelves, frying chips or whatever the fuck you used to do up there. Until the day you die – probably at age fifty-five through a combination of abysmal Northern lung cancer and thirty-odd years of back-breaking work – you will bore your friends rigid with stories about your twelve months on top of the world, snorting lines in the toilets of London nightclubs and getting your dick sucked by some skanky monster on a tour bus parked behind Northampton Roadmenders. The time you spent with us playing at being pop stars will probably be the high-water mark of your entire life. Someone like me will probably be somewhere among your dying thoughts.

So, y'know, just don't do it. Go and become an accountant, or an IT guy or something. *Get a fucking job, you stupid cunt.*

*'I love sports because I'm a total competitor. If we're
playing tennis and you're winning, I'm going to get my
cock out and piss on the goddam net.'*

Don Simpson

'Ladieez an gennelmen, we are now beginning our descent
into Nice. Please return to your seats and fasten . . .'

She goes on. I look out of the window as the plane
continues to bank left, falling out of the sky towards the
runway that juts out into the Mediterranean. Dusk is
hitting the sky over to our right, the sky above Africa, and
turning it incredible colours – purple and gold and orange
and red. We yawn and quickly turn back to our copies of
Loaded, NME and *Music Week.* 'Ze local time is now five
twenty pee em.'

'All righty!' says Trellick in the seat next to me. 'The
cocktail hour!'

MIDEM. Sometime in the middle of the swinging sixties
a couple of Frog fruits decided it would be cool to have a
little convention in the South of France for the music
industry. Thirty years on, last week of every January,
something like ten thousand freeloading madmen descend
on Cannes from all corners of the globe and go crackers.

Champagne is drunk, lobsters are chomped, coke is honked and expense accounts are wildly abused in a week-long orgy of networking and deal-making. The Palais des Festivals on the Croisette houses hundreds of stalls where record labels, publishers, CD manufacturers and merchandising companies – everything central and peripheral to the music business – hawk their wares and ply their trades.

The plane is *rammed* with industry. Had this flight gone down, London's cocaine, prostitution and private members' club industries would have been devastated.

With a comic, a cartoon-strip 'EEEK!' the wheels rubberise the tarmac and we're already popping buckles and reaching for bags. (Hand baggage only for us on these trips. If you were to check a piece of luggage in our company you might as well be caught on your hands and knees in the bathroom blowing one of the stewards.) The major-label guys favour luggage by Mulberry and Prada while the indie boys all have record bags with the their label logos stitched or transferred on them: Soma, Talking Loud, Nova Mute, JDJ, Rising High, Moonshine and lots more. These guys will also have checked hulking great boxes of records, the promos and white labels they'll be hawking around the stalls for the next few days as they desperately try to license some piece of shit track for a couple of hundred quid to help cover the cost of the trip. This is how the indie boys do business. Those of us higher up the food chain will take meetings in the chill, air-conditioned suites of the big hotels.

I look around as my fellow A&R men – all smudged with champagne, spangled with vodka tonics – begin braying at each other. This is the sharp end of the record industry. The front line. We're the SAS. Fucking Delta Force. Our jobs involve making fast decisions with hundreds of thousands, often millions, of pounds at stake. These decisions are often predicated on no more than a hunch or a rumour and are often made under the influence of drugs, alcohol, peer-group pressure and fear.

The fear is constant because, and you must understand this, *no one really has a clue what they are doing.* There is no training programme. No manual. To say that the job (the art of predicting why husky-female-singer number 3 will sell more records than numbers 1, 2 and 4 through to 99, or why loutish-group-of-youths-with-guitars C will, six to twelve months from now, bewitch the nation's youth to a greater extent than groups A, F, P or Z) is an inexact science is like saying that Fred West could probably have been a better father. Here's what we, the A&R community, put our money on last year. This is what we reckon you're going to be buying and enjoying in the coming year or so: the Beekeepers, Luna, Feline, Proper, Lower, Arnold, the Dub Pistols, the Hybirds, the Aloof, Spookey Ruben, Sally Burgess, Ragga & the Jack Magic Orchestra, Genaside II, Hardbody, Finley Quaye, Jocasta, Old Man Stone, Ajax Disco Spanner, Gus Gus, Vitro, Travis, Agnes, Monkey, Tiger, Don, the Nicotines, Mantaray, Laguna Meth, Symposium, Deadstar, Foil, Peach, Manbreak, Ether, Charlotte Kelly, My Life Story, Robbie Williams, Aquasky, Code Red, the Driven, Dust Junkies, Silversun, Alistair Tennent, Kenickie, 1st Class, Ryan Molloy, North & South, Olive, Blue Amazon, Nash, Kelly Lorena, Belvedere Kane, Horace Andy, Ariel, Craig Armstrong, Kavana, Lilacs, One Inch Punch, Kings of Infinite Space, Mandalay, the Stereophonics, Akin, Amar, DJ Pulse, Snug, Eboman, M Beat, Slipmatt.

Go on then, *you* pick the change out of that lot. How many of those chancing spunkers will be kicking back in their country pile with a shelf full of Brits and Grammys in ten years? No one knows what they are doing and everyone has to live with the knowledge that they will – one day – be fired.

Right now you can hear fear rattling around the taxiing aircraft in her socially acceptable disguise: bravado.

'Oi! Oi! Oi!' someone shouts.

'Stelfox! You queer loser fool!' shouts another.

'We're larging it, mate!'

'Bollocks, you cunt!'

'Hello, tolers!'

It is the bravado of soldiers in a landing craft about to crunch onto a hostile shore. The few civilians on the plane – mostly rich Frogs with permatanned alligator skin – sigh and shake their heads. Needless to say, the last two hours have not been pleasant for them.

'What time we got this meeting, Steven?' Darren asks me.

'Nine.'

'Coolio.' Darren has been quiet on the flight, nervous. It's his first MIDEM. When he started here as an A&R scout a little less than two years ago, straight from running his own indie fanzine (called something like *Big Growling Pop Thing!*), he actually looked puppyish. He'd never taken cocaine in his life. Wide-eyed, he'd scamper from office to office with his stack of 7″ singles and demos, a constant ball of teenage enthusiasm. Well, we soon knocked that out of him. He looks like fucking Methuselah now: his skin dry and flaking; his eyes bloodshot and sunken; his hands forever trembling as he lights a fresh Silk Cut with the butt of the last one. He stumbles from office to office, nursing a constant hangover and a three-gram-a-week habit, and being shouted at for playing us some crappy record, or not playing us some crappy record, or whatever. When he isn't being shouted at in the office he's standing at the back of some festering indie gig until three in the morning. His glossy mane of tyre-black hair is already streaked with grey fissures. He has just turned twenty-one. I'm taking him into a few meetings with me. He's got good ears.

Parker-Hall stands up and stretches in the seat in front of us. 'Gawd blimey!' he says, yawning. 'Dis is a bit more blahddy like it! Nice an 'ot. Fackin' tayters in London!'

Parker-Hall is about five foot four and looks like an unruly, mischievous child, like one of the fucking Bash Street Kids. He comes from Hampstead. He went to Wellington. His parents own a couple of *streets* in north London. His surname involves a hyphen, for fuck's sake, and yet he often chooses to talk like a kind of blacked-up Dick Van Dyke – the splayed vowels, the vanished consonants – because somewhere around the age of fifteen he heard a hip-hop record and decided that Kaffirs were cool. But Parker-Hall is hot at the moment, very hot. So I laugh and clap him on the back and ask him, 'Where you staying then?'

'Facking Ritz Carlton, innit?' he says and I immediately wish I hadn't asked.

*

The door swings open. 'SCHTEEVEN! FAANTAS-CHTICK! FAANTASCHTICK! COME IN! COME IN!' Rudi Gertschlinger embraces me as he ushers us into his suite at the Martinez.

It's tacky-impressive: a huge lounge with chintzy furniture and floor-to-ceiling bay windows overlooking the Croisette and, beyond it, the sea. It is dark now and the lights of dozens of huge yachts twinkle here and there in the blackness.

The suite is almost as tacky-impressive as Rudi himself. In his late forties, with silver hair pulled back into a ponytail, he has the face of a well-fed concentration camp commandant, a role I am sure a couple of his direct ancestors probably filled.

We take a seat on the floral sofa and a minion fixes drinks as Rudi continues his spiel, his volume going down a notch to the simply unbearable level he uses for normal conversation. 'How have you been, my friend?! It has been too long! I must thank you for what you did with our last record! And thank you for sending the gold discs from the UK! We're trying to get them up but – you know – there is so little space left on our walls. Eh, Günter?'

'*Ja.*' This will be Günter's sole contribution to the meeting. He hands Darren and me tumblers of Buck's Fizz. Fucking Germans. Darren, nervous, knocks back half of the sickly orange jism in one go.

'When did you get here?' I ask looking around. Rudi looks pretty well ensconced; a tower of gleaming black hi-fi equipment is set up in the corner.

'Ach, just this morning. I had Günter and Anna fly ahead yesterday to get things set up. You know me, Steven. Time is money! I am – what did you call it – hardcore? I AM FUCKING HARDCORE!' He laughs his tits off and we cackle along with the mad bastard.

Rudi's company DMG (Dance Music Group. Yeah, must have taken him a while) has a huge building on the outskirts of Hamburg. On the top floor are offices housing his three record labels, artist management and video production companies. (He diversified into music from pornography.) Below that is a floor with several small recording studios and below that, on the ground floor, is Das Technotron, Rudi's nightclub. It works like this: he has teams of writers, engineers and producers working twenty-four/seven in all three studios. They're young kids desperate to break into the music business, so Rudi pays them a minuscule wage and they get free studio time to work on their own tracks. They get next to no income from record sales and Rudi's name appears as co-writer on every track that comes out of there. (In Rudi's defence here he will, occasionally, charge into one of the studios and scream at these guys to make it 'HEAVIER!' or 'FASTER! Or 'CRAZIER!') Amazingly most of them think this is a good deal. Well, for a while anyway. Inevitably they will get wind of how royally Rudi is fucking them and will ask for what's coming to them. At this point Rudi will show them a) the bit of paper they signed when they joined, and b) the fucking door.

And how do you write a song? Well, in the words of a hero of mine, the late, great Morris Levy, you 'get some kids in a room, you get a beat going, you get a few words together. Boom. You got a song.' This was Levy's state-ment to the judge when he was being cross-examined about his role in the creative process behind the many hit records his name had appeared as co-writer on. He had, of course, written absolutely jack. A bunch of spear-chuckers – on breadline wages but kept perfectly sweet with the occasional (leased) Cadillac and the odd chicken dinner – wrote the actual songs of course. Levy simply told them that, if they ever wanted the record to see the light of day, then they'd better be putting his name in the brackets too, and cutting him in for a goodly slice of the publishing. Levy was a music-industry mogul back in the fifties and sixties – the good old days. The Wild West. When artists did whatever you told them to and thought it was fucking Christmas when you paid them a royalty of half a pence in the pound. (Not like now, when every toerag with a demo tape has their lawyer in tow, some lowlife who, when he's not banging on about royalty uplifts, or trying to skank you for a few extra points, is trying to make everything non-recoupable and threatening you with an audit every fifteen minutes.) Back then you could really make some money. So, while Rudi's tactics might seem draconian to someone who dabbled in, say, ethics, they're hardly innovative.

When one of Rudi's kids has a track they are particularly enthused about they will charge downstairs to Technotron on a Friday or Saturday night – when the place is rammed with two thousand gurning, pilled-up Krauts – and get the DJ to give it a spin. If the crowd go uber-ballistic then they know they've got something and the tune will be pressed onto white labels, whacked up to the third floor, and mailed to key club DJs. It is as sure-fire a way to road-test pop-dance records as has ever been invented and has made Rudi one of the most successful producers in Europe and a millionaire many times over. I have licensed several of his tracks for the UK, earning Rudi's undying love by scoring top-five hits with the last two 'My Baby Wants to Come' and 'Doof! Doof! (This Is House)'. (Those titles. Again, fucking Germans.)

'Anyway,' Rudi is saying, 'let me make you happy, Schteeven. Günter.' He nods to his muppet who hits 'play' on the DAT machine. The room fucking *explodes* as a bass drum louder than the march of a thousand Waffen SS crunches out of the speakers. Rudi and Günter nod along. My fillings thrum. After a moment a flummoxing bass line kicks in and then a female voice joins it. It rumbles along like this for maybe a minute as a second, male, voice creeps in, insistently repeating the words '*Why don't you, why don't you, why don't you, why don't you . . .*' before the chorus drops: 'WHY DON'T YOU SUCK MY FUCKING DICK!'

I look up; Rudi and Günter have their eyes shut, completely lost in music. I glance left towards Darren but he won't meet my gaze, clearly too terrified of collapsing in hysterics. Or perhaps just plain terrified. The chorus is continuing to build, tribal drums pounding and a pack of guys yelling 'WHY DON'T YOU SUCK MY FUCKING DICK!' Except . . . they're not just yelling, the fucking thing is actually incredibly tuneful; a nagging keyboard riff twines around the vocal line, sweetening it.

There's a breakdown about halfway through where the inevitable rapper tells the girl to do stuff like lick his balls and stick her tongue up his ass and stuff, and then the chorus comes back in and it all builds to a deranged crescendo before the track stops abruptly and a single, passionate, soulful voice cries out, '*SUCK IT!*' Then it's over.

Rudi sits there for a moment breathing heavily, his

nostrils flaring, his eyes closed in rapt silence. Before I can say anything he leaps to his feet and thrusts his arms in the air as though he's scored the winner in the World Cup final. 'DIDN'T I TELL YOU!' he screams. 'A SMASH! OUR BIGGEST HIT YET!'

A few things are instantly apparent: 1) Rudi is off his fucking chanks (but we knew this already), 2) obviously no radio station in the civilised world will go anywhere near the record, and 3) the tune is insanely catchy.

'Wow,' I say, 'have you played it at the club yet?'

'Last Friday we dropped it for the first time. Schteeven, I cannot tell you. You have been to Technotron, *ja*? You know what they are like in there, they know their music. Well, they went FUCKING INSANE!' He always says this.

'Wow,' I repeat.

'Who's the singer?' asks Darren redundantly, for something to say.

'Michelle. She is, what do you call them, Schteeven, a moose?' He waves a hand dismissively, 'Ha ha! But this is not a problem. We will find someone else to front it.'

'It's fantastic, Rudi. It's just . . .' I spread my palms.

'The lyrics?'

'Exactly, Rudi.'

'Ach, you English! So schquare! It is no problem, we have a radio edit almost finished.'

'Yeah? Wow. Really? How, er, what did you do?'

'We have changed the chorus to "*Why don't you slap me on the ass!*"'

Holy shit. If this isn't the tackiest, stupidest, most unworkable idea I ever fucking heard then it's definitely in the top five. 'Great!' I say. 'That could work.'

'So, what do you think, my friend? You know I will offer this to you for the UK.'

What do I think? The record is absolutely, off-the-scale, demented, tacky, cheesy, single-entendre garbage. But, and never forget this, this is exactly what 99 per cent of the Great British Public enjoy. It is also properly infectious and stranger things have happened. However, I must also be mindful that while Rudi has as good a track record as you can have with this type of crap, he has also shafted a few labels for hundreds of thousands of pounds for records that have charted at 41 before disappearing without trace. (Last year Virgin paid a fortune for a record of Rudi's called 'Happy Song!'. I remember being in Trellick's office when the midweeks came in showing it at no. 46, with a strontium fucking anchor. Laugh? We nearly needed oxygen masks.)

'How much, Rudi?'

'Ach, Schteeven, I do not know. You paid us, what, twenty-five for the last one?'

'Twenty.'

'Whatever. I could not take less than thirty and eighteen points.' (Percentage points – his royalty rate from us.)

I nod. 'That doesn't sound unreasonable.' Like fuck it doesn't. By the time we pay this Nazi paedo thirty grand for the record, commission some remixes, do artwork, promo the record to club and radio, manufacture the stock, take out print and street advertising and make a video, it will cost us maybe a hundred grand to try and have a hit with this piece of shit. This is what is involved every time you say 'yes'.

'Schteeven, it is a fucking bargain. Where are your ears? It's a smash.'

'Tell you what, let me talk to business affairs, crunch some numbers and I'll come back to you tomorrow. OK?'

'OK,' he shrugs, 'but don't hang around, my friend. I want you to have this, I am playing it to you first, but you know what this place is like!' He gestures out the open window towards Cannes. Several floors below throngs of industry people are heading out for the evening, their laughter and chatter drifting up towards us.

'I'll call you,' I say as I get up.

'Good! Good! Will I see you tonight? Where are you eating?'

'I'm not sure yet. What are you guys up to?'

'I will be in the Barracuda! Getting my *FUCKING DICK SCHUCKED*!' he roars, punching me playfully on the arm.

As soon as the lift doors close Darren bursts out laughing. 'Christ, he's off his tits.'

'No shit. But what did you think?'

'It's a fucking tune, mate, no question, but those lyrics, man.' He shakes his head. 'Would this edit work? I don't know. What are you thinking?'

What am I thinking? I don't know. It's my job to know, but I don't. 'I'm thinking . . . two world wars and one World Cup,' I say.

He cracks up. His laughter contains just the right amount of hysteria and reverence due to a superior and benefactor.

Later, looking through some crap in my hotel room (a decent enough, sea-facing room at the Majestic – Rebecca came through), I noticed that there were delegates from no fewer than ninety-one countries attending this year's convention. Apart from the obvious – the Krauts, Frogs,

Shermans, Japs and Brits — there's a raft of the less obvious — New Zealanders, Mexicans, Russians — and a clutch of the downright crazy — Ugandans, Romanians, fucking *Tanzanians*. I mean, I don't know much about the domestic affairs of Tanzania, granted, but I'd have imagined they had more pressing concerns back there — and better uses for their cash — than sending some witch doctor to Cannes at incredible expense so he can watch a load of drunk, chang'd-up fools shout abuse at each other and vomit hundred-quid dinners down the toilets of nightclubs. How high can music be on their agenda?

But everyone gets along. Oh yes. Background and ethnic origin form no barrier to trade here. If there's a deal to be struck, if there's dollar, yen, rouble or franc to be made then differences will be put aside. Diversity tolerated. Look over there — the Arab contingent is uncorking the Cristal to celebrate a potentially lucrative licensing deal for *Ultimate Bar Mitzvah Classics*! In another corner the staunchly Catholic label boss is snapping up the exclusive distribution rights for an exciting new label called Red Hand: Kill All Fenian Bastards. Music really does cross all barriers. Greed is so incredibly inclusive.

The following afternoon, and Schneider and I have a table on the glass-encased veranda of an insanely expensive restaurant at the far end of the Croissette, overlooking the harbour. There's lead crystal, thick, starched table linen and heavy silver cutlery. Personally I think it's an own goal bringing Rage into a place like this, but Schneider, antici-pating a disagreement (because, with someone like Rage, there is only ever disagreement), wanted somewhere off the beaten track, somewhere that wasn't going to be rammed with industry. Which this place isn't – there's just lots of chic lunching Frogs, cracking open the rust-red exoskeletons of big lobsters and scraping the creamy flesh from the softer, mottled-white shells of the langoustines. Rage and Fisher, his manager, are so late that we've ordered: huge tureens of thirty-quid bouillabaisse sit steaming in front of us. We spoon and sip Sauvignon and make small talk about deals and rumours. Schneider is nervous, his foot tapping away beneath the table. He knows he is on ultra-thin ice with this record. Below the ice, waiting to tear him to pieces, are the sharks. Terrible, ravenous sharks with rusted hypodermics for teeth, the chambers of the syringes filled with plague, anthrax and AIDS. They swim in fast circles, coming nearer and nearer to the surface as the ice begins to creak and splinter beneath Schneider's gleaming Patrick Cox loafers.

Suddenly we sense the pulse, the heartbeat of the place, change and we look up to see Rage and Fisher come swaggering in.

Fisher is impressive enough in here – a bald, twenty-stone East End hooligan with a heavy, gold cord around his neck, dressed in billowing, baggy sportswear topped off with dodgem-sized paper-white trainers – but Rage . . . fuck me.

Forget the fact that he's wearing shades, a baseball cap and a T-shirt that says 'NIGGER', it's the *jewellery*. Half a dozen gold studs are punched into each earlobe. Three thick cables of gold hang around his neck. On every finger of each hand is at least one, often two, huge gold rings, all studded with rocks – diamonds, rubies, emeralds. On his right wrist is a custom-made gold Rolex so encrusted with gems that to try and read the time on it might induce a brain haemorrhage. From his left wrist dangles a half-kilo platinum-gold bracelet. Just to take a step must be like a half-hour workout. He looks like he's covered himself in glue and charged headlong through an outlet called Rich Black Bastard.

'All right, boys?' he says, simultaneously slapping my shoulder, pumping Schneider's hand, aggressively tugging a chair out and casting an imperious glance around the place. The rest of the clientele suddenly find things of great interest in their soup bowls and among the dismembered sea creatures on their plates.

Rage's success is recent and he's not used to being in places like this. Consequently he's on red alert, Defcon 3, ferociously on the lookout for any sign of being patronised, any flicker of condescension. He doesn't even look at the menu proffered by the swallowing waiter. 'Burger and chips, mate, yeah?' he says.

Burger and chips. Steak and chips. Always ordered 'well done'. These are the staple restaurant foods that will be ordered by every filthy working-class toerag you will ever sign. (Until they get saddled with some Hampstead girlfriend – some Millie, some Sophie – who starts civilising them, teaching them about wine and telling them what a fish is. Then you've got to put up with the bastards ordering Rioja with Dover sole and talking about fucking restaurants.) The waiter backs away, looking sick and uncertain, and, after the briefest of 'How's tricks?', Fisher gets straight to making his point. It's basically the same point he makes in every meeting: how we should be paying them more money.

'We gotta go out on this fucking tour, right?' he says.

'I don't wanna do it in the first fucking place,' says Rage.

'Easy,' says Fisher, placing one of his massive wanking paddles reassuringly on his client's arm but not taking his eyes from Schneider, 'we're gonna do the fucking tour . . .' he says benevolently. I wonder how thoroughly they've rehearsed this.

'Great,' says Schneider.

'But we ain't gonna dismantle the studio to take it on the road . . .'

'No way, man,' says Rage, shaking his head solemnly, as if we're asking him to sell one of his – surely many and illegitimate – children into sex slavery.

'So we need to rep, repli . . .' Fisher has a quick pop at pronouncing 'replicate', then changes his mind, 'buy all the gear again, you know? To have a touring rig.'

'How much are we talking about?' Schneider asks.

'Sixty,' says Fisher with a straight face, but his left hand goes automatically to his lobe to finger a big gold stud. This tour – with backing musicians, lighting, transport, hotels, crew, catering, sound, etc. – is already costing us something like eight grand a show in tour support.

'Mmmm,' says Schneider.

'Excuse me, sir?' The manager is standing there, our waiter hiding behind him. Rage swivels around, already, always, angry.

'Yeah?'

'I'm afraid, with your order, we are a zeefood restron and –'

'For fuck's sake,' Rage says.

'Peraps sir would like to shoes another dish?' The guy

offers him the menu again. Rage doesn't even look at it.

'Look, you can make me some fucking chips, man. You got potatoes in the back, ain't you? All you do is fry 'em up in . . .' Rage thinks, 'stuff.'

'There are potatoes on the menu, sir, oven-roasted in oleeve oil, thyme and zee salt?'

Rage clenches his fists together, black skin banding white around gold rings. Here we go.

Every time I have been in a public place with Rage there has been an angry, dramatic scene – a walkout, a storm-off, physical violence on more than one occasion. I'm not of what you'd call a 'cheery' disposition myself, but these guys, guys like Rage, you wonder how they do it. What does it take to wake up every morning already furious, and for that anger to increase steadily during the course of *every single fucking day*? He lives in a world where every possible encounter – from parking the car, to buying a pint of milk, to eating dinner, to having a business meeting – is fraught with the potential for real or imagined 'disrespects', which must be immediately, viciously, avenged. How *does* he do it? Then you remember his childhood: the foster-homes, the beatings. His actual conception: a radioactive wad of angry nigger-rapist semen getting pumped into some gibbering crack whore to produce the 'drum'n'bass superstar' sitting opposite me.

Here's the thing. When Rage was a little boy his mother drove them from London up to Manchester for the day. She pulled up in the city centre and made him get out of the car. Then she drove back to London. He never saw her again. He lived on the streets – crying and begging – for a couple of days before the cops got hold of him. They slung him in and out of a bunch of care homes for the next ten years, where he was doubtless constantly beaten and fucked in the ass. Let's face it, that'd fuck you off, wouldn't it? That'd about do it for you with regard to the notion of unconditional love.

But today, surprisingly, he decides to be benevolent. Graceful even. 'Whatever,' he says airily, somehow managing to wave an ingot-heavy hand, 'just bring me some fucking food. Yeah?'

'Couldn't we just hire the gear for the tour?' I say.

Rage shakes his head, sucking air in through a mouthful of chrome teeth. 'Can't work with no hired gear, man. No way.'

'Look,' says Fisher, 'do you guys believe in this fucking guy,' he jerks a pudgy thumb at Rage, 'long term?'

'Yes,' we both lie.

'Then this ain't gonna be the only tour we ever do. It's an *investment*.'

'I just don't think we can justify the additional expense,' Schneider says, nervously. 'The tour support's high as it is.'

'Right,' Fisher sighs as he lays down his last card, 'we'll have to pull the tour.'

We laugh. They don't.

'I ain't fucking doing it,' says Rage. There's a long silence.

'But,' Schneider says, realising they're perfectly serious, 'we've already paid for advertising, we've —'

'Not our problem,' says Fisher.

Would they pull their own tour out of spite? Of course they fucking would. When your own mother tells you to go and get fucked at the age of seven, telling the rest of the world to go and get fucked on a daily basis holds no terrors. I wonder why they bothered with lunch. Why didn't they just walk into the boardroom with stockings over their heads, wielding shotguns and demanding sixty grand?

Schneider pretends to think for a long time. There's nothing to think about.

'Thirty grand,' he says, 'recoupable.'

'Fifty,' Fisher says.

'Forty.'

'Deal, man.'

They shake hands. At some point we'll see a *Fantasy Island* budget from Fisher's management company with a bunch of fake receipts stapled to it for silly money they never spent on gear they do not own. Essentially Schneider has just agreed to give them forty grand, no strings attached. We might get it back if – and it's a continent-sized 'if' – Rage's album ever recoups all of its costs.

Neither Rage nor Fisher really had any formal schooling, but, in their own ways, their backgrounds prepared them thoroughly for a successful career in the music business. There was a visa problem for a trip to the States last year and the legal department had to sort it out. Trellick got to see the rap sheets.

Yes, you guessed it. Back in the day Rage and Fisher were both muggers.

'So,' Schneider says pleasantly, 'how's the album coming?'

'Mate,' Rage says sombrely, slowly removing his Oakley's for the first time and making eye contact with Schneider. His irises are so brown as to effectively be black. A shark's eyes. 'It's gonna blow your fucking tits off.'

'When can we hear it?'

'Soon, mate. Soon.'

The waiter glides into view. With a triumphant '*Voilà!*' he sets an enormous platter of *fruits de mer* in front of Rage. Rage looks at it – at the spines, tendrils and tentacles, the claws, wobbling antennae and glistening jet eyes of dozens of dead crustaceans. He looks up and says to the beaming waiter, 'Are you having a fucking giraffe, cunt?'

Midnight in the lobby bar of the Martinez. There must be at least three hundred people in here – a boiling scrum of booze and noise and networking. Business cards are constantly exchanged, phone numbers scribbled on napkins and punched into mobiles. People hold imaginary receivers up to their ears and mouth 'Call me' across the room while others throw their heads back and unleash torrents of horrible laughter. The roar of forced bonhomie is deafening. Massively outnumbered, a handful of melting, white-jacketed waiters squeeze through the crush with silver trays, bearing bottles of Krug, Cristal, San Miguel, Budweiser, Heineken, Stoli and Johnnie Walker. A beer costs about eight quid. To have a bottle of Scotch or vodka left on your table will cost you about three hundred. Plenty of people are happily paying that rather than trying to tag an exhausted, near-fainting waiter every fifteen minutes.

Dinner had been the usual deal you fall into over here, with fourteen of us sharing a table at a seafood place on the Croisette: Chardonnay, champagne, cognac, cocaine and untouched food. Swearing and shouting and braying laughter. Elderly customers asking to be moved then the tightly smiling maître d' and the trio of harassed waiters hunched over the metre-long bill and the stack of credit cards and francs we've flicked onto the ruined tablecloth.

Trellick and I have shouldered our way in at the bar, passing close to Parker-Hall and Marty Kersch, a senior Vice President at Capitol in LA. Parker-Hall – as I knew he would – nodded politely but made no move to introduce me or bring me into the conversation. In fact, I watched as he quickly thought of some detailed, urgent question he had to put to Kersch and leaned in close to yell it until I passed by. This is SOP; if you are engaged in a visible, centre-of-the-room, high-profile conversation with someone very powerful then you must jealously protect that conversation from interlopers of your own, or lower, stature. Conversely, had Parker-Hall been talking to some muppet – some guy who works in marketing for some tiny French dance label whom he had mistakenly fallen into conversation with – he would have greeted me like a long-lost brother, brought me into the discussion, and then fucked off leaving me with the muppet. And I would do the same to him in a heartbeat.

'How was Rage by the way?' Trellick asks me.

'The usual.'

'And the album?'

'He reckons it'll blow our tits off.'

'Mmmm, odd that.'

'I know. Pompous cunt. Just out of interest,' I say, lowering my voice, 'for argument's sake,'

'Go on.'

'Let's assume the new Rage album is a pile of shit. Unsellable.'

'Assume away.'

'What's that going to do to Schneider's position?'

'Death row. Game over.'

'So if, when, Schneider goes . . .'

'Who's in the frame for Head of A&R?'

'Yeah.'

'Well, it's not fucking rocket science. It's either you or Waters, or they go out of house.'

'Do a Duke of Wellington on Waters.'

'Pros: a couple of years older than you, a little more experienced in making albums, the rank and file think he's a nice bloke. Cons . . . he's a lazy, brain-dead, cocaine addict with the attention span of a fucking gnat who hasn't had a hit record in donkey's.'

'So he could get the job?'

'Definitely.'

I try to run a few Waters-as-my-boss scenarios through my head: Waters shouting at me because we've missed out on some deal. Waters calling me into meetings, locking me out of meetings with important managers and heads of departments, Waters sending me off to, I don't know, fucking Stoke on a Saturday night to see some band. But I don't get very far with picturing any of this, because a crimson mist keeps closing in, a skull-charge of blood keeps dimming my vision. I feel faint. Sick.

Trellick looks at me and realises exactly what I am thinking. 'You know what they say, young Steven. It's not dog-eat-dog around here . . .' He drains his glass.

'I know,' I say, finishing the aphorism for him, 'it's dog-gang-rapes-dog-then-tortures-him-for-five-days-before-burying-him-alive-and-taking-out-every-motherfucker-the-dog-has-ever-known.'

'Any more for any more?' Trellick says, pointing at my glass, signalling with a drinking motion to Darren and Leamington behind me.

'Wifebeater,' I say.

'Rockschool,' say the other two.

Trellick gets the Stella and the Jack and Cokes in.

Three a.m. and we are *ruling* this fucking place.

We're in a big, tasteless nightclub somewhere on the outskirts of Cannes. It must be 120 degrees in here. We've commandeered our own chunk of the packed dance floor right in front of the DJ booth and we are going bonkers.

Underworld's 'Born Slippy' pounds at festival volume from the massive sound system. There are about fifteen of us now, with waifs and strays. I'm leaping around with an ice bucket on my head, Trellick is down on his knees on the dance floor, playing air guitar, Darren is spraying champagne all over the place, Ladbroke is stretched out against a pillar, nearly unconscious.

Schneider and I split another pill and we're all shouting along to 'Born Slippy', which gets mixed into something else which gets mixed into something vaguely familiar – tribal drums, lolloping bass – and we're all grooving along to it for a minute before – *whump!* – the chorus drops: *'WHY DON'T YOU SUCK MY FUCKING DICK!'* The entire room goes absolutely fucking nuts. By the time it gets to the second chorus everyone is singing along. Holy. Fucking. Shit.

I'm staggering off the dance floor, pushing my way through dancing, singing idiots, trying to find an exit, pawing in my hip pocket for the Nokia. Someone puts an arm around me and shouts, 'Hey, Steven! Is this the record you're signing?'

'Yeah. Done deal.' The lie is automatic.

'Congratulations, mate! Fucking tune.'

Darren looks like he doesn't know whether to laugh or cry. I pull him close and – still smiling – scream in his ear, *'We verbally agreed the fucking deal today. OK?'*

He nods and I stumble off towards an exit, dialling Rudi's number. It rings a few times before going straight to message. 'RUDI!' – I bellow over the roar of a thousand people screaming *'WHY DON'T YOU SUCK MY FUCKING DICK!'* – 'IT'S STEVEN. JUST TO CONFIRM – WE DEFINITELY WANT THE RECORD! "SUCK MY DICK"? WE WANT IT! CALL ME WHEN YOU GET THIS!'

I hang up and lean against the wall, catching my breath. The door to the main room opens and some kid I know from EMI wanders out, gurning, with sweat pouring off him and some sour-faced stick-insect cow dressed in nothing but a thong and some duct tape over her nipples on his arm.

'All right Steven?' he says. 'Fucking tune this, ain't it?'

'Yeah, fierce.'

'Graham was quick off the mark, eh?'

'Uh?'

'Graham at Sony. He signed this record tonight.'

'Yeah?' I swallow.

'Yeah, he was cracking the champagne in the Barracuda with Rudi Gertschl—'

'Excuse me.' And I'm off.

This is the problem with chasing hit singles – it's such hard fucking work. And you have to chase them all the time. If you're going to rely on singles to perk up your bottom line then you have to have a lot of them; four, five, six every year.

This is why I must soon find an act that will sell albums. Smack an album into the top ten that stays there for a year or two and you start generating proper turnover. Making real money. You can start to do less work. (You've been watching, you know I'm overworked.) This is why a little fucker like Parker-Hall is revered in A&R terms: he has signed a bona fide platinum albums act. Who are cool and credible to boot. The mother lode. True, the fluky, chancing prick just happened to be in the right place at the right time but who gives a fuck; he is respected as a 'music guy' – the ultimate A&R accolade.

I'm not. Which is why I'm pulling myself out of bed at ten in the morning and, pausing only to throw up, dialling the Martinez with trembling fingers. Some rude, inefficient French switchboard bumbling goes on for a couple of minutes before the receptionist comes back with, 'I am sorry, sir, that line is engaged.' I tell her – with some emotion – that it is a matter of life or death that Mr Gertschlinger rings me back as soon as he is off the phone.

I crawl across the room and rack up a twelve-quid bill in forty seconds by swallowing three mini-Cokes from the minibar. Everything is mini except for my hangover, which is most definitely fucking maxi. I struggle to place the hangover on my personal Richter scale. Eight? Nine? I try to remember how the previous night ended, but it's like I fell asleep watching some movie and I'm trying to recall where I saw it up to. Then I throw up again.

Breathing hard, I rub my pulsing temples and look around. There's a pool of vomit on the floor, a rusty streak of blood on the white sheets, pieces of glass from a broken champagne bottle scattered all over the place, and a woman, a hooker I guess, looking at me from the bed. Other than that the room seems to be completely normal.

The hooker – who is black and fat – starts talking to me in French. I don't get all of it, but the gist seems to be that I still owe her money from the night before, for some unspeakable extra I must have made her perform. I ignore her, lost in wondering exactly how I'm going to pin the blame for us not signing Rudi's track on Darren. The phone rings and I snatch it up.

'Hello?'

'Schteeven? It is Rudi.' He sounds formal, almost stern, and immediately I know it is bad.

'Rudi, listen, I –'

'I know. I got your message this morning. I am sorry to tell you this, but I have done the deal with Sony.'

Fucking Nazi cunt fuck shit. 'But, Rudi, I told you I –'

'Come on, Schteeven, we are big boys. These things happen.'

I close my eyes and ask him, 'Have you signed the contract yet?'

'As good as. We have a verbal agreement.'

Thank Christ. 'How much?'

'Schteeven, it doesn't matter now. I shook hands on it with Graham last night. As you know, I am a gentleman. A man of my word.'

'Come on, Rudi, how much?'

'There will be other records, my friend.'

'*How much?!*'

'Sixty,' he says, almost sounding embarrassed.

'I'll see you in half an hour,' I say, hanging up.

The hooker gets to her feet, wincing, and tiptoes gingerly towards the bathroom. She's clearly having some trouble walking, and I notice a couple more streaks of dried blood on the backs of her legs and buttocks. Her tone of voice is properly angry now and it dawns on me that I must have been going absolutely bananas last night.

The Barracuda is a Cannes institution. You go into the main bar – a black, windowless hole just off the Croisette – and drink yourself senseless for a few hours, ordering bottles of champagne at two hundred quid a pop, before asking for the 'special vintage'. Your credit card is whisked through the machine and you are charged for another bottle that doesn't appear. Instead, you get ushered through to one of the little back rooms where one of the waitresses hunkers down and slides your balls into her mouth, the waitresses being, in fact, top-notch ostros. Hookers. The Barracuda is the music industry in microcosm: the guys are out front dancing around with champagne glasses on their heads while the girls are chained up in the back, gargling with spunk. The best part of it is that the credit-card receipt still reads 'champagne', rather than 'vicious blow job'. Consequently, every MIDEM there is a steady flow of company plastic over the Barracuda's bar. Last year, when Trellick finally left the place after a seven-hour session, staggering into the dawn clutching a bottle of bubbly and a sheaf of Amex slips totalling three and a half grand, the only people left were the cleaners and a few 'waitresses' rubbing their aching jaws. As the madame held the door open for him she playfully thrust her hand between his legs, grabbed the aching, drained raisins he had instead of balls, and huskily intoned, *'Sexos machinos!'*

'I am sorry for the, ah, mix-up, Schteeven,' Rudi is saying.

'Hey, don't worry about it. We got it fixed.'

'I know. You know I always want – ach! Softly, baby, softly!'

'I understand, Rudi, Graham made you an offer and, ah . . .'

'Ja, ja! I was only trying to . . . ach, ah *gut!'*

Rudi and I – both paralytic – are sprawled on facing sofas in one of the back rooms drinking champagne. I take a long swig and look down: an absolutely gorgeous French girl of maybe twenty-one is trying to take her tonsils out with my cock. She looks up and makes perfect eye contact with me for a second or two before her dark brown eyes flip upwards in their sockets and she moans softly, as though my sour prick tasted like cherries and ice cream. Through the beaded curtains that serve as a door we can hear the roar from the bar drifting down the hallway.

I lie back and shut my eyes. We closed the deal with Graham Westbourne calling Rudi's suite the whole time going nuts and upping his offer. Trellick has the signed contracts in his briefcase and Darren has been comprehensively briefed on the need for utmost secrecy as to why my indecision has cost us thirty thousand quid.

Actually, we're now in kind of scary territory – a proper bidding war and a sixty-grand deal for a one-off single means you have to have a proper hit. Number 18 is no use to anyone. This stupid, dreadful, novelty record will have to be top five, minimum, for me to walk away with any kind of aplomb. Top five and we'll make the cash back purely from licensing the utter piece of shit onto dozens of *Now That's What I Call A Total Insult To Fucking Humanity, Vol. 32* type compilations.

But this is all to come. Right now, tonight, we got the record and the competition didn't. This can be savoured for a day or two before you have to worry about turning the fucking thing into a hit.

I become aware of Rudi, only a few feet away, chanting *'Ja! Ja! Ja!'* as he starts to come. I sit up and watch him roar a final *'JA!!!'* as he blasts a jet of hot Teutonic semen into the bobbing French head, which flies back as though a shotgun has gone off in its mouth: 'Ahhgroooughh!' she says.

After a moment Rudi gets up and zips up. We chink flutes over the head of my girl and I watch him – this gentleman, this man of his word – tooling off through the beaded curtains, wiping his forehead with a handkerchief, while his waitress crawls to the corner where, retching and coughing, she spits his cum into a wicker waste-paper basket.

Going home in the morning, I think.

February

Thanks to the Spice Girls, Virgin has an 88.9% share of the singles market. Mark and Lard are confirmed as the new hosts of the Radio 1 breakfast show. EMI's share price is in the toilet. BlueBoy and Vitro are hot new acts. No Doubt have a no. 1 single. Alan McGee is preparing to launch the debut album by 3 Colours Red. He says, 'By the second or third record we'll sell five million. I'm serious. They're going to be huge.' Some guys get done for killing that black kid, Stephen something. The Brit Awards happen.

'A woman's two cents is worth two cents in the music business.'

Loretta Lynn

Everyone is up and out of their seats and table-hopping now. The thrum of conversation is rising and no one is listening to the Bee Gees, who, incredibly, are *still* onstage about thirty yards away, cranking out the greatest hits for the tolers watching at home. Their nerve-shredding harmonies keen out over the disinterested crowd of executives and flutter up into the darkness, disappearing into the steel-and-concrete roof of Earls Court. It'll probably sound fine on television though.

I lean back in my chair, away from my cold, untouched dinner – salmon, broccoli and new potatoes – and pinch the bridge of my nose. I inhale hard and there's a pop in my ears as the rock of coke dislodges and shoots down the back of my throat, pleasingly strong and bitter. I loosen my tie and wash the glob of chang down with lukewarm Chardonnay and pretend to listen to Desoto while I scan the crowd for someone better to talk to: Lucian Grange from Polydor, Keith Blackhurst from Deconstruction, Nancy Berry from Virgin, Colin Bell from London Records and Matt Jagger.

Ferdy Unger-Hamilton from Go! Beat is talking to Derek, Pete Tong and some guy from Island. Unger-Hamilton has his arm around Gabrielle, her statuette for Best British Female Artist on the table in front of them. Rob Stringer is laughing his head off as he talks to one of the guys from the Manic Street Preachers, their awards on the table next to them. Frank Skinner, Vinnie Jones, Simon Cowell from BMG, some soap star, one of the *Trainspotting* guys and Geri Halliwell. The singer from Kula Shaker and Sony's Muff Winwood. Geri from the Spice Girls totters by, a bottle of champagne in one hand and the cheeks of her (massive) arse spilling out of the bottom of the ludicrous Union Jack minidress she wore for their performance. I wave to some girl I vaguely recognise, Anita or something. I think she's an A&R coordinator over at BMG. She's wearing a tight black dress, kind of Chinese-style with gold patterning, split right to the top of her thigh and slashed deeply between her breasts. Her hair is cut in a short bob. Normally she dresses kind of indie, I guess – T-shirts, trainers, jeans. She waves back, blows me a kiss. Hello.

'Oi, loser!' Trellick claps me on the leg, shouting over the music. '*Listen*. This is good.' I turn back and lean in between Trellick and Desoto. Behind them Ross – our Head of Marketing – and Waters are heckling the Bee Gees. Ross is in his early thirties, tall with a businesslike crew cut.

'Right. Strap yourself in,' Desoto says, leaning forward. Desoto – a lawyer, a friend of Trellick's – is coke-sweating, his rugby-player bulk straining against the seams of his suit. His fine brown hair is shorter now than it used to be. Until a few years back he kept it pretty long but he felt, rightly, as he approached fifty, that it was getting a bit undignified.

Desoto went to Harrow, then the Bar, then, briefly, the City. When he figured out that life in the square mile meant that you had to get up in the morning and actually work for a living he soon gravitated towards music industry law. He made a fortune. Then he lost it.

'A couple of weeks ago I put an ad in *Music Week* for a new PA.'

'You're firing Sophie?'

'No. *Listen*,' Trellick says.

'I put the ad in and made it non-specific,' Desoto continues, 'it just said "major music industry lawyer seeks PA blah blah blah". The response is Off. The. Fucking. Scale. I get something like fifty replies in forty-eight hours.'

'Sen-say-shunal,' says Trellick.

'So I go through the CVs, checking out the dates of birth to make sure they're all under thirty, and ring six of them back.'

'But you're flying blind at this point, no?' I say.

'Correctos, but you have to figure that out of six at least one them is going to be doable, no?' We both nod. 'So, I arrange for them to come in for interviews, different days, all at the close of business, around five thirty. Now,' he pushes his glass towards Trellick, who is pouring the three of us more champagne, 'I kick off by saying to them that I'm *really* sorry but it looks like I won't have a job to offer any more.'

'Why not?'

'Oh,' he waves a hand, 'because my original PA just decided that day to stay on.' A bit of bread flies past me. Ross.

'But,' I intone slowly, beginning to see where Desoto is going with this.

'You've got it. *But*, she's probably going to leave in about six months, so if they'd still like to have a chat, then in the future who knows?'

'Good work. Continue,' says Trellick, emptying the bottle and upending it in the ice bucket.

'By this time it's after six so I –'

'Sorry,' I interrupt, 'what's the quality like?'

'*Astonishingly* high. Out of six there's only one monster, two are doable and three of them are sen-say-shunal.'

'Fucking result.'

'So, it's after six now –' Suddenly, thankfully, the Bee Gees finish playing and Ben Elton walks back on and starts crapping away. Desoto lowers his voice a little. 'It's after six, so I play the "shall we go over to the pub for a chat?" card. Not one of them, *not one*, says no.'

'So, how many did you fuck?'

'Three. Two of them played the boyfriend card early on. The others, it was four or five vodka tonics, back to my place – bosh. Thank you very much and see you later Sooty.'

'You didn't even have to buy dinner?' I ask, genuinely impressed.

'Once. One of them wanted dinner.'

'How much was the ad?' asks Trellick.

'Couple of hundred.'

'And you got laid three times?'

'Correctos,' says Desoto, trying to hail a waiter.

'Bargain of the fucking millennium,' Trellick says.

'Couldn't you get sued?' I ask.

'Bollocks. What am I going to get sued for?'

'Fuck knows. Misrepresentation?'

'Listen, clown, I told them very clearly, upfront, "I'm really sorry, *there's no job.*" They're not doing me thinking it'll get them anywhere. In fact, one of them actually *thanked* me for "being so honest"!' The idea of a girl existing somewhere who is dense enough to believe that Desoto is honest is so lunatic that Trellick and I both burst out laughing. 'Two hours later, I'm doing her up the fucking Gary.' Desoto drains his flute and thumps it down, looking very pleased with himself

'Did you wear a condom?' I ask.

'Oh yeah,' says Desoto, with no sincerity whatsoever as he leans back in his chair to survey the room.

Desoto only got divorced last year. It was a blinder. He'd packed the family off to Italy for a holiday, telling the wife he had to stay on in London for a few days. Work. He'd meet up with them. The wife, nanny and kids fuck off out of it and Desoto gets stuck into a forty-eight hour crack bender.

He hadn't got the wife's messages – the unacceptable hotel, the lost luggage, the heat, the kid's illness – because he'd lost his mobile somewhere along the line. Nor did he check the home messages. He was so cracked up and the music was so loud, that he didn't hear the front door, then the feet on the stairs.

Desoto's wife opened the bedroom door and the children – aged five and seven – burst out from behind her, laughing at the thrill of surprising Daddy. Daddy gradually came into focus through the children's watering eyes; watering first chemically from the rubbery stench of burning bicarbonate of soda, then watering naturally through tears of confusion and anguish: Daddy was naked with a jutting, Vigara-fueled erection. Daddy was propped up against the headboard, almost in crucifix position with a Coke-can crack pipe in one hand and a shit-streaked dildo in the other. Daddy had a dreamy grin strung across his face as he watched two young Latvian girls – hired cheaply from an agency he favoured – furiously 69ing each other across the foot of the bed, their heads coming up, their mouths both slick with cum as the scream began to rise from Mrs Desoto.

The divorce was swift and financially close to ruinous. Among many other things she sought, and secured, an enormous monthly payment towards the cost of post-traumatic stress counselling for the children.

We sit and scan the room and gossip and bitch. It's very easy – everyone falls neatly into one of two categories: winners and losers. People on the up and people on the down. The winners are 'fucking cunts' and the losers are, well, 'fucking losers'. At a nearby table Schneider is talking to Nick Raphael, an A&R guy, recently installed at BMG with Christian Tattersfield. Raphael, in his turn, is monitoring the room over Schneider's shoulder, casually yet fiercely casting about for an upgrade. He doesn't need to be caught having a high-profile conversation with a loser like Schneider. Like being caught cracking jokes with a rabbi in downtown Berlin in 1938. Desoto nods towards Schneider and says, 'Dead man talking.'

Trellick, catching the drift, waves a hand in the air and says 'Waiter? A bottle of *Schadenfreude* for my friends here.'

A few yards away Ellie Crush is interviewed by some TV girl. '*Very* exciting,' the interviewer gushes breathlessly to the camera, 'twenty-one-year-old Ellie Crush taking home Best British Breakthrough Artist tonight. Ellie, just quickly, what does winning this award mean to you?'

'Oh God,' says Ellie, hefting the silver statuette into view, 'I'm speechless, Jo! Honestly, I can't even begin to tell you how much this means to me.' She glances around the babbling throng. 'I'm going to have a find a safe place to put it, mind you!'

'Thanks, Ellie.'

'Cheers!'

'Doable,' Trellick says thoughtfully. 'Very doable.'

'Mmmmm,' I say as Crush comes towards us through the crowd, the statuette cradled against her chest, a bottle of champagne and lit cigarette dangling from the other hand. 'Hi, Ellie,' I say as she passes.

'Oh, hi . . . there!' her face explodes into a ludicrous smile. 'Mwwwah, mwwwah.' She smacks the air either side of my cheeks.

'Congratulations.'

'Shit, I can't bloody believe it! Will you pinch me? I feel like I'm dreaming!' Her face is just an exclamation mark.

'Nah, you deserve it.'

'Aww, thanks, love.' She tries to take a swig of the champagne but burns her hair with the cigarette, dropping her award in the process. Her press officer steps in to help manage the crisis as, right on cue, Parker-Hall emerges from the throng, accepting handshakes, his features a picture of benevolent indulgence. It's always worse when they're magnanimous. 'OI! OI!' Ross shouts in greeting.

'All right, lads? Steven,' he says, shaking my offered hand. 'What a fucking result that was, eh?' he says, rubbing his hands together briskly and accepting a cigarette from Trellick. 'Done them other cunts up like kippers, didn't we?'

Remember, Parker-Hall comes from Hampstead.

'You fluky cunt,' I say.

'Suck my root,' he says, lighting up.

'What you up to later?' Ross asks.

'We got a party on. Up West, innit?' Parker-hall says, reaching into his pocket and handing out a brick of laminates to his after-after-party. 'Right, better do one. Ellie's got to meet the press while she can still fucking speak. C'mon, love.' As he ushers her off Crush turns to me and says 'Bye . . . um, Alex.'

Trellick is still laughing when we reach the green-and-white EXIT sign which glows in the distance on the other side of the auditorium, showing us the way to the after-party.

After the awards ceremony proper finishes the floodgates open and the cannon fodder pours in: the secretaries, marketing assistants, junior PRs, make-up artists, runners, stylists, hairdressers, accountants, legal assistants and friends-of-friends who could only get after-show tickets. Clearly you or I would, upon being told that these were the only tickets available to us, simply climb into a warm bath and open up our veins. However, these losers consider themselves lucky, fortunate even, to be able to get within two bouncers of Robbie or Liam. To be allowed to pay for their own drinks. The secretaries in our building spend *months* planning for tonight. They buy new clothes, they get haircuts and facials, and they pool their miserable salaries to buy a few grams. It's a boiler-fest in here.

Now, you keep reading things – in magazines, in newspapers – about how the nineties are turning out to be, well, nice. According to these articles, men in the sharing, caring nineties have rejected the hollow materialism and sexism of the eighties and embraced women as equals. Partners. You read these things and you wonder – where the fuck are the people who write this stuff hanging out? Primary schools? A rural Greenpeace office?

My industry, always resistant to change (in the fifties we hated the idea of singles, in the seventies cassettes were the enemy, initially CDs were the Antichrist in the eighties – boy, we soon got our heads around that one), hasn't really bought into all this nonsense yet.

Thankfully, very few women seem to have understood it either. There are lots of them already here and thousands more clamouring to get in. Every day piles of CVs tumble into the office. Fresh-faced young girls with excellent qualifications, all hungry to get a job where, in return for working twelve-hour days, being sexually harassed from dawn till dusk, having to cope with all manner of coked-up, coming-down, hung-over, flaky, irrational, abusive, demanding behaviour from people like me, they will be rewarded with maybe fifteen grand a year, the odd backstage pass and occasional glimpses of pop stars in the building.

In toilets, offices, broom cupboards, hotel stairwells and on the chill leather seats of BMWs, Saabs and Mercedes coupés, they will suck cocks and take it up the arse. Their twenties will flash by in a holocaust of parties, hangovers, semen and bad champagne until, one fine morning some-where down the line, they wake up to find themselves thirty-five years old with sagging tits, a cancerous, shrivelled womb, tired, fucked-out eyes, and a complexion battered by late nights, drugs and cocks. A lucky few of these girls will, through a combination of low cunning and viciously skilful fellatio, manage to marry one of the executives they serve and hang on to him for – at best – a decade, raising his children and decorating the house while he works late at the office pumping his way through her successors. Eventually, either she will put her foot down or (more likely) he will upgrade to one of the Sophies or Samanthas who replaced her. They will get divorced somewhere in their mid-forties and she will find herself standing in the kitchen of a big house somewhere in Buckinghamshire with two nasty, pre-pubescent monsters whingeing at her as she haplessly uncorks her second bottle of white wine at half past four in the afternoon.

A very, very few of these girls will manage to marry one of the pop stars. The Meg Matthews deal. This is the record-industry boiler equivalent of winning the lottery – the *Pretty Woman*, rags-to-riches story that surely keeps so many of these girls choking down warty cocks, swallowing spunk and throwing themselves down on all fours like it's going out of fashion for the best part of twenty years. It. Could. Be. You. For the tiny minority of Cinderellas who pull off this incredible coup the life pattern will be much the same as it is for the ones who marry the executives, although the time frame of the marriage will be greatly truncated and the remuneration significantly enhanced.

We're hunkered around a corner table in another cavernous room. Billowing white drapes have been hung, candles lit and carpeting laid down. There are blackjack tables and roulette wheels but, here and there, you can still see the cement floor, the steel poles and corrugated metal of the roof and the gloomy dark above the canopies. You remember that the hulk of Earls Court looks down impassively on everything from car and boat shows to international widget manufacturers conferences – all of them filled with the same kind of guys trying to figure out if Susan from accounts is really up for it or not. Echoing behind the crack of champagne corks, the supercharged laughter, the crackle of suits and sparkling dresses, there is a tinny, reverberating sound. It is the sound of people trying to have a really good time in a lightly decorated under-ground car park.

Pete Dunn rocks up to our table, arms raised, a bottle of Perrier Jouet in each fist. 'AHHHHHGH! Wahey the lads!' he screeches. He's a big guy, Dunn. Once chunky and, back in the eighties, ponytailed, he's now bald and running, sprinting in fact, to fat. His broad Geordie face is ruddy, the stubble greying and the eyes puffy, set back in little pouches. Dunn is our Head of Radio and TV Promotions. He has spent his adult life wheedling and begging radio DJs and programmers and kids' TV producers and presenters to put our acts on their shows. I'm sure he loved his job when he was twenty-six: falling out of nightclubs with Radio 1 DJs and flying to the south of France with pop stars. Now pushing forty-six his every waking moment is a nightmare. Told to fuck off and die on a daily, hourly, basis by TV and radio executives, he must then drive back to the office where he is – far more robustly – told to fuck off and die by Derek.

How much better his job would have been back in the good old days of the fifties – the golden era of payola and 1 per cent artist royalty rates. Now payola was a genius idea, wasn't it? Tell me that wasn't a winner for everyone involved? You didn't have to take anyone out to dinner and suck their dick. You didn't have to laugh at Chris Evans's jokes. You just paid the cunts. Here's the money, now play the record and fuck you. *Fuck you.*

Not too bright to begin with, a decade of grovelling and sucking dick has turned Dunn into a sort of failed light entertainer with a melancholic streak. He pours champagne into all our glasses, singing, 'Here we go, here we go, here we go.' Shouldn't he be at home with the wife and kids? Then you remember – he went upgrados and left the wife and kids two years ago, to go balls-deep in a twenty-year-old dancer he met at the taping of some Saturday-morning kiddie moronathon. She, in her turn, left him for some photographer's assistant six months later. His upgrade upgraded him.

Dunn actually raises his glass to propose a toast – something only the truly suicidal ever do. 'To the lads!' he shouts.

Waters joins in like a retard, pathetically clunking his plastic flute against Dunn's. Leamington from Virgin materialises through the crowd and sidles over to me.

'Oi oi,' he says.

'All right, mate? Two awards for those cows?' I say, nodding across the room towards Mel B, 'You're having a laugh, aren't you? They must think it's fucking Christmas.'

'Nah, I think Geri's off crying somewhere.'

'Ah, fuck her. Congratulations.'

'Nothing to do with me, mate,' he says shrugging, 'but cheers.' We clack tumblers. 'Here,' Leamington says, 'is it right what I'm hearing about your old mucker Rage?'

'What are you hearing?'

'That it's all gone Colonel Kurtz – he's upriver, gone fucking native. Off his nut on the nosebag, months in the studio, no contact with anyone.'

'Fuck knows. Schneider's problem.'

'When's the record due?'

'Three months ago.'

'Could be Bad News Bears for Schneider.'

'Mmmm,' I say. As we drink and gossip and bitch I look over at the recently clean and sober Robbie Williams, who is sitting at a table a few feet away. He's fiddling with the label on a bottle of mineral water, smoking two-handed, and nodding while some guy I don't know – some manager, some lawyer – explains something to him. Williams periodically turns away to stare hard – a hard stare I know well – at the glittering rump of some boiler standing near him. Poor bastard, I guess that's all he's got now, isn't it? The pumping. Can you imagine it? You're not even thirty and you can't do *anything* any more. No nose-up, no pills, no frosty beers, no warming shots of Jack or Rémy. You're just sitting there, completely sober, in your fuck-off mansion, dressed head to foot in all the finery you spent the morning trawling New Bond Street with some stylist for, you've just given up trying to read some book for the umpteenth time, because it's too *hard*, you're turning on Sky Sports again, or forcing some underling to drink fruit juice and play cards with you, and you're thinking – another forty years of *this*? You're just some stage kid, some poor song-and-dance spastic with a cheeky grin who fate threw a whole bunch of sevens. And now you're staring down the wrong end of four decades with just your own thoughts for company when you don't really have two fucking thoughts to rub together. Nasty.

Danny Rent sidles up. He's a scumbag, a real rapist of a manager, one of those old-school Tin Pan Alley guys that you just don't see much any more: late forties, stubble, well-worn Armani suit with hash burns all over it, heavy *gold* Rolex (so wrong) on his right wrist. He looks like a down-on-his-luck nightclub owner from *Miami Vice* and smells like he just went on a four-day Scotch binge and then jumped into a vat of aftershave.

'Hey, Stelfox, how's tricks?' he says.

'Oi oi,' I say.

'Listen, I been meaning to call you. Got a bit of a band coming together just now that's right up your *Strasse*, mate.'

'Yeah?'

'Fucking yeah. Four birds. Girl power. Innit.'

Christ, I bet no one else is thinking that, the week the Spice Girls go to no. 1 in the States. 'Any good?' I say.

'Fucking useless at the minute, mate, but you'd do the lot of them. We're working on it. One of em's got sumfin.'

'Yeah? What they called?'

'Get this – Songbirds. Gerrit?'

'Yeah.'

'Right, do you want a fucking nose-up or what?'

Girl power. Do me a fucking favour. However, there's going to be a bunch of these whores having it away over the next couple of years. No question. One thing you learn when you're in the business of selling utter shite to the Great British Public is that there's really no bottom to where they'll go. Shit food, shit TV, shit bands, shit films, shit houses. There is absolutely no fucking bottom with this stuff. The shittier you can make it – a bad photocopy of a bad photocopy of what was a shit idea in the first place – the more they'll eat it up with a fucking big spoon, from dawn till dusk, from now until the end of time.

It's too good.

Come the early hours we wind up at the Met Bar and then up into the hotel above, to Parker-Hall's suite for his 'after-after-party'. We're all chang'd up to the eyeballs by this point and listening to a chang'd-up Parker-Hall go through a variant of his 'How-I-Did-It' speech for, surely, the billionth time tonight. Now and again Chalmers, Crush's Product Manager, will boringly interject details about the marketing plan, how big the TV ad spend is going to be, the increased poster campaign, who they're getting to direct the next video. Chalmers is just one of the thousand fathers suddenly lining up to stamp their parentage on Crush's success. 'We're looking at doing thirty thousand albums a week from here on,' he says.

I'm trying not to hear this. The expression on my face is pleasant while, inside, I feel like the village girl as she stares at the face of the tenth soldier in the raping queue – blood on her thighs and half a pint of semen already up her. *I'm not here*, I tell myself. *I'm walking in a forest. I'm walking in a forest . . .*

The room is crowded – industry, random girls and a few fairly well-known musicians. Trellick is sitting on the ledge of the tall windows which overlook Hyde Park, arms folded, nodding earnestly as some girl talks shit to him. A few feet away from Trellick, Damon Albarn is engaged in exactly the same sort of conversation. I tune back in. Parker-Hall is telling us, '. . . the fucking mixes were all over the shop. I says to Flood and Moulder, "Listen, cunts . . ."'

'Excuse me,' I say.

In the bathroom I sit down on the toilet, put my head between my legs, and take deep, steady breaths. I'm sweating. *Thirty thousand a week. That fluky little prick. That chancing mockney wanker.* In Mission Control there's a red wash of colour, alarms sounding, the screens all flashing deranged, bloody images of Parker-Hall and Chalmers being forced to gobble and bum each other before a shotgun is slipped in each of their mouths and, simultaneously, their heads fly apart in a pinkish mist of viscera. The technicians are thumping their monitors, twiddling knobs, but they can't shake the pictures.

I splash some water on my face and hold my wrists under the cold tap for a long time and finally I start to feel better. I'm scraping some powder out from the wrap and carving out a heart-stopping elephant's leg when I become aware of a gentle tapping at the door. I open it a crack and squint out, trying to focus into the dark hallway. 'Steven?' a girl says.

'Yeah?'

'It's Anita. From BMG? Can I come in?'

I pull her in and point her towards the coke.

Maybe fifteen minutes later, as we're leaving, I take a quick look around for Trellick. I wander along a hallway and try the door to one of the bedrooms. It opens silently and I hear a girl's voice breathlessly chanting a mantra of *'oh fuck, oh fuck, oh fuck'*. I peer in. A huge bed is lit by soft halogen spots. On the bed Ellie Crush is naked on her hands and knees. There is a black kid – one of the singers in this new boy band Leamington has signed — crouched behind her, doing something to her with his fist. As I softly close the door something silver flashes under the amber halogen glow.

Yes, twenty-one-year-old Ellie Crush had definitely found a safe place to put the statuette for Best British Breakthrough Artist.

'The thing is,' she says, 'no one over there takes my opinion seriously.' Anita and I are at opposite ends of my sofa, an oversized number from Heal's in heavy caramel cloth. A gold disc for some dance record I signed, flecked and streaked with cocaine, lies between us. Jeff Buckley warbles soft in the background as we discuss her career prospects in A&R. Given that she has none it is a remarkable tribute to both my patience and the focusing power of the drug that we've managed to keep the conversation on the rails for a good three hours. Outside, horribly, dawn is beginning to crinkle through Maida Vale. The clock is ticking, but there's still some crap I have to listen to.

'Oh, I'm sure they do,' I say, standing to pour cold shots of Stoli and then flopping back down a little nearer to her. When we got back, remembering that she's really an indie kid, I quickly washed and changed my shirt and tie for a Radiohead T-shirt.

'No they don't. I was the first one saying we should sign Mansun the other year. Look at what that turned into.'

'Really?' I say.

'Oh, there's been loads,' she says and goes onto reel off a list of bands she loves, all either total or demi-turkeys, while I chop more lines out.

'Well,' I say, handing her the furled twenty, 'what are your plans? Where do you want to go from here?' She stands up and bends over right in front of me to snort her line. Her rump – which is near perfect by the way – strains against the tight, shiny dress. I wonder – knickers? thong? nothing? The slit falls open to the top of her thigh, laying bare a yard of brown flesh. 'Ahh . . . thanks,' she says, throwing her head back. She sits down beside me and passes the gold disc. 'I've been A&R coordinator for three years now,' she continues, snuffling, 'I could do it in my fucking sleep. I mean, I'm nearly *twenty-three*, Steven. What am I doing?' She looks at me with sad, damp eyes. Her breasts – which are pushed tight together by one of these new superbras I've been reading so much about, some triumph of geometric wiring and tit-engineering – are straining hard against the gold-speckled satin of her dress. She's really packed into it. I am so thick, so angry, with lust that, just for a moment, I think I may attack her.

'Well, listen,' I say, 'off the record?' She nods, wide-eyed, and I realise that I have absolutely no idea what I'm going to say next. But it's no problem. I lie constantly, I lie all the time. The very fabric of my daily existence from breakfast until bedtime, from toast until tranquillisers, is a finely woven torrent of utter shite. So I know, I'm reasonably confident, that when I start speaking the words, the lies will tumble from my mouth and arrange themselves into a convincing sentence that will take me nearer to what I want. 'Well,' I say, 'we're about to promote Darren to Junior A&R. He doesn't know that yet so you can't tell anyone.' She nods solemnly. 'So we're going to be hiring one, possibly two, new scouts sometime in the next few months. I think you'd be perfect, but the thing is,' I say, completely free-forming now, 'it'd probably mean a drop in salary.'

'I don't care about the money,' she cuts in quickly, leaning towards me, smelling of perfume, sweat, cigarettes and vodka, 'I mean, you only get one life and you have to make sure that whatever you do makes you happy. I've always loved music and I know that, if someone would just give me a shot at it, I'd make a brilliant scout. I spend half my life going to gigs anyway. You couldn't name a new band in London I haven't seen in the past twelve months. The Audience, Bellatrix, Cuff, AC Acoustics, Basement Jaxx . . . Even when I was a kid, I'd listen to the *Top Forty* every Sunday because I wanted to hear what records were going up, what was going down and all that. I've got my own account at Rough Trade. I pay for it myself. BMG won't let me have one because I'm not technically A&R staff – hey, I've got perfect pitch too, did you know that? – and I'm so sick of it there that I've been thinking about just packing it all in and going travelling. A couple of my friends are out in Goa right now and sometimes I just think, "Fuck it, why spend the winter here? You're worth more than this." I mean, what am I doing? Booking studio time and booking cabs and biking bloody tapes around London and all that crap. My dad died last year and we never really got on and that really made me take a look at things because at the end of the day if you're not happy then, basically, what's the point? Do you know what I mean?'

'Anita,' I say hoarsely, 'can I suck your tits?'

*

Fucking cocaine.

Two hours later and she's *still* trying to mangle my cock into something in the vicinity of a hard-on. We're both naked, slick and salty with sweat, and she's going at it like a *demon*: flicking at the tip with her tongue, nibbling the shaft with her teeth, blowing on the helmet gently, viciously gobbling up and down the whole thing, kissing it as softly and tenderly as a mother soothing a crying infant, biting and gnawing on it like an angry pit bull, spitting on it, greasing it with baby oil, making direct eye contact and moaning with pleasure as she sucks, rubbing my cock greedily against her clit, pussy-lips and arsehole, and sliding it between her heavy, lubed breasts. At one point she crams the entire package – prick, balls, the lot – into her mouth and churns them crazily like an overdriven washing machine. Finally she goes absolutely bananas and simply begins furiously wanking me off. For a long, sorry time – teeth gritted, sweat flying from her – she pounds her clenched fist up and down on the melted ribbon of plasticine I have instead of a cock. Somehow, somewhere into about the fifteenth minute of this (by which point she's emitting random screams of pain, her arm just an insane blur, like one of those machines they use to shake paint in DIY shops), my cock stiffens minutely, going from the consistency of – say – jelly into Play-Doh. As she eagerly, desperately, swivels a leg across my chest in an attempt to mount me, I shudder, moan, and ejaculate.

Well, 'ejaculate' is probably over-egging it. 'Ejaculate' is like using 'explosion' to describe what happens when you pierce the foil lid on a jar of instant coffee. What actually happens is that I scream and a drop of semen the size of a grain of rice seeps out the end of my cock. It's not enough to even dribble down onto her hand, the hand which is – still! – frantically trying to guide me into her.

I roll over and gratefully pass out.

When I wake up she's gone. Horribly, inevitably, I have a raging, titanium erection. I roll the sheets back and look at it. My relationship with my prick is beginning to resemble the kind of friendship you have with an old, alcoholic college pal – completely unreliable, always turning up at the worst possible time and costs you a *lot* of money. Yet you're stuck with him. I stare him down. 'What the fuck do you want? You're *late*,' I say. I want to punch him out.

But, with heavy heart and thick blood, I root around on the floor, pluck my wallet from my trousers, and begin dialling the number of a local escort agency. '*Aww*,' I think, folding a cool, soothing fist around my radioactive helmet, '*how could I stay mad at you?*'

A couple of weeks after The Brits we have an emergency marketing meeting, to get a plot in place for Rudi's record. Present are Ross, one of Ross's product-manager muppets, Dunn, the TV promotions girls Hannah and Clare (fucked them both), Barry and Alex, the club promotions kids, who will try to get every DJ in every filthy, tacky toler-infested nightclub in the country playing the record, Bill, who deals with manufacturing, Suzy the press officer (nearly fucked her, blow job) and Nicky. As always I find myself angry at how fucking ugly Nicky is. Usually Ross would chair this meeting, but Derek, sensing a big hit he wants to get his fingerprints on, has decided to sit in.

'Now,' Derek booms, gesturing grandly towards me, 'Steven has recently come back from MIDEM where, I'm pleased to say, he signed the hottest club record of the whole convention.' There is a round of applause and some whooping from Barry and Alex, who already know the record, Barry even implying he had tried to play it to me before Christmas. I move over to the stereo. 'This is the club mix,' I say cueing the track up, 'I'm working on a radio edit.' I am, of course, doing fuck all. One of Rudi's boys will do the radio mix, but these clowns don't know that. Once the thing is a huge hit it will be, naturally, 'my' radio mix that saved the day. I crank the volume all the way to the right, hit 'play' on the CD, and bass flattens the gold discs and posters against the walls. Everyone nods along.

You'd think you wouldn't have to bother with all this, wouldn't you? The process of selling the fucking record to the people in your own company. But you do. Yesterday I picked off Dunn and Ross – playing each of them the record in their offices and telling them both only they could make it a hit. I mean, if you worked at Baked Beans Inc and your job was marketing beans and the guy who made the fucking beans came in with some hot new beans, he wouldn't have to do a sales job on you, would he? He wouldn't have to take you out and get you drunk and slip you a taste of the beans and really try to convince you they were good beans, would he? He'd just say, 'Here's the new beans I've made – which is my job – now sell the fucking things. Because that's your job.' But not in the record industry, oh no. Everyone's got a fucking opinion, everyone wants to be an A&R guy and – most importantly – *everyone wants you to fucking fail.* Do any of the poor cunts around this table (some of their faces – Hannah, Nicky – now twitching with horror as the chorus unfolds) really need to be seeing me striding around the office with a no. 1 record going on? Do they fuck. I'm kind of unbearable when I'm having a hit.

'*SUCK IT!*' reverberates around the boardroom and then it all goes quiet.

Ross breaks the silence – 'It's a smash!' – and then we're all talking about practical stuff; release dates, lead times and artwork.

Derek loves the record. The marketing department love the record. The club promotions department love the record. The radio department love the record. I love Rudi. I have tooled back from Cannes bearing the cure for cancer.

March

Lucian Grange becomes Head of Polydor. The single 'Local Boy in the Photograph' by hotly tipped new act the Stereophonics stiffs at 51. Cast release their second LP. The Manic Street Preachers album goes double platinum. Lots of people want to sign the Audience, an indie band with this girl singer who's the daughter of the boiler who used to present Blue Peter. *Steve Allen, an A&R guy at Warner Brothers, says, 'I see her developing the way Madonna has. This is probably the dance album of the decade.' He is talking about Gina G.*

'I don't know anything about music. In my line you don't have to.'

Elvis Presley

'. . . very much like the early Jam, but more *angular*, and you'd need to find a producer who was sympathetic to that. I don't think . . .' Waters craps on about the band we've just watched in the Dublin Castle as Parkway at closing time creeps past – the Spread Eagle, a kebab palace, three drunk girls in short skirts, another gigantic poster of Tony Blair, the Labour guy, his red devil eyes burning out of the tear across the poster, scaring the shit out of me.

Waters and I are both coked up in the back of a hot stinking minicab, on our way to the Falcon to see some band called Kidnapper, who are meant to be a bit like Elastica. There's the usual gibbering Paki at the wheel, the usual distorted ragga fizzing out of the tiny plastic speakers behind us. Waters is still talking. '. . . his mixes are just too . . . middle-y . . .' I turn to look at him for the first time in a while. He's just a madman with double-glazed pebbles for eyes. He's talking to the air. He may as well be talking to Abdul in front. 'Too middle-y?' I repeat.

'Yeah. You know, not enough top or bottom end . . .'

I nod slowly. 'Sorry, who are we talking about?'

'Mike Hedges.'

'Right. Too . . . middle-y?'

'Yeah.'

Waters is saying that one of country's most respected producers – a guy who has been making records since Waters was a child – is incapable of turning out a mix with the necessary levels of bass and treble. Waters is not saying this because he believes it or because he has given the matter any serious thought (an endeavour he is, in any case, incapable of). He is just saying it to have a *view*. Views are very important. You should always have one.

I say, 'Shall we fuck off this band at the Falcon? Go back to yours and have a think about producers? Draw up a shortlist? Get some more bugle in?'

He grins. Well, he gets as close to a grin as his coke-blasted features will allow, like he's trying to eat his top lip with his bottom teeth. Actually, he looks like he's having a fucking stroke. But he's nodding.

Waters leans forward, causing a fresh torrent of sweat to pour off him, and gives the driver his address in Notting Hill. We make an illegal left up Camden High Street, past the tube station, the Brassiere, teenage goths outside the Electric Ballroom, a woman tramp with a filthy bandage around her arm rooting through a rubbish bin.

By one we're well into the third gram. Waters is still talking – I don't think he's stopped talking since we left the Dublin Castle – and pouring drinks while I root through his record collection. He has about twenty-five CDs – mostly major label promos and a few Greatest Hits collections: Fleetwood Mac, Japan, the fucking Doors. For some reason

— some inexplicable, haunt-you-to-the-grave-unfathomable reason — he has a copy of *Nuisance*, the debut album by Menswear. I also see an advance copy of the new Jam box set Polydor are bringing out and a copy of the Gang of Four's *Entertainment*. My copy of the Gang of Four's *Entertainment*, the one that went missing from my office a couple of weeks ago. This explains Waters earlier, mystifying, spastically inappropriate use of the word 'angular'. I put disc two of the Jam set on. 'Thanks,' I say, taking the tumbler of vodka tonic he hands me and sinking into his ludicrously oversized sofa. 'Right, where were we?' says Waters, tapping his teeth with a biro and staring at the piece of A4.

We've been 'brainstorming' for nearly two hours now. There are two names scrawled in Waters' mutated handwriting on the grimy sheet of paper: Ed Bueller and Dave Eringa, both my suggestions. Waters' dog lies sleeping on the sofa. On the coffee table between us is the coke-flecked mirror, the heaped ashtrays, the empty bottle of Stoli. Copies of *Music Week* are scattered all over the floor, all opened at the album charts where we've been scanning the producers' names for ideas. Waters thinks hard. Or rather he makes the expression he imagines humans use when thinking — furrowed brow, gaze focused somewhere in the mid-distance — while whatever goes on in his mind goes on. I picture the inside of his head as a sleeping donkey, a 747 exploding on the tarmac, a nuclear winter. 'How about . . .' I say sitting forward, picking up his Amex, scooping some powder towards me, pausing dramatically as Waters looks up hopefully, '. . . Guy Stevens?'

I wait a few seconds while his brain turns, as swift as a container of near-set concrete tipping over. There's the vaguest light somewhere in his eyes, the tiniest hint that something like a mind lives and functions in there. 'You know,' I say helpfully, 'he produced *London Calling*. Mott the Hoople.'

'Oh, Guy *Stevens*!' the clown exclaims, as though I'd said Guy Stephen*son*, or Guy Simons or something. 'Yeah, great idea,' he says, enthusiastically writing down the name of a man who has been dead for nearly twenty years. 'I'll get the drinks,' I say.

Waters' kitchen is chrome and marble, clean-lined, halogen-lit and never-used. An aluminium baseball bat with a navy leather grip leans against the fridge. 'Home security,' Waters had said casually when we came in. I grab his mortar and pestle and quickly grind up three more Valium, two Es, a tab of acid, and a scoop of ludicrous-strength, Trade-certified, hardcore-queers-only ketamine. 'Fuck it,' I think, breaking open two big, egg-shaped temazepam with my thumbnail and squeezing the viscous, gluey liquid into the chalky powder. I dump the lot into his glass and fill it to the brim with neat vodka, adding a splash of tonic as an afterthought.

'I'm a bear! I'm the dancing bear!'

We were both dancing to some rave compilation when the furious cocktail of class As kicked in and Waters started tearing his clothes off. I suggested to him that he might like to pretend he was an animal of some sort. Now, an hour or so later, I'm lying back contentedly in Waters' huge leather beanbag, watching him capering naked around his living room pretending to be a circus bear. He is fucking *deranged*.

I shout instructions and encouragement to him, making

the most of the short window I have before he collapses. 'Bear eat CDs?' I suggest, chucking a handful at him.

'Bear eat CDs!' Waters shrieks delightedly and stuffs a copy of Pulp's *Different Class* into his mouth. He crunches right through it – jewel case, sleeve, CD, the lot. 'Mmmm,' he says, turning to me and rubbing his naked belly happily, bits of paper and plastic falling from his bleeding mouth. A worried expression crosses his face. 'Bear need . . .' He's trying to say something, his eyeballs flipping back in their sockets, as though he's trying to look at whatever is left of his brain.

'Bear need what? What does bear need?' I say encouragingly, like you would to a confused child.

'Bear need –' Abruptly he squats down and unleashes a torrent of foul shite all over his nice sea-grass carpeting. Then he loses his balance and falls into his own effluent.

The stench is incredible, arousing the sleeping dog. I lock him in the bedroom.

I check my watch – four a.m. Enough's enough. 'Here, thirsty bear,' I say, lifting his head up – being careful not to get shit on me – and holding a mug to his lips. It's filled with Evian in which I've dissolved a further two dozen of his Valium. Waters greedily gulps it down. 'Good bear,' I say, patting his head, 'good bear . . .'

An hour or so later I watch him sleeping – dying – while I snort the last of the coke and listen to the Menswear album. What the fuck was he thinking with this? 'Roger! What the fuck were you thinking with this?' I shout, slapping his face with the CD case.

'Mmmmmm?' he mumbles, face down on the carpet, death nuzzling up close by, putting his feet up.

I turn the TV on and watch VH1 for a while – the Cardigans, Radiohead, Texas, the new Blur single – as Waters' breathing goes from loud, laboured snoring to a rattling whisper to absolutely nothing. Satisfied he's dead I get my cock out and piss all over him.

Then I go and root through his bedroom drawers, hitting pay dirt when I find a sex-trove of porn mags, videos, toys and lubes at the back of his wardrobe. I pull out a butt-plug. It's about the size of a champagne cork and is attached to the handle/battery compartment by a grey wire about four feet long. I click it on. It thrums feebly so I replace the batteries with the ones from the remote control for the flat-screen TV in Waters' bedroom. Much better – it's like holding a small, angry frog. I get rubber gloves from beneath the sink.

Before I leave I flip through the channels until I find *Red Hot Amateurs*. Some spotty-bummed housewife in cheap red underwear smiles coquettishly into the camera as she fingers a dildo, like a flautist preparing for a tricky recital. I leave the TV on, bluish light flickering across Waters' piss-spattered, shit-flecked corpse, the empty bottles of Valium and vodka atop the cokey mirror, the cord for the butt-plug trailing out from between his cheeks, a faint, muffled hum audible beneath the moans and groans from the TV.

I walk home to Maida Vale, the sun coming up and 'Beetlebum' in my head as I cross the Harrow Road. The long, festering strip studded with fried-chicken shacks and everything-a-quid emporiums – a greying London wound which gentrification will never reach – is deserted except for a solitary double-decker bus. It slams past me, rattling the pavement. It is full of tolers: poor people, their faces as grim and stark as pornography, as blunt as final demands.

They flash by me on their way into W1, where they will do whatever they do all day for no money. Yellow letters glow feebly on the front of the bus, telling me that these people have come from Kensal Rise, Cricklewood, Wembley and other places, poorer, more terrible places, that I don't even know about.

*'If you are a fierce competitor then you want to beat the
other guys' brains out, because that's what you love doing.'*
Al Teller, former Columbia Records President

'What do you think? Honestly?' one of them – the bass
player? the singer? – asks as the last blips of feedback fade
out.

I look around my office. The four musicians (early
twenties, thin, anaemic, torn clothes) sit on the sofa and the
floor while their manager (a couple of years older, a little
better dressed) sits in the chair across the desk from me.

Waters' non-appearance in the office this morning caused
. . . nothing. I guess that, in most workplaces, it's unusual,
reprehensible even, when people just don't turn up. Or turn
up so hung-over all they can do is vomit and cry. But not
here. Not in the record industry. ('Industry'. That's blinding,
isn't it? *'Diligence or assiduity in any task or effort.'* I look through
the glass wall of my office at all the diligence and assiduity
going on around here: Rebecca, laughing her head off as she
feverishly types a gossip-laden email to some whore she
knows; Darren and Stan, our scouts, chasing each other
around with water pistols; Schneider berating Nancy for
failing to secure him a necessary restaurant reservation.)

What do I think? Honestly?

I picture the expressions which would appear on these earnest faces if I even *began* to tell them what I was thinking while we listened to their demo. *'Well, kids, during the ludicrously overlong intro to the first number I started wondering if those fucks in the car department had finally gotten around to installing the new CD changer in the boot of my car. By the time your clichéd, long-overdue first "chorus" was finally dropping, I was mentally re-enacting a recent coke- and E-fuelled gang bang I had with a pair of cheap Eastern European prostitutes. Then I started worrying because I realised I'd forgotten to drop a suit that I want to wear to the* Music Week *Awards tomorrow night into the dry-cleaner's and could they do it same day or should I have Rebecca pop by my flat at lunchtime and take it in for me? Or should I just buy a new suit? I saw one in Paul Smith I liked the other day, but could I possibly have any alterations done in time? Then Lisa from finance walked past the window wearing her low-cut jeans — the piano-wire of her thong just visible above the denim — and I started working her into the East European hooker gang bang, having her being fucked by one of them with a huge strap-on while I'm ejaculating an* astonishingly *large payload into her gagging mouth and blinking, grateful eyes while the other ostro eats her out from beneath. By the time I was standing there in my mind's eye, sweat-glazed, panting and triumphant, over the three tearful, naked semen-encrusted bodies, your last overwrought ballad was spiralling to a close and I hadn't really heard a fucking note. Sorry.'*

What do I think? Honestly? I think I would like to see you and the rest of your band die screaming in agony from something like testicular cancer. I think that last week I spent a hundred and eighty pounds on a necktie and lost it a few hours later, drunk in Soho. I think about telling these hopeless, penniless cunts this. But instead, pointlessly, I say, 'Great guitar sound.'

'Yeah,' the manager says, and he starts crapping on about how Doug – or whoever – has been playing guitar since he was a fucking foetus or something. Doug looks up from the floor and smiles bashfully. It's about all I can do not to punch his stupid, talentless face in. To stand up, run the length of the room, and boot him full-force in his pasty, pimply, stinking indie chops. But – ever reasonable – I just nod and listen and say things like 'yeah?' and 'yeah' and 'great' and 'really?' for a long time.

I *hate* indie music. Until a couple of years ago you didn't really have to think about it. It was just a couple of hundred losers fucking around in Camden. Then a pair of Mancunian losers rock up clutching a Beatles songbook and suddenly you've got to listen to all this shite and take all these meetings in case you miss the next one. It's a fucking nightmare.

I'm tired. I got home from Waters' place and managed just a few hours' fitful, cokey sleep before I had to get up and drive over to the new house, where there was another problem.

I've bought a toilet at the top of Ladbroke Grove. Desoto hooked Trellick and me up with a bent estate agent, one who specialises in finding 'undervalued development opportunities'. What this means is that he convinces derelict pensioners (ideally ones without immediate families) who have been in their derelict houses since the dawn of time that the place is worth a lot less than it really is. You buy it, gut the place, lick of paint, couple of real fireplaces, do the floors up, and flog it a few months later for a sickening profit.

I pulled up at the place and walked through a trio of builders on the front steps — astonished-looking Albanians, buckled over tea and tabloids, smoking like lab beagles — down the hallway, where a couple more Albanians are hunkered down either side of a tea chest savaging a stinking parcel of vinegar-sodden fish and chips, and into the living room where Murdoch, their boss, my builder, stood in a large pool of water gazing thoughtfully at a wall.

A section of plaster around six feet in diameter had been hacked away leaving a black, gaping wound, exposing the guts of the old house; a hydra's head of ancient wiring, rusted copper pipes. One of the pipes had been hastily bandaged, but a thin trickle of water still ran from it down into the wall cavity. 'You're joking?' I said.

'Dinnaeworry,' Murdoch replied cheerfully, 'Plumber's-cummin'rooninnaminnut.Jistasweelwefunoutthenoo.'

'Found out what?'

'Thonpipe'sbinleakin'furdonkey'san'it'sweekendyer halewathere.'

Murdoch was saying that the pipe has been leaking for a long time and has caused damage to the entire wall. It's taken three agonising months but I'm now fluent in the kind of horrible, guttural Scottish Murdoch speaks. It's like I've been forced to learn a language I will never use again.

There's no point getting angry at Murdoch. He just talks more. You just have to ask the question. 'How long and how much?' I said.

'Well . . .' He fired up one of his unspeakable cigarettes

— a Raffles, a Mayfair, a Concord, a Savoy — and started talking.

I didn't listen — it's not worth the effort. It really isn't. Whenever a problem comes up with the building work — which it does on a weekly, sometimes daily, basis — Murdoch will crap on for eternity, giving me several options. He'll then tell me why the cheapest option isn't worth bothering with. And then why the mid-priced option isn't really what I'm after either.

It's all good for Murdoch though. No matter how tits up anything goes — he just keeps raking in cash. He has squadrons of crazed Albanians all over north-west London. Some of them do very well, Murdoch's Albanians. Strong work ethic. You come over here and you work your balls off from dawn until dusk — plastering and painting and bodging and fucking up — while the wife (or sister, or mum) does her bit across town, ankle-deep in spunk in some massage parlour off the North Circular.

I say Murdoch gives me options, but he doesn't really. He just talks shit for a while until I wind up spending more money. But what can I do? What do I know about this stuff? Murdoch could lift up some floorboards and show me a pair of elephants, chained to a tandem and frantically pedalling, and tell me that the building is, in fact, elephant-powered and that we need to replace one of the beasts. I'd display irritation, but only mild surprise, as I scribbled out a cheque for the most costly house-powering elephant on the market.

'Abootseevenoreightthoosanahreckon . . .' he finally said.

'Fuck me.'

'Ayeit'sbadnewsrightenuff.'

'Right, whatever. Do it. And will you please tell your guys to stop eating that stinking fucking takeaway food in here?'

'Ayeah'lltellthemtaewatchitbuttheboayshuvgotaeeatlike.'

I'm now three months and a *lot* of money into this nightmare. I've reached the point where just the sight of Murdoch's mobile number popping up on the screen of my Nokia makes me feel sick.

Murdoch went on, talking about skylights and RSJs and supporting walls, about hardwood flooring and cornices. About new windows and planning permission. And it's all expensive. None of it is cheap.

The funding for this whole farce is, of course, borrowed. Just a few years back it would have been impossible to do this at my age and income. To obtain the financing you'd have needed guarantors, collateral and accounts going back to the Stone Age. I just told them a mad pack of utter crap – I'm Senior Vice President of A&R for the Fucking World – and I earn a billion quid a minute. Bosh. Done Deal.

I drove back to the office, for this meeting. Crawling along Ladbroke Grove with the top down I got stuck in traffic across from a pub; until very recently a crunchily carpeted pit of bitter, satellite TV and boil-in-the-bag pies. Now there are polished oak floors and pan-fried, line-caught Scottish trout. Frosty bottles of champagne and Sauvignon gleam in glass-fronted coolers. An ancient local, baking in his tattered overcoat and cap, stands on the pavement outside, frowning at the braying laughter and the Propellerheads pumping from the jukebox. He's easily eighty and squints through thick glasses at the chalkboard menu, which is telling him that today's special is seafood linguine with Irish lobster, scallops and prawns. The chalkboard may as well read 'go home and die, you fucking old cunt'. I smile. What wars and depressions, what hardships and indignities has this poor bastard lived through, coming of age as he did during unarguably the worst stretch of the twentieth century, to end his days having to witness this shit?

I think about money. I'm running two mortgages, a bridging loan, an overdraft and six credit cards, as well as all the usual monthly outgoings: large and regular tabs must be settled with west London's cocaine dealers. Drinks, fine dining and regular exotic holidays must be factored in. Monthly, it seems, I must write cheques (or rather, Rebecca must before I sign them) to various London parking authorities for hundreds of pounds' worth of fines. There are clothes, gadgets and impulse buys in Heal's and Harvey Nicks of a Saturday morning – last weekend a pair of cherrywood bedside cabinets, snapped up for just twelve hundred quid when I was hung-over and showing off in front of Trellick, four hundred quid the week before on a set of Japanese butcher's knives which sit gleaming and never-used on the black granite breakfast bar. There's the cleaner, a witless Colombian demi-hooker whose efforts in the flat seem to diminish in direct proportion to the wage increases she regularly demands. Some days I bowl through the door and the only significant difference to the place is the fact that she's lifted the money from the kitchen counter. I jump into Sainsbury's for a pint of milk and stumble back to the Saab three hundred quid later, juggling bottles of champagne and Ecuadorian kiwi fruit, foie gras, fresh Loch Fyne oysters, Jerusalem artichokes, Belgian chocolates, sushi and dinky miniature vegetables. The champagne is drunk and the food is tossed straight into the bin from the fridge by the cleaner a couple of weeks later after it's started to fester and turn incredible florid colours.

Because I'm never home, of course. I sometimes think I am buying all this stuff solely to impress the monosyllabic retards who work the supermarket tills. I smoke three packs of Marlboro Lights every day – my tabs tab is approaching four hundred quid a month. An average night out with the lads – drinks at the Atlantic bar, dinner some-where new and ludicrous, more drinks at Soho House or the Groucho, coke, cabs and boilers – clocks in at about eight hundred quid. It's no wonder I'm trying to keep it down to two or three nights out a week. Even though a fair chunk of this can be punted onto expenses, it still takes a lot of fucking dough to keep the wheels on the wagon. My bank manager stutters in disbelief as every month brings the same request to maintain, or increase, my overdraft. He knows what I earn. (About five times what he does.) He can't believe I'm getting through it either. On the plus side my hooker expenses do seem to be steady and manageable at around a grand a month these days. Maybe it's the cold weather. Sometimes, in the feverish months of spring and summer, I have to admit I go a bit bonkers.

Anyway, the answer to all of these problems is simple enough: Big. Fucking. Hit. Records. Have a few of those and – bosh – no more problems.

I edge along Ladbroke Grove – at one point ecstatically managing to get into third gear – and I keep seeing them; hunched on doorsteps with their tabloids and their tea,

smoking their Raffles or Coliseums as they heft rolls of
seagrass matting and lengths of hardwood flooring in and
out of the dusty old houses. The builders. You see?
Everyone's doing it. It's like you can look along the road,
through the leafy trees towards Holland Park, and see the
fireball of cash come flaming down the hill, burning out all
the tolers: the Kaffirs, the old people, the welfare families.
They've had it around here. Finished.

Finally, blissfully, the meeting is ending and I'm saying
things like 'let's do some demos' and 'see you soon'. They
hand me a flyer – a picture of Malcolm McDowell from the
movie *If*, presumably a totem of cool in whatever sorry
universe these jizz-rags inhabit – for their next gig as they
leave.

I flop down on the sofa and start rolling a spliff. There are
days at work, whole days, where nothing seems to happen.
All morning long there is coffee and cigarettes and phone
calls where I say things like 'send it over' and 'in last week's
NME' and 'shipping a hundred thousand' while I watch
MTV – Foo Fighters, Daft Punk, the Chemical Brothers –
and think about lunch. Somewhere in the mid-afternoon I'll
have a spliff and a belt of Scotch, or a line of gak, and the day
will look a little brighter, sharper. I'll make the same calls
and watch the same videos with a little more enthusiasm.
Or sometimes I'll just crawl behind my sofa for a nap after
lunch, the blinds drawn against the outer office and music
whumping from my stereo. Later I'll start to drift up,
suspended in that sweet honey-drop between waking and
sleeping, to see that the street lights have started to come on
along the park across the road.

Darren comes in and starts banging on about new bands

he wants me to listen to; Athletico Strip, Dragdoll, Magoo, Starfish.

I flip through *Music Week* while he talks and slips cassettes and CDs into my machine. Lucian Grange has been promoted to MD at Polydor. He is only a few years older than me. This news mixes with my simmering hangover and fills me with a depth, a profundity, of sorrow I cannot adequately describe.

'What the fuck is this?' I say to Darren, nodding towards the stereo at some tuneless pile of shite he's stuck on the turntable.

'Ah, the Lazies, American band. Fucking cool.'

'It's an insult. Take it off.'

The racket stops and he rummages through his pile of 7″ and CDs for something else.

My mobile chirrups. 'Hello?'

'Christ, big night or what?' a thick, hoarse voice says.

It takes a few seconds for me to register it, to believe it.

'I . . . how do you feel?' I manage finally.

'Bit rough.' He goes on for a while, talking about a gig we're meant to be going to tonight, some band called Bellatrix at the Bull and Gate and finally I hang up, numb.

I'm thinking a couple of things. 1) Fucking worthless Thai Valium. 2) From the sound of things it is not that unusual, it is not completely out of the normal run of things, for Waters to wake up naked and covered in his own shit with a thrumming butt-plug up his arse.

Like Freddie, or Jason, or Michael Myers, he is probably unkillable.

The greenery of Oxfordshire blurs past the tinted windows

of our people carrier. Derek is shouting on his mobile, ranting about some artwork he's unhappy with. Ross taps away at his laptop while Dunn, Nicky, Waters and I read the trades. Schneider has headphones on, listening to Christ knows what on his Discman and trying to act relaxed.

We're all headed to the Rage playback. No one's heard a note yet, but the album will be a key summer release for us among what is a pretty thin-looking release schedule and expectations are running pretty high.

We bowl through the studio – where wine, beers and nibbles have been laid on – and into the control room where Rage, Fisher and two engineers are waiting. Rage sits in a huge leather chair at the centre of the mixing desk.

The first thing I think as he swivels round to greet us is – *fuck me*. His nose is dewy and leaking, his eyeballs vibrating marbles, his left leg stutters and pumps uncontrollably, his jaw is locked forward and set hard, frozen by cocaine. Ross and I exchange a quick, incredulous look.

'Right,' Rage says once we're all seated on two huge leather sofas at the back of the room, glasses of warm Chardonnay in hand. An engineer hits 'play' and Rage moves a trembling hand towards a fader, pushing it all the way up.

Forty minutes into the thing I sneak a look around at the expressions on display. Most people just look blank. Ross is fighting laughter. Derek looks like he might burst out of his seat and kill someone at any moment. Schneider's face is harder to read. It is buried in his hands.

The first five or six minutes of the song were simply annoying – a hi-hat pattern and some abstract tweeting sounds. Somewhere around the fifteen-minute mark a bass line arrived and Rage began conducting the music with his hands, his eyes closed, lost in some mad rapture over this abortion he's created. People cross and recross their legs, sip their wine and pray for it to end. But it doesn't. It just keeps on going – drum loops clattering randomly, snatches of vocals, jarring keyboard stabs.

As the track approaches the one-hour mark and *nothing* has emerged that vaguely resembles a hook, or a chorus, or a recognisable melody, it collectively dawns on us that we're listening to the sonic representation of someone's mind coming apart. On a positive note I'm thinking that I must get the name of Rage's dealer, because the chang the cunt is getting his hands on is clearly fucking phenomenal.

In the end I simply stare at the red, digital numbers on the tape counter, watching the minutes, the money, Schneider's career, tick away. The counter reads '64.33' when it all finally ends in a mad, juddering flourish, like the crescendo at the end of 'A Day in the Life', played on broken computers by mongoloids. Rage has his hands extended, trembling, his forefingers pointing skywards as he wrings the last notes out of his cocaine-induced hallucinatory mind-orchestra.

I look over at Schneider. He has tears in eyes. He is finished and he knows it.

Rage swivels around in his chair to face us. 'It's called "Birth",' he says.

Of course it fucking is.

It gets better when Rage corrects our assumption that we've just heard the whole album, segued together in its entirety. No, he tells us that this will be a *single*, the first single to precede the album in fact, that he *will not* allow an edit of any sort, and how pleased he is that we've been the first witnesses to the world's first drum'n'bass opera. Then he runs off to the toilet. There's a lot of polite nodding and words like 'interesting', 'radical' and 'challenging' get thrown around.

The second we're all inside the people carrier and the driver slams the door shut Schneider turns to Derek and says, 'Look . . .' It will be his longest contribution to the conversation for some time.

'WHAT HAVE YOU DONE? *WHAT THE FUCK HAVE YOU DONE!* THREE AND A HALF MONTHS IN ONE OF THE MOST EXPENSIVE STUDIOS IN THE COUNTRY AND WE DON'T HAVE A FUCKING THING! I'M TELLING YOU RIGHT NOW THAT THERE IS NO WAY ON EARTH THIS LABEL WILL EVER RELEASE A FUCKING NOTE OF ANYTHING WE HEARD TODAY! HOW COULD YOU LET IT GET TO THIS? HOW?'

Schneider tries to speak but Derek's already on the phone to Trellick at the office, telling him to get Rage's contract out and firing questions at him. What's the unrecouped balance? How cheaply can we get out of the deal? Can we, in fact, make any case for suing Rage for breach of contract for delivering material which is so blatantly uncommercial? Is there a sanity clause?

Janette from press leans forward and pats Schneider comfortingly on the knee. 'Actually, I quite liked it,' she says quietly, but he doesn't reply. He just goes on looking out of window as we thread our way back along country lanes towards the M40. Dead Man Staring.

*

Danny Rent brings his girl band, Songbirds, in for a meeting.

The four of them sit bunched up on my office sofa, scowling and chewing gum, looking like they've been kept back in class. Three of them are white and one black, but the white girls all act like Kaffirs — they kiss their teeth and click their fingers and say things like 'seen?' They're all aged between seventeen and twenty, all lookers — one of the white girls in particular (Denise? Sonia?) is stunning — but with that working-class whore look. They're genetic time bombs, DNA-Semtex. Every one of them will explode into monsterism the minute they hit twenty-seven. They're all dressed the way these girls dress, tits busting out of T-shirts made for newborn babies and low-slung combat pants which allow their thongs — pink, black and lemon — to jut way up above the waistlines. I mean, they look like they'd let you do *anything* to them these girls; fuck them in the arse and punch them and stuff.

We're watching a 'video' Danny has had made, to try and sell them to record companies — the four of them, dressed in cheap, nasty, high-street clothes, grind their way unsteadily through a really tacky R&B number.

The video finishes.

'Mmmm,' I say, 'who are your influences then?'

Silence. They shift uneasily. I realise they do not understand the question.

'Steven's saying,' Danny butts in, 'what music do you like?'

Another gargantuan pause. ''Ip op?' says a brunette, uncertainly.

'Madonna,' says the blonde.

'Good,' I say, nodding, 'good.'

'Ere, mate,' the black boiler says, 'Danny says you signed Rage. Yeah?'

'Yeah,' I lie and they all murmur approval.

'Wot's e loike?' one asks.

'Rage? He's great. Really clever guy.'

Another long silence. 'So,' the blonde one, the really attractive one says, fingering a trainer lace and nervously looking up, making eye contact with me through her fringe, 'what chew fink of our stuff then?'

What do I think? I think you look like the worst sort of sink-estate, single-mother, benefit-fraud trash imaginable. I think that your 'music' is about the biggest insult to humanity since a roomful of Nazis first cooed over the blueprints for Auschwitz.

But I'm also thinking that, if we bring in real songwriters, session musicians and a decent producer, if we throw suitcases of money at stylists and hair and make-up artists, if we hire world-quality photographers and video directors, if we get personal trainers in and manage to keep you all off the KFC and the vodka for a few months, if we can find someone to teach you how to speak properly, if we spend eye-popping sums on retainers for press officers and pluggers, and if they can somehow convince enough journalists, radio programmers and TV producers that you're not really talent-free sluts who would gobble a donkey just to meet Chris Evans, that you are, in fact, 'the real deal', then maybe, just maybe, with the wind behind us and a couple of breaks, I think we could probably sell a few fucking records.

'I think it's great,' I say, getting up and showing them out. I mean, it might be worth a pop.

Girl power, innit?

Rebecca is holding a phone towards me. 'It's Barry from club promotions.'

'Barry?'

'Steven, hi, I got the club reactions in on "Why Don't You . . .".'

These are A4 sheets, like little report cards that all the club DJs fill in to tell you what they reckon to the track.

'Well?'

'Ah . . .' In a nanosecond my blood turns to antifreeze.

'Barry?'

'Yeah, they're all right. They're all right.'

All right? Just *all right*? This is bad. This is very fucking bad.

We have a second 'Why Don't You' marketing meeting. It is markedly different from the first. Dunn kicks off.

'Sorry, Radio 1 don't think it's for them. If the record had been bigger at club then we'd have some ammunition. As it is . . .' He spreads his hands.

Barry pipes up, 'It just seems to be the kind of record that . . . we'll need a bit of radio before we can get a lot of the commercial club DJs to pick up on it.'

Hannah: 'MTV quite liked the video. But they're not going to playlist it until we get some radio.'

Through all of this Derek just glares at me. With the video (hastily shot, at my insistence) we have spent well over one hundred thousand pounds on this turkey. Turkey? That's an insult to turkeys. It's a fucking dodo.

Ross: 'No point in doing much advertising or a big poster campaign until we've got some awareness at radio and TV . . .'

Suzy: 'Not much interest at press, I'm afraid. We're getting reviewed in *Mixmag*.'

Nicky: 'I'm afraid there's not much I can do with this at the moment.' She tries to look sympathetic but the bitch can hardly keep the smile from creasing her fat fucking face in half.

Finally Derek hits critical mass: 'ARE YOU TELLING ME WE'VE SPENT OVER A HUNDRED FUCKING GRAND TO GET A FUCKING REVIEW IN FUCKING *MIXMAG*?! JESUS CHRIST!

I stare at the glass table – through the glass table and onto the carpeting where I uselessly notice that Dunn is wearing the same Prada shoes as I am – and say nothing. There is nothing to say. If there was something to say I'd be saying it.

Derek hates the record. The marketing department hate the record. The club promotions department hate the record. The radio department hate the record. I want to kill Rudi, that Nazi-scumbag-fucking-child-molester-fucking-animal. In a bizarre alchemic process perhaps unique to the entertainment industry the cancer cure I brought back from Cannes has mysteriously morphed into something closer to the cause of AIDS.

Finally Derek looks around the room and says, with absolutely no enthusiasm, 'So where do we go with this record now?'

'Lourdes?' Ross suggests, unhelpfully.

Sure enough it comes to pass. Schneider's contract, due to expire later this summer, will not be renewed. They pay him off and he clears his desk out. I go for a drink with him on his last day. It is three in the afternoon and the pub is empty. Outside, rain falls lightly across Hammersmith. It's warm though; the pub doors are open and cars sizzle by on the wet tarmac. Schneider sluices the ice around in his vodka tonic and tries to be upbeat, giving it the whole 'best-thing-that-could-have-happened-in-a-way' type shit. 'What are you going to do?' I ask.

'I've had a couple of interesting offers,' he lies. I mean, fuck. He hasn't had a proper hit in years. He's *thirty-nine* — wife and two kids — and suddenly — bosh! — it's Goodnight Vienna. At best he might land a sympathy job with some reissues label, hawking back catalogue and farting about trying to secure the rights for Eddie and the Hot Rods live LPs. As he craps on about the non-existent offers he reckons he's had, Alisha's Attic, then Kula Shaker, then Mansun blare from the jukebox. It dawns on me that they are all bands that Schneider (and, by extension, me) either turned down or failed to sign in the past year or two. All of whom are having hits now. Any one of them might have saved him. But he went with Rage. The man who put it all on red . . .

'For what it's worth,' he says, 'I told Derek they should make you Head of A&R.'

Fuck. Support from a loser like Schneider can probably only weaken my case right now. 'Really? Thanks. What did Derek say?'

'That they're probably going to give it to Waters.'

He drains his glass, bangs it down on the wet mahogany, and signals wearily for another. 'Sorry,' he says, not looking at me, 'bad timing there with that record of Rudi's.'

*

Sometimes you need to act fast. You really do. 'A good plan today is better than a perfect plan tomorrow,' and all that crap.

The celebration for Waters' promotion began in the fifth floor bar at Harvey Nicks at lunchtime with the whole of the A&R department plus Trellick and Derek. From there onto Quo Vadis for dinner and then Soho House before Waters and I – absolutely smashed beyond human belief by this point – ducked out and caught a cab up to Camden, to see some useless band who are playing at the Dublin Castle. We last two songs before we hail another cab on Parkway and – stopping briefly outside the house of a dealer we both know in Chalk Farm, where we score three more grams – head back to Waters' flat off Westbourne Park Road.

'You know how much I respect you,' Waters says, sniffing and screeching out big lines on the big mirror while I pour the vodka. 'I don't want you to feel that you're suddenly working *for* me. We're working *together*.'

I close my eyes and swallow about a quarter-pint of neat Stoli.

'I want to try and build the kind of culture where . . .' Waters goes into an idiotic rhapsody about his 'vision', about the kind of A&R culture he plans to establish at the label. Words like 'organic', 'Chris Blackwell', 'synergy' and 'John Hammond' are freely tossed around. His stupid fucking dog snoozes at his feet while he snorts and sweats and theorises. The conversation drifts and rambles, landing on the subject of Great British Songwriters, the kind of people Waters wants us to sign. Waters is struggling for actual names. I mention Paul Weller.

'Uh, yeah. He . . . he writes most of his own stuff,

doesn't he?' Waters says, his head thrown back as he sucks a gooey wad of snot and gak down his throat.

CDs are scattered all over the place; on the low coffee table, the sofa, the floor. I pick one up at random, to have something to read while Waters craps on – he's now literally talking about how his daddy laughed when he fell off his bike when he was nine, or some fucking thing – and find I'm holding a copy of the last Prodigy album, *Music for the Jilted Generation*. I open the gatefold inner sleeve and stare at the painting which covers both panels. Or rather 'painting'. The crude piece of artwork depicts a raver – long, straggly hair, trainers, sweatshirt, etc. – who is standing on one side of a dark chasm. On the other side of the chasm a huge group of riot police are wielding truncheons and Perspex shields. Their faces are obscured by the black visors of their helmets. On the raver's side of the chasm is an idyllic green field with a sound system, a DJ and other ravers dancing around blissfully. The sun is shining. Back on the other side, behind the coppers, is a dark industrial city: hulking tower blocks, ominous skyscrapers and factories retching sulphur into the blackened sky. The two sides of the chasm are connected by a rope bridge, which the coppers are preparing to cross, clearly in order to give the raver a good fucking beating. But hang on, the raver is holding a sabre to the rope bridge, about to sever it and thwart their plans. He is also giving the coppers the finger. The quality of the actual painting is *appalling* – like some handicapped kid's O-level art project.

Waters looks up from shaping more lines and peers over my shoulder. 'Good that, isn't it?' he says.

I stare at the picture, dumbfounded, for a long, long

time. All I can think about is how much – if you were somehow forced to live in the world depicted on the Prodigy sleeve – you'd want to be on the coppers' side of that chasm; in the filthy city with its casinos, hookers and petrol stations. Its five-star hotels, sex shops, nightclubs and banks. I am also filled with a great and unexpected affection for Britain's riot police.

I look up at Waters. 'How?'

'What?'

'How is this picture good?'

'It's . . . y'know. It's got a message.'

'What fucking message?'

He craps on with some anti-Establishment balls for a while as I sit there getting angrier and angrier. To calm myself down I try and think of all the words I know for cocaine – gak, chang, nose-up, bag, beak, charlie, krell, powder, chisel, bump, posh, bugle, sniff, skiwear, schniff, Bronson, Bolivian, toot, junior (crack is called senior), chas, nonsense, bounce, blow, Vim – but it's not working.

'Oh fuck off. You know what I mean,' Waters says huffily. 'Anyway . . .' he tries to change the subject.

'Excuse me,' I say as I get up and leave the room.

It's hard to say what does it. Whether it's his views on the Prodigy sleeve, or the fact that that dismal spunk-worshipper Derek could choose to make this guy Head of A&R over me, or the fact Waters doesn't even know that Paul Weller is primarily known for being a songwriter. I mean, don't get me wrong, I don't give a good drop of spunk about the Prodigy, or about Weller or his music – although it was certainly impressive that Go! Discs managed to resurrect the fossilised mod cunt and grind a million albums out of him – it's just . . . the indignity of the situation suddenly hits me. No one knows what they are doing, yes, granted. But Waters . . . Waters really doesn't know *anything*. And now he's my boss. For a second I almost experience sadness, a sense of loss, regarding Schneider.

I walk into the kitchen. There, still in the corner by the fridge, is the blue-and-steel baseball bat.

Home security.

I come back in. He's sitting on the floor with his back to me, hunched over the mirror on the low coffee table, already – always – shaping more lines. I check my watch. It's almost 6 a.m. A dance compilation plays softly. Waters is still talking, gibbering. To me? To the sleeping dog? To the wall? Who knows?

I walk up behind him. I start the bat back, swinging it so far over my head that I'm sure I feel it touch the heel of my right shoe. Then I bring it down with humming force. I can hear the air being moved aside. Waters is saying the word 'crossover'.

Sound of Impact.

Now, I expected there to be some crunchy give as his skull caved in and he slumped forward. Goodnight Vienna. But no. There's a loud clear 'thwock' – like hitting a very hard piece of wood – and Waters immediately *howls* in agony, grabs his head, and starts staggering to his feet, knocking glasses and ashtrays noisily onto the polished wood floor. The bastard dog explodes into life and starts yelping and growling. Stunned and shaking, it takes me a second or two to recock the bat, by which time he's on his knees, halfway up. I swing down again, this time the bat glances off his forehead, which is already slick with blood, and sends him reeling into the middle of the room. He looks up, right at me. Then he looks at his trembling hands, which are covered in blood. The expression on his face . . . he looks confused, horrified. Like when you open your bank statement thinking you've had a quiet month, and scan down the tumbling debits, to the unthinkable figure at the bottom with the letters 'OD' beside it. The dog is barking its tits off, going crackers.

For a second I think he's going to charge at me, and he's a big guy, Waters. Then the force of the blow, the shockwave, hits him, his eyes start vibrating, his legs spastic about and he wobbles onto his knees, making a terrible 'ohhhh . . . urrrr' sound. Blood is pouring down his face now and it looks like oil under the soft halogen spots. I run towards him. He manages one actual word – 'please' – as I bring the bat down for the third time in a massive, terrible arc. He's on his knees, at around waist height to me, and I connect right in the centre of his dome. This time there is *lots* of crunchy give and his skull caves in. A jet of blood sprays out of his nose and he goes over, falling onto his side and twitching on the floor.

Bear eat CDs!

'You stupid fat cunt!' I scream. 'Paul Weller writes *all* his own songs! *He's one of the foremost singer-songwriters of his generation!*' Just to be on the safe side, because the anger is fizzling out now, the adrenalin going, my blood clotting, becoming thick as tarmac in my veins, I smash the bloody bat down once more, onto the side of his head this time. With the sound of a loud, wet fart, a mess of grey-white 'brains' spurts out of the crack in the top of his head. The dog stops barking and growling and starts licking and nibbling at the spreading puddle of blood and brains which is oozing out of his master's broken head. Disgusted, and with about the last of my strength, I smash the Jack Russell incredibly hard over the head. Its skull just explodes, the eyeballs both flopping out and dangling down its face and then it's nice and quiet, the only sound that of the house compilation, Frankie Knuckles' 'Your Love' playing softly.

There's something small, pink and bloody on the floor next to Waters' mouth and I realise he's bitten the tip of his tongue off. It's just lying there, a few inches away from a bloodstained paperback copy of *Fever Pitch* by Nick Hornby.

April

London Records terminate their deal with Tony Wilson's label Factory Too. R. Kelly is no. 1 for a fucking month. XL spends a lot of money signing some band called Stroke. Whispers start to circulate that the new Radiohead LP is off its tits — an unlistenable prog-rock nightmare. Andy Thompson's label VC Recordings prepares to launch an album by dance act D*Note. Thompson says, 'I can see D*Note at the Royal Albert Hall. The sky is really the limit for them.'

*'Lemme tell ya something — if a guy's a cocksucker in his
life, when he dies he don't become a saint.'*

Morris Levy

The day after I kill Waters I have to go to Dublin to see a
band.

I *hate* the cab ride into Dublin. It's a bitch. I mean, it'll
soon be the twenty-first century and these worthless Paddy
tramps can't even get their diseased, potato-ravaged arses
into gear and build a fucking motorway. You have to sit for
eternity on some two-lane B-road that winds through
housing estates, high streets and Christ knows what, all the
while with some lobotomised fucking Mick asking you all
manner of crap about yourself.

'AndwillthisbeyerfirstvisittoDublinnow?' the horrible
tip-scrounging cunt has the balls to ask me.

I just groan and crank up my Discman, turning to stare
silently out of the window at the dreadful shops, bars and
inbred mutants that crawl past in the rain-streaked grid-
lock. But the guy, the cabbie, swings round from the wheel
again and keeps asking me something. I slide the head-
phones down.

'Andwhichhotelwasityewereafternow?'

'What?' I sigh.

He says it again, slower.

'The Clarence.'

'Ohverynicenowyeknowit'syermanfromyewtoowho . . .'

But I don't hear the rest of this because I slip the head-phones back up over my ears and Richard Ashcroft's singing 'You're a slave to money . . .' as I return to staring out the window through cracked, stinging, hung-over eyes: a big Guinness poster, a dirty child on a mountain bike, an old man bawling in the doorway of a pub, and a bright red butcher's shop with carcasses hanging from hooks and gleaming entrails piled in plastic trays.

I check in at the Clarence.

I go to my room, masturbate, and fall asleep.

I wake up and realise I've missed the gig.

I go back to sleep.

I get up the next morning and eat a late, expensive breakfast.

I lie in bed and watch a film called *Outbreak* starring Dustin Hoffman on pay TV.

I fly back to London.

I tell Derek the band were 'promising'.

He nods, like he understands something.

I waltz into the office around lunchtime the next day, sucking on an ice lolly and wearing shorts and sandals – London's having one of those early-spring mornings where it thinks it's summertime. As I round the corner towards my office I see Rebecca and Pam. They're huddled over Rebecca's desk, their faces red, both clutching wet, shredded Kleenex.

'Oh Steven,' Pam says, a catch in her voice, 'it's terrible . . .' She bursts into fresh hot tears.

'What?' I say.

'It's . . . Roger . . .' she manages between sobs.

'WHAT?' I say.

'He's dead!' Pam says.

'No!' I say. (I thought about saying 'NO!', but then I thought, *no*.)

She just nods, blubbing, shoulders shaking, crinkly tissue pressed to her face. I like girls' faces when they've been crying – hot, soft and pulpy. I wonder if Pam – in her grief – is recalling the night after the Ivor Novello Awards last year when she rashly went home with Waters and he tried – at length from what I heard – to cajole her into anal sex. She pulls herself together a little, sweeping wet strands of hair out of her face and taking a deep breath.

'A neighbour found him this morning. It looks like someone broke into his flat, a burglar, and Roger must have disturbed them. Or he tried to stop them or something.'

The idea of Waters being confronted in his living room at 3 a.m. by a couple of big, angry tooled-up niggers and doing anything other than begging for his fat, sleazy life is so laughable I have to bite my cheeks. Pam collapses forwards again into me, shuddering and sobbing as she buries her face in my neck. As I comfort her, and quietly enjoy the press of her (decent) rack against my chest, Rebecca and I look at each other. Rebecca's eyes are red like Pam's, her cheeks slick with tears too, but she's looking at me strangely, with an expression on her face I can't quite place.

Hastings comes out of his office. 'Isn't it terrible?' he says. I put a hand over my face and say, 'Excuse me, please.'

I run into my office, slamming the door behind me, and throw myself face down on the sofa, my shoulders shaking and my whole body convulsing. I can feel Hastings, Rebecca and Pam watching me through the glass partition. I can feel their buffoonish concern upon me.

It must really look like I'm *crying*.

Later, seven o'clock, after everyone's gone home and the place is empty, I go and sit in Waters' office. It is strange to sit there as it slowly gets dark, surrounded by the things he saw and touched every day – his computer, his diary, phone and stereo – and think about how he said 'please'. On the wall is a framed gold disc from the one (almost) successful act Waters signed. (They're 'bands' or 'groups' when you're trying to sign them, and 'acts' once you have. I don't know why that is.) Scattered around his desk and perched on his shelves are various *Star Wars* products; little X-Wing fighters, a Millennium Falcon, a big R2D2 that's actually a phone. Like many men in the record industry in their late twenties/early thirties Waters thought *Star Wars* was cool. Just looking at his dismal toys feels like justification enough for killing the cretin.

I'm bound to get a few of his acts dumped on me. But that's not so bad – most of them are so fucked that they're beyond rescue. 'It was broke when I got here' stuff. I plan to suggest we drop pretty much all of them.

A Jiffy bag, with an EMI address label on it, is propped up on his keyboard. I feel inside and pull out a promo CD. I squint at it in the half-light: Radiohead. Their new single, which isn't out for a month or so and which I haven't heard yet. Dunn says most radio stations are giving it the fuck off.

I slip it into Waters' machine and a strange, terrible noise fills the room. I turn it down.

I open the top drawer of his desk and have a root: taxi and restaurant receipts, half-completed expenses claims, cassettes and CDs, pens and pencils, a couple of empty cocaine wraps. One half-full wrap . . .

I do a line off his mouse mat. The mouse mat is a picture of Hervé Villechaize, the midget actor who played Nick Nack in the James Bond film and Tattoo in *Fantasy Island*. (Like many men in the record industry in their late twenties/early thirties Waters thought that shit TV shows from the seventies and eighties were cool.)

Hervé was three foot ten and weighed four stone, but the mad dwarf cunt fell in love with, and married, a fully grown woman. When she divorced him and took all his cash he went mental; he hit the painkillers, the Scotch and the chang and wound up topping himself. He taped his own suicide too. Honestly. He got hold of a tape recorder, pressed 'record', put a pillow against his chest, held a big fuck-off gun up to the pillow, and he said, *'Goodbye, my darling. I could not satisfy your love,'* and shot himself through his tiny heart.

Or rather, he tried to. Somehow he missed everything vital and had to cock the gun again and shoot himself a second time. Apparently the tape ends with him moaning and groaning, saying, 'O*hhh it hurts, it hurts. I am dying . . . I am dying now.'*

The Radiohead track, which is called 'Paranoid Android', has built through an appalling crescendo of arty noise into a kind of washed-out coda with Thom Yorke, bleating and warbling the words 'rain down' over the top. What the fuck

were they thinking with this nonsense? They're finished.
Surely no cunt's going to be having this?

I turn it off and just sit there in Waters' office in the quiet
dark, doing the last of his chang and thinking about Hervé
Villechaize, until it's time to go to the Borderline, to see
some band called the Hitchers who Lamacq has been
banging on about.

The car from the airport seems to take a long time and we
pull up at the church already – always – late. While Trellick
winds up a call on his mobile I get out the car and look
around: grey skies, windy, brutal. Down the hillside, off in
the distance, is a big, dismal city. Sheffield or something, I
suppose.

Christ, I hate being out of London.

The cabbie is saying something to us but he's Northern
and none of us understand a word. Ross slips the guy a fifty
and tells him to wait for us. The cabbie blinks at the big,
unfamiliar, strawberry-coloured note and carefully folds it
into his shirt pocket, like it's an old, delicate parchment or
something. 'Pay your mortgage off, mate,' Ross says as
we walk away. We go through the gate and up the path
towards the grey stone building, towards soft, horrible
organ music.

Inside it's busy – a couple of hundred people – and we
have to stand at the back. A minister, a vicar or something,
is crapping on about Waters: '. . . in London, in the music
industry, where he enjoyed great success and made a great
many friends, so many of whom have travelled here to be
with us today. As a boy Roger was always a huge fan of
music and it was because of this . . .'

It's been a far easier ride than I ever imagined. Two policemen came to interview me as I'd been out with Waters on the night he died. I told them we'd gone to see some bands in Camden and I'd dropped him off in a cab before going home. They'd nodded away, made some notes and that was that. They reckon it was a burglar. Then again, perhaps this isn't so odd:

Schneider had his mobile and wallet taken from him at knifepoint on Hammersmith Broadway a few months ago. The Kaffir doing the mugging even let him finish his call.

Darren was knocked off his bike in Kentish Town. He got up, dazed and bruised, to find himself surrounded by a mob of teenagers, who proceeded to kick the shit out of him, dip his pockets, and ride off on his bike.

Leamington got back from holiday and walked into his basement flat in Fulham. Everything gone and the proverbial smoking log in his bed.

Rebecca was waiting for the bus in Shepherd's Bush. They punched her in the face and grabbed her handbag.

Nicky from International was sitting at the lights on the Cromwell Road when the car door burst open and the kid – a snarling mess of gold teeth and sportswear – took her bag, phone and a handful of CDs. ('I thought he was going to get *in* the car. I thought he was going to rape me,' she said, telling the story in a meeting. Trellick and I looked at each other, both thinking the same thing – *you're fucking dreaming, love.*)

Daily, it seems, you walk out to your car in the morning to find your feet crunching on the tiny pebbles of glass, then the brick on the passenger seat, the wires hanging like guts from the dashboard, and your Blaupunkt being flogged for a tenner's worth of rocks in some local ragga den.

It serves me well, London: the streets crawl with suspects. The houses and the cars gleam with motive.

I look around the church at the people who I guess Waters grew up with. The girls, apart from the industry whores who made the trip up, are all utter fucking monsters. I'm guessing that most of them are around thirty, Waters' age, but Christ, they look like pensioners – lined, wrinkled faces, massive sagging teats, arses like busted sacks of gravel. The kind of working-class sows who stop being doable around the age of twenty-one. You look at the guys who are with them, guys around our age (but poor guys, failures) and they look innocent. They look like they don't know what's going on. Like they're unaware that they've married some disfigured atrocity. I mean, you look at these guys and you'd expect to see a little shame. Self-consciousness at the very least. If I was one of them I wouldn't be able to look a stranger in the eye without gesturing to my monster and saying, 'Sorry, mate, I don't know what I was thinking.' Maybe they don't. Maybe they look at these women and see the girl they met at school. Is that even possible? That kind of . . . well, love, I suppose you'd have to call it. I shudder at the word, at the thought. No wonder Waters got the fuck out of here as soon as he could.

It occurs to me, not for the first time, how strange it must be not to come from London.

After what feels like a long, long time it's over and we all bow our heads as what I presume is Waters' immediate family file out behind the coffin. There's two girls (his sisters?) who look bad, they're shaking and crying and holding onto each other and stuff, and, behind them, the parents. The father looks like he isn't quite there – red-rimmed eyes set in a thousand-yard stare – but the mother. Jesus wept, *the mother*. She's this tiny woman crumpled into a ball, half clinging to her husband's arm, half being carried along by him. She's clutching a soaking handkerchief in each fist and is making this noise. It sounds like the noise ghosts make in old horror films, a sort of wobbly moaning, whining 'woooo-aahhhh-ooohh'. I mean, she looks fucking insane.

The guys holding the coffin have to pause, to get something out of the way, and she comes right up against the coffin. She starts screaming – *'No! No! My son! My son!'* type stuff – and this triggers off loads of the girls in the crowd crying even harder until a couple of old hags calm her down and they get her out of there.

Going outside a few minutes after this we have to pass in a line by the family. I shake the dad's hand and tell him how sorry I am, that I knew his son through work and all that, and he just nods and doesn't really say anything. The mother isn't in the line-up, it's just the dad and the sisters, one of whom looks doable: big tits strapped tightly into a black dress that's a little too small for her and bright red lipstick on. I hug her quite hard and then I'm out on the steps of the church, lighting a cigarette in the hateful Northern air.

Ross goes off to try the office again, to see if they've got the midweeks yet. Trellick has to get hold of Fisher and I call the office to speak to Rebecca, to make sure she's booked me a cab to Heathrow in the morning. (I am off to

Miami in the morning, for the Winter fucking Music Conference – which is like MIDEM, but with just dance music – and then onto Texas for South by South-fucking-west – which is like the Winter Music Conference, but with indie music. They're all the same thing: a tide of net-working cunts going bananas.) The three of us stand off to one side smoking and talking on our phones as more people file out of the church and the coffin is carried out.

So. Much. Fucking. Respect.

I listen to Rebecca reminding me about connection times and check-in baloney as the coffin is rolled into the big hearse. People are scattered around crying and hugging each other. Waters' mother is sandwiched between the two old girls on a bench. She twitches like some bar-rattling inmate from a Victorian asylum, literally *demented* with grief.

Wow, I think to myself, remembering the expression on Waters' spastic face when he died, it really is something to kill somebody and create all of this.

'You can't spell "star" without A and R.'

Ronnie Vanucci

'Maybe we should go out,' someone says.

'No . . . I . . . that would be bad,' someone else says. It might be me. It's hard to tell who is saying what because all our voices are the same now – all cracked, ghosted whispers, static crackling across the room. Fragments of several different conversations ricochet around, over-lapping, out of sync, at cross-purposes.

The suite is dark, the curtains drawn, the only light coming from a couple of table lamps and the gently strobing pornography on the TV screen.

'We'll need more coke soon.'

'The guy's bringing it.'

'The black guy? Oh fuck . . .'

'Go in the bathroom.'

'And we need more fucking booze. *I need a whiskey.*'

'Have you heard that Stardust bootleg?'

'I can't face him . . .'

'Get room service to fill the minibar again.'

'Hide in the fucking bathroom.'

'Fucking tune.'

'Oh God. I can't face room service. I think I'm having a heart attack.'

'*Hide in the bathroom, you cunt.*'

'I think we should go out.'

'Fuck off.'

'Right, you cunts. I'm calling room service!' Leamington says this.

We've been in Miami for thirty-six hours now and I have yet to leave this room. I move across the darkened, fetid suite (we're in the hotel, where they filmed some of *Goldfinger*, as someone uselessly points out every five minutes) to the window and very nervously pull the curtains a couple of millimetres apart. A thin band of intense toxic sunshine lasers across the room and, just for a second, I glimpse sky, green palms and, beyond them, the beach and the ocean before everyone is screaming for me to shut the fucking curtains. 'Just . . . um, checking,' I say. It is around thirty degrees outside, but we have the windows all sealed and the air con on full crank. I reach behind the curtains and open a window. Ten floors below you can hear the roar of chattering delegates intercut with splashes as people dive into the pool.

I walk about the room swinging my arms, kicking my legs, my chin tucked tight into my chest. I'm beyond wired – pure current.

'I think if I did a couple of pills I could go out,' someone says.

'That's not totally crazy,' someone replies.

'Fatboy Slim tonight,' someone else says.

'Roni Size.'

'Where?'

'At the Cameo Theatre?'

'Fuck that.'

'We *have* to go out tonight.'

'Size at the Cameo?'

'Maybe we should get some hookers in.'

'No Fatboy.'

'He's at the Delano.'

'Or strippers anyway.'

'Do you mean where he's staying or where he's playing?'

'Eh?'

We started on the chang somewhere over Ireland. When we landed – having raped the Virgin Upper Class bar for ten hours straight – we were met by this dealer someone knew. We got a limo and continued with the chang on the drive into town. I don't know everyone here. There's some guy from some indie (XL? Mo Wax? Rising High?) and a publisher kid (Warner Chappell? BMG?) and a couple of ex-pat Brits, drug-dealer types, who someone vaguely knows who've attached themselves to us. Darren hasn't spoken for five or six hours. He just sits there, rocking back and forth. At one point I made an attempt to go downstairs and register at the convention, to pick up my delegate pass, so I could attend the showcases and discussion panels (where gak and pill-lobotomised fools will ruminate on worthy topics like 'How Will Internet DJing Affect the Economies of Former Soviet Bloc Countries?' and 'Is the SuperClub Killing Club Culture?'). The lift doors opened and way across the lobby I could see some of the Brit contingent – Dave Beer, Kris Needs, people like that. I glimpsed a sober, businesslike Parker-Hall striding up to reception. I pressed the button for our floor again and *ran* back to the fucking room. 'You don't want to go down there,' I told everyone. That was, I think, sometime yesterday afternoon. The outside world now looks like an abstraction; a dream you had when you were a kid. Intangible, a few blurred images, the faintest tang of an aftertaste.

'Ritchie Hawtin,' someone says.

'Dimitri from Paris.'

'Get the Yellow Pages.'

'He shit his pants in CentroFly.'

'More coke.'

'Peanut Butter Wolf.'

'Todd Terry.'

'Carl Cox.'

'Basement Jaxx.'

I think someone is crying.

'Grooverider.'

'A case of fucking Cristal.'

'Maybe sushi.'

'Ritchie Hawtin.'

'Double-ended her.'

'Propellerheads.'

There's a fierce, copper-style rap at the door.

'Oh fuck.'

'Jesus fuck.'

'Who's that? *Who is it?*' someone asks in a whisper.

'It's room service, you clown,' says Leamington – incredibly the only person seemingly in control – as he heads for the door.

'Fuck that. You're kidding, aren't you?' I say.

Three or four of us hurdle furniture, elbowing each other out of the way, as we scramble into the bathroom. We bolt the door and crouch down in the milky plastic light.

'Oh God, oh God, oh God . . .' someone keeps saying.

'It'll be all right, it'll be OK,' someone else says soothingly.

'Is this your first time in Miami?' some bloke whispers to me. I shake my head. I'm off my nut, but I'm vaguely aware that this isn't a reasonable way to earn a living.

A long time passes. You can hear everyone's heart beating. The tap drips.

There's a knock on the door, Leamington's voice, the all-clear. We open the door and creep out.

Christ.

A black waiter – a young guy, tall, thin – is standing in the middle of the suite unloading cocktails from a tray onto the coffee table. He turns and sees us. We all freeze.

'Have you got the coke?' one of the bathroom idiots says to the waiter, just seeing a Kaffir and mistaking him for the dealer, despite his tray, and his purple-and-black tunic and the gold name tag on his chest. And the fact that he's *clearly a fucking waiter.*

'I'm sorry,' I say, 'I'm so sorry.' The black kid takes his unloaded tray, and the proffered twenty-dollar tip, and fucks off out of it, looking scared.

'You cunt,' I say to Leamington, who is laughing his head off.

'Oh God, we're finished now,' Darren says.

'Have a drink,' Leamington says.

'Don't you understand, *it's over!*' Darren is actually becoming hysterical. 'He's going to go back downstairs and he's going to tell them what's happening and they're going to come up here and they're going to come in and –'

'Shut up and have a fucking cocktail, you twat. Here, have a Cosmopolitan.' Leamington hands Darren a gigantic Martini glass full of thin, pale blood. He seems to have ordered every cocktail on the menu.

'Do we have any fucking pills?' I ask.

'Yeah,' someone says.

'Should we switch rooms?'

'Maybe if we take some pills we could go out.'

'Have you heard that Stardust bootleg?' someone asks.

'Here.' Someone presses an E into my hand and I suck it back with a gulp of Tequila Sunrise.

'Hey, did you know they filmed *Goldfinger* here?' Leamington says, still laughing.

That evening and the next day become what they always become: a series of blurred snapshots, random shreds of CCTV footage, shakily pixellated stills from a bootleg video I don't remember starring in. I was dancing in the DJ booth to 'Praise You', clinking pills with Leamington as we both double-dropped, vomiting out of a moving cab on the Strip, throwing an ice cube across the lobby of the Delano at some DJ (Rampling? Oakenfold?), being thrown out of a DJ booth somewhere, an alleyway behind the Strip, buying glass vials of coke, buying an E that came individually wrapped in its own cellophane bag, wanking in a private booth at a lap-dancing club, the Propellerheads onstage, lying on the floor of someone's hotel room watching a stripper do herself with a beer bottle, dawn on the beach – Leamington and I looking out to sea dumbstruck as an oil tanker the length of the Westway slunk across the horizon – a breakfast pint of rum and Coke at that bar in the middle of the hotel pool.

The next morning and early afternoon are fine. I sleep right through both of them, missing both my original flight to Texas and the rebooked flight. I finally make it to the airport late in the afternoon where, of course, the flight I've made is delayed.

I find a quiet corner in the BA exec lounge and crumple into an armchair. The screen hanging from the ceiling silently wipes itself and unrolls the revised flight times: AA157, MIA to Houston, Texas, is now leaving at 6.10 p.m.

I settle in and inhale a long chain of Bloody Marys. I thoughtfully chew half a Quaalude and try to place my hangover on my personal Richter scale. Twenty minutes later, when I still haven't come with an answer, when I still don't understand the question in fact, it dawns on me why I can't properly evaluate my hangover. I'm not having it yet. I'm still completely off my fucking nugget.

'Sir, excuse me, sir? Are you OK?'

I look up – he's about my age, airport uniform, concerned expression. 'Uh, yeah,' I cough. Urine-temperature drool flecks from my chin. Outside, sunny Florida has vanished, there's just darkness and lights; lines, grids and blocks of them. 'What time is it?' I ask, my voice a tramp-rasp produced by broken piping, blocked air passages. There's a modulating whine in my ears, a rising note, searching for its rightful, most painful, key.

'It's just after six, sir.'

'Shit.' I swing into action, swivelling up and onto my feet, grabbing my jacket and scooping up my bag. The guy helps me up from the floor. 'Sir . . . *sir?*'

'Which way to Gate . . .' I'm fumbling for my boarding pass.

'Sir, it's six in the morning. Six a.m.'

I look at him. The whine in my ears finally finds its pitch and something pops somewhere deep in the centre of my face, some blockage behind my nose clears as a small dam bursts.

'The next flight to Houston isn't for a few hours.'

Fucking Quaaludes. The Shermans know how to put a tranquilliser together – you have to give them that.

'Uh, sir, you've got a . . . Christ.' He's fumbling in his pocket.

But I can already taste the blood, sharp and salty in the back of my throat, as it begins its warm, oddly pleasant, cascade across my top lip and spatters down onto the T-shirt I'm wearing. The T-shirt has a picture of Al Pacino as Tony Montana. He's holding a huge fuck-off gun. *'Say hello to my leetle fren.'*

Sometimes, when they're trying to understand what A&R means, people who don't know anything about the music industry will say, 'Ah, so you're talent spotters?' This is inaccurate. Madonna, Bono, the Spice Girls, Noel Gallagher, Kylie . . . do you really think any of that lot are *talented*? Don't make me fucking laugh. What they are is ambitious. This is where the big money is. Fuck talent. Forget Rock and Roll, if he'd just turned the other way out of the schoolyard Bono could have been a very successful

CEO of a huge armaments manufacturer. The Spice Girls? How driven are those boilers? You get these fucking indie bands moaning about having to get up before lunchtime once every three months to appear on some kids' TV programme. In return for her fifteen minutes I guarantee you that Geri Halliwell would have risen at the crack of dawn every morning for a year and swum naked through a river of shark-infested, HIV-positive semen – cutting the throats of children, OAPs and cancer patients and throwing them behind her as she went – just to be allowed to do a sixty-second regional radio interview.

This is the kind of person you want to sign. You've got a shot with that kind of attitude. Talented? Fuck off. Go and work in a guitar shop with all the other talented losers.

'I'm telling you – Pawl? Steve? – there are piracy issues involved that we're only just beginning to understand. The long-term implications could be catastrophic. Cat-a-stroff-ick.' Some cunt from our American label has been dribbling on for a fortnight about the impending devastation the Internet will wreak on the record industry. I can't see it myself.

The stench of burning flesh fills the air and it's hot. It's like being in hell. We're in the grounds of one of the big hotels, attending a barbecue some publisher is throwing. Whole hogs – basted in barbecue sauce thicker than melted chocolate – are crackling and spitting over flaming pits. Steaks the size of babies sizzle on hotplates. A slaughter-house of ribs is piled up next to rows of silver dishes containing refried beans, coleslaw, fries, chicken wings, cornbread, mashed potatoes, chilli and gravy. Now and then the warm, feeble breeze changes direction and I get a whiff of this lot and nearly throw up. Everyone of the English contingent here is either coked up or hung-over. Either way, we're not eating a fucking thing. You look around at these things and you can spot the Yanks a hundred yards away. They're the ones who actually look like they've been to bed in the past year. They look tanned, fit and rested and they want to talk business. Players – or thinking they are – they came to play. We – the Brits – look like we've just staggered off the set of a snuff film after a meth-driven four-day shoot: blood in the eyes, skin cracked and yellow, nostrils inflamed and blood-caked. We look like ghosts. We came to play too.

'Mmmm,' says Trellick nodding to the Yank like he gives a fuck, 'it could be problem.' I nod solemnly too and drain my fifth glass of cold white wine.

As we leave, the Mexican busboys are shovelling tons of uneaten food into plastic garbage bags. I see one of them pocket a steak.

Later we're all at one of the hundreds of gigs taking place across the city. There's a band on the stage, some four-piece punk rock kind of thing called the Lazies, I think. The very doable girl singer is screaming over a splintering tower of glassy feedback. There's a couple of rows of kids going crackers at the front, like there are at every gig. Abortion, I think to myself. Derivative, tuneless abortion. I start polishing and sharpening a few caustic phrases to toss off later. She's on the floor now, the mike lead wrapped around her body, sweat pouring down her face as she screams something like 'fuck me in the ass' over and over.

She's wearing fishnet tights that are shredded to pieces, half an arse cheek is bursting out. Very fuckable, but still a derivative, tuneless abortion.

Finally, mercifully, they finish. I walk through a crunchy sea of plastic beer mugs to the bar. Leamington, Trellick, Parker-Hall and Simon Tench, Parker-Hall's scout, are all at the bar. I also see Miles and Dan from Parlophone, Steven Bass from Go! Beat, and a few others. Someone hands me a drink. A tequila shot.

'Capitol just offered two hundred, US only,' someone is saying.

'What did you think?' that weasel Tench asks me.

I think I want a nose-up. I think my hotel room isn't big enough.

It really gets tedious sometimes – being paid primarily for your opinion when you very rarely have one. Or frequently have the wrong one.

'You'd do the singer,' I say, sagely. Everyone nods. 'And I liked the "fuck me in the ass" song. You ain't getting it on the radio though.'

'Which song?' says Leamington.

'The one where she says *"fuck me in the ass"*.'

Leamington laughs. 'It's *"love me, make it last"*. It's the single.'

'Haven't you got it?' Tench asks.

'Yeah, whatever,' I say airily, knocking back the oily, bitter spirit, 'fuck them.'

Trellick sidles up to me as we leave the venue to look for cabs. 'I don't know,' he says quietly, 'they all seem to like it. Should we be in on this?'

'I was downgrading it, you clown. I've already got a

meeting set up.' The lie slides softly out of the corner of my mouth. The lie itself is effortless, but, sadly, it means I'll actually have to do some work.

'Good boy,' says Trellick, his hand in the air as a canary-yellow taxi comes towards us out of the jungly Texas night.

'Best live band I've seen in a long, long time.'

'Yeah?' The manager – a stringy, indie, vegetarian-looking anorak cunt – doesn't look up from spooning pulpy melon into his mouth. He couldn't look less enthusiastic if he tried, which is fucking cheeky considering the effort, the time, I've put into arranging and preparing for this lunch.

When I got back to the hotel last night – tramp-drunk at 3 a.m. – I rang Darren. While I should, by rights, have been snorting inhuman amounts of chang and trying to negotiate the local ostros down to a hundred bucks for uncovered oral, I was on the phone, working. After berating Darren for not already being on to the Lazies (the lying prick claimed he tried to play me the single) I told him I needed to know who managed them, I needed his phone number, I needed a potted history of the band, and I needed him to find a record store in Austin who had the band's records and then he had to buy the records over the phone with his credit card and have them cabbed to my hotel.

Then I passed out.

I woke up five hours later. The fax with all the info was in an envelope that had been pushed under my door. A package containing the band's slender catalogue – one single and an EP – awaited me behind reception.

I rang the manager, the kid Jimmy now sitting opposite me, and here we are. I gave the music a cursory listen earlier – it's all right. I don't know really. Who knows? But enough people seem to be interested. We're having lunch in the restaurant at the hotel. Good PR for me to be seen lunching with the manager of a hot band.

'What was your favourite track on the EP?' he asks.

Shit. 'Track three,' I say, 'definitely.'

'Yeah? That's interesting.' Is it?

'Are you going to be playing in England soon?' I ask.

'Uh, yeah. In a month or so. Glastonbury. We're doing some warm-ups first. At the, uh, is it the Borderline?'

'Yeah. Good venue.' Stinking fucking toilet.

He finishes his fruit salad and surprises me by lighting a cigarette. 'So, man,' he says, leaning back, pushing long, unkempt hair from his face, 'what's your favourite album of all time?'

The fucking nerve. I pretend to think for a moment, then say, '*Marquee Moon*.' With a certain type of indie loser you cannot go wrong with *Marquee Moon*.

The clown nods and says, 'Cool.'

He starts talking about how hard the band work, how little they're willing to compromise, how great their debut album's going to be. All the usual shit I've heard a billion times before. I nod away, looking like I'm listening, generally doing a reasonable impression of a normal human being.

Across the restaurant I see Parker-Hall and Tench walking towards us. 'All right, lads?' I say magnanimously, chewing on a toothpick, 'this is J—'

'How you doing, Jimmy?' says Parker-Hall. Jimmy's

already on his feet and they're embracing warmly. 'Hey, Tony! My man! What's up?'

'Me and Si are just going for a bit of a stroll. Catch some rays.' Jimmy, the Yank cunt, is lapping up Parker-Hall's Dick Van Dyke schtick. I cannot believe he gets away with this shit. 'We still on for later?' Parker-Hall asks him.

'For sure. I've just got this meeting to finish up with . . .' the manager has forgotten my name, '. . . ah, with Steve here. Then I'll be back at my hotel.'

In the background I'm sure Tench is smirking as they say their matey goodbyes and tool off.

'You know Tony then?' I ask.

'Yeah, we talk on the phone a lot. He was a big fan of the first single.'

'Right.' Cunt. Fucking fuck.

'Hey, Steve, I've really got to run too. We're playing again tonight at this thing, it's a little way out of town . . .' he writes the address down on a napkin.

'Yeah, great. How far along are you? You know, in terms of other companies.'

'Well,' he says grinning, shaking his head, 'I've got to tell you, we've got a couple of really interesting offers on the table already. I wouldn't want you to get your hopes up.'

I laugh. 'Another offer wouldn't hurt though, would it?' I am going to fire Darren. Why weren't we on to this fucking band earlier?

'Maybe not, maybe not. Thanks for lunch.'

We shake hands and I watch him fruit off through the restaurant, stopping halfway to shake hands with some girl.

A waitress appears. She's cute, huge rack.

'You're finished?' she says.

No, I think. Not completely. Not yet.

With the indie kids you have to remember this: they really think that what they do matters in some way. They reckon that history will care. (They don't know that history will have other shit to be getting on with.) The indie kids figure that they're passing on the torch or some fucking thing. That, just as they were influenced by someone – the Velvet Underground, Jonathan Richman, the Stooges, whoever – then, in the future, young bands will be influenced by them. Maybe so. Maybe a few thousand malnourished cockless freaks scattered around the globe will give a shit. So what? Real people don't care, do they? Real people put stone cladding and UPVC double-glazing on their council houses, they buy four albums a year and they want to be able to hear all the words. And there are fucking *billions* of them.

That's why I like it when you deal with a genuine pop act. It's so refreshing and honest. Some greasy demi-paedo of a manager flops down in your office with three fit fifteen-year-old sluts on his arm. Half a GCSE between them, they say, 'We want to be famous and make a lot of money.' You know what? No problem. *Let's fucking rock.* I might thereafter have to have the odd conversation about, for instance, do we need to Photoshop someone's jugs to make them look bigger or firmer? What I *won't* have to do is sit in some toilet flat at three in the morning, listening to tuneless B-sides and talking about, I don't know, Tom Verlaine's guitar solos. Because, really, who gives a fucking shit?

Here – you want to say to these indie kids – have a *steak*. Let's go to Harvey Nicks and buy you some decent clothes.

Here's three hundred quid – go and get a hot boiler to suck your dick properly for the first time in your life. *Live a little, son.*

May

Talk of EMI/Seagram merger. Spice Girls do massive Pepsi deal. Lots of interest in Ultrasound now. The Jamiroquai LP goes triple platinum. Audioweb's single 'Faker' charts at 70. Deconstruction signs this girl singer called Sylvia Powell. The label's MD Keith Blackhurst says, 'I'm sure her songs will make it onto TV and radio and that the album will be huge.' Echo and the Bunnymen look like making a comeback. Labour wins the election.

> '*The nature of show business means that people within the business feel that if someone else fails, they move up a notch.*'

Tom Arnold

A few days after I get back from Austin I go on a *date*. Yeah, I know.

The thing is, if you just fuck an awful lot of whores all the time then you kind of need to go on a date now and again, if only to prove to yourself that you can still do boilers without a fistful of grubby fifty-pound notes changing hands. Also, sometimes I'll look at people who have girlfriends and I'll think, 'That doesn't look so crazy.' Who knows, maybe it's worth a pop.

I've been listening to this girl (she's literally called Sophie, for fuck's sake, a friend of a friend, works in international at . . . Warners?) crapping on about something – an argument she had with the singer from some band about, I don't know, maybe the quality of cheeseburgers at Oslo airport, or the purity of bottled water in Auckland – for what feels like a decade. This is the thing. You're expected to make conversation, aren't you? Beyond the level of 'here's your money, now suck this, you rancid fucking slut'.

'Hey,' she says, waving a hand across my vacant face as a fawning spic plonks her dessert in front of her, 'what are you thinking about?'

Gak, chang, nose-up, bag, beak, charlie, krell, powder, chisel, bump, posh, bugle, sniff, skiwear . . .

This is the thing about girlfriends. They'll say to you: 'What are you thinking?' I am always thinking about cash and fucking, but you can't really say this, can you?

But people do it, don't they? You see it all the time. There seem to be definite upsides, financially and health-wise at least. I mean, you're unlikely to come in from work of a Friday evening and – during the course of a quiet weekend with your girlfriend – spend nearly two grand on coke, crack, booze, Viagra and hookers. I don't imagine that's how it goes, is it? Your girlfriend is unlikely to suggest the kind of evening out that will terminate sometime the following afternoon in an Albanian knocking shop in Brixton, up to your nuts in an illegal immigrant. You don't do that nasty stuff with a girlfriend, do you? You . . . What do you do? You go to, I don't know, the cinema? Or maybe for a walk? Stuff like that?

But then I think about the downsides. The talking. They're really into the whole talking thing, girlfriends. Ross has a girlfriend. He tells you about the things they do, the stuff they say. They try and talk to you about complicated weekends away in three months' time over breakfast. About wallpaper colours. They ask things like, 'How was your day?' and 'How did your meeting go?' What do you care how the meeting went? *I* don't fucking care how the meeting went and I was there.

Why? Why would they ask these things? What can they

possibly have to gain from the answer? At least with hookers I find the banter, the discussions, manageable: *bend over . . . put your leg there . . . good . . . suck harder . . . faster . . . lick my balls . . . piss on me.*

I mean, I can just about manage that.

I tune back into the present, into the restaurant, the date. She's saying, '. . . and anyway, these days BA's business class is *almost* as good as first.'

You're wrong, I think. But I don't correct her. I just listen, wondering how much more of this I will have to sit through before she will be drunk enough to let me fuck her. Tiredly I reach for the Pinot Grigio and refill her glass.

'What are you thinking?' Well, I'm thinking about having some big hit records and then upgrading your pock-marked arse for someone younger and fitter. Now, what film did you want to go and see? Shall we get a takeaway? Do you really want to go for a fucking *walk*, you horrible cow?

I'm lying on the sofa in my office, half listening to demos, mostly playing Fifa '97 on the PlayStation, when Rebecca, ridiculously serious-faced, pops her head around the door.

'Steven?'

'Yeah?' Just the defender to beat, if I . . .

'There's someone in reception who wants to see you.'

'Tell them to fuck off.' That's it, scoot along the edge of the box . . .

'Actually, I don't think that's a good idea.'

'Why not?' He shoots . . .

'It's a policeman.'

. . . he hits the post.

The guy comes in. Plain clothes, a nasty-looking Next/ Marks and Sparks type suit on. He's young, maybe just a couple of years older than me. 'Mr Stelfox?' he asks needlessly, extending his hand. Rebecca hovers in the doorway.

'Steven,' I say.

'DC Woodham. Thanks for seeing me without an appointment. I could come back another time if this is inconvenient?'

'No, no. It's fine. Can we get you anything?'

'No, thank you.' Rebecca shuts the door and Woodham folds himself awkwardly into the chair opposite me. He's tall and gangly, all limbs and angles in his nasty, ill-fitting suit. He's fair-haired, but it's not the thick Aryan blond you see on someone like Trellick. This is pauper's hair – thin, pale and frayed into a cheap, bad cut which (surely unusually for a copper) touches the collar of his shirt here and there. His face is thin and pinched, kind of sad-looking. But that's fair enough. If I had to tool around in a Next suit dealing with the world's sewage for – what? twenty grand a year? – I'd be looking fucking sad too.

'Wow,' he says, eyeing up the pile of gold and platinum discs stacked beside my desk, 'shouldn't they be up on the wall?'

'Oh, I'll get round to it,' I shrug bashfully. 'I'm sorry, is this about Roger? Because I already spoke to –'

'Yes, I know you've given a statement. I just had a couple of questions about the – hey –' he breaks off, pointing to the pinboard on the wall behind me – 'is that . . . is that you and *Joe Strummer*?'

I turn. He's pointing to a photograph of me and Strummer – arms around each other, both in wellies and

macs covered in mud, both out of our poor minds –
standing behind the Pyramid Stage. I'd been looking at
signing him last year but the demos were a pile of shit. But
young bands often respond well to that photo. Good ice-
breaker. 'Yeah,' I say chuckling, 'backstage at Glastonbury
last year. We'd had a few.'

'Wow. What's he like?'

A washed-up cunt. 'Joe? He's a sweetheart. Are you a
fan?'

'God, not half. I saw the Clash live when I was fifteen,'
he beams proudly.

'Really?' Jesus wept, what a waste of fucking semen this
cunt is. 'Bit before my time I'm afraid.'

'Oh, best live band in the world, I reckon.'

'A few people say that. Sorry, Officer, I do have a
meeting starting shortly.'

'Of course. Sorry. What it is, I'm following up with a
few people and . . . I believe you told one of my colleagues
that you,' he consults a notebook he's pulled out, 'you were
with Mr Waters on the night of his death?'

'Yeah.'

'You'd been to . . . the Dublin Castle in Camden?'

'That's right. Then we shared a cab and I dropped him
off.'

'See anything good?'

'Anything good? Oh, the gig. Band called Rape Squadron
I think. They weren't bad.'

'Bit of an old toilet the Dublin Castle, isn't it?' he grins.

'Oh, you know it?'

'Yeah. Well, I played there a few times. Back in the day,
you know.'

'Really? You were in a band?' Mother of fucking uncontrollable God. 'What did you play?'

'Guitar. And songwriting. We still play a bit as it happens, in our spare time and that. We've all got jobs now. Wives and kids and all that.'

Fuck me. 'Yeah, it can be tough.'

'Tell me about it,' he says, shaking his head. 'Anyway, I really wanted to ask you about Mr Waters' state of mind that night.'

'In what way?'

'Well, did he seem worried about anything? Did he have any enemies that you know of? Debts? Money problems?'

I pretend to think for a moment. 'No. Nothing like that. He's unlikely to have had any money problems.' The fat overpaid spastic.

'Yeah, I didn't think so. Expenses all the way in this racket, isn't it?' Woodham laughs.

I laugh too. 'Yeah, we've been known to claim a few beers back.'

'You'd been drinking?'

'Yeah, we'd had a few. He'd just been promoted. We were celebrating.'

'Drugs?'

'No.'

'Really? The autopsy showed considerable levels of cocaine in Mr Waters' bloodstream.'

'It must have been after I left him. I don't take cocaine.'

'I thought all you guys . . .'

'Oh, that's a myth. It's not the eighties. You have to work too hard these days.'

'But you knew he took drugs?'

'Well . . .'

He writes something down and goes on to ask me a few more vaguely Waters-related questions before getting onto what he really seems to want to talk about: what kind of bands were getting signed these days? How many demos did we get a week? How many gigs did I go to? Who have I worked with? What kind of music did I like? (The Clash, Bob Dylan blah blah blah . . .) Finally I email Rebecca telling her to come and get me for a non-existent meeting.

She pops her head around the door. 'Sorry to interrupt,' she says, leaning in, giving Woodham full cleavage, 'but you've got that meeting starting now, Steven.'

'Thanks, Rebecca.' She ducks back out.

'Well, thank you, Mr Stelfox,' Woodham says, getting up.

'Steven's fine. Sorry I couldn't be more helpful,' I say walking him to the door.

'No, you've been very helpful. Just one last thing. This is a bit awkward.' He reaches into his jacket.

Fuck. Here it comes, the fucking Columbo bit. He's almost out the bastard door when he turns round and produces the smoking gun. 'Could you tell me what you think of this?' he says, holding something towards me.

Oh God. I look down.

It's a CD. 'It's just some rough mixes we did at my mate's home studio, but I'd really like, you know, a professional opinion about the songs. If you could spare ten minutes to have a listen sometime . . .'

I look at him for a moment.

'Sure,' I say, taking the CD. 'Is your number on here?'

Seconds after he leaves Rebecca comes in to find me

standing up at the window. 'Is everything OK?' she says, sounding genuinely anxious.

'It's nothing. Just some questions about Roger.' She joins me at the window and we watch Woodham walk to his car – a shitty Ford of some description.

'Quite cute for a policeman,' she says.

'Mmmm.' We stand there for a moment in silence.

'Are you all right, Steven?'

'I'm fine.'

She raises her hand, as if to stroke my arm, then thinks better of it and leaves.

I often wonder what sort of life people like Woodham end up having. I don't mean policemen, I mean guys who toiled away in pointless bands for years, never getting anywhere, until they got some hag up the duff. Are you one of them? How do you get through it? You turn round and – bosh! – you're nearly thirty and standing in line at some fucking B&Q at nine o'clock on a Sunday morning, a giant monster holding your hand while your five-year-old runs around smashing the place up and another brat howls in a papoose round your neck. You've maybe got two hundred and fifty quid in your current account until the end of the month. I mean, what keeps the noose from around your neck, the razor blade from your veins? Love? Don't make me fucking laugh. Look at how you're *living*.

Without warning, with no warning at all, winter just becomes summer somewhere in the middle of May. There is no spring. The heat does what it does to London; cars become boiling torture boxes as – and everyone is surprised about this, no one thought it possible – the traffic slows even further. *Everywhere* seems to be under construction; the navvies, stripped to the waist, or wrapped in fluorescent yellow and orange vests, scratch their heads as they stare at some mad coil of piping they've dragged up through the broken bubbling tarmac. They stand on the hard shoulder, on the pavement, in the middle of the road, chewing gum and insolently holding up their circular red 'STOP' signs, or – rarer and briefer – their bright green 'GO' signs. All the slip roads lead to despair. In their torture boxes the people sluice Evian, light cigarettes, drum their hands on the wheel and fiddle with the radio and all the time you hear the sampled string loop and Richard Ashcroft singing 'Bittersweet Symphony' and you punch through the stations and you hear 'Things Can Only Get Better'.

The summer does something else to London too. You've noticed, haven't you? How could you not? Look at them appearing; pouring from the tubes and buses, emerging from doorways and office blocks, chattering and stretching out in wine bars and at wooden tables outside the pubs: the fucking boilers.

I mean, girls, where do you all *go* in the winter? Fill us in. October rolls around and you all vanish underground. Or you fly off to some island somewhere, some girls-only paradise where you work on your tans and leaf through lingerie catalogues, planning the summer attack. From October until May the female population of London is composed entirely of octogenarian Polack hags wearing carpet-thick tights and growing beards. You look around Oxford Street and you think – what the fuck is going on? It's just blokes, benders and beasts. Then the sun comes back and — bosh — it's a boiler-fest, a sea of silicone-jugged teenage porn stars in micro-skirts, sawn-off tops and thongs. Taunting midriffs, heckling arse-cheeks and abusive nipples all over the fucking shop. Even Nicky has abandoned her traditional fat-chick black leggings and has taken to parading around the office in some kind of condom-thin kaftan, her gigantic, nightmare paps sloshing around beneath it like a couple of carrier bags filled with glue.

It gets worse every summer. It fucks us up. It interferes with work. The needle of my libidometer, which is generally nudging 'RAPIST' at the best of times, is jumping off the scale. The other night, stumbling through Soho, I became so enraged with lust that I had to dive into one of those festering doorways off Berwick Street to spend fifteen minutes and fifty quid having my pulsing balls drained by an East European teenager in a grubby satin slip. (In London after midnight, as in many capital cities, it is far easier to get your cock sucked by a pair of terrified fourteen-year-old immigrant twins with a gun at their heads than it is to buy a bottle of Chardonnay. And there are lots of young fit Bosnian and Kosovan chicks on the game at the moment — a pleasing by-product of the recent punch-ups over there.) And, yes, of course I feel guilty about contributing to the sum total of this kind of human misery and all that. But, come on, what are we meant to do? I mean, have a heart. Put some fucking clothes on.

It gets hotter and things happen.

Rage is arrested for attacking a British Rail employee who asked him to put his cigarette out. We still have no plans to release his album.

It looks like Seagrams will buy EMI.

Ellie Crush's record goes gold – half a million – in the US. Parker-Hall is officially the industry fucking wonder boy.

I have a couple more meetings with Danny Rent about Songbirds. A couple of other labels are interested in them now, which is always good news as it means I'm not completely off my nugget, but . . . I just don't know. They're so fucking bad. Having said that, apparently Tracy Bennett over at London Records has just signed some cobbled-together bunch of sows called All Saints, so it looks like a few people will be having a pop with the Spice Girls cash-ins. I need to be signing something soon.

Neither Waters nor Schneider has been replaced yet and I am de facto running the department, although there is no official recognition of this and no extra remuneration. If 'Why Don't You . . .' was shaping up to be a hit I reckon I'd have been offered the job by now.

Trellick gets some girl from Sony pregnant. But he does the decent thing and forks out for a top-drawer abortion, an overnight-stay job at the Wellington near Regent's Park.

The Lazies fly into the country soon. They're doing a short European tour, playing a few warm-up dates for Glastonbury and meeting record companies. No less than seven labels are now trying to sign them. Apparently Parker-Hall is all over them. With the possible exception of Ultrasound, they are now the hottest unsigned band on the planet. I have managed to convince Jimmy, their indie-manager loser, to let me take them to dinner while they're in town.

I quadruple-park the car on Parkway across from the Spread

Eagle, which is already rammed with summer drinkers, and run into the off-licence to buy cigarettes and whisky. Waiting for my change I happen to glance along the top shelf, at the glut of hardcore: *Cum Sluts, Anal Housewives, Fifty-Plus, Suck. Pump. Grinder.*

My eyes settle on a pair of brown cheeks, thrust high in the air, a red satin G-string splitting the cleft, barely covering the faceless boiler's gleefully proffered anus. The strapline reads: '*She Wants You Up Her. Now!*' I am immediately overwhelmed by a sickening rush of lust so powerful as to be indistinguishable from total rage. The shopkeeper – a toothless, octogenarian Paki – doesn't bat an eyelid, doesn't register a flicker of alarm or interest as I add an armful of the most hardcore titles to my purchases, even though the top magazine is called *Asian Whores* and features one of his Sikh or Hindu sisters naked and fingering herself while sucking greedily on a huge orange plastic prick.

'Sorry, sir. No bags,' he says.

I stagger out to the car, teetering with fags, Scotch and hardcore, and there he is: a hulking Nigerian monstrosity in serge blue uniform, frowning at my licence plate as he punches numbers into his little machine. 'Come on, mate,' I begin.

'No parking,' he grunts, not looking up.

'I was only in there a minute.'

He just repeats the two words. The only two words of English he knows.

I mean, Jesus Christ. They bowl over here, straight out of some boiling HIV cauldron, some genocide-rape-famine meltdown entirely of their own making, and are they grateful? Are they fuck. They go to some language class (probably at the taxpayers' expense) to learn how to say 'no parking', and then they march around London fucking you up.

'Look,' I say reasonably, 'fuck off, cunt.'

'No parking.' The ticket whirrs out of the machine.

He holds it out to me. I throw it on the ground and spit on it. He shakes his head and starts writing something in his notebook.

'Oh yeah?' I say. 'You can *write*, can you, you fucking animal? Why don't you –'

'Hi, Steven.'

I turn. It's a girl called Charlie, or Chrissie or something. She's a scout somewhere. Sony? EMI? 'Ah, hi there,' I say.

'You going to see Ultrasound?' she asks me brightly.

'Ah, yeah. Trying to.' I shift the magazines, trying to huddle them in towards my chest, but it's too late, her gaze is already ambling down towards the glossy pile of total disgrace.

'Right . . .' She says uncertainly, already backing away, 'maybe I'll see you in there.'

'Yeah, see you there.' I turn back, but he's already across the street and the spittle-flecked ticket has been fixed to my windscreen.

The Ultrasound show is rammed: A&R people from Virgin, Island, Warner Chappell. I see Nick Mander, Andy MacDonald, Andy Leese and Malcolm Dunbar from Mother, Leamington, Dave Gilmour. No Parker-Hall, who is already on record as saying the band are 'pony'. Across the room I see Rebecca talking to some girl I don't know. I wave hello and she smiles back. You often see Rebecca out at gigs. Why the fuck does she bother? I mean, I wouldn't be here if I didn't have to be.

I'm in a filthy mood, lounging at the bar sipping a triple Rockschool when someone taps me on the shoulder. 'Hi, Steven,' this guy says. He's in his late twenties, a bit old to be in here. I've no idea who he is, probably some manager, some agent. 'Hi,' I say shaking his offered hand, no light of recognition whatsoever in my eyes. He senses this and says, 'It's Alan Woodham.'

Nothing.

'DC Woodham? I came to interview you about Roger Waters?'

Fuck, the copper. 'Oh, hi! Didn't recognise you, you know, in civvies.'

'What do you think?'

'About what?'

'Err,' he looks confused, 'about the band,' he gestures towards the stage where the singer of Ultrasound, who must weigh twenty fucking stone by the way, is screaming over an angry fizz of noise.

'Oh them.' I pretend to think. Maybe I actually am thinking. I don't know the difference any more. 'Not bad. Angular.' He nods, like this means something. 'What brings you here?' I ask.

'Oh, I'd heard some good things about them. Thought I'd check it out.'

Christ, what a fucking loser. What the fuck is he doing here watching some poxy unsigned band? Shouldn't he be out cracking crime?

'So,' he says grinning, 'what did you think of our demo? Be frank, I can take it.'

'Actually,' I say, putting my drink down on the bar for emphasis, 'I was going to call you about this, but I couldn't find your card. I have to say . . .' His face is doing a good impression of passive, professional disinterest but you can see the ticks and judders of fear and apprehension in the way his eyeballs flicker and dart, the way his lips squirm and quiver. They all look like this just before you tell them what you think. Obviously I have no idea what I am about to say. I listened to about half a song of his demo — worthless sub-Oasis drivel — before I pegged it into the bin. So I say, 'I was really impressed.'

'Really?'

'Yeah. Great songs. Honestly.'

'Any song in particular stand out?'

Fuck. 'Track three.'

'"Time Keeps Moving"?'

'Yeah. That's the one.'

'Yeah, I like that too. I was trying to . . .'

He starts to crap on about whatever influences he was trying to merge in the song or something. It's good because I can stop listening now. It's just a bunch of self-serving toss requiring no comeback, no specific rejoinders. I nod away, looking across the room at some girl's arse and thinking about an Asian boiler being smacked repeatedly in the face by a very stiff cock. I catch Rebecca's eye across the room and she looks away quickly. Finally Woodham finishes speaking so it's my turn.

'Listen,' I say, 'the only thing that's letting you down is the production.' He nods eagerly. 'What if I spring you a little demo money? Put you in the studio with a decent engineer for a couple of days?'

'Really? Shit, that would be great.'

'Give the office a ring and ask for Darren, yeah? I'll get him to sort it out. Have you made any progress on finding out what happened to Roger?'

'Not really. None of the neighbours saw anything, we don't have any witnesses. It was most likely a disturbed burglar.'

'Fucking bastards,' I say, draining my glass and plonking it on the bar. 'Well, keep me posted, won't you?'

'Of course. And thanks, Steven. Thanks for the chance. I mean, obviously with the job and the kids and everything and being, well, *nearly* thirty, I'm not still harbouring any illusions about being a rock star . . .'

No shit, mate. You look like a fucking copper. No – you *are* a fucking copper.

'. . . but I thought,' he continues, 'with the songwriting, maybe I could get a publishing deal? Write songs for other people?'

Fuck me. *Fuck me.* 'Yeah, definitely,' I say instantly, 'I mean, don't give up on it just yet, Alan. Noel Gallagher was, like, twenty-eight or something when he got signed. And Mark Knopfler. And Sting was old *and* he was a fucking teacher!'

We share a laugh and I can see he's thinking the same crazy shit that they all think. It goes something like this: *'Yeah. It happened for them, it could still happen for me. Why not? I'm talented. You just need the break. Right place at the right time. It's not* what *you know, it's* who *you know.'*

They really do think like that these people. They think that Dame Fame and Lady Fortune are going to loaf into the room and single them out. You wouldn't fucking believe it.

I'm making my way through the crowded bar towards the door when, for the second time that evening, a heavy hand falls on my shoulder. Wearily I turn round – straight into a snarling mess of burnished fangs, a pair of burning devil's eyes. Tony-Blair-poster eyes.

'Oi, cunt, what the fuck is going on?' Flecks of spittle hit me.

'Ah, hi, Rage.' What the fuck is he doing here?

'Don't fucking give me that. What the *fuck* is happening with my album?' There's a couple of big darkies with him. One of them carries a record box. Rage must be DJing somewhere later.

What is happening with the album is nothing. We're sitting on the abortion until the cretin speaking to me writes something approaching a hit single.

'How do you mean?' I say innocently.

'Are trying to be fucking funny?'

'No.'

'Schneider gets fired, that fucking queer Sommers ain't returning our calls, I ain't got a release date, I ain't been fucking paid, I . . .' he goes on and I see now that he really is angry.

'Listen,' I say, interrupting, 'can we go somewhere quieter and have a chat? I need to speak to you. Alone, yeah?' One of his boys glares at me and kisses his teeth but Rage waves them away and leads me off towards the dressing room, managing to get into only two serious arguments with security guards on the way there.

Soon enough we're hunkered down over the nosebag and, once he's got a thick line of my chang into his greedy fucking face, I hit him with the truth. Schneider *hated* the record. Derek's on the fence. I think it's a masterpiece. I tell him that I have some strong ideas on how to market it properly. That we *have* to get it released.

'That cunt of a fucking Jew-boy,' Rage says.

'I mean,' I say incredulously, 'he wanted you to fuck about writing some pop single! The fucking cheek. I kept telling him, you're an *albums artist*.'

'Yeah. Fucking straight up, blood.'

'We'll get great press and build it from there. Fuck Radio 1. *Fuck them*.' I smack a fist into my palm. I'm getting into it myself now, almost believing the utter shite I'm spewing.

'Yeah, fuck radio,' Rage says.

'Listen, when we came to the studio, to that playback, that track you played us, "Birth", yeah?'

'Yeah.'

I shake my head solemnly. 'I had tears in my eyes,' (this much was true) 'fucking goosebumps, mate. I mean, who gives a fuck if its sixty-four minutes long? It's a classic.'

'Yeah? Cheers, Steven.'

'Look, everything's fucked right now with Schneider going. But it ain't gonna be that way for long.' I have started to speak like Rage, a trait I have when talking to bands. If this conversation goes on much longer I'll be breaking out the fucking boot dubbin. 'I'm not saying I've got the job yet, but when – if – I do, I want you to know you'll be a priority act, mate. A priority act.'

Rage looks at me for a long moment, the silence dripping with cocaine. Finally he points a finger at me. The finger has three heavy gold rings on it. 'I always said to Fisher that you fucking understood what I was doing,' he says.

'Yeah? Cheers, Rage,' I say raising my glass.

'I'll tell you what I was trying to do with that track . . .' He starts talking about the piece-of-shit song in mind-frying detail, but it's OK because I don't have to listen any more. It's fine. I can just stand here, nodding, and moving frozen shards of coke around the roof of mouth with my tongue while saying over and over to myself *you black bastard, you black bastard, you black bastard . . .*

The following morning, in business affairs, I whole-heartedly add my vote to the unanimous landslide as we decide to drop Rage from the label. 'All righty,' says Trellick rapping his notes on the table '. . . moving on, boys and girls. Unsigned bands . . .' Within a few months Rage will probably be back to whatever he did before – chiselling stereos out of dashboards, holding Stanley knives to the throats of terrified pensioners, and filling council flats with half-caste babies.

Darren and I take The Lazies out to an insanely expensive Russian restaurant on the Embankment – caviar and thirty-seven different kinds of vodka and private dining rooms where you can do nose-up right off the table without being seen.

'Jimmy! Good to see you again, man,' I say, getting up and slapping him on the arm, trying to remember what we talked about over lunch in Austin the month before. 'How's things? This is Darren,' I say as Darren gets up and extends a hand.

'Uh, hi, guys. Darren? Yeah. I'm good man. This is Greg, and Adam and Kevin . . .' He introduces a shy, gangly, six-legged tangle of pimples, torn jeans and BO. The musicians.

We shake hands and do the 'hi, how are you' stuff. None of them makes eye contact. It is probably blowing their minds to be ordering a meal somewhere you don't just put the handbrake on and speak into a grille. '. . . and this is Marcy.' The singer comes out from behind them. She's tiny, stunning. Skin white as a fridge and perfect features half hidden under thick black, bowl-cut hair.

We do the small talk – how was your flight? Been to London before? Bish, bash, bosh. What you're trying to figure out here is: who am I talking to? Whose band is it? You can usually – not always – forget the drummer and the bass player. It's normally a guitarist/singer deal. I make sure I'm sitting next to Adam, the guitar player, and across from Marcy. Darren gets plonked with the rhythm section, the Muppet Show.

A waiter appears in full Cossack rig and dispenses menus. 'May I get you some drinks?' the fruit asks.

'Yes,' I say, 'can you bring us the vodka menu? You have to check this out, guys, they've got over thirty –'

'Could I just have some water please?' Marcy says.

'Yeah me too,' from Adam.

'We got an early start tomorrow,' Jimmy explains, 'gotta drive to . . . Dover?' (he pronounces it 'Daw-ver') 'to get the ferry.'

'No problem, water's good for me.'

Water. Waters. He *liked* the Prodigy artwork.

It's a fundamental – if they drink, you drink. If they don't . . . dear sweet mother of teats-blown Jesus. I am going to have to spend a couple of hours with these cunts sober.

The drummer – Greg? Kevin? – orders a beer and they fall to frowning over the menus.

'So,' I say, 'are you looking forward to Glastonbury?'

'Shit, man,' Adam says, 'it'll be . . .'

'Wild?' one of the other guys suggests.

'Yeah, wild.'

'We are going to rock that motherfucker.' The drummer. Obviously.

Marcy doesn't say anything. She stares at a hole in her shoe, a chunky, scuffed DM boot. I try to visualise her in heels.

We order and I make a big show of ordering nearly everything on the menu – beluga, sevruga, blinis, smoked salmon, chops, goose, baked fucking pike. Ominously the band order mostly salads.

'What's the vibe like at Glastonbury?' one of them asks. *Vibe?* It is a fucking insult that I am sat here having to live through this. For the umpteenth time today I lament the fact that I am not more successful and above all this.

'Oh, Glastonbury? It's just the most incredible . . . atmosphere.' (If you reckon that the atmosphere in medieval England – plague, filth, disease and billions of mud-spattered tolers everywhere – would qualify as incredible, then Glastonbury is indeed incredible.) With an upward surge of nausea I realise that, if we're going to have any chance of signing these clowns, I will probably have to go to Glastonbury.

The food starts to arrive. Darren talks indie with Adam. I watch Marcy pick at her salad. 'You must have had a bellyful of those record company dinners by now?'

She smiles for the first time – nervously, hesitantly, but still a smile – revealing a row of gleaming teeth whiter than her skin. A shred of purple lettuce is stuck between the front top two. Nice lips too. I can't make out the jugs because she's wearing a baggy sweater but, if I remember rightly from the gig in Austin, she's well stacked for a boiler her size. I don't remember any of the fucking songs, but I remember that.

'Nah,' she says, removing the strand of lettuce, 'it's nice, y'know? People being interested.'

'Have some caviar.' I push a dish of beluga towards her.

'No thanks. I don't eat fish.'

'So . . . tell us about your label,' Jimmy says.

'OK . . .' I clear my throat.

But what is there to tell really? We'll manufacture your records and put them in the fucking shops. We'll try our best not to spend a red cent unless we're sure we'll get it back with interest. We'll second-guess you and interfere at every conceivable stage of the artistic process. We'll edit and remix tracks without your permission. We'll force you to appear on appalling, degrading kiddies' TV programmes where you will shake hands with Dobbin the Donkey and have to explain yourself to a teenage VJ with the attention span of a Ritalin-fuelled infant. We'll work you until you can't stand up. In collusion with your publishers we'll try and license your music to TV adverts for everything from banks to multinational petrochemical companies. (We'd license it to whaling fleets and arms dealers too if only they advertised on TV). We'll under-account to you and charge you for every recoupable expense from the staples used to knock your horrendous contract together to the Coke you had from the fridge in my office. And if it doesn't all work out, you'll be dropped faster than a Plymouth hooker's knickers when there's a big ship in town.

Howzat, you pasty-faced vegetarian hippy cunts? Strap that on for a fucking laugh.

But, sadly, you can't say that these days. So I sip water and talk and they all nod away as I drone on about 'artistic freedom' and 'creative control' and 'long-term artist development' and all the usual balls until I'm nearly crying with boredom. Finally, when I can stand it no more, I get up and say, 'Excuse me.' I head for the Gents, leaving Darren to continue his part of the conversation − B-sides and the guitar solos of Tom Verlaine.

On the way to the toilet I stop at the bar and drink three double bison grass vodkas. In the toilet I deftly roll a fifty, lean close into the cistern lid, and snarfle up a heart-stopper. 'Right, you cunts, *let's fucking rock . . .*' I say, before − pausing only to vomit about a kilo of black sturgeon roe down the toilet − I'm striding manfully back to the table, sweat breaking out on my forehead and clear bubbles popping and exploding in my brain.

Well, things livened up after that, I can fucking tell you. I order a massive round of vodkas and a couple of the band even join me. I crack a few jokes. One contains the punch-line, 'No, that's my flask.' I talk about making them 'bigger than U2'. I get more drinks in . . .

Things get blurry and I find myself sitting next to Marcy, pressing myself closer and asking about her childhood and shit like that. Christ, she's fit. Maybe if I . . . no, must remain professional.

I get the Russkis to turn the music up and I drag one of the waiters in and make him Cossack-dance for us, throwing twenty-pound notes at him and laughing my head off. I start singing Clash songs with the drummer but I keep getting all the words wrong. I start Cossack-dancing myself, trying to drag Marcy up but she's not really into it. I order more vodka and then Jimmy is turning to me and saying, 'Hey, thanks for dinner, man. We gotta run.'

'Fuck off. It's only eleven.'

'No really, we've got an early start.'

'Come on . . .' But they're all getting up now, pulling jackets on, gathering bags.

'Right, no problem. I'll give you a call. We'll send our offer to your lawyer.'

'Sure.'

'Thanks for dinner, man,' one of them – Adam? Doug? – says and they're gone. I mean – who fucking farted?

'That went all right,' Darren says, not convincingly.

'Yeah. Fine. Fucking Shermans.'

'You got any bugle?'

I toss him the gram and he heads for the bogs. I get up and duck out into the hallway. Marcy is pulling her jacket on. 'Hey, you're not really going back to the hotel, are you?'

'Yeah,' she smiles, 'I'm beat.'

'Bollocks. Come for a drink. I know this place. Members only.'

'No thanks.'

'Come on, love, you know you –'

'Are you, like, hitting on me?'

'Am I . . . ?'

'Look, thanks for dinner. Goodnight.'

I wander back into our room and neck a stray vodka. A grinning waiter appears and a silver dish with a long strip of paper on it is plonked down in front of me.

The bill is just over seven hundred quid.

When I get into work in the morning there's a message on my machine from Jimmy. In a flat tone he says:

'Uh, Steven . . . I just called to say thank you for last night. We, uh, as you know we've still got a few other labels to meet so . . . you could have your guy send your offer to our lawyer if you like and I . . . I'll try and give you a call and let you know what's happening. OK. Bye.'

So that's over, then.

June

The Ivor Novello Awards are held at the Grosvenor House Hotel. Ken Berry becomes Head of EMI. 'MMmm Bop' by Hanson is no. 1. A lot of people are talking about Basement Jaxx. The Ultrasound deal is really heating up — Simon Williams, Head of Fierce Panda, says, 'It is clear that this band will be around a lot longer than eighteen months . . .'

'A lot of people are singing about how screwed up the world is. I don't think that everybody wants to hear about that all the time.'

Mariah Carey

The tailback is long and we're surrounded by tolers – goths, ravers, punks, hippies, everything – carrying their back-packs, tents, huge plastic bottles of cider, cases of cheap lager, acoustic guitars, ghetto blasters, all that crap. They stumble along the sides of the road, pressing around the cars, all of them soaking wet and spattered with mud. Through the softening quartz of the windows of Trellick's Range Rover it feels like watching a CNN bulletin about an evacuation, a refugee trail somewhere. Incredibly enough it has stopped raining for a few minutes. The sun filters through weakly and all the losers cheer.

I pull the handbrake on just enough to allow me to turn on the dashboard TV. Trellick, in the driver's seat, is patiently arguing with *another* security guard ('We're from the record company. One of our acts is playing in fifteen minutes. We need to get in *now*'), while, in the distance, the boom of the festival shudders around the hills and vales of Somerset. In the back Ross and Darren – already drunk

– are 'ironically' singing 'Here we go, here we go, here we go . . .'

A guy suddenly bangs on my window. He's stripped to the waist, tattooed, crew cut. I press the button and the window hums down a few inches, admitting a reek of lager. 'Fucking hell!' he says to some people behind him, pointing at the dash, 'There's a fucking telly in there!' I just look at him. 'All right, mate!' he says cheerfully. 'What you watching then?'

I make sure the door is locked before replying. 'Dole office is that way, mate,' I say, pointing back down the road as I hit the button and the window slides efficiently back up. The guy pumps his fist, wanking an imaginary cock off at me, as he falls back into step with the other losers.

Finally the security mutant, having examined our VIP tickets and backstage parking pass for an hour or so, seems satisfied and waves us out of the queue and towards a closer, more discreet entrance. 'Thank you *very* much,' Trellick drawls, then, when we're a few yards away, he adds, 'you fucking loser.' There is a banner over the main entrance – the entrance where thousands of weary, footsore tolers are being herded in – which reads 'Greenpeace Glastonbury Festival 1997'. 'It should read "*Arbeit Macht Frei*",' Ross says sourly.

We come to another gate, endure more tedious negotiations, and then we're on the site proper, driving past rows of tents. Scumbags and jizz-buckets sit around their tents drinking Stella and Woodpecker and Christ knows what. I see a guy drinking fucking *Newcastle Brown*.

I do not understand the festival experience. These people, these disgusting lowlifes we're driving through, they *fought* to get in here. They think they're *lucky*. They spent hours on the phone trying to get tickets, happily paying hundreds of pounds for a pair when they managed to find some. Now they're *celebrating* being here, celebrating the fact that they can lie around in urine-flavoured mud drinking warm lager and eating burgers prepared by some syphilitic gyppo while fucking Cast knock out their greatest hits in the distance.

I turn round in my seat and give Darren a playful slap.

'Get the fucking pooey open and rack 'em out then!'

He pulls another bottle of Mumm's from a cooler at his feet while Ross digs the corner of his Amex into a huge bag of chang and we all do a quick card-edge.

'All righty!' Trellick shouts, thumping the wheel. *'Let's fucking rock!'*

Darren hands me the champagne and I shake the bottle up a bit before I fire the cork out of the open window of the Range Rover 'Oi! Oi! Oi!' we shout in delighted unison as a few scumbags look up from their cups of piss and tinfoil barbecues to give us what they imagine are withering looks. 'We're larging it, mate!' Ross shouts into the uncomprehending face of a passing middle-aged hippy.

The champagne cork sails up in a high arc over a row of filthy tents and disappears into the sun, finally, one hopes, hitting some filthy toe-rag right in the fucking eye. We roll off, clanking along the metal vehicle path towards hospitality parking.

The backstage beer tent is *rammed*. We elbow our way into the crush at the bar. Ross, viciously drunk by this point, says, 'It's like fucking Hillsborough in here,' to the clear disgust of Tony Crean, who literally *is* a fucking Scouser. Debbie Harry from Blondie walks by, dressed head to foot in crimson — topped off with a bunch of red roses for a hat. She looks shocking, like an old hooker who's fallen on hard times and gone crazy. 'Oi, love, how much for unprotected anal?' Ross shouts after her.

Across the bar I see Dean Wengrow, recently moved from London Records to Island. He waves and then mimes bending over and slapping his arse while giving me the thumbs up and pissing himself.

Last week, after I put the release date back four times in the demented hope that something, *anything*, positive might happen around the record, 'Why Don't You Slap Me on the Ass?' was finally released. It sold 1,112 copies and charted at no. 68 for a week before disappearing forever. We spent about a hundred quid for every copy of the record we sold. We might as well have made the sleeves out of jewel-encrusted platinum.

Finished. Game over. See you later, Sooty.

I mime wanking an imaginary cock in Wengrow's direction.

We get absolutely fucking *mullered* at the bar and then someone's saying that the Lazies are about to go onstage in the new bands tent.

'Hang on,' Trellick says as we finish up our drinks.

We huddle in a corner of the muggy, crowded bar. Darren — who has been deputised to carry the bulk of the drugs — produces a bag of Es and we all bosh one, washing them down with a swirl of flat, sour lager. Ross produces a bottle of Jack Daniel's, we buy a load of Cokes, tip the last of our lager out of the paper cups and improvise pints of

Rockschool. We lean in for another quick card-edge and we're ready to go.

Walking from the backstage area at Glastonbury into the main arena is like stepping from a drug-addled village fete into the Holocaust. Or from a field hospital onto the battlefield itself. The mud, the devastation, is incredible. It's only Friday afternoon but already, everywhere you look, you see the casualties: tripping, wall-eyed Scousers who haven't slept in three days; Jocks who've been living on speed and lager and who have, somehow, even with the downpour, *still* managed to get sunburned; and crying teenage girls. Unconscious bodies (corpses?) lie broken in the mud and hooded Kaffirs stand by the walkways, muttering their *'speed? 'ash? aceed? coke?'* mantra out of the sides of their mouths. You see forty-five-year-old blokes with their faces painted; accountants and estate agents off their nuts on mushrooms, having their one big weekend of the year.

Clean and shining, bright with coke and bourbon, it all looks very funny to us. 'Hello, tolers!' we chirp as we pass by. *'Arbeit macht frei!'* we say brightly to their red, confused faces.

The Lazies are on early, it's only four o'clock in the afternoon, but there's an incredible surge into the tent. It takes us forever to crawl around the side and then push our way in at the front. Steam is rising in great clouds off the crowded bodies at the crash barrier. I count no less than fifteen other A&R people around us as the band walk onstage. No Parker-Hall in sight. Got to be good news. (Or is it? What if he's changed his mind? Maybe the Lazies are actually shit. How can you tell?)

Marcy runs out last. She is wearing a black catsuit as tight as a surgical glove and now, elevated by the stage, italicised by the lights, she looks about twelve feet tall.

'Sen-say-shunal,' says Trellick. People start yelling and screaming.

'What's she like?' Ross asks me.

Are you hitting on me? 'Bang up for it,' I reply automatically.

Marcy grabs the mike from the stand, 'Hey, Glastonbury!' she yells over a deafening squawk of guitar, two ribcage-moving thumps on the bass drum, 'are you motherfuckers ready to fucking rock!'

'NO!' shouts Ross.

'FUCK OFF, YOU SHERMAN CUNTS!' some wag shouts and then the drumsticks click together fast – one, two, three, four times, the wooden slap echoing through the huge walls of speakers in front of us – and they pile into the first song. The place goes *berserk*.

Two songs in and people are being pulled out of the crowd unconscious. People are stage-diving. For a band just two singles old, it's an incredible reaction.

Ross: 'They are going to be fucking massive.'

Trellick: 'We have to get this deal. We should up the offer.'

Me: 'I'm all over it.'

Later in the evening I find I can't remember much about their set because I was so traumatised by what happened at the end of it.

What happened was this: the last song was grinding and juddering to a climax, the E was kicking in so I was actually, incredibly, just enjoying the music. I had my eyes closed, swaying, when Trellick tapped me on the shoulder and pointed to something. I followed his finger woozily, looking along it like a gun barrel towards the stage where the band were flouncing off, waving and blowing kisses to the baying, ecstatic crowd. I watched as Marcy skipped offstage and jumped delightedly towards someone standing at the side of the stage, someone with a stage-laminate dangling around their neck, the only pass greater than ours.

With gut-pummelling agony I recognised the shaved head and grinning features of Parker-Hall, as Marcy embraced him.

Outside the tent the rain has stopped again and a weak purplish sun is setting over the fields. Time to spend the summer's evening experiencing all that the biggest, most diverse music festival in the world has to offer. We stomp sulkily backstage to someone's Winnebago where we pull the blinds and spend the next five hours angrily drinking brandy and snorting cocaine.

It's all broken, out-of-focus snapshots from there. We're in the backstage bar; we're walking across the site, through lakes of mud and along rattling metal paths; we're buying mushrooms (mushrooms?) and pints of cider (cider?); and we're walking, walking, walking and then I'm tripping my nut off in the middle of a huge crowd *are you hitting on me* and the rain is falling lightly on us as we strain to see something in the distance, something far away in the dark, glowing red and blue and gold and green and there's music and *fucking Parker-Hall* it's getting louder and there are people singing something I can't make out and hugging each other all around us and *120 grand unrecouped* this music is building and building and then suddenly it all pulls into focus *crossover* and brilliant white light washes over the crowd and you can see the raindrops – billions of them – suspended in the light above us and I realise we're watching Radiohead and he's singing 'Rain down . . .' everyone's singing 'Rain down . . .' and I don't like Radiohead because I don't know what they *marketing spend* want but it's really beautiful and Darren turns to me and I think he's crying and maybe you are not alone in the universe *sound of impact* and for a moment there I lose myself.

But then we're off again. We're dancing in some packed, steaming rave-tent and I'm kissing some rave-boiler, then I'm pulling her zipper down, freeing her breasts and trying to suck them right there on the heaving dance floor and there's a slap and some rave-guy wading in and then we're heading somewhere else and I'm high on a Ferris wheel with Ross, snorting poppers and roaring with laughter as the cold black air swirls around and around us, and there's thousands of orange fires and coloured lights stretching off into the night, and then there's an argument with the owner of an ethnic foods stall, who goes lunatic after I career into his falafel wagon or tofu cart, smashing it to pieces and simply thrusting a bunch of fifties into his hands in lieu of an apology, and all the time I'm thinking *'fucking Parker-Hall, fucking Parker-Hall, fucking Parker-Hall'*.

Now the dawn is coming up and a bunch of us are stretched out up in the Green Field. For some reason I can't remember we're all wearing hats – huge felt jester caps in grape, canary yellow and red. How did we get them?

I'm lying flat on my back and listening to a three-way

conversation between Darren, Ross and Leamington that goes something like this:

'How long do you reckon it takes to clean this up?'

'Wimbledon?'

'The hats?'

'No, I mean . . .'

'On the centre court?'

'Hats?'

'Cheese?'

'I want to know what's happening at Wimbledon . . .'

I don't know who's saying what and it doesn't really seem to matter much.

'Oh God . . .' I moan quietly and I sit up and survey the field in the chill dawn mist. It's an almost clichéd post-apocalyptic landscape. Doomed, lonely figures wrapped in tattered blankets stumble through the cold mud. Bodies are littered all over the place. The smoke from all the thousands of fires has created a battlefield pall over the place. It's like someone dropped the bomb.

'Is this the Green Field?' someone says.

'Who gives a fuck?' says Trellick, pulling his Nokia out, the screen already glowing a beautiful civilised green, like it's the only piece of technology to have survived the epicentre. In the context of where we are Trellick's mobile looks like the black obelisk from *2001*, gleaming in the desert among the apes.

'Shall we do one back to the hotel, boys and girls?' he says, dialling calmly.

Barely an hour later Ross and I are neck-deep in hot, bubbling water, clinking brimming flutes of Bollinger. A few feet away, Trellick, snugly wrapped in one of the hotel's thick, white towelling robes, chops out some lines and bellows at room service for more, colder, champagne. Burt Bacharach purrs smoothly from the Bang & Olufsen.

'Oh, I *love* Glastonbury,' Ross sighs contentedly.

Trellick's phone rings. He picks it up and looks at the screen. 'Shit, fucking Derek.'

'What the fuck can he want at this time?' Ross says.

'An AIDS helpline?' I reply before slipping down under the surface, my temples throbbing as the hot water loosens the grime of the festival from my skin.

Trellick is gone for a while. When he comes back he looks stunned. It takes a lot to stun Trellick.

'What's happened?'

'Strap yourself in, matey boy,' he says, looking at me, allowing a dramatic pause.

'For fuck's sake, James . . .'

'Listen! It looks like we'll be signing the Lazies after all.'

'Go on!' I yell, leaping up in the tub and pumping my fist. I am the King. I am the King of fucking Rock. Fuck Parker-Hall. *Fuck him.* Ross starts clapping and whooping.

'Hold your horses,' Trellick says, starting to laugh now, 'Parker-Hall is actually signing them.'

Eh? 'What do you –'

'The band want to sign with Parker-Hall. No one else. It seems Derek's been talking to Parker-Hall for a while now and, well . . . he's our new Head of A&R.'

'I don't under . . .' The words dribble off because my mouth isn't working properly. I am just standing there – literally up to my knees in hot water.

'Derek, our Managing Director, has just hired Anthony

Parker-Hall,' Trellick says, speaking simply and clearly, as you would to a child. 'Parker-Hall is coming to work for us as Head of A&R, effective immediately. He is bringing the Lazies with him as his first signing.'

They both look at me, standing there in the middle of the hot tub, my mouth hanging open.

'He's your fucking boss,' Ross says.

They both start pissing themselves.

Parker-Hall — younger than me — chewing me out in meetings. ('*Gawdnbennet, Steven, wot da fuck's appening wiv dem poxy remixes?*')

Parker-Hall parking his car so much closer to the building than me.

Parker-Hall questioning my expenses.

'How much?' I say in a strangled whisper. I'm trembling now too. 'How much are we paying him?'

Trellick: 'I've been told not to discuss it and, trust me, you don't want to fucking know.'

I am Hervé Villechaize.

It hurts.

I am dying now.

July

Simon Cowell signs a boy band called Five. For reasons I can't quite work out there is a lot of interest in this Paki band called Asian Dub Foundation. (Who the fuck is Satpal Ram?) Sony are about to launch a pop singer called Jimmy Ray, who is managed by Simon Fuller who manages the Spice Girls. Sony's marketing guy Mark Richardson says, 'I dare anyone to listen to the single "Are You Jimmy Ray?" and tell me it's not going to be a hit. It's both retro and contemporary.'

'After you've finished being smart in the record business you've also got to be lucky.'

Dick Asher, MD of CBS Records

'As you all know,' Derek announces, standing up at the head of the big conference table, his eyes – predatory eyes, queer's eyes – flickering around the boardroom, 'it's been a very difficult year so far for the company, what with Roger's tragic death . . .' Everyone nods sadly. I look around the room. Pretty much the whole company – about thirty people – are crammed in here, for this miserable 'celebration'. I catch Rebecca's eye and she looks away. '. . . and Paul Schneider's decision to move on,' ('Move on'? Yeah, right), 'we've been missing . . .' he searches for the right word, not wanting to put the boot in on me and Hastings too directly, but wanting to put it in a bit no doubt, 'leadership in the A&R department. Well, I'm very pleased to say that's all about to change.' He drops his hand onto Parker-Hall's shoulder, who has been sitting next to him throughout this, looking embarrassed. 'As I'm sure you all already know Anthony signed his contract last week and is officially our new Head of A&R.' Derek leads the applause as Parker-Hall squirms in his chair, gesturing for people to stop. The applause goes on for a while. In Stalinist Russia, if you were the first person to stop clapping after one of old Joe's speeches, they came and got you in the night. A few weeks of solid dawn-to-dusk beatings with a car battery permanently hooked up to your shaved nuts, and then you were off to the salt mines for the next forty years. Top lad, Stalin.

'I won't embarrass Anthony any further by listing his résumé here but, as I'm sure you all know, he's just had an incredibly successful run over at EMI where he signed – among others – Ellie Crush whose album has now gone double platinum in the UK and sold over a million copies worldwide.'

But everybody knew this. Last week it was the front-page story on *Music Week*. There was a big photo of Derek, Parker-Hall, Trellick and Marcy from the Lazies and an accompanying story saying how Parker-Hall's contract had expired at EMI (he'd let it run out), how he had been unable to agree new terms, how we'd come in just at the right time, with the right offer – (*How much? How much are we paying the little bastard?*) – how excited Parker-Hall was to be able to make the Lazies his first signing . . .

The story went on to list Parker-Hall's A&R achievements, focusing on Ellie Crush's continued US success, and stressing the fact that he has just turned twenty-six. It concluded with a horribly magnanimous and ominous quote from Parker-Hall:

'I'm really looking forward to the challenges of my new role. The label already has a vibrant A&R culture, one I'm aiming to take to the next level.' ('The next level'! One of those spastic music-business phrases – like 'does what it says on the tin' and 'it's not rocket science' – that spill from your mouth in meetings. Meaning absolutely fuck all.)

After I read the story I spent forty-eight hours in bed.

Parker-Hall stands up and does a bit of awkward shuffling, really laying on the 'I'm not worthy' crap. 'Thanks, everyone. I'm not much for big speeches, so I'll just say how excited I am to be here and how pleased I am to have a fantastic band like the Lazies to bring to the table . . .'

More applause, led now by Dunn. The next Lazies single is already recorded and Dunn is convinced that it's going to stroll onto the Radio 1 playlist. Consequently he's been licking Parker-Hall's Ronson like it's going out of fashion.

'Obviously I already know Steven and Rob,' he indicates me and Hastings, the broken men, 'and I'm looking forward to getting us all pulling in the same direction so we can get stuck in and sign a few more great bands for you all to work on. Thanks very much.'

Cue applause and cheers and Derek nodding as though he's just negotiated world fucking peace.

I'm walking in a forest. I'm walking in a forest.

Later, on the stairs, I pass Nicky. Normally the most I ever get from the monstrous diesel is a tight little smile but today she's beaming, I mean fucking *beaming* at me. Her smile says: 'End of the line for you and your turkey acts, loser. There's a real A&R guy in town now. How can you even stand to come into work?' The urge to kick her down the stairs, to jump on her head, to pummel her gloating dyke-face into an unrecognisable porridge of blood and bone, is tremendous. But, using incredible reserves of will-power, I manage to ignore her and continue on towards marketing.

Rebecca comes in. Today she's wearing leather trousers. I'm not kidding. Leather. Fucking. Trousers. If I had any self-respect left I'd fire her.

'That policeman's here to see you again,' she says in what she imagines is a meaningful tone of voice. I just yawn and click the mouse to close the window on my laptop. A graphic close-up – too close in fact, I'd zoomed in until the image was just a smear of pixels – of a bull ejaculating a ludicrous payload of glutinous semen into a Latino girl's grateful face vanishes. A Mexican website Trellick turned me onto.

'Send him up,' I say, pushing the screen down, the laptop closing with a snick.

I knew Woodham was coming. I've finally agreed to see him to talk about the tracks he recorded for us a few weeks ago. I'd been dodging his calls.

Basically, figuring there was no downside to keeping him sweet, I sprang five hundred quid from the demo fund and he went into the Stoneroom in Acton with his band where the mad cunt managed to bang down something like fourteen songs in two days. I've managed to listen to two or three tracks and they are *appalling*. You couldn't have got arrested with them even last year, when any scavenger from north of Watford with a fucking giro in one hand and a semi-acoustic guitar in the other was getting on the cover of the *NME*. Woodham's demo is so bad that there can be no prevaricating, none of the 'lots of potential' crap. I'll just have to be honest and tell him straight out to forget it.

He comes in and we do the hey-how-are-you-can-I-get-you-anything stuff before I say, 'Look, Alan, about your demos.'

'Actually, before we get onto that, I need to talk to you in connection with Mr Waters.' His tone is different. Formal. Less matey.

'Roger?' I say.

He takes out his notebook and flips to a page. What the fuck is going on here? 'There's something that's been puzzling me. You said that the last time you saw him alive was when you dropped him off in Notting Hill around 11 p.m. before you took the cab onto Maida Vale.'

'That's right.'

He consults his notebook and taps his pen against his leg. 'You were at the Dublin Castle on Parkway, weren't you?'

He looks up at me. He looks like a different guy now. He's suddenly older, more serious. He's suddenly very fucking serious.

'Yeah . . .'

'And you caught a cab on Parkway?'

'Um, yeah. I think that's right.'

'It seems a long way round, doesn't it?'

'How do you mean?'

'Parkway's one-way. You'd have had to head up further into Camden and then up towards Chalk Farm.'

'Sorry, Alan, I'm not quite following you.' But I'm beginning to.

'Well, you said you dropped him off. But you live in Maida Vale. To Maida Vale from Chalk Farm via Notting Hill? You pretty much have to go through Maida Vale to get to Notting Hill from there, don't you? Why didn't you get dropped off first?'

'Ah . . .' I am dying here. My head is pounding. Think. 'Why didn't I get dropped off first?' I repeat while, in my head, Def Con 3 goes on. A long time passes. Woodham says nothing, looks straight at me. The silent close.

'Ah!' I say, and I actually snap my fingers together. Jesus Christ, this is like a fucking masterclass in bad acting. 'Sorry, we were going to drop me off first but neither of us had any cash,' this is so *lame*, 'and I'd left my wallet in the office, so we went onto Roger's place, he had some cash in the house and, yeah . . .' he continues to look at me evenly, 'that was it. Sorry, I'd had a few.' I laugh. He doesn't.

'So – you dropped him first and then went back to Maida Vale?'

'Yeah, that's right. Sorry.'

He writes something down. Jesus Christ. Jesus fucking Christ.

'OK,' he says, snapping the notebook shut, 'so what were you going to say about the demos?'

I clear my throat. 'I have to be honest with you . . . I think the songs are incredible. Some of the best material I've heard in a long, long time.'

'Really?'

'Yeah. What we should do, what I think we can do, is we should look at trying to get you a publishing deal.'

'Seriously?' he says, smiling now for the first time since he came in. 'Well, that'd be great, Steven,' he says getting up.

'Yeah, let me look into that. Make a few calls. And, sorry about the confusion there, with the Roger stuff.'

We shake hands. 'Don't worry about it,' he says and he leaves.

I close the blinds, avoiding Rebecca's concerned gaze on the other side of the glass. I cross the room to my little fridge, chug a bottle of Beck's in one go, and open a second one. I sit down and torch a Marlboro Light with a trembling hand and I try to work out if what I think was just happening was actually happening.

So, on top of everything else, on top of Parker-Hall, on top of the hundred-grand dance single that stiffed at 68, on top of the bridging loan for a ruined house that a gang of speed-fuelled Albanians are busy dismantling, on top of the American Express and Visa bills totalling six and a half grand I received this month, I now looks like I'll have to find a publishing deal for a copper who thinks he's Noel fucking Gallagher.

Cheers.

Meet the new boss.

Parker-Hall takes me and Hastings to the River Cafe for lunch. A sort of getting-to-know-you combined with 'here's my vision' deal. We have pasta and Hastings fidgets and looks uncomfortable the whole time, probably wondering why there's no chicken fucking tikka on the menu. We're all drinking Evian. 'Bottle of still water, mate,' Parker-Hall had said when the waiter rocked up and I looked up from the wine list I was examining and said, 'Same.' If they drink . . .

'The way I see it,' Parker-Hall is saying, 'there are two categories of acts; there are entertainers – Robbie Williams, Spice Girls, what have you – and there are artists

— Radiohead, Weller . . . Ellie . . .' *You pompous little cunt.*
'Now —'

'What about the Beatles?' I interrupt. 'Weren't they
both?'

'Well, if you wanna split hairs, Steven, they were
entertainers who later became artists. Anyway,' he waves it
away, *you pompous smart-arsed little cunt*, 'a label needs both.
You need the entertainers in the short term so you can
develop the artists for the long term. Now you guys both
have different strengths; Rob, you're coming from an indie
guitar-band area,' Hastings nods enthusiastically, 'and,
Steven,' he indicates me, 'your roots are more in the pop-
dance area of the marketplace. So . . .'

He goes on, but I don't hear much more of it. I get lost
in a rapturous fantasy vision where I'm grabbing the steak
knife from the table in front of me, I'm vaulting across and
burying it in Parker-Hall's jugular vein and throwing him to
the floor, then I'm jumping up and down on his head,
slipping and sliding in his blood as I pound his stubbly,
shaven little elfin head into fucking jelly, the other diners
looking on in horror as I scream, '*Shut the fuck up! What the
fuck do you know about anything, you jammy, fluky chancing little
prick? Ellie Crush? You won the fucking lottery with that cow. Fuck
you. Fuck you. Fuck you.*'

'Do you know what I mean, Steven?'

'Umm, yeah. Definitely,' I say, tuning back in, having no
idea what I'm replying to.

'Good. Because there's rumours doing the rounds that
I'm going to poach so-and-so from Island, that so-and-so
from EMI is going to come over with me. All the usual
bollocks. I just want you two to know that your jobs are

safe. I'm gonna have complete faith in you until you give me a reason not to. Right?'

'Yeah,' Hastings says, 'thanks, Tony.'

'No problem, Rob. Steven, I hear you've been looking at signing Songbirds, them girls Danny Rent's managing?'

'Yeah, I've been thinking about it. What do you reckon?'

'I didn't reckon much to any of the songs on the demos.'

'Me neither, but –'

'But that ain't necessarily a problem with that type of band, is it? And they're lookers, the girls. Trashy, but lookers.'

'Yeah.'

'What kind of advance is he looking for?'

'Fuck all really.'

'So, do we wanna be doing the deal or what?'

'What do you think?'

He laughs. 'I'm asking you, mate. It's your call,' he says, signalling for the bill.

Do I want to sign them?

I really don't know. It's so much easier not to sign bands. Signing bands can cost you your fucking job. Also, I must be mindful of Parker-Hall's intentions here. He could be privately convinced that Songbirds are grade A, oven-ready turkeys with lead wings and hobnailed boots on. He could be cheerfully doling me out enough rope here to hang myself properly once and for all. What does he care about the advance? It's not his fucking money. Having me sign a pop act also makes practical and political sense for him.

Practical sense because he's just signed a three-year contract and you can break a pop act in six months to a year. As for breaking a 'proper' band . . . the Manic Street

Preachers were signed in 1991 and only started properly selling records last year. Same kind of time frame with Radiohead. Do you really want to be fannying about for five fucking years trying to break something like that? Chances are they'll be a billion quid unrecouped and you'll be clearing out your desk before they sell one record.

Political sense because, if Songbirds are huge, he looks the King of Rock because he authorised the deal and supervised the project. If they go down like the *Titanic* with boulders strapped to it he'll say something about how he had to allow me the autonomy to make my own mistakes, how he always had his reservations, etc., etc.

However, on the other hand, I've got fuck all else going on at the moment. If I don't sign Songbirds and some other fucker does and then they're huge, then I'm dead anyway. You're the guy who passed on the Beatles. It's a fucking nightmare. Poisoned chalices and loaded dice all over the shop.

My call. What do I want to do?

'Yeah,' I hear myself saying, 'I think we should sign them.'

'All right then. Get Trellick to put an offer in.'

The bill arrives and Parker-Hall nimbly presses his plutonium credit card down on top of it. His card is from Coutts and I am raped by envy.

The last one of the girls puts her childish uncertain signature on the contract (the 'i' in 'Debbie' is a little balloon), 'That's your career over then,' says Trellick, cracking his usual gag and the cork cracks out of another bottle and goes flying across the boardroom as the other girls – Annette,

Kelly and Jo – shriek piercingly for the umpteenth time.

I hate signing celebrations. You get drunk and do coke and have to listen to some manager, some singer, some *drummer* even, crapping on about how great you both are and how you're going to rule the world. I often think back to these moments when we're dropping the cunts a year later.

Crammed into the boardroom along with the girls and Danny Rent are Trellick, Derek (who, perhaps thinking/ hoping that this bunch of dogs are doomed from the off, kept his ludicrous 'we're going to rule the world' speech mercifully short), Ross, Darren, Rebecca, a couple of junior muppets from press and radio and Parker-Hall. Dunn isn't here but should be. Where is the Geordie cunt?

Everyone is smiling and laughing, but, to the trained eye, to the practised ear, there is a marked difference in the quality of the happiness: that of the band and the manager is of a genuine, top-of-the-world, time-of-your-life quality. They're thinking that they've won the lottery. The laughter and smiles of the executives is brittle and plastic; we've done this so many times, often for bands and singers who turned out to be about as commercial as tooth-kind drinkable HIV for children. Ours is the forced jollity of the whore, cracking a joke as she tiredly addresses herself to the fifth or sixth cock of the evening. Everyone is thinking something like 'What are the chances of this piece-of-shit band actually happening? How can I position myself so that if – when – they go down screaming in flames I don't get burned, *but,* at the same time, if by some miracle, some unforeseen quirk of taste and radio play they actually sell a few fucking records, then how can I have some of the glory spatter onto me?'

Parker-Hall gives me a wink from across the room and raises his glass. Congratulating me? Or congratulating himself on letting me trowel a few more bricks onto my DIY mausoleum? I smile back at the lowlife and take a seat next to one of the girls. Jo, I think. 'Congratulations,' I say clinking her glass.

'Oh fank you, Steven,' she says all breathy, her eyelashes fluttering and her hard little peasant's eyes glittering, 'we won't let ya down, mate.' She smiles at me from under her fringe, tracing her finger around the rim of her champagne flute. I suppose she's being as subtly and classily flirtatious as she can be, given that her teenage sexual 'awakenings' probably consisted of hiking her jeans down in a car park under some tower block and bending over while a trio of thugs lined up behind her.

The door bursts open and Dunn strides into the room looking incredibly pleased with himself. 'Hi there!' he brays, shaking a few hands. 'Sorry I'm late, just got back from Radio 1.' There's a hush of anticipation.

'The Lazies single?' Dunn continues, looking around the room, savouring the moment. 'Straight on the fucking B-list, *six weeks upfront*!' he says, punching the air. The room explodes – Nicky shrieks, literally *shrieks* with joy – and Derek is immediately by Parker-Hall's side, clapping him frantically on the back as everyone whoops and cheers.

Fucking. Shit.

'Nah,' Parker-Hall says, stretching back in his chair, 'that's pony. Take it off, Darren.' Darren, manning the stereo, takes whatever demo is playing off and slips something else in. I'm sitting on one of the sofas in Parker-Hall's office

(Schneider's old office), Hastings is on the other sofa, Parker-Hall sits at his desk reading emails, and Darren and Stan are on the floor with a pile of demos and records.

'This is Coco and the Bean,' Stan says, getting up, 'Edinburgh band, a few people are talking about this.'

A&R meetings are now weekly under Parker-Hall, rather than whenever we felt like it under Schneider. They are also driven by a new focus and clarity: he's right up every lawyer, agent and manager in town. He's on everything early and he has a sharp idea of what he likes and what he doesn't like. What he thinks will work in the marketplace and what won't. One and a half songs into the Coco and the Bean demo he says, 'Next,' and we listen to Polar Bear, Earl Brutus, Catch, the Low Fidelity All-Stars and many more. Parker-Hall tells us why none of them will sell records.

In the last couple of weeks I have sent Woodham's demo over to a few of the big publishers; Island Music, Sony, BMG, Warner-Chappell. I struck out everywhere. I put a call in to Woodham and told him I've been getting some good reactions, people like the songs, but it'll take some time. I'll get back to him. He's perfectly pleasant.

Maybe I was being paranoid. Maybe he doesn't . . .

A further indignity. The Lazies signed their deal and we had a party at the Halcyon in Holland Park. The night before the party Parker-Hall shuffled into my office and said he thought it'd be a good idea if I didn't come. 'I can't come anyway,' I lied, 'I've got a gig to go to. But, just out of interest, why the fuck not?'

'No offence, mate,' he said, 'and I don't know what happened, but Marcy says she gets a bad vibe off ya . . .'

'Right,' Parker-Hall says after we've listened to all the new music kicking around this week. 'I've been thinking about producers for the Lazies album and wondered if any of you lot had any bright ideas . . .'

Fortunately this week's *Music Week* is open on the floor next to me at the top hundred albums and I hastily run my eye down the page, over the names of producers, which are listed in brackets after the albums themselves, while Hastings craps on.

'Steven?' Parker-Hall says, swivelling in his chair to face me.

'Bird and Bush? Bacon and Quarmby? Gil Norton? Dave Bascombe? Langer and Winstanley?' I say, reeling them off.

'Why?' Parker-Hall says, looking blank.

'Why what?'

'Steven, mate,' he sighs, 'it sounds like you've just stuck a fucking pin the *Music Week* directory and come up with a list of people who've produced a few records that are in the charts this week.'

'No, I . . .' My face is colouring. This answer would have worked fine under the old regime. 'Well, who are you thinking of?' I say.

'Steve Albini,' Parker-Hall says.

Hastings nods solemnly. I do too, while thinking, 'Who the fuck is Steve Albini?'

'He produced *In Utero*, the last Nirvana record. He rocks up with a box of microphones and records the band live. Don't take points either.' Eh? This guy Albini must be out of his fucking mind. 'The way I see it,' Parker-Hall continues, 'we're gonna have enough of a buzz on the band to have a gold record with this one whatever it sounds like.

Let's make an extreme record, establish credibility, and then we can look to make something more commercial with the second one. Yeah?'

He's thought all this through. He isn't really asking our opinions on anything.

It is just some horrible test.

I go into the studio with Songbirds.

Now, I hate going to the studio. (Unlike Parker-Hall who seems to love it. Also – and check this out, you won't believe it – he goes away for the weekend *with his artists*. Honestly. Picture it, if you will. They sit around and get stoned and talk about . . . I don't know. I guess they talk about chords and middle eights and B-sides and stuff. I've tried to imagine doing this myself but, come on. There's a limit.) In the studio nothing happens for four days and then they play you something and ask for your opinion and you pretty much tell them to make it shorter and make the vocals louder. I mean, there's not a lot to it. But I need to fill the days somehow, so here I am. (*'How do you write a song? Well, you get some kids in a room, you get a beat going . . .'*)

On the other side of the glass the girls have been trying to record some harmonies for the past four hours. I'm reading the *FT* while Allan, the producer, fucks around with the Autotune – a studio device that, in theory, should allow a tramp gargling with razor blades and spunk to sound like Pavarotti.

The Dow hit a record high the other week. People I know are making money and I'm sinking in a quagmire of delays and debt. I had another heart-caving conference with Murdoch at the new house last week. Another wall may have to come down. I am haemorrhaging cash I do not have and if I do not turn this bunch of whores around soon it is possible I will be finished before the building work is. I take some comfort from the fact that Trellick bought a load of EMI shares recently, thinking they'd hit the floor. He was wrong. They're still going down. Every morning he's waking up to find his dough has been gang-banged over night. *Schadenfreudes* all round.

'Shall we see if that's any better, Steven?' Allan says after a while. 'Yeah,' I say sullenly, swapping the *FT* for *FHM*. He hits a button somewhere on the huge desk and music fills the room.

The girls' harmonies . . . it's hard to describe. Imagine you'd got four fishwives together, filled them full of Special Brew, and told them to scream random, primal abuse at each other. It sounds absolutely satanic. Allan turns it down and looks at me sadly.

'I don't see that we have any other option,' he says.

'Fine,' I say getting up and slipping into my suit jacket, 'let them fuck around a bit more, tell 'em it's great and send them home. Then we'll get some singers in and get it done properly tonight.'

'Right,' he says with visible relief.

As soon as he kills the track shouting can be heard coming from the live room, even through the phone-book-thick glass. I squint through. Two of girls, maybe Annette and Debbie, are screaming and pushing at each other. Allan hits the talkback and the sound of the playground comes out of the speakers.

'FACK OFF, YOU FACKING SLAAAG!'
'YOU'RE THE FACKING SLAG, SLAG!'

'At least they're taking it seriously,' I say to Allan as microphone stands and sound baffles get knocked over.

'I'M WEARING THE FACKING GREEN ONES!'

'YOU LOOK LIKE A FACKING FAT COW!'

I realise as they really go for each other – nails flailing, feet lashing out – that they are actually fighting over a consignment of shoes a stylist has brought down for a photo shoot. I swivel round in my chair to Rent who is stretched out on a sofa at the back of the control room reading *Billboard*.

'For fuck's sake, Dan,' I say wearily.

'All right, all right,' he says getting up and slouching off towards the sliding glass door to go and break it up.

'And talk to them about the fucking cab accounts.'

'OK. Christ.'

Since the stupid whores got signed – sluts who had never seen the inside of a taxi in their lives – they've been using company cabs for *everything*. Going to the corner shop for a pint of milk seems to involve a people carrier on wait-and-return. Fucking bands always do this. Us too. Every few months a memo will go round vetoing all cab use without the signature of a head of department. Then, gradually, it slips back to the old ways. This climaxed a couple of years ago when a secretary in the marketing department used company cabs *for her fucking wedding*.

And then the cretins wonder why they don't make any money. Let's see, your album sold eight copies and you spent fourteen thousand quid a month on cabs.

Later that week, sitting at the traffic lights off Shepherd's Bush, staring at the blue water in the huge ornamental syringe they've stuck in the middle of the roundabout, I hear the Lazies single for the third time that day on Radio 1 and I come to a painful conclusion about Parker-Hall. He's actually very good at his job and – unlike Schneider – is not going to simply destroy himself through incompetence.

So, the following night, I drive across London to a seedy Internet café in Whitechapel: filthy, slow, old computers and a few Pakis scattered around scrolling through search results for cheap flights.

Although the place is almost empty I still make a point of choosing a screen in a far away corner. I log on and start doing some research, prepaying for my user time with cash.

I do not want to leave any sort of paper trail.

August

Epic trumpets the launch of the new Echobelly LP. MD Rob Stringer says, 'What a fine act they are. I was very involved in the signing.' Andersen Consulting and Sun Microsystems are to spend 50K hosting a Music Industry Trust dinner in honour of Jonathan King. All the time you hear Will Smith singing 'Men in Black' and you hear 'Tubthumping' by Chumbawumba.

'It's a mean industry – especially when you're on the outs.'
Richard Dobbis, former Sony Music President

By the time the Reading Festival and Carnival roll around
the Lazies single is shaping up be a proper hit – possibly top
ten – and they're getting ready to record their debut album,
which is already being freely talked about around the office
as being 'a landmark', 'a classic' (Parker-Hall) and, from a
coked-up Derek, as 'the best debut album since *Nevermind*'.
(And nevermind that the homo-fool doesn't know that
Nevermind wasn't a debut LP.) Meanwhile, over in the
Songbirds camp, I'm onto the second producer, third
studio, and fourth or fifth lot of songwriters – and well into
six figures' worth of recording costs – and I still don't have
so much as a B-side.

It's Sunday morning and everyone's in the bar at the
Ramada, a few miles from the Reading site.

Cigarette smoke and hoarse laughter in the air and groups
of people buckle over their Bloody Marys. The place is
packed with scouts, journalists, press officers, managers,
agents, A&R guys, guys from bands – all talking about bands
they saw the previous day: Symposium, Kent, Pavement,
Remy Zero and Les Rhythms Digitales. They enthuse about

Cha Cha Cohen, Chicks, Space Raiders, Delgados, Smog, Seafood, the Webb Brothers and Dawn of the Replicants. About Rosita, Seafruit, Cinerama, Skinny and Indian Ropeman. We have opinions about Lit, Black Box Recorder, Cornelius and SubCircus. Now, most of that lot will probably end up going down the tubes for a small fortune, probably taking a few people like me out along the way. This is why you have to watch it with signing bands – they can literally cost you your fucking job. One minute you're nodding away at the back of some indie gig. A rash wave of a recording contract later and you're down the dole office, shouldering your way between a couple of stinking tolers and a bunch of teenage mothers.

I see Darren, Leamington and a couple of people at the bar. As I make my way towards them Jon Carter passes me. 'All right, mate,' he croaks, his voice a shredded bark – a dog who has been in kennels all night, howling and yelping along with his cell mates. I nod hello.

'Large Bloody Mary,' I say to the bartender, who looks crippled with exhaustion, like a soldier who's been left too long on his own to guard some remote outpost of the empire.

'Who are we seeing today?' I ask, lighting a Marlboro and taking a swig of Leamington's beer.

'Cornelius,' Darren says.

'Arab Strap,' someone else says.

'Buckcherry later,' Leamington says and he starts singing, '*I love the cocaine, I love the cocaine.*'

My drink arrives and I gratefully sink a third of it in one go. The guys are all talking about what Carnival parties will be worth going to. Christ, Carnival. It's Bank Holiday weekend and there's still another two days to go. I had two hours' sleep last night, none the night before. I pull myself up onto a bar stool. It's already hot and bright outside, the sun filtering through the slatted blinds, smoky beams and bars falling across the sofas and tables, trying to land on the vampires and the damned. In a room full of people who've been up all night, it's like the air itself is sweating, grimy and tired.

I run a quick mental feasibility study on just fucking off out of there: concierge gets me a cab, back to London in about an hour, hit the sack for a bit, shower, food, then over to Notting Hill for Ross's Carnival party. Doable. Very doable. Sensible shoes option.

'Oi, Stelfox,' says Leamington, clapping a hand on my shoulder, 'do you want a fucking nose-up or what?'

'Yeah,' I say. And then I'm following him to the toilet, my hands on his shoulders as I bounce up and down, both of us singing, *'I love the cocaine, I love the cocaine,'* and the girls on reception can hear us and everything but we don't give a fuck. As we barge into the toilets Brett Anderson from Suede and Justine Frischmann from Elastica come staggering out looking fucked out of their skulls. She gives Leamington a sloppy kiss and then follows Anderson off towards the elevators.

The world is much brighter – sharper and clearer – as we jump out of the taxi and crunch our way through a wasteland of plastic glasses towards the backstage bar. It's pretty much a freak show in there. We say hellos and hit the bar and then a cubicle for another bump. Darren and I split an E and then we bowl off across the site towards the Evening Session stage because a couple of people want to see Ultrasound again for some fucking reason. Why? They just signed to Nude for fuck's sake.

'Hey,' I say as we make our way there through a sea of broken tolers, 'I've got an idea . . .'

We root through a few stalls, people selling T-shirts, hash pipes, Rizlas, soft drinks and crap like that, until we come to a fifty-year-old hippy with a shameful tray tucked among his flea-bitten merchandise — a few rows of tiny brown bottles with names like 'Bolt' and 'TNT'. (American poppers have far better names. In direct acknowledgement of the huge faggot market for the popular quasi-legal heart stimulant, they're called things like 'Locker Room', 'Cruising' and 'Rectal Trauma'.) As I hand over the money I notice that the guy has a little sign up advertising his amyl nitrate. 'Room Odorizer' it says.

'Hey, cunt,' I say as the guy hands me two bottles of Liquid Gold, 'who do you know whose room smells *so fucking bad* that drenching it in amyl is actually going to be an upgrade?'

Early evening and it's still hot and clear and sunny and I'm stretched out in the back of a chauffeured company people carrier with Leamington. Darren sits up front with the driver, the windows down and the M4 sizzling by outside. The only other sound is the soft hiss of the radio. We are all fucking destroyed. I tilt back in the leather seat and look out of the back window, at the sun sinking behind us as we speed towards London. The sun seems huge. I mean it looks fucking enormous; a scarlet ball that's about to touch the ground. It looks like Armageddon falling over Bristol, over Reading.

Energised by a knuckle of coke as the driver pretends not to notice we pass a bottle of Maker's Mark back and forth and talk random industry gossip: Who's going to win the Mercury? Beth Orton? The Chemical Brothers? Are Nude going to have it away with Ultrasound? Will Kylie's new indie stuff work? Are the Prodigy going to sell records in America? Money. Will London have a hit with All Saints, this new girl band they've signed? If they do will it clear the pitch for Songbirds? (Unlikely. Remember – there is no bottom to this crap.) It looks like Ray Cooper at Virgin is signing this new band Catch, who are managed by Hall or Nothing. My head starts swimming, that last pill kicking in. 'Martin Hall reckons the singer kid, Toby, is a star . . .' Darren says. 'Yeah?' I say. Or maybe I just say, 'Yeah.' I don't know. I feel funny. Leamington craps on, he's telling some story I already heard the night before, about something that happened at Tracy Bennett's wedding the other week. (Subtext from Leamington: I went to Bennett's wedding.) I nod and just stare through my Aviators – we are all wearing sunglasses – at the back of the driver's head, at his cracked, seamy neck. I need to make more money. It occurs to me – and the realisation is in no way an epiphany, it just dawns on me in the same way you might idly realise one day that you really prefer linguine to spaghetti – that, were I forced to choose between Leamington's life and my own career success, then I would happily watch Leamington die. I am now experiencing auditory hallucinations. I can hear feedback and the beating of helicopter blades. Watch? I would kill him myself. And I quite like Leamington. 'They sound like the fucking Police,' Darren says, talking about some band. The Police.

Woodham. Fuck. Money. Waters. I think I am going to be sick. A helicopter chops right by my head. I flinch and whisper something.

'What?' Leamington says, turning.

'What?' I reply.

'Did you just say,' he lowers his sunglasses, 'kill them all?'

'No.'

I feel this volume continue to build and swell behind me, beneath me, the sound of chopper blades and feedback shimmering up through the car, and I think I may be losing my mind. Then I see that, in the front, Darren is dialling the volume way up on the stereo, Leamington's hands are shooting up into the air, he's flicking his fingers Manc style and they're both laughing. I lean forward and squint through the windscreen glare and I see a sign appearing out of the dusk: the comforting forestry green with white lettering which says 'NOTTING HILL' and now the Westway is opening up in front of us and the driver floors it and the feedback and helicopters resolve themselves into drums and guitars.

'*Turn it up!*' I yell at Darren. He cranks it all the way and then the three of us are singing, screaming, *'All my people right here right now . . .'* and I've ridden it out and everything is OK again.

I fucking love the new Oasis album. Masterpiece. Three hundred and sixty thousand over the counter sales on day one? You can't be arguing with that, can you?

We edge along the pavement. You can actually feel the heat of the pavement through the soles of your Birkenstocks. All you can move is your head, your arms are jammed down by your sides, your legs crushed together as everyone sways from side to side, rotating from the feet up, like one of those inflatable kiddies' toys with a weighted base. Like a Weeble. Looking up the hill, all the way along Kensington Park Road, all you can see is bobbing heads. I'm trying to keep my hand in my right pocket – the pocket with all the drugs and cash in it – because we're surrounded by greedy, shifty-looking darkies. As the crowd moves, as the breeze changes direction, you get hit by different smells – dope, beer, vomit, frying chicken. The shrill *rakka-ta-takka-ta-tak* of calypso drums meshes with the subsonic whumf of dozens of sound systems cranking out dancehall, drum'n'bass, two-step and ragga, creating a chesty slur of noise. All around us grinning, sunburned middle-class losers – Rorys and Camillas – bop up and down cheering and blowing their stupid fucking whistles while they clink Red Stripe cans with the indulgently smiling brothers. (Who, in their turn, are wondering if they can get Millie's handbag away without being caught.)

Whose bright idea was all this? I picture a bunch of old Rastas, hunkered on a doorstep on Ladbroke Grove on an August afternoon a long time ago. 'Leroy,' says Winston, passing across the dachshund-sized reefer 'suppose we be holding dem carnival and all dem white batty boys be spending dem money?'

'Righteous,' says Leroy, shivering under the weak London sun as he takes a big, Jamaican toke. Half a century later on the Portobello Road some student hands over a tenner for a burnt piece of plantain and a couple of warm lagers and steps around the corner to be mugged.

You've gotta hand it to them, Carnival is definitely one–nil to the Kaffirs.

I'm wired from the coke, taut and angry, on the verge of going nuts and smashing an elbow into somebody's face, doing anything to bust out, when there's a change in the pulse of the crush, something weakens and opens up on my left. I grab Darren's arm and manage to pull both of us through and out onto Talbot Road, where it's quieter, where the crowd is just insanely – as opposed to life-threateningly – big. A few mounted policemen trot around smiling benevolently, their horses braying, their hooves clipping on the cement. Carnival's a PR job now for the filth; you're in shirtsleeves, you get your picture taken with a big fat mama who's wearing your helmet. I even see a young constable taking a matey swig of Red Stripe.

But now and again, on the faces and in the eyes of the older coppers, you see flashes of how it used to be. Some young ragga will flounce by, nonchalantly billowing clouds of ganja smoke, his gold teeth shining and his trainers gleaming in the sun, and there'll be a tightening of the jawline, a contracting of the pupils, and you can see these old boys thinking, *'Come on. Come on, you fuckers . . .'* High up in the saddle they glaze over as they reminisce about the Perspex shields and the baton charge, the pleasing give of black skull beneath lead-tipped truncheon, and then a leisurely hour in the cell with the rolled-up phone book and the rubber hose. The good old days.

'Fucking hell,' says Darren as we press on, edging our way along the Portobello Road towards the Earl Percy.

Shouts of 'Oi! Oi!' rend the air as we shoulder our way into the pub. Trellick stands on a chair, his arms outstretched, a bottle of champagne in each fist. Behind him, crouched down, Ross is furtively doing a bump off the back of a girl's hand. Tench is sprawled across a row of seats, his face buried between the miniskirted thighs of some shrieking boiler. Parker-Hall is holding court at a corner table with a couple of girls, what's-his-name from Chrysalis and one of the guys who writes songs for Ellie Crush. Rebecca and Katie and Sophie and Pam and a bunch of other girls we know all dancing in the corner. Someone throws an E at me. That guy Richard Bolger from London Records pours a drink over himself. Derek DahLarge is talking to the wall.

Thank Christ, I think. Civilisation.

Ross's party at his place on Colville Terrace goes on until Tuesday morning. At some point, somewhere into the early hours, I turn round and realise I am crapping away to Parker-Hall. I don't know what we're saying or how long we've been talking. We're both off our tits but he's clearly in better shape than me. In a moment of pilled-up, cracked-up, coked-up, boozed-up, sleep-deprived, woolly false-bonhomie, I put my arm around him and say, 'I'm really enjoying us working together.'

'Me too, mate,' he replies, smiling as he pats me on the knee, untangles himself from my arm, and waltzes off, disappearing into the smoke and music.

Granted, I'm off my fucking head and might be paranoid, but even so, I'm sure there's a terrifying lack of sincerity in Parker-Hall's voice. I watch as across the room he talks and laughs with Ross. It's important for A&R to have a good relationship with marketing.

I'm not sure I like the way all this is going.

*

The following Monday, having slept through all of Sunday, I stroll into the office late, hung-over and grouchy. Rebecca and Pam and a couple of the other boilers are sitting around in tears. Nothing unusual there – I figure that Derek has just blazed through the department on one of his scorched-earth rampages, a search-and-destroy mission because of an errant bar code on a single, or a wrong release date on a poster. However, it is unusual that *all* of them are crying. Then Rob Hastings comes towards me. The clown looks genuinely shaken.

'What's up?' I say.

'Haven't you heard, man?'

'Heard what?'

He pulls me into Waters' old office where a few wet-faced secretaries are gathered round the TV. Paris, an underpass, a mangled Mercedes, Kensington Palace, crowds of wailing tolers.

I hit the phones and make a few calls. Radio playlists are being suspended and reconfigured, release dates are being put back and cancelled. BMG are in trouble – the new Kylie LP, titled *Impossible Princess*, will have to be pulled, retitled and re-artworked. Death in Vegas have had a record hauled off the radio because of their name. The new Prodigy single is fucked because the sleeve featured a crashed car.

It is a fucking nightmare. Thank Christ I don't have a record coming out in the next few weeks.

Parker-Hall and I go along to Trellick's office. Ross is already in there and we join him on the sofa as Trellick flips between CNN and BBC. Peasants all over the country are losing their fucking minds. In Newcastle, Milton Keynes,

Coventry, losers are crying in the fucking streets. A fat toler appears on the screen. Tears are pouring down her face. Her face. Fuck me – it's a real forty roll-ups and a bottle of cheap vodka a day monstrosity, honeycombed with broken blood vessels, fucked in from not having enough cash or sense. 'She . . . she . . .' the mad cow stammers, hardly able to get the words out, snapped with grief, '. . . she done *so much good* for people.' We fucking piss ourselves. It's happening here too. Along the corridor in accounts the secretaries are all snuffling and comforting each other. It takes my breath away – genuine grief, upset, over something which does not directly affect you in any way whatsoever. But, a golden rule of showbiz states, whenever there is a massive outpouring of collective emotion among the lower classes – Christmas, the World Cup, summer holidays – there are records to be sold and money to be made.

'Surely we want to be cashing in on all this?' Ross says. 'A tribute LP? A charity thing?'

Trellick thinks for a bit. 'Nah,' he says finally, 'too much scrutiny. It'd be impossible to skim any cash off. Maybe in a year. Anniversary thing . . .' He's probably right, but it's a pity because in the past, thanks to a little creative accounting, we've been very successful at skimming cash off of a couple of other charity records we've been involved in.

'Yeah, not worth the grief,' I say.

'I dunno,' Parker-Hall says, lighting a cigarette, 'the sales would still count towards our market share, wouldn't they?'

'Good point,' Trellick admits, nodding.

'Yeah, but,' I start to say, but Parker-Hall has the floor. He's talking about licensing, about appropriate tracks for a nation in mourning, about marketing. Trellick and Ross are nodding away, swept up with him. I sit there and read *Music Week* and get angrier and angrier.

Trellick makes a few phone calls, but it turns out that it looks like Elton's doing something and he's signed to Mercury so the project will probably happen over there. 'Fuck it,' Parker-Hall says, 'worth a pop. Wanna get lunch, James?'

'Sure,' Trellick says. I wait for Parker-Hall to extend the invitation. He doesn't.

'I've got to go,' I lie, 'meeting in town.'

'Oh, Steven?' Parker-Hall says as I leave. I turn round and without looking at me, not taking his eyes off the TV, he says, 'Can you make sure you get them demos off Coalition for me? That band Rob was talking about? Thanks.'

I nod, turn, and walk on down the hallway. There is a roaring noise in my ears, a metallic taste in my mouth, and I cannot see properly.

I drive through Stratford and Leytonstone – cancerous high streets choked up with PoundSmasher! shops and AlabamaFriedChicken dives – and take the M25 South.

I come along a flyover and, for a moment, the Saab is suspended so high in the air that it feels like you are in a video game. On my right, stretching back towards Docklands and the City, and on my left, oozing out into Kent, is the nuclear winter of east London – hundreds of square miles of power stations and freight yards, pylons, construction sites and chemical plants, motorway and flyover, ring road and tunnel, endless miles of red tail lights, yellow headlights and sodium street lights. The air outside the blue-tinted windows of the car is smoke, dust and dirt. Out in that air, in grids and blocks, the lights are coming on in houses.

Houses.

You realise that people actually have to live in among all this and that east London is the bill, the tab that these cunts are picking up so that you can live in west London.

I take a left onto the M20 and drive on towards Dover in the dark. The guy – 'Charlie' – meets me, as arranged, in the lounge of an unbelievable pub on the Dover Road. He's in his forties and unshaven with stains (egg? curry?) on his cheap, bobbled sweater. It has taken me several weeks to meet Charlie. Weeks of furtive emailing – from a dummy Hotmail account, set up under a false name and accessed only from the computers in a random, disparate chain of internet cafés – to get to this point.

After the briefest of drinks and a minute of the most innocuous conversation (literally 'Wot about them Arsenal then?'), we exchange envelopes. The one I hand to Charlie contains an awful lot of fifty-pound notes. The far slimmer envelope he hands me contains only a computer disk.

I will not look at what is on the disk until later – again, in a remote corner of a remote Internet café – and even then I will only do so for a split second, just to make sure. After that I will never look at it again.

The contents of the disk are, as I'd been promised, beyond description.

September

Roni Size wins the Mercury Music Prize. Dave Gilmour leaves Island Records to become Head of A&R at Independiente. Lots of interest in some Jocky band called Idlewild. Phil Howells over at London Records signs Asian Dub Foundation. He says, 'I'd have to be mad not to have signed them.' Mercury launches this pop singer called Thomas Jules Stock. And 'Candle in the Wind', 'Candle in the Wind', 'Candle in the fucking Wind' . . .

'I'm basically in the David Geffen business.'

David Geffen

It was Bournemouth last year, so it's Brighton again this year.

The TV set in my room says that the Grand Hotel welcomes 'Mr S. Stalefox'. I pull back the net curtains to check the view again, to check that it really has happened.

It has: brick walls, heating ducts, pipes. This is my 'sea view'. I am overcome by another seismic jolt of fury. How could Rebecca have allowed this to happen? I try her mobile again and it just goes straight to message for the umpteenth time. Hatefully I picture her; on the train down here, or in the bar at Victoria, drinking wine and gossiping with the other sows while I am forced to live through this.

They'll be excited, of course, all the PAs and marketing assistants love the company conference. It's an excuse to spend a couple of days wallowing in a five-star hotel, getting manicures and facials and fuck knows what by day, then agonising over what to wear in the evening before spending the early hours of the morning sweating over some guy's coke-broke prick.

My rage only increases the moment Trellick – wearing a

dressing gown, his hair wet, his mobile cradled in his shoulder – opens his door. The chinless bastard has lucked into some kind of suite, with double French windows opening out onto a balcony overlooking the seafront. 'Fuck you,' I say, taking two Scotches from his minibar.

I take a seat by the open window, the chill September breeze filling the room as Trellick strides around, simultaneously talking on his mobile, smoking a cigarette and putting on his suit. I'm wearing a suit too, by the way. I flip through Trellick's copy of *Music Week*. As has been known for a couple of weeks now, Neil Ferris, recently installed as MD over at EMI, has been hiring and firing people like a madman. He's made Tris Penna Head of A&R. Incredibly Nick Robinson, the previous Head of A&R, has not been fired. He's been demoted. He's going to work under Penna. I mean, where's your fucking self-respect? Wouldn't you just top yourself?

'What's your problem, loser?' Trellick asks, hanging up.

'Nothing,' I say. 'When did you get here?'

'Just now.'

'Anyone around downstairs?'

'I saw your mate,' ('your mate' is now the official euphemism for Parker-Hall), 'in the bar, talking to Derek.'

'Oh yeah?' I say casually. The networking little prick.

The objective of the annual company conference is straightforward enough: you gather together all the sales reps from all over the country – along with key players from retailers like Our Price, Virgin, HMV and the like – and everyone from the label above the rank of janitor, you bang them all up in some five-star atrocity by the sea for a few days, and bombard them with speeches about how great we all are and show them videos and presentations of your new acts.

Some of the acts, the priority acts, will play live at the conference. If you are in a band this must be your worst nightmare. Imagine striding onstage to belt out your heart-felt anthems of youth and alienation to a hotel conference roomful of sales reps: a roomful of Mondeo-driving, Next-suit-wearing, pebble-dash-semi-and-two-kids cunts. Some bands have kind of an existential meltdown about playing at conference. It's too funny. It's like they know it's the antithesis of rawk and roll, playing for a roomful of 'suits', but they all want to sell records too, so they fret and moan for a while before, inevitably, agreeing to do it. They're all good little capitalists at heart, bands. Even Thom fucking Yorke, when he's not crying and wringing his hands about what kind of coffee beans you should be using so some cunt in Outer Mongolia can afford to put an inside toilet in his filthy gaff, even he's wondering what the marketing spend is looking like. He's wondering about venue sizes, about playlists. He'll tell you – with a straight face no less – that he thinks about all this stuff because he wants to 'get the message across'. He wants to 'reach as many people as possible'. That's what he'll tell you.

But it's bad news for us too, conference. In the evening, at dinner, in the hotel bars, you have to mingle with the reps; the retards who pound up and down the motorways in their two-litre Vauxhall mongol-wagons, desperately trying to get some cunt at Bob's Records in Ipswich to take a few more copies of the new Mansun LP. You stand with an aching fake smile strung across your face as you listen to their stories about how many Celine Dion records they sold in a week, about what local bands from up North they reckon are going to be big next year, to their dismal, Chardonnay-fuelled views on the way the music industry is going.

Finally Trellick is dressed so we do a quick line and hit the bar.

I decided not to have Songbirds appear at conference. True, we finally have a single ready to release, a fizzy slab of pornographic dance-floor baloney called 'Fully Grown' (the lyrics rammed with near-the-knuckle plays on how close to the legal age for fucking the girls are), but if anyone actually heard them sing live, the jig would be up in a nanosecond. Derek, desperate to fill out the upcoming releases roster, begged, nearly demanded in fact, that they do a mimed PA instead, but I held out. This too would have been fraught with danger because it would have involved the girls dancing in public.

I'd assumed that, like most teenage girls, they'd be able to stomp and bomp around in some sort of coordinated fashion and that eventually, with the aid of some pricey choreography and dance gurus, we could knock together a couple of routines. I was disabused of this notion when I attended one of the dance rehearsals. It was like watching . . . carthorses won't quite cover it. Annette and Kelly at least had a basic move they could execute, a sort of running up and down on the spot while grinning their heads off kind of routine. Jo had this whole other thing going on – it was like watching a baby horse, a five-minute-old colt, still gloopy from the womb, trying to stand up. Her legs, absurdly too long for her body (like all the girls in Songbirds she has freakishly pronounced sexual characteristics: their arses jut out like ledges, the tits are gravity-insulting miracles, even through baggy combat pants you can make out Debbie's pussy lips) twanged and skittered away from her as she tried to keep her balance while she shadow-boxed, furiously thrashing the air with her tiny fists. Dance? Jo could barely fucking walk.

All this, however, was prologue to Debbie. Perhaps having already realised and come to terms with her inadequacies as a dancer she abandoned all pretence at the choreographed routine and chose instead to concentrate on the sexual angle of the performance. All the time rocking epileptically to the music, she slid her hand down her pants and worked two fingers in her crotch. She massaged and tweaked her own breasts so hard that the choreographer (who by this point was watching the whole thing from behind his clipboard, a clenched fist in his mouth, salty tears of anguish running down his face) thought she might perform a half-arsed mastectomy on herself. She started dry-humping the microphone stand. As the track climaxed, she dropped onto all fours and swivelled round to present her rump to us, shaking it madly while she tugged her G-string up and down her butt crack in wild frottage. The whole time, all around her, Annette and Kelly jogged resolutely up and down on the spot with idiotic fixed grins on their faces and Jo skittered around like a Glaswegian drunk on ice.

It was like watching CCTV footage of the tail end of a twelve-hour hen night in Liverpool.

But we should be able to cobble some kind of video together . . . and I still have this feeling. Instinct, I suppose you'd have to call it. I instinctively know that I'd love to fuck every one of them (particularly Debbie) in a vicious and degrading manner. I am nothing if not resolutely populist in my tastes, so I have no reason to believe that any other guy in the country would feel any differently. If we can just get them to put one foot in front of the other and then throw in some nice ditties and some cool clothes for the little girlies to like, we might just have a chance. We might just have it away with this piece of shit.

A guy I vaguely know, some marketing guy from some other label in the group, comes up to us in the crush at the bar. 'Hi, Steven, how's it going with those girls you signed?'

'OK,' I tell him. 'It's going OK.'

Dinner is hell. I get sat next to some rep who talks to me for a long time about the new GPS system in his car. I'm not making this up. He really talks about it. Derek gets up and makes a ridiculous speech in which he actually singles out Parker-Hall for praise, for 'injecting a new energy and focus' into the company's A&R. Jesus Christ. Parker-Hall acts embarrassed, pulling his sweater up over his head, but you can tell the little fucker is loving it.

As soon as it's respectable – i.e.: the moment a waiter holding a dessert plate walks into the ballroom from the kitchens – I'm out of my seat and heading for the toilets.

Derek has a party in his suite – a massive lair on the top floor – and, in the early hours, I find myself in the bathroom with Ross. I'm sitting on the edge of the huge circular tub, sipping Jim Beam straight from the bottle, while he racks them out on the counter. For some strange reason we're reminiscing about Waters.

'Remember conference last year? In Bournemouth?' he asks me. 'When everyone ran out of coke and he had that guy drive halfway down from London with about twenty grams and he drove halfway up and met him at a Little Chef or something?'

'Christ,' I laugh, remembering Waters' reappearance a few hours later, when he'd literally been attacked by a coke-ravenous mob. 'Yeah,' I say, 'he was a proper fucking gakhead, wasn't he?' (A proper gakhead: someone you do not like who does exactly as much coke as you do.) Ross snorts a line and sits down on the toilet, passing me the note. I reroll it carefully.

'Yeah,' Ross says, almost wistfully, 'that was a shitty way to go, wasn't it? Getting your head caved in by some fucking burglar?'

'Yeah,' I say, leaning into the powder, remembering the expression on Waters' face as he turned, after I'd hit him the first time, the tiny tear of black blood appearing at his hairline. How he just looked shocked, his eyes wide, his mouth a tiny little 'o', like the blow hadn't hurt him. Like it had just really . . . surprised him. 'It might have been, I don't know . . . drugs?'

'Drugs?' Ross says.

'Yeah. You never know. Drug debts, some mad dealer . . .' This is all pure malicious invention, but I quite like the sound of it. Might be worth putting it out there, it might well gain some credibility.

'Fuck,' Ross says.

I perch up on the counter and tip my head back, sniffing, feeling my throat constricting and numbing, feeling the trickle of cold, bitter froth. I stare into one of the spots sunk in the bathroom ceiling until it hurts my eyes and then, blinking, I turn to face Ross. 'Hey,' I say, 'I know you shouldn't speak ill of the dead and all that, *but*, Waters *was* a fucking idiot. All we ever did was bitch about the fat cunt.'

'Christ, Steven,' Ross says, laughing, 'you *are* fucking hardcore.'

There's a knock at the door. Ross unlocks it and Rebecca pops her head around. 'Room for two little ones?' she asks mock sheepishly. 'Quick, shut the door,' Ross says as Rebecca hops in trailing this girl Grace, who we know a bit. She's a press officer or something. Rebecca goes to get a gram out of her purse but I motion her towards our pile as Grace hops up on the counter beside me. Rebecca has a short skirt on and I'm wondering if it's tights or stockings. I have to admit it, she can look pretty doable sometimes. 'So,' Grace says, 'what are you freaks talking about?'

'Waters,' Ross says, climbing fully clothed into the tub.

'Oh please don't,' says Rebecca, already scrubbing her room key against the back of a fifty-pound note, 'it's too horrible . . .'

There's another knock at the door. 'Fuck off!' I say.

'Stelfox?' Derek asks gruffly through the door. Shit. Ross is already scrambling for the lock. 'Ah,' Derek says brightly as he comes in, 'making yourselves at home? Like everyone else he's coked up, sweating like a fucking rapist.

'Yeah, sorry,' I say.

'Do you want a line, Derek?' Rebecca says, pointlessly, as he's already squeezing greedily around her towards the pile. He claps me on the leg as he passes. I try to imagine the number of cocks his hand has closed around in its time, but it's unimaginable. 'How are you, Steven?' he asks, genuinely friendly for some reason.

'I'm good, Derek. Great,' I say unconvincingly.

'Ross!' Derek says abruptly, looking in the huge mirror and seeing Ross sprawled in the bathtub behind him. 'Tell me, what's the projected marketing spend on the Lazies LP up to?'

Derek has left the bathroom door half open and out in the darkened hallway of the suite I can just see Trellick, smiling and nodding as he listens to something that black girl from finance is saying.

I wake up the next morning – just, it's 11.58 a.m. – to a ringing phone. 'Hello?' I groan.

'Wakey-wakey!' Parker-Hall shouts brightly (he doesn't really do coke). 'Get your arse in gear! I'll see you downstairs in ten.' We're flying up to Glasgow together, the idea being that we can catch up on the flight, discuss progress on various acts on the roster, and generally 'review A&R strategy'. I was clearly off my fucking nut when I agreed to this nightmare.

I hang up and look around the darkened room at the usual debris – suit trousers and jacket strewn across the floor like a police outline, clutch of bottles and glasses on the table, coke-spackled CD case on the bedside table next to a bottle of Valium and a half-full whisky tumbler. There is a G-string on the lampshade.

I sense the extra warmth as I turn over and lift the covers a little. A naked back. She's well tanned, just the white 'T' that runs around the waist and down the crack of her arse. I prop myself up on my elbow as she rolls over to face me.

'Hello you,' Rebecca says.

Doing your secretary is a shocker. Worst-case-scenario shit. Here's how it happened:

We went back to my room in the early hours, to have a chat about 'a few work things', or some such nonsense. We lay on the bed drinking and nosing, getting closer to each other, and the conversation turned into what it always turns into in those situations.

'What's your favourite position?' Rebecca asks me, giggling coyly.

Bitch tied up with a knife at her throat, I think, but, ever reasonable, I say, 'Doggy,' then ask her, 'Do you masturbate?'

'Of course I bloody do! Come on, it's *the nineties* for Christ's sake! Have you ever done a hooker?'

'No.' (Tip: never tell the truth here.) 'Have you ever done two guys?'

'Ummm . . . pass,' she says, hiding her face.

'Really?' I say. What a fucking spunk bucket.

'Have you ever done two girls?'

'Yeah. How about anal?'

'What about it?'

I raise an eyebrow.

Rebecca reaches into her handbag and rummages around. 'Do you want one of these?'

I look down at her hand. There, in the middle of her outstretched palm, is a big, blue triangular pill.

'What is it?'

'Viagra.'

Well, I don't mind telling you, I got greedy. Very greedy. Greedy? I went fucking berserk – pumping, sucking, grinding, fisting. Rebecca, as it turned out, is a *demon* in the sack. I got the fucking mother lode – soup to nuts. At one point as I was viciously doing her from behind, she reached down and – unprecedented this – began to guide my cock towards her arsehole. Bosh! I started furiously pummelling her up the Gary and the next thing I know she's screaming, 'No! No!'

I stop.

'What are you doing?' she asks, looking back over her shoulder, breathing hard and still pushing back against me. I am up to my nuts in her dung funnel.

'I . . .'

'Please keep fucking me up the arse.'

I resume. 'No! No!' she starts screaming again, really enjoying it now. Wow, I think, sometimes when they say 'no' they really do mean 'yes.'

'Talk dirty to me, Steven.'

'You nasty bitch.'

'Yes . . . oh God . . . fuck me.'

'You dirty fucking whore . . .'

'Oh God, I'm . . .'

'You slut . . . you whore . . . you . . .'

But that's the problem with talking dirty. You're hardly going to start out with 'you very badly behaved girl' and gradually crank it up, are you? No. You go straight in at the deep end with 'you dirty fucking slut' and stuff like that. And then there's not a lot to move onto later. I pump her harder and try for a bit of variety.

'You fucking . . . idiot.'

'Don't call me an idiot!' she says, stopping her thrusts, sounding genuinely hurt.

'Sorry. You fucking . . . cow?' This restores order and she pushes back onto me again. Bit close to the bone there possibly.

Well, things degenerated from there. I mean they really went downhill – coke, Valium, more Viagra and amyl were all relentlessly produced from Rebecca's handbag and the minibar was thoroughly emptied as we got off our chanks and went properly crackers. Somewhere around dawn, even with the cock-pills, my prick is destroyed. It's a cautionary tale – a bloody, red-raw, still-erect slab of disgrace. And still Rebecca wants more. She's lying back, eyes closed and a couple of pillows underneath her as she busily works the index and middle fingers of her right hand over her pussy. 'Please keep fucking me,' she moans.

Fuck her? *Fuck me.*

I root around on the floor of the bedroom. Nothing – I thought there might be a champagne bottle, but we've been drinking the mini-splits of Moët from the minibar. And I don't think a mini-split is going to do it here. I mean, she wants a fucking battleship up there. She wants the Death Star.

With Rebecca still moaning and writhing on the bed I charge into the bathroom and still find nothing. There's no deodorant cans, no big bottle of shampoo, not even a bog brush – nothing which could make for a reasonable facsimile of a functioning cock. In desperation I throw open the wardrobe. Coat hangers. 'Hang on a minute . . .' I say.

A few grunts and twists and turns (and in my memory

I'm not sure what Rebecca's up to during all of this, whether she's aware of what I'm doing or not. I think she's wanking herself off. Or doing coke. Or both). I manage to fashion a strange cock-like contraption from a wire coat hanger. I mean, it looks exactly like a long, thin, cock. The only real drawback, I suppose, is that it is flat and two-dimensional. But we give it a go anyway, both us mad and sweating and naked; me kneeling on the floor at the foot of the bed, frowning – tongue between my teeth in con-centration – as I grimly work the contraption into her, looking for all the world like a backstreet abortionist on an emergency call-out.

After a while, as her moans decrease, I said, 'It's not really working, is it?' and, shortly after that, thankfully, we both passed out.

'Hello, you,' she says and leans in for a kiss. Mindful of all the utter disgrace her mouth was put through just a few short hours ago – at one point it felt like she was trying to get her whole head up my arse – I manage to just graze her lips before blurting out, 'Shit, I'm late,' and running for the shower.

I lean tiredly under the stinging needles and think about how quickly I can have Rebecca fired. Fired? No, not these days, you're joking, aren't you? You'll be up in front of some tribunal before you can say, 'She loved it, Your Honour.' With a sigh I get a foreboding glimpse of how very badly I am going to have to treat Rebecca in the coming weeks and months in order to get her to quit.

I tiptoe back into the bedroom, praying she'll have fallen asleep. She hasn't. She's propped up on one elbow on the pillow watching me carefully. 'I've got to go,' I say, 'Glasgow.'

'I know,' she says, tonelessly. I bend down to pick up my trousers. There, on the floor next to them, is a strangely bent coat hanger. The contraption. Queasily I kick it under the bed. 'Steven?' Rebecca says.

'Mmmm?'

'You killed Roger. Didn't you?'

Total silence. Somewhere outside the window, a seagull squawks. I blink at her, too hung-over to think, to lie. I manage a hoarse, feeble laugh as I say, 'What?'

'I don't care,' she goes on, matter-of-factly, 'he was an idiot.'

I sit down and we look right at each other for a long time, neither of us saying anything. It is like I am really seeing Rebecca for the first time, seeing some reserve of strength, of will, that I never knew she had.

'Why do you think I killed him?'

'I follow you sometimes. I go to all these stupid gigs because I know you're going to be there. I was parked across the street from Roger's house the night he died. Just watching the flat because I knew you were in there. I saw you leaving.'

'Why would you . . .'

'I love you, Steven.'

I sit there basking in this fresh hell while I allow myself time to register the new information: *Rebecca is insane.* It's a long time before I speak.

'What do you want to do?' I say.

She tells me. I can't believe I've heard her properly so I ask her to repeat it.

'I want us to get married,' she says for the second time.

'OK . . .'

'And then we'll never talk about Roger again.'

'OK . . .'

A few traumatic hours later (I lost my car keys so we have to get a cab to Gatwick while the Saab stays in Brighton; squatting in the NCP, racking up thirty quid a day in charges) I'm standing at reception at the Glasgow Hilton trying to check in. There's a braying mob five-deep in front of me, all waving credit cards, travel vouchers and confirmation slips. The girls behind reception look like the last few Redcoats left at Rorke's Drift, trying to front out an angry mob of spear-chuckers with two bullets and a tattered Bible.

Behind me the bar, lobby and reception area have all merged into one drunken scrum and Parker-Hall is already working the crowd. ('All right, geezer! Nice one! Fack orf, you cant!') I just want to get up to my room. To think. To try and plot some way forward through the chaos.

Parker-Hall and I were late getting up here because of our conference. Some people, a lot of the scouts, have already been here a couple of days. Pete Tong says hello. Nigel Coxon from Island strides by. Matthew Rumbold from Food waves hello. A bunch of publishers are huddled at the bar; Mike Smith from EMI is talking animatedly to Bruce Craigie from Deceptive and that lawyer from Russell's, the one who is handling the Idlewild deal. Rob Stringer is listening, angrily, to his mobile phone. Ian

Brodie from the Lighting Seeds shuffles by. People are talking about bands. They're talking about Idlewild, the Lanterns and the Smiles. They're talking about Magicdrive and Dawn of the Replicants. They're talking about the High Fidelity, Tam and Fat Lip as 'Candle in the Wind' is piped through the lobby, swirling beneath the roar of conversation.

In The City again. In The Fucking City.

In The City is an annual music industry convention that was knocked together in the early nineties by Tony Wilson, who used to run Factory Records – until those cretins the Happy Mondays skanked the whole label down the shitter for a bag of rocks. Then Wilson somehow chiselled a deal out of Tracy Bennett and Roger Ames over at London Records for a new label, the hysterically named Factory Too, which also recently went under, having produced zero hits in three years. Laugh? I nearly bought a fucking round.

Anyway, it seems that all this wasn't quite enough to fill Wilson's days for him so, a few years back, he decided that what the music industry really needed more than anything was *another* fucking convention. Hundreds of bands playing in dozens of venues all over the city, networking opportunities (have Hans from Düsseldorf palm you a 12″ of some mad techno you will never listen to), and discussions and debates on things like 'Is the Remix a Valid Artform?' 'Will the Internet Engender a Pan-Global Dissolution of the Record Industry?' and 'Darkies: Have They Been Ripped Off Over the Years, Or What?'

Every year now you have to sit through this shit. (And

have you ever tried to get hold of a decent hooker up North? Fuck me. A couple of years ago, desperate in Manchester, I pulled this toothless pig into the cab off the street. She started undressing in my hotel room and, for a second, I thought she was wearing some artful, designer bodice. It turned out to be a lattice-work of stained, seeping bandages. The AIDS, I supposed, literally leaking out of her. I threw her a tenner and kicked her into the elevator rapid-style.)

The whole thing would be just about tolerable if they had it in Soho but, no, every September we all have to troop off to Manchester, or Dublin, or Glasgow. You check into the Holiday Inn, or the Ramada, and bowl around a skanky Northern city – getting in and out of taxis in the rain, standing in drizzly guest-list queues, having damp business cards thrust into your hands by stinking amateur hour 'managers' and indie label 'bosses' – for a few days, seeing a load of unsigned bands. They're unsigned for a reason, of course. Every single one of them is fucking shit. Cheers, Tony.

Leamington comes over to us through the crush. 'Oi oi,' he says.

'Oi oi,' I reply.

'Did you hear about your boy? Well, former boy.'

'Who?'

'Rage. He was DJing here at this thing last night. Gets into an argument with some bouncers, starts giving it all the "do-you-facking-know-who-I-am" business – the usual – anyway, they beat the fucking shit out of him.'

'Good on them,' I say.

'Nah, mate, I mean they *properly* beat the shit out of

him. They're talking about fucking brain damage and the like.'

Wow, I think. How can they tell?

When I get into the room the message light is flashing on the phone. I hit the button and put it on speaker while I get a drink from the minibar. As I rummage among the cool shelves I get this:

'Hi, Steven, it's Alan Woodham. I gather you're up at In The City.' Woodham's tone is flat, neutral. 'Listen, you said you'd get back to me about this publishing deal before the end of August. It's now the middle of September and I haven't heard anything. I've tried ringing you several times now. I left a couple of messages on your phone. I need you to call me back because . . .'

I cannot bear long phone messages. You want to kill, don't you? What's wrong with 'Call me back?' Why crap on for a fortnight? It's like directions, as soon as someone gets past the third 'and then a left at that roundabout and then –' you just want to cut their tongue out and fucking feed it to them.

The Woodham situation: after striking out with all the big publishers I actually sent his miserable demo round some of the smaller independent publishers – Complete, Rondor, Notting Hill Music – and got told to fuck off there too.

'. . . there's something else I need to talk to you about. In connection with the Roger Waters murder.'

Hang on a fucking minute.

'So please call me back as soon as you get this.'

I pick up the receiver and drop it back down, cutting the

message off, and start scrolling through my mobile for his number. Outside, the sky is the colour of smoked glass and it is starting to rain. Christ, I hate Scotland. What a nation of fucking losers.

I twist the caps off of three tiny bottles of Johnnie Walker from the minibar, pour them into a dirty glass and neck the lot. I start smoothing the coke out, covering the powder with a fifty and then scrubbing my room key up and down the note. I snort the line and sit back and give my problems free rein to strut and preen in my head.

As problems will, they soon settle themselves into a swirling, but definite, hierarchy. At the bottom level, coughing and grumbling and looking for attention, are all the constant, normal, low-level issues to do with work and money: Who can I get to remix the Songbirds single? How big is the Lazies LP – and subsequently Parker-Hall – going to be? How much more cash will the house haemorrhage? I must do my expenses. I should be getting paid more.

Floating above all this, sharper, clearer, more insistent, are the newcomers: My car is still in the NCP in Brighton. It is possible that Parker-Hall thinks I am a loser and will soon fire me. Does Woodham really know anything? And – straight in at no. 1 with a fucking bullet – Rebecca has been stalking me. She's gone round the bend, figured out I killed Waters and yet she wants to marry me regardless. (On reflection perhaps this isn't quite as crazy as it seems – didn't Ted Bundy get inundated with marriage proposals? And he was properly hardcore. He killed and raped dozens of women. Top lad, Bundy.)

I glug a belt of Scotch, honk a stupefying line of chang, and dial Woodham's mobile. He answers on the second ring. 'Alan? Hi, it's Steven. Listen, sorry for not getting back to you sooner. It's been mental recently. I –'

'Mr Stelfox,' (no 'Steven', 'Steven' is long gone), 'can you tell me why one of your neighbours claims that they saw you entering your flat at 5.30 a.m. on the morning of Roger Waters' murder when you already told me you'd arrived home around 11.30 the previous evening and gone straight to bed?'

He just rattles this off, staccato, machine-gun style. The blood in my head starts pumping so hard behind my eyeballs that I think they're going to burst out of my skull. 'I . . . I got up early and . . . went for a paper?'

'Where?'

'What?'

'Where did you buy this newspaper?' This is a different guy I'm talking to.

'At the newsagent . . . on the corner of Shirland Road and Elgin Avenue.' Fuck, fuck, fuck – are they even open at that time? This will be so easy to check.

'Alan, is everything OK?'

'I don't know,' he says, 'is it?'

I think hard, and then I'm talking. 'Listen, Alan, I'm sorry I haven't got back to you, about the demos. It's . . . it's looking good. It's just taking a little time. We'll get there. '

'Whatever you can do would be great.' He hangs up.

Woodham's new voice is clipped and formal, so much older-sounding than his indie-kid-down-the-Monarch voice. His new voice is the leathery whisper of gloves coming off, the hard-edged crack of cards being slapped on the table.

I'm shaking. It all comes crashing in and the precariously balanced hierarchy of problems comes tumbling down. The mortgages, the credit cards, Woodham, the coke, the never-ending building work, the whores, the overdraft, the bridging loan, the holidays, the private members' clubs, the coke, the whores, the restaurants, the airily picked-up four-hundred-quid bar tabs, the coke, the whores, Rebecca . . .

I just make it to the bathroom before I jackknife over, spewing a torrent of searing broth over the floor and down the toilet for a long, long time until I collapse onto the soothing tiled floor. I stare at the sour orange-brown puddle, recognising a few things; a bit of potato, peas, a chunk of what likes like chicken that I can't remember eating. Then I lie on the floor crying for a long time.

Much later – it is dark outside – I am sitting at the little desk up by the window of my hotel room multitasking. I am simultaneously drinking Scotch straight from the bottle, smoothing out another line, and scanning through the *Music Week Directory*.

Publishers. I'm looking for publishers.

Currency begets currency. We all know that Parker-Hall is a useless mockney twat; however, he has just signed the coolest band in the country and has also had a big commercial hit with a half-arsed soul/pop diva that he's somehow managed to hoodwink everyone into thinking is hip. So people want to meet him. People listen to what he has to say. As we make our way from elevator to pavement people stop him to talk. 'What do you reckon to them?' they say. Or 'I hear you're looking at . . .' or 'How's the album going?' or 'Hi, I sent you a demo of . . .' I stand there nodding while he pontificates.

This is what I've become. I am Parker-Hall's muppet.

We're just about out the revolving doors when we run into Derek. I look pretty rough, Derek looks . . . insane. Hitler-in-the-bunker insane. He clearly hasn't been to bed.

'Anthony! Steven!' he barks. 'Come with me.'

Back up in the elevator and we walk into his suite behind him. Little Stan, one of junior scouts, is in there. He's sitting at a coffee table in the lounge. In front of him is a gigantic pile of rocky cocaine which he's attempting to chop into finer powder. He looks up as we enter and we see real fear in his eyes. He can't actually speak, but with his eyes he's begging us to help him, to get him out of there. 'Stan!' Derek barks. 'A line for Steven and Anthony.' Stan, chained and shackled in Derek's mad gak factory, immediately begins drawing out a couple of fat lines for us. 'So,' Derek says, sitting down and motioning for us to do the same, as though everything is perfectly normal, 'what's our strategy here this week?' For the first time since he's joined the company I see that Parker-Hall is getting the true measure of Derek. I think up until this point he thought all the Derek stories were just that: mad stories. But here he is looking like death whacked out of his fucking mind on chang and asking us, sincerely, what our 'strategy' is.

Parker-Hall begins mumbling a response, some bunch of shit about 'A&R culture', while Derek nods and tightly rolls a fifty-pound note. He passes it first to Stan, who leans towards the powder and then stops. He looks up at Derek, fear and shame colliding across his face, and says, 'I'm sorry, Derek. I can't do any more.'

There's a pause.

Magnanimously Derek dismisses him with an airy wave of the hand. Passing the note to Parker-Hall, Stan gets up and timidly asks Derek, 'Do you have a hairdryer?' Stan's hair is perfectly dry.

Derek, confused himself now, says, 'In the bathroom.'

Parker-Hall and I quickly split one of the elephant-leg lines between us, tell Derek we're running late for a gig, and fuck off out of it.

As we leave we can hear the whirring blast of the hairdryer coming from behind the bathroom door.

'What the fuck was all that about?' Parker-Hall says after the lift doors close.

'Weird scenes inside the gold mine,' I say.

We go out and rattle around the freezing Glasgow night, climbing in and out of cabs (where the suspicious Jock bastards expect you to pay them *before* you step out onto the pavement) and seeing pointless band after pointless band.

We return to the Hilton and hit the bar where we drink and do coke before I finally slope off upstairs with some girl – some publisher – just before dawn.

I hold her hand as we cross the lobby, take the lift, and stumble down endless corridors of halogen and beige, seeing only old people at this hour – pensioners driven from their beds at 6 a.m. by the death fear, sleep becoming too close to the real thing for them now, what with the real thing snuffling right outside the door.

Back in my room she talks about girl power for a while and then I'm ripping her Wonderbra off and fucking her from behind. I spit into her arse and try and stuff my cock up there but she's not really having it and I think I remember punching her in the back of the head a few times (playfully but not really) and when I wake up she's gone and it's *still* raining outside.

October

Virgin Records' Ray Cooper and Ashley Newton move to LA to run Virgin America. The Verve album is no. 1. Daniel Miller at Mute Records, talking about the new album by an act he's signed called Peach, says, 'It is a timeless record. The album is packed with hits. I'm so confident.' Gary Glitter is honoured by the MCPS with a lunch at the Savoy.

'Artists and executives come and go. Record companies are forever.'

Anonymous lawyer

Friday night on Regent Street and I light the fourth cigarette of the tailback and engage second gear for the first time in forty-five minutes. This has to stop. We can't go on like this. You can't drive anywhere any more. You can't park anywhere. In central London now you can't even *walk* anywhere. For a mile radius in every direction from Oxford Circus it's like being down the front at Glastonbury. The shops are all rammed with filthy tolers, every last one of them wielding a sweaty handful of tacky credit cards – their Bank of Toytown Gold Card, their DSS Mastercards – as they hurl themselves at the counters, desperate to cram their blubber into another new and lurid outfit. I mean, I hate to sound like a killjoy, a party-pooper, but it's Tuesday afternoon, for fuck's sake. What do these losers all do? *Where's all the fucking dough coming from?*

Because everyone reckons they're a player nowadays. Everyone thinks they're big time.

You live in an eighteen-foot-square toilet in Dagenham with your eighteen-foot-square girlfriend. You work as a crate packer in a warehouse and she's part-time behind the till at Iceland. Effectively the two of you earn about a millionth of a pence a year. Your net worth is zero. Yet you think it reasonable – perfectly acceptable – to stroll down to the George & Dragon dressed like some bad-acid version of Tom and Nicole at the Oscars, matching his and hers Rolexes on your wrists and freshly tanned from your four-star week in Ayia Napa.

The clothes are on the plastic.

The holidays are on the plastic.

The plastic is on the plastic.

I'm having drinks at Momo with Paul Dex and Terry Del Mar, a DJ/producer duo who I am going to commission to remix the Songbirds single. We're in a booth downstairs, an ornate Eastern lamp dangling above our heads. There are patterned rugs on the walls, some of the walls themselves appear to be made out of mud, and somewhere I think incense is being burned. Dex and Del Mar are about my age, 'geezers' who've been through the whole acid-house thing, and they use expressions like 'massive tune' and 'it drops big time'.

Deafening hip hop plays and, were I remotely interested in anything these clowns have to say, I'd have to really strain to hear it. Thankfully I'm not. None of the A-list DJs we approached could remix the tune in time. These mongo-loids were top of the B-list, available and – relatively – cheap. They're hired, this meeting is a formality.

'Massive props,' Dex is saying.

'An underground vibe,' Del Mar chips in.

I nod and sip my vodka tonic.

Earlier today, at lunchtime, I waited until Parker-Hall

strolled downstairs for a meeting I knew he had scheduled. I slipped across the hallway into his office and hurriedly got to work on his computer. I uploaded the contents of the Dover disk onto Parker-Hall's hard drive. I buried the disk in a file I named 'Personal', then buried that file in a deep, remote corner of 'My Documents'. There are hundreds of files in there and I'm sure he won't notice one tiny new addition. The whole thing took less than two minutes and then I was back in my office flipping between MTV and VH1.

I drift back into the conversation. Del Mar is saying, 'Soma, Basic Channel, Peace Frog . . .'

Dex says, 'Hooj Choons.'

'Lads,' I say, getting up and peeling a fifty from my wad to cover the drinks, 'I gotta run.'

Upstairs as I leave I see Paul Oakenfold sitting in the restaurant. Coincidentally he was one of the DJs who turned down the Songbirds remix. On the table in front of him is an ice bucket containing a bottle of Dom Pérignon. Beside it is a Dictaphone, its red light glowing. A young guy faces him, chewing on a pen, nodding. An interview, then. As I pass, Oakenfold stabs the table with a pudgy finger, looks the journalist right in the eye, and says, 'I am the biggest DJ in the world. *In. The. World.*' His teeny little legs dangle over the banquette seating, his feet – kiddie's feet – barely touching the ground.

Yeah, beware the small man, I think to myself. Always beware the small man. He'll fuck you every time. Because they never forget, do they? All that grief they got at school. Over and over, and for the rest of their miserable short-arsed lives, someone's got to pay.

*

Autumn really gets going and things happen, mostly bad.

An entire wall in the house will need to be replaced. Weeks – months – and thousands and thousands of pounds before I can sell the fucking place for anything like a decent profit.

'Fully Grown', Songbirds' debut single, is taken up to Radio 1 for playlist . . . and swiftly rejected. Even *Music Week* – usually a publication that gives every record released in Britain a little gold star – describes the single as 'somewhat lacklustre'.

The Lazies are offered the cover of *NME*. Demand for their debut LP is at such a pitch that it is sure to go straight into the top ten. There is a passing reference to Parker-Hall in the *Sunday Times* where he's described as an 'A&R guru'. After I read this – at eleven o'clock in the morning – I drink half a bottle of vodka and cry for a while.

Rebecca bustles around the office jangling with happiness. We went out for a drink and a long talk after I returned from Glasgow. She doesn't see the point in a long engagement. While telling her I agree I also point out that I want to do things properly, ask her father's permission and all that, and that this will take a little time. I manage to get her to agree that we will keep our 'engagement' under wraps for the time being.

Incredibly, this strict *omertà* seems to be holding fast. Had she confided in anyone it would most likely be Katie, Trellick's PA, in which case it would have been around the business affairs department in seconds and Trellick would immediately have hauled me down to Full and Frank's. In the normal run of things asking Rebecca – asking any secretary – to keep quiet about something like this would be about as effective a silencing tactic as taking out a full-page ad in *Music Week* to announce your engagement.

Because that's what they do. That's *all* they do. They talk to each other about the shit we do. Over salads and Diet Cokes, around photocopiers and water coolers, across wine-bar tables littered with Chardonnay bottles and packs of Marlboro Lights, they talk and they rant and they dissect the shit that we do to them. If you removed the phrase 'and *then* he said' from the language every one of these fucking sows would have a hard time kick-starting a conversation. And then – I guarantee it – the ones who have boyfriends go home at night and some poor bastard will have to hear the whole thing again, with whatever refinements and embellishments they've dreamed up on the tube thrown in. I mean, the sheer fucking *arrogance* of it, to think that anyone wants to hear about your miserable day.

Infuriatingly, when no one is around, she twirls into my office and gives me a peck on the cheek. On the plus side I have had her over to the flat once or twice, late at night, when I've been off my tits. Like many crazy girls she is truly gifted at fucking.

Rumours abound that Derek is going to leave the company, to move into management or something. Up until recently the only possible internal successor to him would have been Trellick, which would be an incredible result for me. But, the way things are going, Parker-Hall might just get offered the job. A nightmare beyond description. Managing Director by the age of thirty? Could it happen?

How in the seven names of fuck am I going to get

Woodham a publishing deal? Does he really know anything about Waters? What's he going to do?

Out of all this crap the most pressing problem is the Songbirds single. We've got the Dex and Del Mar remix in, which we're going to 'put out to clubs'. Is it any good? I haven't a fucking clue. I should know, I suppose. I'm paid to know these things. But I'm tired. It's so *tiring*, not knowing anything the whole time. You're meant to listen to your 'gut instinct'. 'Go with your gut instinct,' they say. But I don't know . . . all I hear from my gut are vague unhappy rumblings that I should be making more money, fucking more, and cuter, boilers, eating in better restaurants, getting more respect from quarter-wits like Dunn.

Dunn. The spastic was almost cheerful when he told me Songbirds didn't get playlisted. Like everyone else at the label he is in love with Parker-Hall and thinks the Lazies are going to be the next Led Zeppelin.

He will pay. They will all pay.

As requested Ross calls me the minute he gets the midweeks in. 'Sitting down?' he says. Jesus, this must be bad. 'Three,' he says bluntly. I don't think I've heard him right.

'Thirty?' I say, hopefully.

'*Three*,' he repeats, 'it's number three.'

Numbly I hang up. The midweek chart prediction for the Lazies single is number three. A stupendous result for Parker-Hall and a disaster for me. Well, anywhere in the top ten would have been a disaster for me but this . . . it's terrible, a living nightmare I am praying to awaken from. I only really have two options: 1) slink out of the office, take the rest of the week off with a mysterious illness and wait until all the fuss dies down a bit, or 2) go along to Parker-Hall's office, right now, and congratulate him. Play the magnanimous card.

His door is open. I take a deep breath, will my features into an idiotic grin, and pop my head around. 'Hey!' I say. 'Congratulations on . . .' Derek and Dunn – horrible success vampires – are both already in there, the three of them are deep in conversation.

'Yeah, cheers, mate,' Parker-Hall says breaking off in mid-flow. 'Can you just give us a minute? Thanks.' Neither Derek nor Dunn even look at me.

I turn to go but – 'Sorry, Steven, hang on a minute.' I turn back. Parker-Hall is holding a piece of paper up. 'Have you spent four and a half grand on club promotion on this Songbirds single?'

Dunn and Derek look at me coolly now. Can this really be happening? 'Umm, yeah,' I say shrugging, 'what's the problem?'

'In future,' Derek says, aggressively, 'anything like this will have to be signed off by either Anthony or myself.'

'Right . . .' I say.

'Just run it by me, mate,' Parker-Hall says airily. I nod. They resume their conversation – Derek literally turning his back on me and saying 'Anyway' – and I stumble off along the hall, numb, beginning to realise just how far I have fallen.

The tiny file squats on Parker-Hall's hard drive, inert and unnoticed, waiting for me to push the button.

Not yet, I think. Not just yet.

*

I somehow manage to add a new, alarming vice to my already jam-packed roster. In addition to the chang, the booze and fags, the ostros, the online dog and pony shows, the sex lines and whatever else opportunity, cash and technology throw my way, I am now compulsively overeating. In the car on the way to the office, idling in fogbound traffic, I cram buttery croissants into my face, washing them down with litre-and-a-half vats of full-fat latte. Standing at my office window, listening to demos and gazing at the bend of the Thames, I follow triple-decker BLTs with a couple of rounds of chocolate brownies. At lunch with Trellick and Ross, with Darren and Leamington, I bulldoze through plates of gnocchi and pasta, covered in oozing tomato sauce and hidden under drifts of Parmesan. I tear apart side portions of heavily buttered bread and inhale gallons of Diet Coke. ('I see they're working,' Ross commented one lunchtime, patting my burgeoning paunch as I drained a third silver-and-red can.) The other night the normally inscrutable kid from the Thai takeaway did a slight double take as he set the groaning bags (tom yam gai, green curry, special rice, spring rolls, three orders of dumplings) on the kitchen counter and realised I was eating alone. It's the cold, I suppose, I reflect as I wait impatiently for the evening's second tub of Belgian chocolate ice cream to complete its twenty-second thawing in the microwave.

With all this going on New York is probably the worst place on earth for me, yet here I am, sprawled on my bed at the Soho Grand – a tub of minibar M&Ms in my left hand, my softish prick in my right, and some hardcore on the TV. I'm tiredly watching some brick-shithouse darkie slide his horse-prick (the vein running down it is like a section of garden hose) in and out of a traumatised arse when the phone rings, its tone soft, purring, apologetic, like it doesn't really want to disturb you. Still half-heartedly masturbating, I pick it up. 'Band's on at half seven,' Parker-Hall says, 'then we got dinner with the American label, yeah?' He's not asking me.

'See you downstairs,' I say and hang up.

We're here for CMJ, which is kind of the same deal as In The City, which was very much like Sound City, as was Pop Komm, which bore a stunning similarity to South by Southwest, which merges in my head with the Winter Music Festival, which wasn't all that different to MIDEM. New York, Glasgow, Cologne, Bristol, Texas, Miami, Cannes: you shout at waiters and sign credit-card slips and all that really changes is the quality of the porn.

Parker-Hall really does work. I don't know that he actually likes going to gigs, but he certainly sees it as a necessary part of the job – which is why we're enduring a forty-minute cab ride to some venue way uptown, where we'll watch some fucking band for twenty minutes before another forty-minute ride back downtown to meet some people from the American label for dinner at a restaurant five minutes from our hotel. Had Parker-Hall not been here the chances of me going to this gig would have been . . . minimal.

He strides into the lobby, flipping his mobile shut. The hotel – the city – is rammed with Brits. In the bar I can see a couple of guys from Virgin laughing and drinking beer with the tall blond-hair-and-specs guy from the Chemical Brothers, Ed, I think. The Chemicals are on the verge of actually taking off properly over here – half a million albums or so, about the same as Ellie Crush. That's the thing about America. It's shit or bust. Fuck all or a couple of million albums. I physically have to shake my head to knock out a vision of Parker-Hall having that kind of US success.

'Should we be signing these cunts?' Parker-Hall asks as an opener as we clatter down the hotel's ludicrous industrial-metal stairwell.

'Who?'

He holds up a CD of some band.

'Nah, pony,' I say.

'It's OK. Like the new Radiohead with some tunes. Can't see it being good for more than a hundred thousand though. Do you wanna see if we can get a meeting? Just for a laugh, fuck every other cunt up?'

'Yeah,' I say as the doorman hails us a cab.

Parker-Hall turns to me as we edge into traffic. 'What's happening with the Songbirds single?'

'Starting to get some good club reactions in,' I say. This means fuck all. Without radio play it means absolutely nothing, unless you have a *monstrously* huge club record, the kind that can become a hit with minimal radio. 'Good reaction at club' is the kind of thing you say when there is nothing else to say. I know this and Parker-Hall knows this, but he chooses to nod and say, 'Yeah?'

'Yeah, still early days,' I say. Too right it fucking is – I have already put the release date back twice.

'And the album?'

'Still writing. Trying a few different writers.'

'What's the recording budget again?'

'One twenty.'

'Gonna come in at that? Be realistic.'

'I should think so,' I say with a straight face. I reckon, once everything is in, I'll have spent that on the fucking single.

'Coolio,' he says in a completely neutral tone. What to read into it? It is just about possible that he's backing me here, being supportive of my instincts in an area of the market – pop-dance – that isn't really his field. It's also possible – it's far more likely, it's practically a fucking banker – that he's doling me out a colossal amount of thick, oily rope and watching with amusement as I coil it over my arm and climb the steps towards my shaky, home-made gallows.

Outside, the brownstones of the Village give way to the wide, loud cord of Broadway as we whip uptown through light rain and suddenly, without warning, we're in the open space of Times Square, which squats neutralised, bereft, in the daylight. Off to our left 42nd Street snakes down towards Chelsea and I experience a sudden, intense pang of pornography, a yearning for fisting, for lurid plastic dildos and ben-wa balls, to see someone other than myself being defiled and degraded.

Parker-Hall's mobile trills, interrupting my reverie – 'All right geezer!' he says delightedly – and then he's talking to someone back home, his affected, brutalised vowels flouncing off some satellite miles above us and passing silently through cold, cold space before they flutter out another chunk of plastic somewhere in London, where it will be bedtime.

*

Having managed to drink pretty heavily at the gig (four double Rockschools and a couple of beers in less than an hour), I continue drinking heavily in the bar at the restaurant – some place called Balthazar, a recently opened pseudo-French shithole that seems to be the toast of every flaming virus carrier in the fucking Village – before we sit down to dinner with the American record company, which is where I *really* kick things up a gear.

Refreshed by repeated hops to the bathroom I begin double-fisting red wine and Scotch as well as popping back stinging tequila shots whenever I (frequently) swing by the bar to smoke another cigarette. I'm not eating and food – seared foie gras, steak frites, a salad of asparagus and fennel – builds up in front of and around me. Along from me Parker-Hall is having the *fruits de mer*; two sparkling tiers of iced crab, crayfish, clams, oysters, mussels and shrimp tower in front of him. 'Are you having a fucking giraffe, cunt?' I think and I briefly wish that someone who would appreciate the Rage anecdote – Trellick, say – was here.

Because the dinner is mind-numbing. Parker-Hall sits between Ashley Werner, chairman of the American arm of our company, and Russ Koppel, Head of Promotions, the guy who gets your signings on the radio over here. He's like an even more game-show version of Dunn. There's a couple of junior A&R guys from the American label beside me and, across from me, some woman manager – in her forties, well heeled, big glasses, serious – and a couple of other boilers I don't know. All the Shermans are drinking water and eating salads and the conversation consists of listening to Werner and Koppel pontificate away and waiting for your turn to nod. They're all Ellie Crush fans and treat Parker-Hall as though he were the young Ahmet fucking Ertegun. Parker-Hall, in his turn, drones on about how much he values their input or something.

I lean across the table to the cutest girl here – a blonde in her mid-twenties, denim jacket, small tits perky beneath a tight vintage Rolling Stones T-shirt – and whisper 'Hey . . .'

'Mmmm?' she ducks towards me, smiling uncertainly.

'Wanna do a bump?'

'Sorry?'

'A bump? You wanna do a bump?

'Uh, whaddya mean exactly?'

'Do you want some bugle?

'Huh?'

Fucking hell. 'Gak? Racket, chang, beak, bag, nose?'

Nothing.

'Charlie?'

'Do you mean coke?' she says, her face scrunching, starting to look like someone's farted.

'Oh yeah.'

'No thank you.'

'Ah, come on . . .' I say playfully.

She shakes her head and resumes listening to one of her bosses who is talking about 'Madge'.

Fucking Shermans. They hit the Stairmaster, make a quick stop at Tofu World to pick up their lunch, and are at their fucking desks by 8 a.m. It makes you sick. Fuck you then, you dyke cow, I think.

By the time dessert appears I'm translucent with booze and coke and I'm drawing the odd glare from Parker-Hall. Leaning across the table to squeeze the last few drops from a bottle of Rioja, I tune into the old manager chick's conversation. She's talking about some slag she looks after – Marianne Faithfull? Joni Mitchell? Kate Bush? Some ancient munter or other – and how hard it is to get exposure, press or radio, for them in this day and age. What a disgrace this is, living legends that they are and all. 'It's a different story,' she says, 'when it's Clapton, or Rod Stewart, but for the women . . .' she trails off, shaking her (big) hair sadly.

'Well,' I say, reasonably, 'it does get harder for women as they get older.'

She turns towards me and through the booze and gak I see properly the angles of her spectacles, the sour, rock-critic cut of her dish.

'I beg your pardon?' she says, as if I'd just said, 'I've done your mother up the coal-hole, no lube.'

'Come on,' I say addressing the table now, 'it's a tough break in general, being a chick and getting older. Being a pop star? It's gotta be a nightmare.'

'Why would you say that?' she asks, genuinely curious. A bunch of people are listening now, out of the corner of my eye, shimmering, I see Parker-Hall looking my way, his cutlery suspended over his tart. (My entire meal has, of course, gone completely uneaten.) Fuck him. Why does he care what this miserable spunk-bucket thinks?

'Why on earth,' she continues soberly, 'should things be any different for a female musician than they are for a man?'

'I don't know,' I say, 'but they are.'

'Are you saying,' the dyke in the Stones shirt chips in, 'that older women in music should be afforded less opportunity for exposure and respect than men?'

'I'm not saying they should, but,' I gesture with my glass, suavely throwing red wine across the tablecloth, 'they fucking are.'

'Why do you think that would be?' The horn-rimmed spectacled sow asks patronisingly.

'Well,' I say, marshalling my argument, 'it's like, you don't mind seeing Jagger, or Bowie, fruiting about at fifty, do you? There's a certain . . . charm there. Or Clapton, he's just a muso, isn't he? You don't give a shit what he looks like. But, say, Debbie Harry at sixty?' A couple of people shake their heads, affecting disbelief at my cynicism. A cynicism they all share but are too reasonable (i.e. sober) to articulate. Fuck this, I think. In for a penny . . . 'Cher,' I continue, 'at seventy? Playing keepy-uppy with her fucking jugs? Cunt like a wizard's sleeve? Face like a melted bucket of concrete? Fuck that.'

There's a gasp. Literally a gasp. The manager woman looks like she's about to cry. 'What . . . what,' she says banging the handle of her fork on the table, sending shreds of pastry flying, 'what about women who're still producing important, artistically valid work? Nanci Griffith? Emmylou Harris? Chrissie Hynde?'

'Come on,' I say good-naturedly, 'who really wants to want to fuck any of those cows?'

There's a bunch of shouting – I think she actually tries to hit me – and then Parker-Hall is helping me up and we're out on the street, the cool night air of Soho washing my face as he shouts for a cab.

Americans, I reflect as some Paki drives me back to the hotel, they're so fucking *serious*.

*

Morning manages to find a crack in the heavy drapes and comes crawling across the bed, waking me up. The TV is still on. The adult channel, obviously. I groan and engage the memory banks, fast-forwarding through the previous evening: drinking in the room, cab, gig, drinking, cab, chang, another bar, drinking . . . the restaurant, after that, nothing. Wait a minute, the restaurant. Go back. My leg gives an involuntary twitch, a physical spasm of pain as I freeze-frame on an image from last night: the manager chick's face, twisted in disgust. Bad, something pretty bad happened.

I'm just finishing up a spectacular bout of vomiting (and noticing that I seem to have managed an even more outstanding – and exotically placed – example during the night: the shower stall looks like someone has dumped a tub of dog food in it) when there's a knock at the door. Blanket-wrapped and trembling, a ball of wet Kleenex in my fist I press a watery eye to the spyhole. There's some old Latino chick there, housekeeping or something. 'Come back later,' I shout.

I collapse back onto the bed, scrabbling with the Advil bottle. She keeps on knocking. These fucking people.

Angrily I pull the door open – the abuse already fully formed in my lungs, barrelling up towards my mouth – and it all happens very fast. A short, stocky woman sweeps into the room (hung-over as I am, I get a strong reek of booze from her), throws her raincoat off, and sits down on the edge of my bed, crossing her white-stocking-clad legs. 'You call for a date, honee?' Eh?

'What?' I say. 'What fucking date? Look, I think you've got the wrong room.'

'Room 335?'

'Umm . . .' I look at the TV screen, now showing an ad for 'Co-Ed Foxes', allegedly 'Manhattan's finest escort service'. 'We visit you,' the voice on the ad says, 'day or night.'

'You are Steeeven, yes?' She leers drunkenly, revealing a battered row of teeth so viciously bucked that, for a second, I think she's slipped a chunk of comedy orange peel into her mouth for a laugh. As an ice-breaker.

Looking past her I see the credit cards and the scrawled scraps of paper by the phone. Understanding, memory breaks in on me as I remember making the call a few hours ago before I passed out.

'Right,' I say, taking her in properly now: a buck-toothed dwarf in her late forties, her stomach a crenellated apocalypse of porridgy stretch marks. Graveyard shift. 'Sorry, I've changed my mind. Can you just . . . how much for you to just leave?'

'Full charge, three hunner dollar.'

'Fuck off. I'll give you fifty.'

She leaps up. 'You pay me! You pay now or I go downstairs and get my driver. I go get Ramirez!' Fucking Americans, so serious.

'OK, fucking hell!' I sigh fishing my wallet out and handing over the bills.

'Thanks, honee,' she says, rubbing up against me, friendly enough now she's got the fucking dollar, 'you sure you no want me to stay? I know we can have a good time,' she says huskily into my face. I don't know what she had for breakfast. Pilchards in garlic semen chased down with a mug of gasoline maybe? Her hand flashes through the sheet

I'm wrapped in and starts massaging my bare prick. A good time? To recap: she's an ancient Latino beast, pissed out of her mind, with a mouthful of Stanley knives and breath like a summer fish factory . . .

. . . who turns out to have an incredibly skilful way with a handjob. (I abandoned the blow job after an exploratory sixty seconds of fretful, white-knuckle gobbling. You'd be more relaxed with your cock in the maw of a ravenous Alsatian.) It only takes her about two minutes – all the time she's shouting 'CUM! CUM FOR MY BIG TITTIES!' while, with her free hand, vigorously working a small dildo into my rectum – before I start to shudder and buck. She pulls down her grimy bra and her burst jugs spill down to her stomach. 'CUM! CUM ON MY BEEG TITTIES!' she screams. I swallow hard against the spiralling nausea and unload a wad of spunk all over her.

I collapse onto the bed, foetal with shame, while she gets busy with the Kleenex. 'You feel better now, baybee?' she says, giving me a playful smack on the arse as she staggers towards the bathroom.

I bury my head under the pillow, groaning, and only hear the knocking dimly at first. By the time I leap up the crazy bitch is already tugging the door open.

Parker-Hall stands there looking clean, sober and rested in a crisp white shirt and jeans. Slowly he takes it all in: me, halfway across the room, naked and sweating, trying to cover my half-erect cock with a T-shirt, and the beast, forty-odd years and two hundred pounds of stinking Colombian whore with blobs of spunk still glistening here and there on the ruins of her tits and her stretch-marked stomach. A few feet away from Parker-Hall, directly in his line of vision, the shit-streaked dildo stands proudly on top the minibar. I notice for the first time that a yellow stud of sweetcorn I don't recall eating is stuck to its tip. The room must smell bad.

She grins at him. 'You his fren? You wanna join us eet's extra.'

'I'll see you at the airport,' Parker-Hall says and then he's gone.

We meet again in the BA executive lounge at Kennedy a few hours later. I'm sitting reading *Billboard* and sipping a quadruple Bloody Mary when Parker-Hall strides in. He gets himself an orange juice and sits down next to me.

'Look, Tony, I –' It's as far as I get.

'Listen,' he says, 'this has gone far enough. I don't give a fuck what you do on your own time, but last night you made an utter cunt out of us in front of the American label and it has to stop.' He looks at me coldly. I am dying here. 'I think you might need help,' he adds.

'Help?'

'With the drinking and the coke.'

'Oh come on,' I say, 'I was just taking the piss. She was a pompous old –'

'She's Ashley Werner's fucking *wife*.'

Shit. 'Look,' I say, 'we haven't been working together long –'

'Listen, mate,' he says sharply, cutting me off, 'we might as well get this straight. We aren't "working together". You work *for* me. And as long as you fucking are working for me you'd better shape up. Right? You sign a few fucking hits and then you can get off your nut at dinner and take the piss out of whoever you want because, I'm telling you, you're on thin ice, Steven. Thin fucking ice.'

With that he drains his glass and strides off across the lounge, out through the opaque glass doors, and disappears into the busy terminal.

He's right. This has definitely gone far enough.

I get back to London early the following morning – Parker-Hall and I sat well away from each other on the flight, we avoided each other through the plastic tunnels of Heathrow and took separate cabs in the wet dawn – and get into bed. I don't get out of it for a week.

I call Rebecca. 'A fever,' I tell her and she offers to come over. 'No,' I say.

She cancels meetings and I crumple back down beneath the duvet where I sleep feverishly for short stretches, often waking screaming from terrible dreams: there are dreams where Trellick and I are working in a concentration camp, butchering babies, dreams where I am being raped by a handicapped man, dreams where I am standing on the top of Centre Point watching a shower of nuclear missiles – thousands of them – falling over London, dreams filled with sly, grinning dogs with hypodermics for teeth, dreams where I am married to Rebecca and our babies are crawling all over me and the babies have no eyes, dreams where I cradle Waters' body while I reach into the hole in his skull, almost up to my elbow, scraping around in there for a long time before finally pulling my bloody arm out and seeing that I am holding a fistful of tiny silver statuettes: little Brit Awards, each one the size of a jelly baby.

I wake up screaming – the only light in the room coming

from the TV screen; either a fizz of static or a hardcore shot, as I almost always have a pornographic film on. I watch the video of Annabel Chong fucking three hundred guys five or six times a day. Over and over she pumps and sucks and grinds. Over and over semen is sprayed across her face, belly, breasts and bum. I watch a scene where she upends a used condom over her mouth and greedily slurps down the contents perhaps a hundred times, my thumb shuttling numbly between the play and the rewind. I watch the Rape Tape repeatedly: a compilation Ross had some guy at an edit suite knock up for him; basically all the classic rape scenes from modern cinema – *The Accused*, *Straw Dogs* (is it or isn't it up the Ronson?), *Salvador* (nuns – awesome), *Leaving Las Vegas*, *Clockwork Orange*, *I Spit On Your Grave*, *Thelma and Louise* (well, the bloke nearly gets in there before the dyke shoots him) – spliced onto one video. We wondered about the possibility of selling it commercially. I reckon there's a market but Trellick said you'd have too many clearance and distribution problems.

Every few hours I ring for food and a guy – some gook, some dago – will come to the door with Chinese, Thai or pizza.

Between meals I dry-swallow Valium.

I cry a lot.

A few days into this – having smoked nearly the entire two cartons of cigarettes I brought back from America and needing to freshen my crackling stack of overused hardcore – I try to go the corner shop and find that I cannot leave the house.

So I stay in bed, my hair greasy, my fingernails encrusted with filth, rancid semen-cracked tissues balled up all over the bedroom, overflowing ashtrays teetering on piles of unwashed clothes, waxy pizza boxes and fungal takeaway cartons littered across the floor.

I have been reduced to the bare fundamentals of human existence: eating, smoking and wanking.

Somewhere around the end of the week I am crumpled in a corner of the living room, naked, when I begin to have, well, epiphany is a very strong word, but I'm thinking about all the wrong, all the evil I've done. I'm haunted by an image of Waters' mother at his funeral – trembling her way along the aisle, emitting that crazed, inhuman *woooohooo* sound. Maybe it could be undone. Some kind of atonement? I'm looking at the Karma Bank and it's bad. It's fucking bad. It's like looking at one of my own bank statements; the tumbling, unreal zeros, DR stamped everywhere. Debit, debit, debit. Maybe if . . . if I stop. Change. Do good. Charity. Join the VSO and go and work abroad, nursing swollen-bellied babies, helping African villagers rebuild, I don't know, a dam or something? I could volunteer for spoon-feeding lukewarm soup to skeletal pensioners, or going around the underpasses and subways of central London on January nights, handing out sandwiches and blankets, tucking in freezing derelicts, my only reward being allowed to bask for a moment in the warmth of their grateful smiles. I could move to the country and raise children, try to live happily on the other side of the Prodigy sleeve, the side with the green fields and the smiling people.

The phone rings. Or rather, I become aware of its ringing. It might have been ringing for two days. I crawl across the floor towards it and watch it with dread: six, seven rings and then the machine clicks on.

'Hi . . . Steven? Uh, it's Barry from club promotions. Listen, I need to speak to you. I don't know if you . . .'

I pour a litre of Evian over my head, breathe in deeply a few times, pick the phone up and croak, 'Barry?'

'Oh, you're there. Christ, you sound like fucking shit, mate!'

'Yeah. Flu or something.'

'I've been trying to get hold of you, your mobile's off. Anyway, what are you doing Saturday night?'

'What? Why?'

'You won't believe this . . .'

And Barry tells me first good news I've heard in a long, long time.

'Oh my fucking God,' Trellick says from the back seat, 'will you look at this . . .' We turn a corner and come onto what I guess is the high street. It's eleven thirty on a Saturday night and the tolers – hundreds of them – are doing what they do up North: an overweight girl wearing a thong, a boob tube and high heels is vomiting over a Keep Left sign. A bunch of lads are pissing against a shopfront in full view. Another girl lies unconscious on her back in the gutter, her skirt hauled up and her tights shredded, a bottle of some demented alcopop, some estate juice, still clutched in her hand. 'Are those . . . *chips?*' Ross asks. The four of us squint. As far as you can see, for a few hundred yards in front of us, the air is filled with flying chips, bags of them being hurled upwards as dozens of fights break out. A kid staggers in front of the Saab, blood pouring from a cut in his forehead. He's pulled off the road and disappears under a flurry of fists and kicks as three blokes pile back in, kicking the shit out of him. A handful of chips spatters off the car and I put the foot down.

'Welcome to Rotherham,' Barry says laughing.

'Should have left the car at the fucking hotel,' I say.

The club is a giant metal hangar on the outskirts of town. From the outside it could be a bowling alley, an ice rink, a swimming pool. The giveaways are the dull whump of bass coming from inside and the angry mob fighting to get in. A clutch of bouncers, all in black bomber jackets, all with little earpieces in, stand at the top of the stairs, chewing gum. Their faces are blank, mongoloid. We hang back and Barry talks to one while the tolers of Rotherham look at us strangely – in our dark jeans and black and navy cashmere V-necks. We're the only guys not wearing untucked knock-off Ralph Lauren shirts in head-splitting iridescent shades of lemon, violet and turquoise. It is almost freezing and we're the only people wearing coats.

Finally, with some grunting into headsets and gruff 'excuse mes', a two-bouncer escort is moving us through the throng, the velvet rope is lifted and we're being escorted along a stickily carpeted hallway towards the music by some guy called Steve, the promoter I guess. He seems very pleased to have some London industry types in his shithole. 'You'll 'ave a fooking good crack tonight, lads. The birds in here? Un-fooking-believable, like. We had that FFRR mob up here a while back. Pete Tong's lot, you know 'em?' Barry fields the loser's questions as the music grows louder and louder.

'Here we go, best cloob in't North,' Steve says as he throws a set of double doors open and we bowl right into Hades: two thousand bikini-clad girls and Teflon-shirted

Northern arguments for mass sterilisation are going fucking bananas to some awful cheesy house record. The DJ is suspended high above the crowd in what looks like a metal egg. He is wearing a baseball cap with a giant foam cock-and-balls on top of it. I'm not fucking kidding. Steve the promoter grins proudly.

'Wow,' Trellick says.

'I say we take off and nuke the entire site from orbit,' Ross whispers.

We get given a table in their 'VIP' section: actually a tiny bar roped off to one side of the club with a few fag-burned, booze-stained sofas dotted around. It's rammed with what can only be local VIPS – hairdressers and third division footballers. A few of the boilers are doable in an utterly disgraceful filth kind of way.

'It's grim up North,' Ross says laughing as he opens the bottle of Moët Steve has proudly placed on our table.

We make the best of a terrible situation, talking crap, chatting up girls, draining bottle after bottle of complimentary pooey and ducking down to sneak surreptitious card-edges of chang.

It's nearly 2 a.m. – everyone in the place is *incandescent* with booze: boiled on Stella, Breezers, vodka Red Bulls and speed and Es and all the other terrible crap the penniless spastics in places like this shovel into themselves – when I hear a familiar drum loop and a breathy female vocal. 'Come on,' Barry says, pulling me after him as we head out into the club proper. Packs of girls are charging towards the dance floor, pushing us aside. Guys follow them. Whoops and cheers are going up. Trellick and I look at each other. Then the track kicks in properly.

The whole place goes fucking *ballistic*. We watch open-mouthed. Every girl in the place knows all the words. Dozens of them are doing this funny little dance. It is, without doubt, the biggest reaction to a record I have witnessed in a super-toler nightclub since we all heard 'Saturday Night' by Whigfield for the first time, in some cattle market outside Marbella a few years back. Barry appears, sweating and drunk through the crowd. 'What did I tell you?' he shouts over the Dex and Del Mar remix of 'Fully Grown' by Songbirds.

Ross charges up. 'They've got a dance!' he screams. 'They've got their own fucking dance!'

'Maybe it's just this club . . .' I say.

'Bollocks,' Barry shouts, 'I was in Leeds last weekend. Glasgow too. *It's like this everywhere!*'

Trellick slips an arm around my shoulder, 'This, matey boy,' he says gesturing towards the music, the tolers, all of it, 'is going to be *a fucking smash*,' and then the four of us are dancing a jig, holding our champagne flutes on top of heads and laughing so hard that tears are running down our faces.

Immediately – and without consulting Parker-Hall or Derek – I authorise Barry to *treble* the club mailout. To get the record to every cock-and-balls-on-the-head DJ in the country, to every Ritzy-Cinderella-Rockafeller piece-of-shit, stab-you-in-face-with-a-broken-Beck's-bottle nightclub from Land's End to John O'-fucking-Groats.

Because I got blindsided, didn't I? Sidetracked by detail and nonsense I lost sight of the big picture. Only one thing matters in this racket: Big. Hit. Records. And plenty of them. Sort that out and you can do what you fucking like.

Back at the hotel I turn it all over in my head –

Woodham, Waters, Rebecca, Parker-Hall — and the same question keeps coming back. How far? How far can you go? I root through my bag, take out the dog-eared copy of Hauptman's *Unleash Your Monster* and flip back and forth until I find the passage. *'In every difficult, worthwhile endeavour there will come a point when the easiest course of action is to abandon forward motion, to allow inertia to take over and to return to the status quo. It is the brave and great man who, upon recognising this point, resists inertia and smashes on through to the far side. No matter the cost. I call this juncture the critical moment of will.'*

I underline the last four words several times.

Payback time.

I take Rebecca out to dinner at an obscure Sudanese restaurant to discuss our 'wedding'. Rebecca does most of the talking and I do a lot of nodding. 'We can announce it,' I say grandly, 'at the company Christmas party.'

'*Yeah!*' she coos, excitedly — doubtless imagining all her tunnel-cunted, doomed-to-childlessness, thirty-something secretary friends shimmering with envy as she waltzes around showing off the ring — and continues blathering about arrangements for her wedding that will never happen.

'. . . in gold, or ivory, and then there's place settings, and napkin rings and the like to think about . . . possibly Claridge's — or Babington — but I suppose we'd need to book the whole place out, and then there's the question of how late you can go on . . . DJs or band? Oh! Maybe we could get . . .'

It occurs to me that this is why boilers like Rebecca want

to get married so much – it is the ultimate organisational hard-on.

Earlier today I called Woodham. Without preamble I said, 'Do you want the good news or the bad news?'

'Bad news first,' he says.

'Well, the deal isn't huge and it's with a pretty small publisher.'

'What deal?'

'Your publishing deal.'

A pause while he takes this in. 'Seriously?' he says finally.

'Congratulations,' I say.

'You got me a publishing deal?'

'Yup.'

This was almost true. Having been laughed out of town by every real publisher in the business I rang Benny Gold.

Benny's an old-school has-been who copped the publishing on a couple of big novelty records in the seventies. He's made a little money on property since then but, like a lot of old-school fools, he likes to reckon himself still 'in the business'. He runs a tiny publishing company called Cloudberry Music: going to MIDEM every year and scratching around for deals no one else wants. He's a nice loser, the kind of guy you end up getting pissed with in the Barracuda – hundred-franc notes and whores all over the shop.

The deal I make with Benny is straightforward enough. I will personally sink twenty grand into Cloudberry to become a sleeping partner. I'll then punt acts his way, give him tips on hot bands and stuff. In return Benny agreed to make Alan Woodham our first joint signing (Benny's nearly sixty, he thinks Joe Jackson is a hot new artist, he had no idea if the demo was good, bad, or whatever) and to pay him an advance of ten grand out of my twenty K seed money. The only other condition I imposed was that Woodham never knows I'm involved in the company. He must think the whole thing was Benny's idea. Under the deal we have to pay Woodham five grand of the advance on signature and I max out my overdraft writing the cheque for this. I am up to the hilt on the cards. I am teetering right on the fucking brink, no question.

Woodham is beyond excited. 'How much?' he stammers.

'The advance is only ten grand, but –' I begin.

'Really?' he says, excited, and I have to remind myself that this is probably half his annual salary.

'Yeah. Sorry, but –'

'Oh fuck the money,' he babbles, cutting me off, 'all I ever wanted was a chance.'

Woodham is thinking about fame and success. I am thinking – will this be enough?

'Alan,' I said, my knuckles whitening around the phone, 'about this neighbour of mine who saw me coming home early the morning Roger was murdered.'

A pause while he adjusts to the twist in the conversation. 'When you went out early to get a newspaper?'

'Yeah, but, well, am I in trouble here?'

'Why would you be in trouble for that?'

'I just thought, when we spoke about it on the phone the other week, you sounded a bit . . . pissed off.'

'No.'

'So everything's OK? We're good? I mean, you don't think . . .'

'We're fine, Steven.'

And I want to believe him. I really do.

'Oh no!' Rebecca says suddenly, looking up at me, her fork suspended halfway to her mouth. 'That won't work, will it?'

'What won't?'

'Announcing it at the Christmas party.'

'Why not?'

'Darling, your memory! I won't be here, remember? I told you, I'm going to see my parents. I leave on the first and I'm not back until the new year. Bugger!'

She had told me. Rebecca – like me – is an only child. Her parents live in Melbourne. It's their anniversary soon and she's taking a month off, to fly out unannounced and surprise them. I think quickly. 'Tell you what . . . tell you what. You know I'm going to Thailand with the lads on the 15th?'

She nods eagerly.

'Why don't I cut it short with them and come to Australia for Christmas? I can meet your parents and we can tell them together? I mean, thinking about it, we should keep it under wraps until then, shouldn't we? Your parents should really be the first to know.'

She looks at me in gaping, wide-eyed adoration. 'Sweetie, that's a *marvellous* idea! I'll look into flights in the morning for you. Bangkok to Melbourne. Oh, you'll love my dad!'

She starts talking about her dad, about how funny he is, how laid-back he is, and it's good because now I don't have to listen any more. I can think. I'm thinking – this could actually work out really well. But there are questions. At the flat? Or a hotel suite? And just how hardcore is Woodham? How much does he want it? I think about all this as I push rice around my plate and Rebecca talks on in the background. She's saying, '. . . and you don't want a stretch limo, *so* tacky, but maybe a Lincoln Town Car, we can use Addison Lee for the guests and if we . . .'

As she talks I look up into her face, which is lit a soft orange from a candle which is floating and glittering in a bowl of water in the middle of our table. Rebecca's eyes are bright green. They are glittering too – the zinging glitter of utter madness.

November

Michael Hutchence tops himself in some demented wanking frenzy. The Teletubbies are no. 1. Chris Evans buys Virgin Radio. Martin Heath is fired from Arista. A&R guy Jono Cox is given a label deal by Deconstruction/BMG on the strength of this band he's signed called Superstar. He says, 'This is very much a long-term relationship.'

'Whatever it takes . . .'

Casablanca Records motto

Woodham signs his publishing deal. He takes the day off and I take him to the Groucho for lunch.

We're barely into the second bottle of Perrier Jouet when he starts coming out with all the crazy shit they all come out with – '. . . things are gonna happen now . . . I've been trying so hard for so long . . . all I needed was a break . . .' At one point he even starts talking about the 'craft' of songwriting. You what? I think. You're a twenty-eight-year-old *copper.*

As I upend the second empty champagne bottle into the ice bucket and signal the waitress (the cute one I always overtip) for a third, I ask him about his kids. He goes misty-eyed and starts blathering on like they all do, thinking that you give a shit about the howling brats they've conjured up out of some sloppy fuck. He talks on while I think about house prices and money and remixes and chart positions and stuff. I catch the odd phrase – '. . . such a clever little boy . . . takes after her mother . . . the thing about being a parent . . .' Fucking spare me.

'Do you plan on having kids, Steven?' he asks me finally.

'Oh, definitely,' I say. Then, quickly, I add, 'Do you want some fucking chang?'

He doesn't understand so I explain, employing a more widely used noun. There's a pause.

'Here?' he says, glancing around the half-empty bar.

Downstairs into the little bathroom with the little stack of books in it and soon I'm watching the detective constable snort up an icy line of very decent cocaine.

Of course the downside to this is that I soon have to listen to the cunt talking an *incredible* amount of balls: how much he owes me; how, in ten years, I was the first A&R guy to give his music a chance; how he gets laughed at by the other coppers for persisting with his dream in his spare time; how they call him 'Noel'; how his – now dead – father never understood his drive to make music. 'He told me it was a waste of time,' Woodham says sadly, and suddenly I feel a great surge of affection for his dad, for old man Woodham, sagely telling his worthless son what they should all be told really – '*Get a fucking job, you stupid cunt.*'

We're literally a breath away the same story about how he fell off his bike when he was nine when I interrupt him. 'Listen, Alan,' I say, swallowing and slapping on my gravest expression, 'now we're getting to be . . . well, friends, I suppose . . .'

He nods eagerly and with utter conviction, the coked-up, brain-dead fool.

'There's something I've been wanting to talk to you about but . . . it's difficult. I . . .' I trail off.

'What?'

'Christ, I . . .'

'Come on, mate,' he says, his jaw is set at a mad gak-angle and I am pretty sure he will believe anything I am about to tell him.

'It's just, when you were talking about how much you loved your kids earlier . . . it got me thinking. Oh God . . .'

'Steven,' Woodham says, setting his drink down, putting a hand on my shoulder, 'what is it?'

I wait for a long time, looking like I'm really weighing it up, before I say, 'There's this guy at work . . .'

I tell him.

He sits there for a long time. He looks very angry. Finally he says, 'Are you sure about this, Steven?'

'Pretty sure. Things he's said, when he's drunk.'

'Right. What's his name?'

I spell it for him.

'I'm going to make a phone call. Right now.' he says, pulling his mobile out.

'No phones in the club, Alan.'

'Oh, right.' He sways off towards reception, dialling as he goes.

Afternoon drinking blurs into evening drinking and I take Woodham on a whirlwind blitz of the West End; from the Groucho to Soho House to Black's to the Two Bridges club before cabbing it up to Hyde Park Corner, to the Met Bar.

It's Friday night and the place is *rammed*. Scary Spice has a big corner table with a gang of minders and shrieking drunken mates. Jay Kay from Jamiroquai is on the dance floor, wheeling about like a fruit. For some reason all the male members of the cast of *Friends* are hunkered around one of the central banquettes. We elbow our way in at the bar and Woodham stands there, bathed in the light from the backlit spirits bottle – the golden glow of the Scotches, the emerald of the gins, the platinum white of the vodkas – taking it all in, astonished. 'Shit,' he whispers out the corner of his mouth, nudging me, 'that's James Dean Bradfield, from the Manic Street Preachers.' I look down the bar to see that Bradfield is indeed buying a round a few feet along from us.

'Oh yeah, you a fan then?' I say, cracking a credit card down.

'God, not half.'

Jesus wept. Bradfield comes through the crush beside us, heading for his table. 'Hey James,' I say, extending my hand. He shakes it and it takes him a couple of seconds.

'All right . . . Steve? How you doing, mate?'

'Good, thanks. Out on the town?'

'Ah, me and the Hedgemeister just came out for a couple.' He indicates Mike Hedges across the room, the man-mountain who produced the last Manics album. 'Too middley,' Waters had said. Waters' tongue, the tongue he had used to say those senseless words – and millions more – lying on the floor next to the Nick Hornby novel. While Bradfield and I exchange pleasantries Woodham is twitching and shuffling spastically, begging to be introduced.

'James, this is Alan.'

'All right mate?' Bradfield says, extending his hand to Woodham. Woodham shakes it reverently and then he slurs the following. Oh yes he does.

'It's an honour to meet you, Mr Bradfield. I have to say, I think you're an amazing guitarist.'

I close my eyes but Bradfield just laughs it off. 'Ah bollocks,' he says. 'Have a good night, lads.' And he's off.

A sour-faced bumboy materialises behind the bar.

'What can I get you?'

Woodham dives in. 'I'll get this.'

'No, my treat tonight Alan.'

'No, you've been buying all the drinks. My turn.'

'OK. Double vodka and tonic.'

'Same for me please.'

The guy goes off to fix the drinks. Woodham leans into me and says, 'I suppose that wasn't very cool, was it? With James just then.'

'Ah, don't worry about it. I'm sure he gets it a lot.'

'I had to tell him.'

'Sure.'

'How do you know him?'

How did I know him? I didn't really. 'Oh, just from around, you know.'

Woodham nods and says, 'It's another world.'

The virus carrier returns with the drinks, which come in huge, heavy ice-packed tumblers. Woodham holds a tenner out and the barman looks at him like he's lost his fucking mind. Woodham reaches into his wallet and upgrades to a twenty, which still isn't going to cut it. 'I'll be back in a minute,' I say and head for the toilet for a bump, leaving the barman talking Woodham through the bill.

When I come back ten minutes later Woodham is still blinking at the receipt.

It's midnight when we get back to my place and Woodham is *hammered*.

We're sat on high stools at the granite kitchen counter which separates my kitchen area from the living room. On the worktop between us is a CD case (*Give 'Em Enough Rope*, which we are listening to, Woodham's choice) with a mound of gak on it, my Amex, a rolled fifty, a bottle of Stoli, a bottle of tonic, a half-full ice bucket, some sliced limes and two heavy crystal tumblers. Woodham is getting a bit giggly now, possibly feeling the effect of the half E I ground into his first drink almost an hour ago. (I thought it best to slip him small and gradual doses.) 'I *love* this song,' says Woodham, leaping off his stool and stumbling over towards the massive speakers. He turns it up.

My mobile rings and I look at the screen. Rebecca. Bang on time. 'Hi there,' I drawl.

'Hello, sexy,' she giggles, 'are you home yet?'

It's Rebecca's last night in London before she goes to Australia, to surprise her parents on their anniversary. She wanted us to spend it together but I told her I had a couple of gigs and a meeting. Why didn't she go out with the girls and we could meet up later at my place? Have a late supper? She could stay the night and I'd drive her to Heathrow in the morning. She thought this was very sweet of me.

'I'm a bit tipsy and feeling very naughty . . .' she giggles. She sounds smashed beyond human belief. Sen-say-shunal.

'Really?' I say. 'Get your arse in a cab then.'

'Do you need anything? What's that racket?'

'Ah, I've got a mate here. He'll be leaving soon. Oh, you could get some champagne. That place on the Harrow Road will still be open. I'll pay you back when you get here.'

'Mmmm, lovely. OK, sweetie, see you in twenty. Big kiss, Mwwah.'

I hang up and watch Woodham, who is swaying in the

middle of the room, eyes closed, as he plays air guitar along to the Clash. What a fucking loser.

Later, in the bedroom, I look up at Woodham and he looks back at me. The look on his face is an incredible cocktail of expressions: joy, terror, pleasure, embarrassment, confusion, shame, panic, hilarity, disbelief . . . they're all fighting for position. I look down, at Rebecca's naked rump, at my cock appearing then disappearing into her, at the back of her head, her dirty-blonde hair bobbing as it moves rapidly up and down over Woodham's crotch. Rebecca is on all fours on my bed with Woodham and I positioned at either end of her in classic double-ender stylee.

Don't get me wrong, it wasn't easy to pull this off. It took *two fucking hours.*

Rebecca had been a little surprised when she toppled in the door – pulling her little trolley-suitcase behind her, and carrying two bottles of champagne (fucking Moët) – to see Woodham there. But only a little. I'd mentioned a few times that I'd been seeing a bit of him, and she knew I'd demoed his songs. Woodham, pilled up, drunk, chang'd and randy, had been *delighted* to see Rebecca.

The three of us did more coke. We had drinks and danced around to disco records. After an hour or so of this I convinced both of them that we should all do an E (*'it's Friday night for fuck's sake!'*). I took an aspirin while Rebecca necked her first pill and Woodham chucked a whole one back on top of the one and a half I'd already slipped him.

More drinking, dancing and coke until, an hour later, the

three of us are stretched out on the big sofa, Rebecca in the middle.

'It's . . . another fucking world,' Woodham says, gazing around at the flat, his pupils like manholes as he takes in the gorgeous girl, the drugs and empty champagne bottles, the evening meeting pop stars. The kind of life he thought he might have when he was a guitar-strumming nineteen-year-old? Woodham told me he lives in Forest Gate with the hag and kids. I nodded, but I do not know where Forest Gate is.

'Listen,' Rebecca says, taking Woodham's hand, her jaw juddering, 'if Steven believes in your music then it's got to be good. He's got the most *amazing* taste.'

I smile, allowing the compliment.

'I know,' Woodham says, looking like he might cry. 'C'mere, mate . . .' He lurches towards me. Oh Christ. Woodham hugs me passionately. 'I fucking love you,' he says into my neck.

'Hey,' says Rebecca, as she squeezes in and the three of us hug. Woodham – almost delirious now – buries his face in her cleavage and makes moaning noises. Rebecca shrieks delightedly. I leave them rolling around on the sofa and tool over to the breakfast bar, to the mirror where I've prepared three big, chunky lines. The three lines are near identical, except for the fact that one of them is simply cocaine while the other two are a brain-rupturing blend of 70 per cent pure ketamine and 30 per cent cocaine. I snuffle up the coke-only line. 'Here,' I say turning back to the sofa, holding out the mirror.

A few moments later Rebecca is lying back in my lap, her eyeballs vibrating gently. I've freed one of her breasts from her dress and am slowly massaging the dark brown nipple while Woodham watches stupefied. I mean, he's foaming at the fucking mouth.

'Shall we adjourn?' I say thickly and I lead the two of them into the bedroom, carefully stepping over the broken champagne bottle which lies on the floor at the foot of the bed.

So, here we are. The three of us are buckled and sweating and exhausted in a heap on my bed, the detective constable having just sprayed a goodly load all over my 'fiancée's' breasts and chin. 'Oh God,' Rebecca says, giggling and dabbing at herself with a Kleenex, 'how did this happen?'

'Holy shit,' says Woodham.

'Go get us some more drinks, Alan,' I say.

'Uh, sure. Vodka and tonic?' I nod and he stumbles off, leaving us alone.

'I love you,' Rebecca says.

'I love you too,' I say, before adding, casually, 'could you pass me up that glass of water?'

She crawls to the edge of the bed, hangs over the side and reaches down. Somewhere down the hallway I can hear Woodham clattering around in the kitchen. Music – fucking Radiohead now – hums from the living room. '*Rain down . . .*'

I jump on top of Rebecca, pushing her down into the mattress, grabbing her hair and pulling her head back. 'Ooof! Gerrof!' she giggles, thinking I'm fucking around.

Critical moment of will.

With my free hand, I bring the thick, jagged stump of the Dom Pérignon bottle up hard and plunge it into the base of her throat, ripping it upwards towards her chin, feeling the flesh tear, feeling her larynx come apart. There's a terrible, flapping, sucking sound as she gasps and breathes in, the breath going into her body now through the fist-sized slash in her throat. It sounds like when the waste disposal gets blocked. Then she breathes out and a wash of syrupy blood sprays everywhere, all over the bed, the seagrass carpeting and the twelve-hundred-quid cherrywood cabinets from Heal's.

I throw her forward – naked – into the pool of her own blood and she writhes onto her back, kicking and thrashing, her hands scrabbling at her throat, trying to get hold of the stump of the bottle, which is jutting out of her neck like a mad, half-arsed tracheotomy. Apart from a frothy gurgle she makes very little noise, I guess because I've just slashed her voice box to pieces.

Hello, you.

Very quickly – the whole thing has taken less than a minute – her kicks start to subside, becoming little random jerks as her staring, incredulous eyes begin to glaze over, and I take off – running full pelt and blood-spattered down the corridor and screaming, *'Oh Christ! Alan! Alan! Help!'*

December

Big A&R buzz on Campag Velocet. The Spice Girls LP is certified as the biggest selling American release of the year. Nick Mander, an A&R guy at Epic, signs a band called Headswim. He says, 'We have been developing a strong reputation for breaking exciting new acts. Headswim can be the next one.'

'I'm all in favour of the Conservative values of personal responsibility, hard work and enjoying the fruits of your success.'

Geri Haliwell

London gets really cold and I develop a major thing for Natalie Imbruglia, this Aussie soap star whose debut single 'Torn' is all over the radio. Can she be fucked? I wonder. She's A&R'd by Mark Fox over at BMG who I don't really know. Cowell knows him though. Is it worth calling Cowell and testing the water? Nigel Godrich has worked with her. Is it worth giving him a bell? I think about the ins and outs of it a lot.

'Fully Grown' by Songbirds has been no. 1 on the club chart for two weeks now. Demand filtering in from the shops is starting to look huge and I've put the release date back to the week before Christmas. It's a gamble, but if it comes through . . .

I pull into the car park early, around half ten. There are two police cars parked close to the front door of our building. Two uniformed coppers come out of the entrance; the first one is carrying a computer monitor, the second has the keyboard balanced on top of the hard drive. As I lock the

Saab I watch them carefully loading the stuff into the boot of one of the squad cars, overseen by some older plain-clothes guy.

I stroll into marketing on the first floor. It's a morgue, no music playing, people sitting about in shock. 'Morning, all,' I say brightly, as I cross the open-plan space. I've been a bit of a god in marketing lately, a few of the girls have even put bets on Songbirds being the Christmas no. 1. But, this morning, I get no reaction beyond a couple of muted 'hellos'.

I stick my head around Ross's office door. He's on the phone, talking quietly. 'Listen, hang on,' he says as soon as he sees me, 'I'll have to call you back.'

'What's up with the coppers?' I say, strolling in.

He looks at me for a moment before asking, 'Have you been upstairs yet?'

'No, I just . . .'

'Shut the door and sit down.'

I do it.

'Strap yourself in,' Ross says standing up.

'For fuck's sake . . .'

'The police arrived about an hour ago, no one's been allowed to go up to A&R since then. We only know because Jeannie came down and told us. It's . . .' He stops, shaking his head in disbelief.

'For fuck's sake mate, *what is it?*'

'Parker-Hall's been arrested. They've found obscene images of children on his computer. I mean, proper hardcore stuff. Babies and shit like that.'

I let my jaw drop. 'You. Are. Fucking. Joking.'

'I swear to God, Steven. The cunt's a paedo.

*

So Woodham came crashing and stumbling down the hallway behind me. I stood aside and let him see. Rebecca, naked, dead and twisted in a mad heap, her green eyes staring and the green stump of the champagne bottle still jutting out of her throat, blood still pumping weakly over her brown freckled skin and trickling down her breasts and belly.

'Oh my God. Oh fucking Christ.'

'We were messing about, play-fighting. She . . . she fell off the end of the bed. The bottle . . .'

He inched towards her and extended two trembling fingers to the side of her neck. I picked up the phone and started to dial.

'What are you doing, Steven?'

'Calling an ambulance.'

'She's dead.'

'We need to –'

'Don't be fucking stupid.'

He took the phone from me and sat down. 'Fuck!' Woodham said. 'Fuck it!'

'We have to –'

'Think. I'm a policeman. We're off our heads. There's drugs all over the fucking place, she's full of them. We've both . . . do you know how this will look?'

'Oh Jesus. Oh Jesus, Alan.'

'Shhh. Let me think.'

I sat down on the bed and buried my face in my hands and pretended to cry while Woodham thought.

'Right,' he said, 'give me a hand. Wrap her up in this sheet and we'll, yeah, strip the bed. Here . . .'

Later I sat in my bathrobe, cradling a half-pint of Glenfiddich, chain-smoking and watching MTV with the sound turned way up, the ceaseless din of the videos – Jamiroquai with the floor moving under him (I wonder if we could get Jonathan Glazer to do the Songbirds video?), Pulp, Kula Shaker, Mansun – partially obliterating the sounds of sawing, splintering and hacking coming from the bathroom. Well, I reflected, the four hundred quid on that set of Japanese butcher's knives hadn't been completely wasted after all.

It took almost two hours for Woodham to cut Rebecca up into manageable sections (torso, hips, limbs and head) that would fit into my two biggest suitcases. We sat in silence for a while after he'd finished. Finally he looks at Rebecca's suitcase and turns to me, remembering something we must have been talking about earlier. 'She said she was going to Australia today?'

'Yeah.'

'To visit her parents, but it was a surprise? They don't know she's coming?'

'No.' I'm acting kind of numb.

'She must have her passport on her.'

'Yeah.' It was in her coat. I'd checked.

'How long was she going for?'

'Till the new year.'

'Right. Good.'

Then he got up, got showered and dressed and, just before the sun came up, we hauled the suitcases out to my car. I handed Woodham the keys. He said he had a place in mind and that it was probably best if I didn't know any more.

I watched Woodham drive off, the silver Saab disappearing towards the Harrow Road as the feeble sun came up. Then I walked back through to the bedroom. I picked the digital video camera up – its black eye had been peering through a crack in a pile of sweaters – and turned the little switch from 'record' to 'rewind' to 'play'. I had a decent shot of the naked, bloody Woodham saying, 'Think. I'm a policeman . . .' I put the camera in a drawer and went off to sleep in the spare room.

Remind me not to get sent to prison.

Trellick and I are sitting in the visiting room of Wormwood Scrubs waiting for Parker-Hall to appear and sipping plastic coffee from styrofoam cups. The room seems to be unchanged from the 1960s: brick walls gloss-painted in filthy white and brown, chipped Formica tables, those orange plastic seats with the holes cut out of the back.

And then there's the people – these lifetime losers and their broods. The dads sunk down into their striped pyjama-style prison shirts with their matted hair and stubble, wearily listening to the hags they married banging on about money and gossip, wondering which of their mates or neighbours is lumping it into her in their absence. The wives are, of course, something else entirely. At the top end of the scale there's a couple of council-estate readers' wives (a type I'm not *completely* averse to) *Razzle* rejects, bottle-blonde jobs in tight jeans and crop tops who look like they'd take you into a side room right now and break your cock off for forty quid. Down the bottom end of the market it's the twenty-stone thirty-year-olds who look sixty-five, women who look like they've had their cunts kicked in from dawn till dusk every single day of their lives since birth and who expected nothing else. The kind of women who, when their man looked up and told them 'before we get married you should know, darling – I'm a convicted rapist with a history of GBH who's wanted for armed robbery', replied 'let's do this fucking thing', and started cheerily humming 'Here Comes the Bride'.

Their kids sit sullenly, fidgeting, kicking their cheap supermarket trainers at the worn lino, headphones on, tinny drum'n'bass audible, all lost in their own little ragga worlds, already hatching their embryonic schemes for greatness: cashpoint muggings, ram raids, crack deals and lifting your Nokia at knifepoint. Everyone – even the kids, the babies in their tattered strollers – seems to be smoking roll-ups. I mean, roll-ups for fuck's sake. Where's your self-respect? You'd just quit, wouldn't you? (Then again, self-respect can't be too high on the agenda if you're in here for arse-fucking a struggling nine-year-old, for taking a chisel to a granny for eight and a half quid.) People are shouting at each other and banging the tables. Women are crying. The air is flinty with tension and barely suppressed rage. It reminds me of something. Business Affairs meetings. It reminds me of Business Affairs meetings.

I say we take off and nuke the entire site from orbit.

'Fuck,' Trellick whispers as Parker-Hall appears, shepherded over to us by a warden. He manages a cracked shaky grin as he sits down. Jesus Christ. He's only been here for three days and he looks *appalling*. There is a glassy terror in his eyes, like he's numb with horror, like he can't believe it's happening, and yet he's twitchy, nervy, like he knows it could all get much worse at any moment – the sharpened teaspoon in the dining hall, the ebony hand, black as a grand piano, on his shoulder in the showers.

'You know,' he asks us, head bowed, 'I didn't do anything. Don't you?'

'Course we do,' I say.

'No one believes it,' Trellick lies.

I slide across some magazines I've brought him – *Q*, *Uncut*, *Mojo*, *NME*. 'There's a good live review of the Lazies in there,' I say but he just stares at the magazines dumbly, perhaps feeling too keenly the distance between his old life and his current one.

'Why is this happening to me?' he says to no one.

'Listen,' Trellick says, using his best let's-get-a-grip-shall-we? Etonian voice as he counts off the positives on his fingers, 'a) you'll get bail next week, b) the company will pay it, whatever it is, and c) that was an old computer in your office. Christ knows who's used it over the years.' Trellick talks law for a bit, burden of proof, beyond reasonable doubt stuff.

'But what are people going to say?' Parker-Hall looks very small and very young now. He looks like he might cry.

'Listen, Tony, everyone at the label is behind you,' I say, 'and Derek's totally put a lid on discussing it outside the company. Don't worry, it's not going to get into any of the papers.'

Well, this wasn't strictly true. The first call I made when I left the meeting where Derek put a complete ban on discussing the Parker-Hall situation was to Leamington. His next call, as I knew it would be, was to one of his mates at *Music Week*. Front page next week. With a little luck, if they pick up on the man-who-discovered-Ellie-Crush angle, it will be all over the tabloids in time to coincide with Parker-Hall's release on bail.

'Thanks, guys,' he says to us, wiping his eyes.

'Don't be daft,' I say. 'You're a mate.'

Monica is telling Joey and Chandler off about something. She has her hands on her hips and her hair tied back. The tits are good and high in a tight black vest thing. I'd like to fuck Courtney Cox and idly wonder how the planets would have to align in order for this to be possible. (A huge hit record in the States? I'm on tour with the act, they're in LA playing the Hollywood Bowl, she comes backstage, David isn't there, she gets a little drunk, I'm being charming and 'English' . . .)

It's a Christmas episode; the girls' apartment has a huge tree in the corner and outside, through that big many-paned window, snow is – of course – gently falling on the sound-stage Manhattan. It's almost Christmas here in London too, but no snow. Rachel comes in looking really hot – tiny black skirt with black tights and knee-high leather boots. Yeah, forget Monica, Rachel – now there's a proper fuck-jar. The sound on the TV is off, I'm listening to rough mixes of tracks from the Songbirds LP, lying on the enormous sofa in my new house in Notting Hill, drinking Scotch and eating guacamole. The songs are mostly utter donkey. It doesn't matter. We're about to have a huge hit with 'Fully Grown' and we've got two more killer singles. I've even got one of Woodham's less offensive numbers on the LP, which should recoup the idiot's publishing advance and pay me back.

You should see the video for the single. It's incredible.

Annette, Kelly, Jo and Debbie – dressed as schoolgirls, as pubescent spunk-worshippers, as teenage cock addicts – throw themselves around a gymnasium in tight hardcore porno-choreography. Tanned and toned, rehearsed to death and sumptuously lit, they are a living, grinding-sucking-pumping monument to what can be achieved with crazed ambition and near unlimited funds and bear no resemblance whatsoever to the council-estate prostitutes who fidgeted in my office six months ago.

The girls have been reacting to their sudden success in the usual manner. There have been strops, walkouts and catfights. There have been tears and tantrums. Bulimia and bitching. Less believably they've taken to referring to themselves as 'artists' and voicing opinions about the kind of material they're being offered to sing. There are rumblings from Debbie about her songwriting ambitions. (If they really start selling some albums next year I'll probably have to start listening to some of this fucking nonsense. Jesus wept.) For the moment, however, it's fine. It's all manageable. They've worked hard; let them preen and strut and enjoy the short window they'll be afforded before they're spat out the other end. (Spat reeking into rehab and from there onto the daytime TV confessionals, the presenting jobs, the ghostwritten autobiographies – '*I always knew I was different from the other kids*' – and taking a good fucking kicking from their footballer husbands before drifting into middle-aged mega-obscurity.)

It's some rush, the process of having a hit record. A proper hit record, I mean. Not some stinking indie piece of shit that pops up on the midweeks at no. 12, drops to 17 by the Friday, and charts at 21 on Sunday. No. I mean *a proper fucking hit*: a record that slashes and burns its way in at no. 1 and then plants itself in the top five for weeks. A record that every lowlife toler, spod, pikey, uber, granny and foetus in the country is going to be singing for months to come. You turn on the radio, any station, and you hear it. You flip channels and you see the video. You go into a nightclub and every sour-cunted working-class sow in there is throwing herself around her fake designer handbag, smouldering Kensington in one hand, tumbler of vodka and sugar in the other, all doing some mad quasi-synchronised dance they've invented.

It's at moments like this that you genuinely feel like you've contributed to the culture in some way.

'Fully Grown' is now the most played record on Independent Local Radio. It's the third most played record on Radio 1, who, having blanked the single first time around, have sensed how huge a hit it's going to be and have come on board with a vengeance on the Dex and Del Mar remix.

Daily now Dunn sidles into my office. He joshes. He punches me on the arm and talks about football and fucking as he gives me updates about TV appearances and airplay. He even, over two beers after work, goes so far as to tell me how he knew right away that 'Fully Grown' would be a hit, it just needed a little time. A sleeper. He says he always had his doubts about Parker-Hall. His banter, his forced jocularity, has the desperate tang of a man trying to joke his way out the gas chambers, showing a card trick to the guards even as they're forcing him to strip and are sizing up his gold fillings.

He is a dead man and he knows it.

Through the glass wall at the end of my office the new temp Jo (twenty-five, great rack) taps away at her computer, sucking thoughtfully on a strand of her blonde hair. She treats me appropriately, which is to say she treats me like a god with a hangover. She doesn't know it yet, but in the new year, when Rebecca mysteriously fails to return from Down Under, she will be offered the job on a permanent basis.

Last week Derek invited me to a drinks thing over at his house, his virus pit. I declined, but still. He knows he backed the wrong horse. He knows that the industry perception is that he's the raving iron who hired a rampant paedo. To my surprise a lot of people haven't really needed all that much prompting to put together the desired equation. It's roughly something like this: queer + Internet access x cocaine = potential paedophile. We're having lunch together next Tuesday – right after the Songbirds midweek arrives – to discuss my new job.

He is going to pay.

A few hundred yards away on the Portobello Road people are already buying Christmas tree lights and wrapping paper. They're buying hot sausages with fried onions. My one present was bought some time back: tickets for my mother and her friend to go to the Caribbean for Christmas and New Year. It's a present that works both ways, as it means I won't even have to see her over the holidays, which is fortunate – I won't be here anyway.

Ross – that dickhead – strolls in and joins in the argument, taking the girls' side I think, and Joey and Chandler stomp off to their place, Chandler turning round and getting a good crack in before he goes. I wonder, not for the first time, about the viability of a series of pornographic *Friends* videos; filmed on a replica set, with quality lookalike actors and decent production values, although super-hardcore of course. *The One with All the Fisting . . . The One with Phoebe's Double Penetration . . . The One with the GHB and the Ben-Wa Balls . . .* You could even do a sideline for the faggots and the diesels – Joey and Chandler finally go for it, looking tenderly into each other's eyes, a thick rope of milky jizz connecting Chandler's mouth to Joey's twitching prick. Monica and Rachel in a long, rapturous 69. *The One with the Ten-Inch Strap-On.* Massive legal problems of course, you'd have to keep the whole operation untraceable, but I'm sure there's a huge market.

As someone who makes their living from anticipating, from shaping, the tastes of millions of tasteless morons, you have to tell yourself that the things you feel are universal, that the things you think and feel are thought and felt by millions of other people.

I turn the stereo off with the remote and lie back, looking up at the cream ceiling fifteen feet above me. Six months later than billed, and nearly a hundred grand over budget, Murdoch and the Albanians are finally gone. The room I'm in, the ground-floor living room, is really two rooms knocked into one. It is forty-four feet long and eighteen feet wide, narrowing to fourteen feet towards the back of the house. The huge windows overlook the corner of Basing Street and Lancaster Road. The only furniture in the room is the sofa, a massive hardwood coffee table, and a matt-black wall of TV, VCR and stereo equipment. I won't be here long. Shortly after I get back from holiday in mid-January I'm letting the place to a banker, some Sherman.

The monthly rental is absolutely horse-choking. Foxtons are handling everything.

Next year Trellick and I are looking to buy a bigger place together. Paint the whole gaff cream, seagrass matting throughout, chuck a couple of nice fireplaces in and sell it sharpish.

I top my glass up and wander over to the window. A couple of streets away, along Basing Street, left on Westbourne Park Road, right onto Ledbury Road, is Parker-Hall's place. It's on the market and stupidly overpriced. It would be pleasant to stand here – in this huge, warm, soon-to-be profitable room, with Glenmorangie fumes tickling my nose and tearing up my eyes – and picture him: shivering in the dark, turning over in his bunk to face the cold, brick wall, pulling the grimy pillow over his head to drown out the sound of his cell mate aggressively masturbating, but, sadly, the CPS wound up dropping the charges a few weeks later. Trellick was right; insufficient evidence. Still, there was comfort to be had.

The day after he made bail, the headline on page four of the *Sun* raged, 'PAEDOPHILE POP GURU!' Below two starkly contrasting photographs – one of Parker-Hall with his arm around Ellie Crush at the *Q* Awards and one of him being led into court by two coppers – the story continued, '. . . *the talent scout responsible for discovering multimillion-selling Brit winner Ellie Crush was arrested after police seized computers from his west London office. Detectives later found files containing HUNDREDS of depraved images of child pornography. Managing Director Derek Sommers, 45, confirmed today that Parker-Hall's recently signed employment contract was "under review"* . . .'

Parker-Hall's contract remained 'under review' until the *Star* ran with the story on the front cover the following day. Then it was terminated. Last week, after the charges were dropped, Parker-Hall took a flight to Canada. Apparently he's got relatives out there.

Another funny incident last week too . . .

Saturday night and we – me, Trellick, Ross, Darren, Desoto and a few waifs and strays – wound up, unusually, south of the river, in Club UK. Three a.m. and we were all separated, wandering around, pilled up, moving from room to room, checking out boilers. I was standing by the dance floor, swaying, pleasantly off my tits when I become aware of a black guy smiling at me. There was something familiar about him – beyond the usual they-all-look-the-same business I mean. He continued grinning and began nodding downwards, urging me to look too, his expression saying 'take a peek at this'. I followed his gaze down – half expecting to see a cock or something – and saw another black guy, his head at about waist height. In the dark and noise of the club it took me a few seconds to realise who it was. One side of his face was all screwed up – from the beating? from the brain haemorrhage that followed? – and one side was sort of loose and flabby. It looked like he was sucking a lemon with one half of his mouth and trying to blow bubbles with the other. Something chrome sparkled all around him in the dark. I looked up at the guy pushing him, recognising him now as the guy who kissed his teeth at me at the gig that night. 'It's Steven, ain't it?' he said.

'Yeah.'

'He wanted to say hello,' he nodded at the deformity in the wheelchair.

'Hello, Rage,' I said. Rage tried to say something but only managed to produce a frothy bubble of saliva.

''E don't tawk no good since his accident.'

I nodded. Rage beckoned me closer with a twisted, flopping hand. 'T . . .' he said.

I continued nodding, smiling indulgently, like you do at children and mongoloids. It dawned on me that Rage wasn't just a metaphorical mongoloid any more – he's the real fucking deal.

'T . . . tu . . .' he went on, producing a lot of spit, but starting to get somewhere, and now I noticed that the wheelchair wasn't some vamped-up custom job, with power steering and alloys. It was a bog-standard NHS number. Leather-look vinyl and wheel yourself. Times, I concluded, must be hard.

He finally got it out: 'T . . . T . . . TUNE!' he spluttered, gesturing at the air around us, at the record pounding out of the speakers. Some drum'n'bass nonsense.

'Yeah!' I said, giving him a thumbs up. 'Fucking tune!'

The minder, or helper, or whatever, leaned down to Rage and did two things: first he wiped the (considerable) drool from Rage's mouth and chin, then he held a thumbnail of cocaine up to Rage's quivering nostril. But Rage couldn't inhale it – maybe something to do with the loss of motor functions or something – so the guy just rubbed it into his gums, over the chrome and gold teeth, the teeth themselves now a relic, a reminder of something Rage once was.

The minder glanced quickly around the packed dance floor and held a grubby thumb towards me. 'Bump?'

'Nah. I'm all right thanks.'

He did it himself and we stood there nodding along to the music for a moment, me wondering how quickly I could get the fuck out of there, when we both became aware of a terrible stench. We looked down together. Rage was twisting and puffing and jerking his head about. 'Facking hell. Sorry, mate. Happens sometimes.'

I gave the only possible response. I nodded slowly.

'Do you know where the bogs are?' I didn't, but I pointed off into the middle distance anyway, pointing anywhere away from me.

They trundled off and I stood watching them go, wondering if the minder's just a mate or if he's on the payroll. If so, how much? What's the going rate for scraping the crap out of a former 'drum'n'bass superstar's' caked pants? Well, at least it keeps him off the streets.

Rage, of course, is literally *off* the streets. The cunt's in a fucking wheelchair.

I found Trellick in one of the smaller rooms – his shirt off and going bananas to some techno tune. I leaned in and screamed in his ear, 'Have we actually dropped Rage yet?' I had to repeat it a few times. He shook his head. *'Don't,'* I said.

'Don't what?'

'Do. Not. Drop. Rage. Yet. Got an idea.'

The theme music from *Friends* comes on very softly in the background. *'I'll be there for you . . .'* I walk to the coffee table and drop fresh ice into my glass and then listen to it splinter under the amber wash of Glenmorangie. I walk back to the window and sip my drink, resting my left palm on the windowpane.

It's cold out there.

Generally speaking I don't like Christmas. It reminds me of childhood and me and my mother, just the two of us, exchanging gifts; me handing her the usual box of bath salts or whatever and her reciprocating with the envelope of cash.

This year is a little different. This year I don't mind the half-hearted decorations in the office, or the extra crush and traffic around Regent Street, or the struggle to get a decent table anywhere.

Yeah, Christmas looks a whole lot brighter when you have the Christmas no. 1.

Derek and I go to lunch at the River Cafe. I have duck, he has the penne. We both drink champagne. On the mid-weeks that morning 'Fully Grown' by Songbirds is outselling its nearest rival by nearly two to one. Un-fucking-touchable. Derek does the contrition thing, phrases like 'tremendous asset' and 'great ears' are freely bandied about. At one point the deluded bender – high on the festive spirit and a couple of Bellinis – even goes as far as to tell me he knew we'd 'always had a great respect for each other'. I generously tolerate this nonsense for a while before graciously accepting his offer of the position of Head of A&R.

He stammers and splutters a little as I spell out the insanely avaricious terms of my acceptance – bonkers salary increase, signing-on bonus, profit-share, car upgrade, etc.

– but he pretty much agrees to everything. My lawyer can work it all out with Trellick in the new year.

In the new year I intend to have a platinum album with Songbirds.

In the new year Derek's own contract comes up for renewal. I am going to make life very difficult for Derek.

In the new year I am going to have Dunn fired.

I am going to have Nicky fired.

I am going to fire Rob Hastings.

Everyone is going to pay.

Derek signals for the bill. Outside the plate-glass windows of the River Cafe people, poor people, walk by, their chins jammed hard down into their collars and scarves and their hands in the pockets of thick coats. I'm leaning back from the table in shirtsleeves. Although I can't feel it I know there is a freezing, salty wind blasting up off the Thames and rolling over the pavements and people of Hammersmith. The Thames is not quite frozen yet, here where it bends and heads out towards Oxfordshire. Guys in canoes slide along it. The trees along the riverbank flatten back in the chill wind. A *Big Issue* seller – who looks far too fat to be genuine – has his tattered copy blown from his frozen hand.

The cold doesn't worry me too much. When Derek's paid the bill we'll stroll the three yards across the pavement to the waiting car, a toasty chauffeured Merc from Addison Lee, and trundle the half-mile back to the office, where the temperature is the same every day of the year. Later, when my busy day is done – there are final travel arrangements to be made for Thailand, the interior of my new Range Rover to confirm, the clearing out of my new office (Parker-Hall's old office, Schneider's old office) to supervise, a rough cut of the new Songbirds video to approve – I'll walk the eighteen feet from reception to my new parking space next to Derek's. (Parker-Hall's old space. Schneider's old space.)

No, I'm not worried about the cold at all.

Derek's mobile twitters its deranged ringtone. He pops it open. There are a lot of dusty old houses on these side streets, in the strange hinterland along the river, between Hammersmith and Fulham. Ash-streaked net curtains, non-opening, fifty times painted-over window casements, dead gardens. Probably all full of old boilers who've been living there since the Blitz. Probably all undervalued to fuck. Find yourself a simpatico estate agent – bish, bash, bosh. I must talk to Trellick about this.

'No! Oh God *no!*' Derek says, his hand going to his mouth in that queenly way. My first thought is that something unthinkable, something truly terrible, has happened: somehow one of the records behind the Songbirds single has had a dramatic sales surge and has overtaken us.

'What is it?' I say, but he turns away from me, finger in the ear, still listening. This can't be happening. We were outselling the nearest record by . . .

He hangs up and turns to me, his mouth hanging open.

'Tony Parker-Hall's committed suicide.'

The sensation of relief I experience is tidal, almost orgasmic.

Finished. Game Over. See you later, Sooty.

'Thank fuck for that' almost comes out of my mouth but I manage to say, 'Oh my God,' because I suppose that's the kind of thing you're meant to say.

*

Bangkok Airport on New Year's Eve.

Ross, Leamington and I are knocking back the local brew, which is called – brilliantly – Chang. It's barely lunchtime and already half a dozen fat, brown empties are lined up on the Formica tabletop. We're Chang'd up to the max and waiting for Trellick, whose flight out from Heathrow has been delayed. It's a billion degrees outside but we've managed to wedge ourselves right under the air conditioner, so we're laughing.

I feel great, tanned and fit. We've been here over a week, taking it easy down at Koh Samet. Beer and beach. Books and Discmans. Backgammon, tom yam gai and floating in the body-temperature ocean. No ostros. No class As. No quadruple Rockschools. This is, of course, all set to change with Trellick's arrival. Later today we fly down to Phuket for a fuck-off party; tonight is when the real shit begins. It's a boiler-fest down there – clean-tasting Scandinavian back-packers a go go. We're also planning to pop into the human toilet of Pattaya and catch a few shows: bare-knuckle midget boxing and teenage ostros firing ping-pong balls, goldfish and frogs out of their cunts; pulling razor blades, butcher knives, landmines and Christ knows what out of their arses.

We're larging it.

'Any more for any more?' Leamington asks. We both give him a thumbs up and he pootles off towards the bar, weaving a little.

I'm leafing through a week-old copy of the *Guardian*. Tony Blair is larging it too. He's in the Seychelles, staying at some massive fuck-off gaff where (apparently) they filmed the soft-porn flick *Emmanuelle*. They reckon Tony will have spunked seven and a half million quid on travel and entertainment in his first year in power. Meanwhile, back home, he wants to slash benefits to single mothers. Top lad, Blair.

There's a little piece about the upcoming Brit Awards. I want to be back in London for 12 January, for the nominations at the Café de Paris, where Songbirds are going to be nominated for Best Single. I gave an expansive interview to *Music Week* about the girls just before I left London. I said, 'I've dealt with a lot of bands, but these girls are the best songwriters I've ever worked with.' And I said, 'They're real music fans. Trust me. They can give you the bar codes on their record collections.' Then, refuting a slight accusation that they were just another manufactured pop act, I said, 'You wouldn't believe the IQs of these girls. No one tells them what to do.' Then, finally, I looked the journalist in the eye and, with an absolutely straight face, I told him: 'Songbirds will be around for a long, long time.' Oh yes I did.

We're putting the second single out end of February, album beginning of March. There's two more potential singles to come after that. Bish, bash, bosh.

I've got another big album shaping up for next year too. You won't believe it, but the press have gone mental for the Rage story we leaked out: the whole 'a crippled man dislocated from his environment communicating through electronica' bullshit I drummed up with the press office went down a storm. He's being perceived as some kind of drum'n'bass Stephen Hawking. Front covers with *NME*, *Muzik* and *Mixmag*. They don't know he finished the record months before he got quadra-spazzed. And what does it matter that the record's an unlistenable pile of shite? He's riding his steel wheelchair across a massive wave of PC goodwill. Are you going to be the journalist who sits down and tells this poor, drooling mess that his record sucks? No one listens to this sort of album anyway, do they? You buy them and stick them down on your Habitat coffee table so that the cretins at your dinner party think you are on it. I'm not even releasing a single. We're spending fuck all on marketing. It's all being done via press and word of mouth. I reckon we'll just about ship gold, which is little short of a miracle considering what we had to work with. Rage. The last turkey in the fucking shop sprouts some wings.

Ross drains his beer. 'Ahhh,' he yawns contentedly, 'it's a hard knock life.' I light a duty-free Marlboro as Leamington reappears, three fresh Changs tinkling together on a plastic tray.

'Hey, look at this,' he says, slapping down a copy of the *Sun* he's found. It's dated 28 December, three days ago. Leamington flips as fast he can through the tired, soggy pages until he comes to the half-page story. There's a photograph of Ellie Crush in a black dress and sunglasses. She's a little out of focus, it's clearly been taken with a long lens. Above the photograph, the headline: 'ELLIE GRIEVES FOR SUSPECTED POP PAEDO'.

We all hunker round and read the story. It's the usual guff – *'ace record industry talent spotter . . . Brit winner Crush . . . police seized computer . . . sacked . . . six-figure salary . . . charges later dropped . . .'*

Towards the end there's a quote from Parker-Hall's

father, also Anthony, a solicitor, 57, from Hampstead, north London: *'Anthony was innocent and we know we will clear his name. Now we hope we can be left alone to mourn our son.'* There's no photo of him and I wonder what Anthony Senior looks like.

'Shocker,' says Ross, setting his beer down, 'absolute shocker.'

We're all quiet for a moment. 'Do you think he was guilty?' Leamington says. 'I mean, topping your fucking self? If you were innocent surely –'

'I can't see it,' Ross says, 'I mean, they dropped the charges, didn't they? Now, if it had been Derek . . .' He trails off, leaving us to join the dots ourselves, to make our own solid connections between irons and paedos and demi-paedos. (*Queer + cocaine x Internet access . . .*)

'What do you reckon?' Leamington asks, turning to me.

Gak, chang, nose-up, bag, beak, charlie, krell, powder, chisel, bump, posh, bugle, sniff, skiwear . . .

What do I reckon? I pour more Chang into my plastic cup and the foam volcanoes up, lathering down the sides and running over the *Sun,* darkening the paper, bleeding into the blurry photograph of sad-looking Ellie. He was buried at Kensal Rise cemetery, at the corner of Harrow Road and Ladbroke Grove, near the William the Fourth. Good chips in there. Nice Bloody Mary. Crush's face disappears beneath the expanding circle of golden bubbles. I wonder if Parker-Hall ever fucked her? Surely to Christ he must have? I wonder if he fucked Marcy from the Lazies? Because this is something that's definitely on my 'to do' list for next year. It'll be tough as she hates my fucking guts. But that may all change now, given that I'm her boss. We're meeting soon.

To discuss producers and recording budgets and the like.
I'm thinking Steve Albini.

Woodham called the office just once after that night, to
see if there had been any interest in his songs. I didn't speak
to him. Jo gave me the message. I didn't bother calling him
back. I think we've definitely reached an understanding
there.

We stayed in Bangkok last night, at the Ramada. This
morning I got up bright and early and strolled to an Internet
café near the hotel. I tapped into Rebecca's Hotmail
account (her password, obtained during a little good-
natured pillow talk, is – fairly unbelievably – 'Steven') and
sent the following email:

From: Rebecca_spears21@hotmail.com
To: stevens@******records.co.uk
Subject: I'm sorry . . .

Steven – I'm so sorry, but I won't be coming back to
work after the holidays. I think you'll understand.
What with Roger and losing the baby and everything,
I'm just really messed up right now. I need to be on
my own for a while. Sorry to leave you in the lurch,
especially when you've been so understanding this
year.

Love R x

Back home, after the holidays, I'll be forced to tell people
that Rebecca was pregnant with Waters' child. She
didn't know what to do, whether to have it or not. She

confided in me. Then she had a miscarriage. She was depressed . . .

Other than in these very practical terms I don't think about Rebecca much. And I'm definitely not planning on fucking Jo in a hurry. I mean, there's a level of fallout, of grief, you'll take from doing a secretary – the frosty silences, the substandard work, her sporadic dashes to the bathroom with the red eyes and the balled Kleenex – and a level of grief you won't take. (Like, for instance, a ketamine-addled copper dismembering a fucking corpse in your en suite.)

'I don't know,' I say finally, shaking my head, 'you just don't know about people, do you? Anyway,' I yawn, turning the page, 'fuck him. One less guy we have to compete with.'

'Christ, Steven,' Leamington says, 'you *are* hardcore.'

I *am* hardcore. I am the fucking King.

'OI! OI!' Ross shouts and I turn round.

About seventy yards away, I see Trellick appearing out of the handful of International Arrivals. He comes towards us pushing a trolley. He hasn't seen us yet and he has that air about him that people do when you see them before they see you; alert, scanning, vulnerable, self-conscious.

'OI! *LOSER!*' I shout and a few Thai heads turn.

He sees us now and his face lights up reluctantly. He's grinning as he trundles towards us through all the people, using his elbows to keep the trolley on line as he gives us a really stupid thumbs up. People, mostly Thais in their shitty sub-Western dress – tracksuit trousers and 'The Pope Smokes Dope' T-shirts, like Scousers from 1988 – get out of his way, darting and dodging around his trolley, all smiling their heads off and it strikes me that the airport is pretty busy considering it's New Year's Eve, but then I remember that the holidays don't mean much out here because they're all Buddhists. I mean, they don't give a shit about anything, do they?

About the author

About the book

Read on

Insights,
Interviews
& More . . .

Meet John Niven

Matthew Donaldson

JOHN NIVEN was born in Irvine, Ayrshire. He read English literature at Glasgow University and spent the next ten years working in the U.K. music industry. He has written for *Word*, *FHM*, *Q*, and *Socialism*. His debut novella, *Music from Big Pink*, was published in 2006. He lives in Buckinghamshire, England. ∽

How I Write

"How I Write" appeared in Time Out *(London), January 30, 2008, and is reprinted courtesy of the author.*

How DO I WRITE? This is a very good question, the kind writers like. If you're a writer then it's also one of the few questions that really interests you about other writers. Pen and paper or laptop? If the latter, then what typeface? Morning or evening? How many words a day? How many drafts? Music on or off? Any motivational quotes plastered above your desk?

I had the impulse to write for a long time and made various attempts at novels, screenplays, and short stories throughout my late teens and twenties. However, it wasn't until my early thirties that I had anything like the discipline required to see an idea through. It took me a long time to understand a key fundamental: writing is rewriting. (Just as, as Nabokov pointed out, reading is really rereading.)

A few years ago I left—or rather, finally succeeded in napalming every bridge I ever had in—the music industry and moved out of west London and into the Buckinghamshire countryside. We lived for a while with my girlfriend's mother in a large seven-bedroom house. (Thank you, Sheila.) For a time, there I was living the dream: running three separate studies à la John Updike: one for fiction, one for journalism, and one for reading and buggering about. (This use of the multi-study system is, of course, the only parity I could reasonably claim with Mr. Updike.)

It's a grand system and I can see why he favors it: you walk through a different door and the clutter of the previous room stays where it is, rather than in your head. Using it I wrote three novels and four screenplays in four years.

Alas, seven-bedroom houses in Buckinghamshire lie beyond the means of all but the most successful writers, and when we finally bought our own place I was reduced— the indignity!—to just the one study; clutter ▶

> **❝ It took me a long time to understand a key fundamental: writing is rewriting. ❞**

soon crept onto the bookshelves, onto the desk, across the sofa, and into my feeble, feeble mind.

While I write novels alone, I write scripts with my screenwriting partner, Nick. On one level the process of writing fiction is simply sitting in a room and saying "what if?" (and then its corollaries "how?" and "why?") all day long. When you've been doing this alone for a year and a half it's fun, it's a blessed relief, to have someone to say "what if?" with you for a few weeks. The screenplay is all about economy and compression, while the novel works by the accretion of detail, and I've come to really enjoy jumping between the two mediums. When you're rewriting a screenplay you're constantly trimming descriptions, paring dialogue, removing unnecessary stage-direction-filled parentheses. One of the joys of the novel is that you can follow a character's train of thought as far as you want, into whatever dark corner it wants to go. And sometimes a little beyond that.

And finally, to answer the questions I left hanging in paragraph one, personally it's: laptop (six-year-old PowerBook G4); 12-point Courier; mornings (the earlier the better); a thousand (often a bit more, never less); three (plus maybe a polish); the music is most definitely off; and the quote? I'm afraid it's that hoary old James Joyce classic: "Write damn ye! What else are you good for?" ∽

66 The screenplay is all about economy and compression, while the novel works by the accretion of detail, and I've come to really enjoy jumping between the two mediums. 99

In His Own Words

On Graduating from Glasgow University in 1991

"I strolled through the ancient quads and out into leafy Hillhead, drunk on possibility. And sherry. I had an English literature degree in my fist and not really a thought in my pretty young head beyond that fine old Spinal Tap–age, 'Have a good time all the time.' Bright, ambitious, yet lazy and a moral blank tape, I was, of course, absolutely perfect for a career in the music industry." —*Scotsman*, February 8, 2008

On Being a Young Man with an Old Man's Disease

"I suffer from gout—which some friends have laughed about because it sounds so Churchillian. In fact, it is excruciating. The first attack was when I was thirty-four. I woke up with an extreme pain in my right big toe. It was so agonizing I thought I must have broken my foot."
   —*Mail on Sunday* (London), April 27, 2008

On His Close Friendship with James Dean Bradfield (Singer/Lead Guitarist, Manic Street Preachers)

"When I first met him, the last record his band had made was *The Holy Bible*, which I still think is one of the best rock records ever; I was in awe of James's ability on the guitar. But as we got to know each other, I realized we'd had similar teenage years—me in a small Scottish town, him in a small Welsh town—watching the same movies and playing guitar to the Clash in our bedrooms. Whenever I play guitar with him it depresses me how good he is."
—*The Independent* (London), February 17, 2008 ▶

5

In His Own Words *(continued)*

On the Difference Between Real and Fictional Characters

"Real people are rarely good enough for a novel. Good characters are usually composites. With *Kill Your Friends*, it's now being treated as a kind of higher autobiography, which it's not. . . . Everything in the book is true in that it's an accurate representation of that world."

—*Sunday Times* (London), March 23, 2008

On His Next Novel

"There's also lots of drug-dealing and sex and infidelity, but with golf as the backdrop."

—*Glasgow Herald*, March 24, 2008

'Til Death Did We Party

" *'Til Death Did We Party"* appeared first in The Times *(London), February 15, 2008, and is reprinted with permission.*

AFTER GRADUATION, IN THE EARLY NINETIES, I was certain of two seemingly contradictory things. (1) I didn't want a proper job of any description just yet, thank you very much, and (2) I wanted—after four years of university plus two of playing guitar in a penniless indie band— to earn some money. Both lazy and avaricious, without even knowing it I was already an ideal candidate for a career in the music business.

Shortly afterward I stumbled into a job in the marketing department of the now-defunct major label London Records. London specialized in bright, shiny pop music—Bananarama, East 17, All Saints, Fine Young Cannibals. It was the sort of label that favored that week's chart position over long-term artist development.

The marketing meetings were an eye-opener. Records were "this useless, stinking piece of shit." Artists were "clowns," "losers," and "spastics." Like many a bright-eyed newbie before me I was quickly, viciously, disabused of the notion that record companies loved music.

It also soon became apparent that, if you were lazy and avaricious enough, there was only one area of the music business to be in, the kind of area where you could reasonably expect to be handed a six-figure salary, a BMW, and a bottomless expense account in return for rolling out of bed at noon: A&R—Artiste and Repertoire, to give the full handle—which is responsible for finding and developing new talent.

The name is a genteel hangover from another era, reeking of civility and respect, of Ahmet Ertegun in a spun-silk suit leafing through some sheet music with Ray Charles. The reality was somewhat different: a generation of twentysomethings blasted to the gills on cocaine, tearing around the world trying not ▶

About the book

❝ I wanted— after four years of university plus two of playing guitar in a penniless indie band—to earn some money. ❞

to lose their jobs by doing something crazy. Like actually signing a band.

Inevitably I bluffed and blustered my way in. In the autumn of 1995 I went to a party in a Mayfair nightclub. The entertainment was provided by an easy-listening orchestra called the Mike Flowers Pops. I thought no more about it until a few days later when Chris Evans played Flowers's version of "Wonderwall" on his Radio 1 show. I gave Mike a call. A few weeks later we (note—when an act is succeeding an A&R man will always use the inclusive pronoun; when they fail they become "they") nearly scored the Christmas number one, shipping nearly half a million singles, and like that—bosh!—I was a major-label A&R man.

There is a Hunter S. Thompson quote that has become the music industry's Magna Carta: "The music industry is a cruel and shallow money trench, a long plastic hallway where thieves and pimps run free and good men die like dogs. There is also a negative side." It's appropriate enough given that the dominant emotions within A&R culture are fear and loathing: fear that you had signed—or were about to sign—the wrong thing, loathing because one of your peers had just signed the right thing.

"No one knows anything," runs the Oscar-winning screenwriter William Goldman's maxim about Hollywood. None of the executives responsible for choosing hit films has the slightest idea what will work and what won't: the effects-laden blockbuster stiffs while the quirky little film no one wanted to make cleans up. So it goes in A&R—the can't-miss band goes belly-up on the first single and that strange little indie record sells by the truckload.

I quickly learned a key fundamental for survival in meetings—say everything with absolute certainty and as though your life depended upon it. I saw a senior industry figure (someone who, in all likelihood, has signed and developed music you own)

66 **Inevitably I bluffed and blustered my way in.** 99

8

throw the first White Stripes record out of a fourth-floor window with the words, "No one will ever—ever—be having this fucking nonsense!"

I went one further. As the last chords of a mildly hot demo hung in the air, I punctured the silence in the conference room with, "Is anyone really going to be having another bunch of sub-Radiohead drivel?" Thus did I terminate our company's interest in the emerging Coldplay.

As you've probably gathered, there was a problem with my A&R career. I was absolutely terrible at it. But then again, so was everyone else. You were a success if you could produce a profitable act every two or three years. Which meant picking the right act just once biennially out of thousands of demos and hundreds of gigs. Of course virtually no one manages this. In a neat twist on "the unspeakable in pursuit of the uneatable," the Wildean epithet about the foxhunting English upper class, here was the unbelievable in pursuit of the unlistenable.

And pursue we did, jetting off every other month to some exotic location for a "convention," a scarcely credible four-day holocaust of drugs and expense account abuse. Miami for the Winter Music Conference, Cannes for MIDEM, Cologne for Popkomm, New York for CMJ, Texas for South by Southwest: hundreds of A&R men spending hundreds of thousands of pounds on flights and entertainment. In a good year these conventions might produce one signing of note.

Of course, spending your twenties flying around the world on a diet of vodka and cocaine while being wildly overpaid does not make for reasonable, well-adjusted people. Arrogant? At a Janet Jackson party in the penthouse of the Chrysler Building I casually tossed my coat to Benny Medina, thinking he was a bouncer. Medina probably had better things to do: he was managing Jennifer Lopez and Mariah Carey at the time.

How were these levels of squander and ▶

> " I quickly learned a key fundamental for survival in meetings— say everything with absolute certainty and as though your life depended upon it. "

buffoonery sustainable? Thanks to our good friend the compact disc. Today you can walk into Asda or Tesco and pick up an LP for seven or eight quid. Back in the mid- to late nineties a new release routinely cost twelve to fifteen pounds—nearly thirty pounds in today's money. Factor in manufacturing costs of a few pence per unit and a royalty rate to the artist of about a quid and you have a profit margin to make third-world sweatshop owners wince.

It seemed that the artificially inflated good times would roll forever. Britpop lurched towards its swollen apogee. I remember standing in the corporate hospitality box at Oasis's Maine Road show in the spring of 1996, being entertained by jugglers and fire-eaters, a glass of cold champagne in my hand. Far below, tens of thousands of tolers (industry shorthand for the lumpen proletariat who buy the product) gleefully smashed up Moss Side. I was thinking, "And when Alexander saw the breadth of his domain . . ." or, more likely, "Where's the dealer?"

But, of course, elsewhere, the meter was running. By the time the new millennium was dawning I had an infant son I barely knew and a karma balance so overdrawn I would need to help several old ladies across the road every day for the remainder of many lifetimes to get it anywhere near the black.

A few years later (I was never any good at leaving a party early), I finally left the music industry for good and began writing. As *Kill Your Friends* started to do the rounds I reestablished contact with a few people from my time in the business and I keep hearing the same things again and again: "It's tough out there . . . redundancies all over . . ."

The late nineties are increasingly starting to resemble a glorious last hurrah for the music industry, a spangled fall-of-Rome era. The sales of CDs have declined year on year since 2000. Profit margins have been decimated. Bands give their music away free with newspapers to drive up ticket sales for their profitable live shows—

❝ Arrogant? At a Janet Jackson party in the penthouse of the Chrysler Building I casually tossed my coat to Benny Medina, thinking he was a bouncer. ❞

a complete reversal of the time when an act lost money on the road in order to drive CD sales.

As an industry acquaintance put it recently, A&R men "used to go and see their band playing at Wembley and think: 'I'm the king!' Now they are thinking, 'I'm the only guy not making any money out of this!'" Somehow I doubt we'll be holding a telethon anytime soon. ◠

An E-mail Conversation with John Niven

The following interview was conducted by Julie Burchill, a controversial writer who once placed 85 in a poll titled 100 Worst Britons We Love to Hate.

Julie Burchill: It must have been fun saying all those rude things and putting them in other people's mouths!

John Niven: It certainly was. It is, as I'm sure you know, one of the great pleasures of authorship. The really boring, obvious way to approach a book like this—and it's the way it's often been approached in the past—would have been to write from the point of view of an innocent who stumbles into the music business, becomes corrupted, and then, maybe, gets his innocence back. You'd give the reader a lens through which to view the horror: a Tim from *The Office*–type perspective. How boring. I thought it would be a lot more fun to write it from the point of view of someone who was within the belly of the beast and who *loved it there*, someone who was completely unapologetic about his greed and his ambition. In terms of saying "rude things," I had a rule when I was writing the book that, if there was something I'd heard colleagues say in a private moment, between friends, behind closed doors, then no matter how racist, sexist, or homophobic it was, Stelfox would be allowed to say or think it. And, believe me, I heard plenty as bad as—or worse than—anything in the novel. In fact, when I sent the book to a former colleague, he said, "The funny thing is people are going to think you're exaggerating. . . ." Also, the bad guys are always more fun to write, aren't they? Writers have been realizing this since Satan in *Paradise Lost*.

JB: Without going into specifics, what proportion of Stelfox's opinions are yours?

JN: A funny thing happens when people talk to me about the book. They'll invariably say, "Of course I thought he was a terrible racist/sexist/

whatever, but I kind of kept agreeing with him." A lot of Stelfox's opinions—about the nature of the music industry, the fevered egos of artists, the general public—are bang on the money. So you drag the reader into an uncomfortable collusion with someone they think they really shouldn't be agreeing with at all. It shouldn't even need saying that I am not sexist, racist, or homophobic; however, most people today don't understand what a novel is, particularly younger men. Because all they read are sports and music biographies, they think that fiction is simply some form of higher autobiography. Consequently, you have to endure idiots thinking that Stelfox = Me. Also, Stelfox's views are reflective of the world he inhabits. I did an interview recently where the journalist was really getting quite angry about the racism and sexism in the book. I had to say to her, "Look, if you really think there's no racism or sexism in the music industry then draw me up a list of all the managing directors of major record companies who are black or female." I'm aware I haven't completely answered your question here. . . .

JB: Did your girlfriend, Helen, start looking at you funny after she'd read it for the first time?

JN: I'll let Helen answer this. Helen, did you look at me funny after you read *Kill Your Friends*?

Helen Sheerin: Umm, I can't remember what I thought. No, I didn't look at you funny. I mean, we'd been going out for years by then. My boss read it and started looking at *me* funny, though. Like he'd figured out what we got up to on the weekends or something.

JN: Helen's a commercial litigator. *Kill Your Friends* is light reading for her, a frothy little boy-meets-girl-then-has-her-body-cut-up-in-his-bathroom number.

JB: When I was in the music business as a teenager, just after the Boer War, my beef wasn't that it was filled with corrupt cynics but rather with vile saps who really *believed* in the music. *Yuk*! Had this changed by the time you came in? ▶

> ❝ A funny thing happens when people talk to me about the book. They'll invariably say, 'Of course I thought he was a terrible racist/ sexist/whatever, but I kind of kept agreeing with him.' ❞

An E-mail Conversation with John Niven
(continued)

❝ I'm rather sad and childish in that I enjoy taking whatever stance is likely to cause maximum irritation to those around me. ❞

JN: I really do think that as you get older cynicism becomes a more and more attractive quality—the old "if you're not a rebel in your twenties you haven't got a heart, if you aren't establishment by the end of your thirties you haven't got a brain." I'm a bit thick and it took me a few years to realize that the Sex Pistols and the Clash were every bit as manufactured as Girls Aloud or Westlife. It's a very teenage thing, actually, thinking that what music you like *really* matters, really defines you as a person. I find it so embarrassing when you see men of a certain age getting incredibly angry because someone doesn't like the same B-sides as they do.

JB: I would have *loved* to have had a Stelfox to go around with when I was a seventeen-year-old music journalist! Are you anywhere near as much fun?

JN: Oh, God yes. And I won't slash your throat in the morning, baby. I promise.

JB: Baudelaire said, "To escape from horror, bury yourself in it," while someone whose name I can't recall—it was probably my mum—said, "There's nothing so sad as the laughter of those who have lost their pet faith." Though I personally found most of what Stelfox thought and did—apart from the killings and that—sexy and/or fun, I sensed that you actually didn't. Are you indeed, as I believe, a thwarted idealist rather than a natural-born amoralist? I won't tell anyone, honest!

Don't miss the next book by your favorite author. Sign up now for AuthorTracker by visiting www.AuthorTracker.com.

JN: I think I can be either one on any given day, depending on the company I'm in. I'm rather sad and childish in that I enjoy taking whatever stance is likely to cause maximum irritation to those around me. So if I were with a group of super-cynical Cowell/Stelfox types, I'd probably choose to believe in music, man. If I were with a bunch of indie kids it's very likely that I'd play the Stelfox part. I really am that pathetic. But, at the same time, there's nothing as tedious as the sound of clucking agreement, is there? ∾

CPSIA information can be obtained at www.ICGtesting.com
Printed in the USA
LVOW08s1113040116

469039LV00005B/12/P